Pelican Books

Defended to Death

Gwyn Prins is a Fellow, College Lecturer and the Director of
Studies in History at Emmanuel College, Cambridge. After gaining a
double first in history from the University of Cambridge, he became a
Research Fellow at Emmanuel College during which time he worked
for his doctoral dissertation in African history. This involved several
years of fieldwork in the Zambian bush. His research has been
concerned with the regional history of western Zambia and, more
recently, with comparative medical anthropology and history in Africa.
Dr Prins is the author of *The Hidden Hippopotamus – Reappraisal in
African History: the Early Colonial Experience in Western Zambia* (1980)
and (with J. Janzen) he edited *Causality and Classification in African
Medicine and Health* (1981).

Notes about the other contributors appear on page 5.

Edited by Gwyn Prins

DEFENDED TO DEATH

A study of the nuclear arms race

from the Cambridge University Disarmament Seminar

John Barber, Pat Bateson, Andrew Collins,
John Griffiths, Robert Hindle, Ralph Lapwood,
Martin Ryle, John Wells, Jay Winter

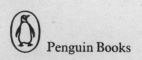 Penguin Books

Penguin Books Ltd, Harmondsworth, Middlesex, England
Penguin Books, 625 Madison Avenue, New York, New York 10022, U.S.A.
Penguin Books Australia Ltd, Ringwood, Victoria, Australia
Penguin Books Canada Ltd, 2801 John Street, Markham, Ontario, Canada L3R 1B4
Penguin Books (N.Z.) Ltd, 182–190 Wairau Road, Auckland 10, New Zealand

First published 1983

Made and printed in Great Britain by
Richard Clay (The Chaucer Press) Ltd,
Bungay, Suffolk
Set in VIP Plantin

The Authors

John BARBER, MA, PhD, University Lecturer in Social and Political Sciences; Fellow and Director of Studies in History, King's College, Cambridge.

Pat BATESON, MA, PhD, ScD, Reader in Animal Behaviour and Director of the Sub-Department of Animal Behaviour; Fellow of King's College, Cambridge.

Andrew COLLINS, MA, PhD, Senior Research Associate, CRC Mammalian Cell DNA Repair Group, Department of Zoology, Cambridge.

John GRIFFITHS, MA, LlB, LlM, PhD, University Assistant Lecturer in Law; Fellow and Director of Studies in Law, Emmanuel College, Cambridge.

Robert HINDE, MA, PhD, ScD, FRS, Royal Society Research Professor in Animal Behaviour; Fellow of St John's College, Cambridge.

Ralph LAPWOOD, MA, PhD, Emeritus Reader in Seismology; Fellow of Emmanuel College, Cambridge.

Martin RYLE, MA, PhD, ScD, FRS, Kt, Professor of Radio Astronomy; Director of the Mullard Radio-Astronomy Observatory; Fellow of Trinity College, Cambridge. Cambridge.

John WELLS, MA, PhD, University Lecturer in Economics; Fellow of King's College, Cambridge.

Jay WINTER, MA, PhD, University Lecturer in History; Fellow of Pembroke College, Cambridge.

Contents

List of Figures

List of Tables

Select List
of Information Boxes

Preface

This book is the product of several hands but is a collective statement. Early drafts of each of the chapters were written by individuals, and then amended in a process of extended criticism. The authors responsible for the text at this stage were John Barber, Pat Bateson, Robert Hinde, Ralph Lapwood, Gwyn Prins, and Jay Winter. However, they would not have been able to complete the work without the contributions of other authors who drafted sections based upon their specialized knowledge. These authors were Andrew Collins, John Griffiths, Martin Ryle, and John Wells. Stan Norris read and criticized the entire manuscript, and the authors are much indebted to him, and also to Christopher Comford for drawing Figure 8. Nor could we have managed without the research assistance which we received throughout the project from Christopher Husbands and Marian Sugden, who investigated and documented specific topics as the need arose. Marian Sugden also prepared the index and coordinated a team of undergraduate and postgraduate researchers. The authors' debt to her is very great. Among the researchers, in particular, Rob Westaway made fundamental contributions to Appendix A1. The other helpers were Richard Bradley, Tim Clarke, Alison Drew, Alison Grant, Richard Kamm, and Frances Laidlaw.

In preparing this book we have incurred debts of gratitude to many scholars. Robert Neild generously allowed us access to his book, *How to Make up your Mind about the Bomb* before its publication. Two research institutes have made contributions to the project. We are grateful to the Armament and Disarmament Information Unit within the Science Policy Research Unit, University of Sussex, for general advice, and for help in preparing the section on Further Reading. The entire manuscript received a critical reading at the Center for Defense Information, Washington, and we obtained a mass of factual material through the formidable expertise of the Center's staff, especially that of the senior analyst, Dr Stan Norris. We are deeply indebted to him, to the librarian, to other analysts and to the director and assistant director, Admirals G. La Rocque and E. Carroll,

USN (Retd), for all their help and guidance. Naturally, none of those who have been kind enough to assist us in our task bears any responsibility for our analysis: this rests with us alone.

We wish to thank Neil Middleton and Penguin Books for their efficient production of this book, and Rebecca Hibbert of Cambridge Word Processing Ltd, for making an ordered final typescript out of a manuscript that frequently changed as it evolved. All the royalties from the sale of this book will be placed in a fund established to promote further research.

Finally, we thank our families for their support and encouragement, and especially we thank Miriam and Elizabeth Prins, who experienced much the worst inconvenience and disruption of family life for the sake of this enterprise.

We dedicate this book to our families for this, and for other more obvious and more sombre reasons.

Cambridge
May 1982

Introduction

In the summer of 1981 an article in *The Times*, entitled 'Academic help sought to explain nuclear policy', reported a discussion paper about NATO nuclear strategy. Noting the increasing public dissatisfaction with the government's attitude, the author, Michael Legge, a civil servant concerned with nuclear policy within the Ministry of Defence, wrote:

The evidence of widespread concern over nuclear war, which has been heightened by recent decisions in the nuclear field, shows that we have to make a major effort to ensure that [NATO] alliance objectives and policies are better understood. I would suggest that the academic community can play a valuable part in ensuring that the debate is conducted on an informed basis.

The Times, Monday, 25 May 1981

This book is an answer to that request. We share with the Ministry's nuclear strategists and their colleagues the desire for a debate well supplied with clear information. We believe that the present situation, its historical roots, and its likely future consequences require careful and clear-sighted examination. We must identify the nature of the dangers that beset us, and decide how we should defend ourselves against them. As the book proceeds, it will become clear that we see the official position, which is the present conventional wisdom of our elected rulers, to be wrong.

We suggest that the official position is based on an inadequate analysis of the actions of both East and West which have led to the present distrust. As a consequence, its basic assumption about Soviet aggressive intentions does not bear close examination. The authors of this book do not deny that there *is* a 'Soviet threat', but there is also an American threat, a French threat, and a British threat, and all these threats are the same: it is the possession of nuclear weapons that threatens the possessor with destruction by those of the other power, which fears destruction by the first party's weapons. The official position is untenable in that it envisages or threatens nuclear destruction as an instrument of policy, when no ends can justify such means. The various strategies which are supposed to govern the possession and use of nuclear weapons can never give that security which all normal people desire. Its expectations of what nuclear war in the 1980s would be like are unrealistic. It fails to perceive the subtlety of the mechanisms which connect overt, declared policies to action in the real world. Its artificial 'war games' approach neglects the ramifying consequences which the arms race has on ordinary people throughout the world, even in the absence of nuclear war, and it is flawed throughout by the uncritical way in which evidence supplied by Western defence 'experts' and officials is often accepted at face value in spite of its track record of unreliability. In this book we examine each of these issues, offering the reasons for our different reading of the evidence.

In making our case, it is not our intention to suggest that Mr Legge and those like him are evil or scheming people. Their failing is more that of narrowly blinkered vision. It is charitable to make allowance for failings, but because the strategists and generals have too much power over our lives, their failings could become our tragedy; believing their view to be inaccurate and inadequate, we must expose its shortcomings. After all, if we are wrong in the prescriptions which we offer in this book, then we or our successors can try again, as mankind has always done. But if the nuclear strategists are wrong, there will be no one left to try again.

In writing this book we expressly contract out of their assumptions and terminology. One of their principal working assumptions is 'the Soviet threat'. Therefore, we devote some space to probing its nature, for it is as dangerous to exaggerate it as it is to ignore it. Within the official terms, to examine and perhaps to question this axiom of a Great Threat is to become either a 'tool of Moscow', a naïve apologist for Communism and/or a wicked agent 'orchestrated' by the enemy; or – which amounts to the same thing – it is 'appeasement', 'going soft on the Commies'. But that we find the claim of aggressive Soviet expansionism deficient is in no sense to be read as mindless approval of the Soviet regime. We reject the primitive world-view which automatically links the differences between Western and Soviet ideologies with aggressive Soviet expansionism. The facile division of mankind into entrenched, mutually alien armed camps, each defended to death, will be the death of us all unless we act soon to stop it.

A National Opinion Poll in May 1980 found that 65 per cent of all those interviewed expected nuclear war in their lifetime. In April 1981, a Marplan opinion poll found that 65 per cent of their subjects believed that prospects for world peace were worse than a year before.[1] Nor is this pessimism to be found only in Europe. Ordinary Americans share it in very similar proportion. A Gallup poll conducted in September 1981 revealed that 68 per cent of those questioned believed that an all-out nuclear war between the USA and the USSR was a possibility (ranging from 'some chance' to 'almost certain') in the next ten years. Nine out of ten believed that their chances of survival were poor or 'just fifty-fifty', pessimism which has increased during the last twenty years since a 1961 Gallup poll.[2] Consider for one moment what, in human terms, lies behind the trend indicated by the polls. Mr Philip Payne, an Essex County Inspector of Schools, felt compelled to write to *The Times* about the insidious effects of the nuclear age upon our children, as well as its future promise of extreme suffering.

Even if the worst does not happen, at least until our present children are grown up, we must still take into account the effect of living one's most formative years under the 'protection' of the nuclear deterrent ... What may our children learn from this? They learn that a community may call itself civilized and yet possess weapons which would once have been regarded as barbarous beyond belief. The middle-aged and old can perhaps preserve their innate sense of what it means to be civilized, having been brought up at a time when an attack on a field ambulance or an unarmed village provoked feelings of indignation. How will it be for our children, brought up to regard the infliction of widespread devastation on civilians as something we, in certain circumstances, may be forced to do? Surely in deploying such weapons, we erode the moral base of what we are out to defend. On several occasions I have sat in on discussion lessons when schoolchildren have brought up the question of the Bomb. Many have come to accept that they may not live out their lives in full; they have also learned (from their elders) that nothing can be done. Some, quite literally, smile about it. Perhaps they confuse violence and death with its image on television, which does not hurt and can even be enjoyed. Others are most painfully aware of what is involved.[3]

Mr Payne's letter stimulated others. The Bishop of Tonbridge wrote:

clergy have told me of children with recurring nightmares about the holocaust. Teachers speak of sixth formers who genuinely believe that the future, if there is one, is short.[4]

But other correspondents reacted quite differently. Mr John Stokes, the Conservative MP for Halesowen and Stourbridge, admonished the Bishop, whom he accused of muddled thinking.

The whole point of the nuclear deterrent in the West is to prevent war and the use of these weapons. This policy has been successful for over thirty years. If the West were to abandon the nuclear deterrent unilaterally there would be nothing to stop a Soviet invasion, with their enormous superiority of conventional weapons – as happened in Afghanistan and may happen in Poland. I think normal children are perfectly capable of understanding this.[5]

It is worth dwelling on Mr Stokes's admonition. Each sentence and each implication will be shown in later chapters to be incorrect: the code words 'nuclear deterrent' are broken open and the full range of their meaning exposed; it will then become apparent that Mr Stokes's view has a shaky basis in the situation of the 1980s. We suggest that there are more convincing ways to view the last thirty years. 'To abandon the nuclear deterrent unilaterally' is another code phrase, pregnant with misunderstanding; we discuss real policies. 'Nothing to stop a Soviet invasion', 'Afghanistan', and 'may happen in Poland' represent a special shorthand which assumes a hostile view of the Soviet Union that is examined carefully throughout this book. 'Enormous superiority of conventional weapons', at the superficial level, appears true, but at a deeper level is seen to be incomplete and false.

It is our intention that this book can be read right through as a linked argument about how to begin the steps to survival, to formulate policies to promote real security in a real world. But it is also our hope that readers will find the format of sections and 'information boxes' easily accessible so that they can readily uncover relevant sources to help them in piercing the fog which envelops the field of nuclear affairs. In addition we have provided some background material in appendices and some suggestions for further reading.

Part One
The Nuclear Arms Race:
Origins

1 Discrepancies

The most immediate problem for the human race is that of the piling up of immense arsenals of nuclear weapons in the arms race. On this all thoughtful people are agreed. Yet there is no agreement as to how to escape from the danger so urgently perceived. Harshly divergent analyses and proposed remedies arise from discrepancies in basic assumptions. These discrepancies must be identified before we can proceed to describe the sequence of decisions and events which led to our present state, or to evaluate the courses of future action.

1 Discrepancies in Perceptions of Threats

Our approach to the history of East/West relations is complicated not only because the sources available to study the Soviet and American experiences are so different, but also because views are framed so heavily in the form of mirrored threats that they seem irreconcilable.

This distortion of perception has deep roots. It is introduced into the mind of each citizen by national history books and patriotic feelings. Consider the question of aggression. Statements from the USA speak of the threat from the USSR. Statements from the USSR speak of threats from the USA. For instance Brezhnev stated, 'At one time we proposed to ban the development of the naval Trident missile system in the US and of a corresponding system in our country. The proposal was not accepted. As a result, the US has built the new Ohio submarine armed with Trident I missile, while an analogous system, the Typhoon, was built in our country.'[1] This implies that the Russians believe that they are responding to the threat of US aggression.

On the other hand, US and British politicians explicitly justify increases in nuclear armaments by reference to Soviet threats. For instance, the US Defense Secretary in 1980, justifying the increases in theatre nuclear weapons, said, 'The Soviet leadership appears to contemplate at least the possibility of a relatively prolonged exchange if a war comes, and in some circles at least, they seem to take seriously the theoretical possibility of victory in such a war. We cannot afford to ignore those views.'

The following are parallel statements from an American history book and two Soviet encyclopedias. These show clearly how each is presented in the popular teaching of the other as the main threat and source of danger.

[After 1950] Stalin's decision to end cooperation with the West was not unnatural in view of communist history. The alliance against Hitler had been strictly a marriage of convenience, and once the Nazi menace was ended, the Soviet leader could see no purpose in continuing the arrangement. He returned to the philosophy which Lenin had developed and which Stalin himself had consistently upheld – except during the brief interval of the Second World War. Lenin had warned, 'As long as capitalism and socialism exist, we cannot live in peace. In the end, one or the other will triumph, a funeral dirge will be sung either over the Soviet Republic or over world capitalism.' As for methods, Lenin put into words the policy which Communists have followed consistently ever since his day: 'We have to use any ruse, dodge, trick, cunning, unlawful methods, concealment, veiling of the truth . . .' Stalin gave full endorsement to Lenin. In his book *Foundations of Leninism*, published in an English translation in New York in 1939, the Russian dictator described his plans with as much detail as Hitler had done in *Mein Kampf*.

The determination to spread Communism throughout the world was not the only driving force in Soviet policy. For three hundred years before the Revolution Tsarist Russia had followed a program of expansion, toward the Far East, toward the Dardanelles, and toward the Balkans. Stalin revived this imperialist policy. Under this double sanction of Communism and Russian imperialism the Soviet Union gave the Western world ample reason to fear for its own survival. The danger was multiplied by the fact that Communist parties throughout the world accepted blindly the leadership of Moscow. Faithful party members in each country were available for use as spies and saboteurs in the interest of Russia.[2]

After the end of the war imperialist circles in the USA began a 'cold war' against the USSR and other socialist states, were the chief organizers of aggressive blocs – NATO (1949), SEATO (1954), etc., of military bases, of the arms race, unleashed intervention in Korea (1950–53), and in the mid-1960s an aggressive war in Indochina . . . In conditions of a change in the world balance of power, chiefly thanks to the growth in the strength of the USSR and of the whole socialist commonwealth, the United States at the beginning of the 1970s had to take a number of steps in the direction of normalizing and developing relations with the socialist countries . . . The further development of Soviet–American relations came into conflict with opposition from certain influential forces in the USA.[3]

In the late 1960s, 'step by step, the US government, while not stopping subversive actions in the socialist countries of Europe, began to implement in its relations with these countries a more flexible tactic of "building bridges" . . . directed at "softening" the socialist order in these countries and weakening their links with the USSR.'[4]

A consequence of these contrary perceptions of threat is that each analyst moves towards the adoption of an extreme view – the 'worst case' assumption. Henry Nash worked once as an 'intelligence analyst' in the Air Targets Division of the US Air Force. He explains clearly how the acquired tendency towards a slogan-based antagonistic point of view was encouraged. The worse the Soviets appeared, the better the chance that Congress would approve the Defense Department's budget. In the 'worst case', there were no constraints on imagination in speculating about future Russian weapons, and 'worst cases' were less susceptible to challenge. Acquired preconceptions and the military/political environment reinforced each other so that the analyst came to be preoccupied not with the enemy's *intentions* (since these were automatically assumed to be the worst possible), but with his *capabilities*. 'Assembling, or at least being familiar with, lists, tables, and catalogues of the estimated numbers and characteristics of enemy weapons was an essential part of being a respected intelligence analyst.'[5] This point is crucial in understanding the differences between the analysis in this book and those of the Pentagon and Whitehall.

This issue was brought home to the authors of this book in a closed seminar with a Whitehall defence expert. 'How exactly did he view the Soviet threat?' we asked. His reply was instructive. 'There was, indeed, no present indication of a Soviet intention to invade Western Europe, but it would be prudent to assume the worst about their intentions in view of Soviet capabilities.' Throughout the seminar, it was to the question of numbers – of capabilities – that he continually returned.

The same point was made more forcefully with the publication by the US Department of Defense at the end of September 1981 of a book entitled *Soviet Military Power*. Complete with many diagrams and photographs, as well as dramatic paintings of all sorts of weapons, this sustained recital of Soviet 'capabilities' was offered to the reader as a self-sufficient description of 'the challenge we face'. The same fundamental confusion between capabilities and intentions was evident, so in fact the book told nothing at all about 'the challenge'. Indeed, when interviewed on American television on the day that the report was released, during a heavily publicized press conference by Secretary of Defense Weinberger, retired US Admiral Gene La Rocque made an essential point that by showing only Soviet forces, without comparison with NATO and US forces, the book 'puts them [Soviet forces] in a very dramatic way simply to scare the pants off the

American public and our European and Japanese allies'. A few months later the Soviets responded with publication of their view of the threat, an equally unbalanced book, this time showing the Western arsenal. Applying the same 'worst case' assumptions to such a book would certainly scare the pants off a Soviet audience. This is clearly not the way to proceed.[6]

2 Discrepancies of Language

Underlying all the differences in analysis between this book and the writings of the Ministry of Defence and its apologists is a shared problem. Key words in any discussion about war and peace have been so distorted by use in polemics and slogans that it is hard to set up a common basic vocabulary of agreed meanings. The importance of this in the present context goes beyond the possibilities for misunderstanding. Language is not just a neutral bland medium for conveying information and ideas. It actually influences what we feel and think.

Four groups of words are essential for discussion of the nuclear question; each word has been touched and transformed. The groups relate to aims, agents, justifications, and uses.

(A) AIMS

'Security' and 'peace' have been differently affected in East and West. 'Security' has suffered worst in the West, where it has been effectively weakened by trivialization. Armies used to reinforce policemen in quelling street riots have come to be described routinely as 'security forces' and so, by loose association, the word has slipped into the description of all armies. It is overused because it has 'good' resonances. Security conveys a picture of a quiet life, free from fear and danger. But while everyone in the West likes security, peace sometimes has bad resonances: in some countries, like Britain, some people associate it with 'pacifism', 'being wet', and 'appeasement', although in countries which have had more brutal experiences of war, peace is less likely to encounter such a reaction. In the East, peace runs into different problems. It has been suffocated in too close an embrace by rigid and authoritarian regimes.

'Freedom' and 'democracy' are words with several different meanings which cannot be reconciled. Indeed, not only is there no agreed definition of democracy but nowadays every kind of regime wishes to bask in the benign warmth of this archetypally 'good' word. So both freedom and democracy can easily be used in consciously dishonest ways.

(B) AGENTS

Who decides upon the policy to be pursued and pursues it? Of course each nation has its decision-making processes, but, according to common usage, it is 'Britain' or 'the USA' or 'the Soviet Union' or 'NATO' which makes the decisions. But what does that mean? In each nation, many forces operate. These forces are often in tension and even in conflict, yet on the most contentious issues the mass media assume and then personalize a remarkable consensus. Countries become honorary people, with minds which are made up.

For example, in October 1979, 'Britain' made up its mind to accept cruise missiles. The news coverage at the time *assumed* a consensus for 'modernization' (another word with good resonances), which subsequent massive public protest has revealed was unwarranted: it has since become known that it was the NATO 'High Level Group', instructing the 'Nuclear Planning Group', instructing member governments, which made this decision. This simple personification of countries obscures the fact that nations are made up of differently thinking people, and differ enormously within themselves – far more than people do.

(C) JUSTIFICATIONS

'Defence' and **'aggression'** are starkly contrasted. **Defence** is splendid, morally justified, manly, honourable, and it is normal for governments to describe their intentions and all their own weapons as 'defensive'.

'We have to deal with the leaders of a closed totalitarian state of hostile ideology, huge military power, and a proven willingness to use that power without scruple when it thinks it can safely get away with it.'

(J. Nott, British Secretary of State for Defence)[7]

'The impression is increasingly being formed in the world of the United States as an absolutely unreliable partner in inter-state ties, as a state whose leadership, prompted by some whim, caprice or emotional outburst, or by considerations of narrowly understood immediate advantage, is capable at any moment of violating its international obligations and cancelling treaties and agreements signed by it. There is hardly any need to explain what a dangerous destabilizing impact this has on the entire international situation...'

(L. Brezhnev, President of USSR)[8]

Aggression, on the other hand, is darkly cruel. No government admits to **aggression**; but governments commonly accuse other governments of **aggression**. In fact it is usual to interpret the actions of an antagonist in the worst light, as the outcome of a spirit of **aggression**. Previously British governments had a War Office; now, like all others, they have a Ministry of **Defence**.

'**Deterrence**' is the central word in the vocabulary of nuclear war and weapons. On the one hand, it expresses the whole antagonistic world-view of the Cold War; on the other, '**deterrence**' makes it possible to regard even those weapons which can have no other use than destruction as defensive (therefore, good) on the grounds that the aim of **deterrence** is to *prevent* war, to resist **aggression**. Quite naturally, people in a country threatened by the **deterrent** weapons regard them as preparations of an **aggressor**. The dominance of the **defence/aggression** polarity translated into **deterrent** threats facilitates greatly a steady increase in the arsenal of weapons of all descriptions.

(D) USES

But what happens if the nuclear weapons in that arsenal are, for whatever reason, released? Einstein said, 'The power set free from the atom has changed everything, *except our ways of thought*.' The noble old meanings of words about war are used without thought, and this has the effect of making nuclear weapons seem normal.

What are the words that make nuclear weapons seem 'usable', nuclear war 'winnable'? There is '**survival**'. The British government has told its subjects to hide under the stairs in order to **survive** in the event of nuclear war. But so callously unimaginative was its leaflet *Protect and Survive* that when it was released for public sale, it provoked outrage. To the generals and strategists, **survival** means the ability to continue resistance, which means survival not of people but of nuclear weapons sufficient for the next stage of a 'flexible response' or a 'second strike'. But for ordinary people the only **survival** that can realistically be imagined in Britain after a nuclear attack would be in conditions where the survivors would envy the dead.

In nuclear war **victory** as objective and **defeat** as penalty no longer have any meaning. There can be no victor, only various degrees of destruction and degradation. In nuclear war you can annihilate your enemy more surely and more extensively than was possible ever before; but just as surely, you kill yourself.

'Defeat is indivisible in a war of nuclear weapons.'
(Lord Zuckerman, formerly Chief Scientific Adviser to the British government)[9]

Since discussion of nuclear warfare deals with events so repulsive that the minds of normal people, including many soldiers, find it hard to bear, many euphemisms have been introduced to soften the impact on the imagination. Instead of the obliteration of great cities, we hear of 'demographic targeting'. Instead of the incineration of great tracts of countryside – of plants, animals, people – we hear of 'collateral damage'; and the phrase 'unacceptable damage' implies that there is an 'acceptable' tally of burned, mangled, and disintegrated bodies, of gravely wounded and grief-crazed survivors, an 'acceptable' quantity of radioactive water, of poisoned ground and food.

SLOGANS

Slogans consist of simple sets of code words all gummed together into easily remembered catch-phrases, but they do not necessarily have a malign intent. 'Peace through strength' and 'Peace is our profession' (motto of the American Strategic Air Command) are intended to inspire. However, all types of slogans obstruct thought and so impede understanding.

Some of the most effective slogans involve *false polarities*, which seal off other possibilities. 'Rather dead than Red!' is the most wizened and celebrated of these, permitting the slur of cowardice and treachery to be applied to critics of nuclear weapons policies.

False polarities soon decay into *false antagonisms*. One above all others, which at present obscures thought about disarmament, deserves closer inspection. The contrast between unilateral and multilateral action is perverse and has been used in the media to create a division in the issue of disarmament: 'Multilateral good; unilateral bad.' As public debate continues to gather momentum, the specious distinction becomes if anything more rather than less entrenched.

In their pamphlet *Neither Red nor Dead*, written for the Social Democratic Party, Lord and Lady Kennet share with us a feeling that words may 'darken the subject', but object to 'unilateral' and 'multilateral' on a curious ground: because they are – polysyllabic. Therefore with the obvious intention of trying to make the contrast appear yet *more* lurid, they substitute 'one-sided' and 'all-round', suggesting that the 'one-sided movement' derives from 'emotional response' and not from any 'political or intellectual claims it makes' – and so, by implication, suggesting that 'all-roundedness' (which every decent chap knows is the mark of a gentleman) is the converse. In fact it is never clear in their pamphlet how their position differs in any important respect from the Whitehall conventional wisdom.[10] In November 1981 this entrenched slogan was further formalized with the creation of the Council for Arms Control, a body funded by individuals and by companies for the promotion of 'multilateral disarmament' through, in the words of the Bishop of Woolwich, at the press conference which launched the Council, 'serious and sensible' government initiatives. Interviewed on the radio, the Bishop revealed that fear of, or hostility to, 'unilateral disarmament' had helped impel the creation of this Council. But the Council's prospectus and an article by its chairman, Professor N. Brown, reveal that use of the false polarity has led to a misidentification of the problem. Indeed, Professor Brown's opinions are even more exotic: unilateralism is, he believes, a type of millenarian religion, akin to the Shia Islam of the Iranian ayatollahs, the Black Muslims of the United States, or the Jehovah's Witnesses. Given this view, his conclusion is that 'for any British government to concede even a portion of the unilateralists' core demands might be to increase the risk of nuclear war by at least a factor of ten'.[11] (Why ten?)

The idea and hope of simultaneous, multilateral, equally weighted *anything* in politics is Utopian. In the real world, when multilateral actions do occur (for they do), they occur as a series of sequential unilateral actions – chain reactions – so the two are in that sense one. There is good reason for this chain of causation: unilateral actions are powerful (look at rearmament). So while unilateral actions can happen independently – hence their power – multilateral action *in practice* is always a sequence; multilateral action *in theory* – the Utopian simultaneity – is at best a sign of political naïveté, usually just hot air, at worst a cynical justification for inaction.

The terms 'unilateral' and 'multilateral' have the specific and limited relationship mentioned. The words are of limited use in analysis, and since their meanings are now so generally distorted, it would be prudent to remove them from the agenda if we wish to have real discussion rather than remain immired in rhetoric.

3 Discrepancies between Declared Policy and Real Practice

We have already referred to the forces that complicate policy-making by any government, and also its course of action. These demand care in the use of such inclusive labels as 'Britain' or 'the British people'. But there are other discrepancies which arise from external pressures, from constraints of developing international relations, and from the inevitable desire of any government to put the best face on its own record, actions, and plans.

Normal diplomatic negotiations are conducted with a mixture of frankness and deception. It is often considered desirable to mislead a potential adversary, and sometimes thought necessary (for psychological reasons) to withhold unpleasant news from fellow-countrymen. So, for example, when in early November 1981 the media reported that Secretary of State Haig had informed a Congressional committee that NATO had an alarming plan to fire a nuclear 'demonstration' shot during conventional hostilities in Europe (only to be flatly contradicted by Secretary of Defense Caspar Weinberger giving evidence before another committee),[12] the British Secretary for Defence castigated the BBC for reporting the matter at all because 'its impact on ordinary people is deeply disturbing ... [it] ... can demoralize the West and weaken its capacity to defend its freedom'. He accused the BBC of biased, selective reporting, a charge which the BBC strongly refuted.[13] A desire to control the flow of information by distortion or suppression is unhappily common to governments of all kinds, and the citizen must be aware of it and try to allow for it.

It may happen that the distortion is so constant and uniform that the government officers and politicians who transmit the information and make the decisions come to believe that their picture of the nation and other nations is in fact correct. They believe their own deceptions. Then the discrepancy between declared policy and real practice may lead to internal muddle and external disastrous mistakes, or, as in the case of Haig, Weinberger, and the 'demonstration shot', to external muddle also.

A CASE STUDY
The exchange about limited nuclear war, October 1981

FRIDAY, 16 OCTOBER 1981
During a luncheon for newspaper editors, President Reagan is asked whether an exchange of nuclear weapons could be limited. A West

German correspondent noted down his reply: 'I don't honestly know. I think again, until some place ... all over the world this is being research going on, to try and find the defensive weapon. There never has been a weapon that someone hasn't come up with a defence. But it could ... and the only defence is, well, you shoot yours and we'll shoot ours' (sic). He continued: 'And if you still had that kind of a stalemate, I could see where you could have the exchange of tactical weapons against troops in the field without it bringing either one of the major powers to pushing the button.'

Asked again whether there could be a battlefield exchange of nuclear weapons without an exchange of strategic nuclear weapons President Reagan replied: 'Well, I would – if they realized that we – again, if – if we led them back to that stalemate only because that our retaliatory power, our seconds, or our strike at them after their first strike, would be so destructive that they couldn't afford it, that would hold them off.'

The Times journalist felt that it was not clear what President Reagan intended by these replies and that therefore the reaction which ensued was not justified. But a little application and thought reveal a simple proposition within them, expressed in the *Frankfurter Rundschau* headline of 19 October: 'Nuclear war in Europe? Reagan thinks that the USA could be spared' (*The Times*, Thursday, 22 October 1981, p. 8). Indeed, this interpretation was confirmed comprehensibly by the President himself in a news conference on 10 November.

Anger about the remarks was not confined to Western Europeans only, for in the same interview President Reagan added, 'I do have to point out that everything that has been said and everything in their manuals indicates that, unlike us, the Soviet Union believes that a nuclear war is possible and they believe it is winnable' (*The New York Times*, Wednesday, 21 October 1981, p. A7).

TUESDAY, 20 OCTOBER 1981
The NATO Defence Ministers of the Nuclear Planning Group were meeting at Gleneagles Hotel in Scotland when the news of President Reagan's remarks broke. It created a furore in Europe. Mr Nott, the British Defence Secretary, described this as a 'storm in a teacup', saying that there had been no change in US policy. The US State Department, amplifying the President's remarks, stated that his remarks 'were completely consistent with the alliance's long-standing strategy of flexible response'. The American administration took the

view that European consternation has been 'orchestrated' by opponents of nuclear weapons.

Meanwhile, the same day in Moscow, President Brezhnev commented upon President Reagan's remarks. He said that he would leave upon Mr Reagan's conscience the remark that he 'supposedly knows what Soviet leaders are talking about among themselves', and added, 'Among ourselves we are saying the same thing that was stated by me publicly from the rostrum of the Party Congress, namely that it is dangerous madness to try to defeat each other in the arms race and to count on victory in nuclear war.

'I shall add that only he who has decided to commit suicide can start a nuclear war in the hope of emerging a victor. No matter what might the attacker possesses, no matter what method of unleashing nuclear war he chooses, he will not attain his aims. Retribution will ensue ineluctably . . .

'It would be good if the President of the United States, too, would make a clear and unambiguous statement rejecting the very idea of nuclear attack as criminal' (*The New York Times*, Wednesday, 21 October 1981, p. A7).

He concluded by asking 'why was the United States not supporting the proposal made by the Soviet Union at the current session of the United Nations General Assembly to forgo any first nuclear strike?' (*The Times*, Wednesday, 21 October 1981, p. 1).

'For if there is no nuclear first strike, then consequently there will be no second or third nuclear strikes. Thereby all talk about the possibility or impossibility of victory in nuclear war will become pointless – the question of nuclear war as such will be removed from the agenda of the day.' (*The New York Times*, Wednesday, 21 October 1981, p. A7).

WEDNESDAY, 21 OCTOBER 1981
Aboard Air Force One en route to the North–South summit in Mexico, President Reagan issued a statement in response to President Brezhnev's remarks. 'Our strategy remains, as it has been, one of flexible response: maintaining an assured military capability to deter the use of force – conventional or nuclear – by the Warsaw Pact at the lowest possible level . . .

'The suggestion that the United States could even consider fighting a nuclear war at Europe's expense is an outright deception.

'The essence of United States nuclear strategy is that no aggressor should believe that the use of nuclear weapons in Europe would reasonably be limited to Europe' (*The Times*, 22 October 1981, p. 1).

However, as *The Times* reporter noted, President Reagan did not respond to the direct challenge to renounce nuclear war.

At the end of that week, massive public demonstrations took place in European capitals. On Monday 26th, the Reagan administration was swift to denounce them. Presidential counsellor Edwin Meese III said, 'we feel this will not impact on our policies'. The European demonstrations were, he added, 'a fairly well orchestrated attempt to influence opinion'. The *Washington Post* observed that 'State Department officials are considering ways of trying to exert counter-influences on US opinion' (*Washington Post*, 27 October 1981, pp. A1, A3).

TUESDAY, 27 OCTOBER 1981
In a final comment on the whole episode, Mr Weinberger, US Defense Secretary, said, 'The simple fact of the matter is that, unfortunate and awful as it would be for the world, it is possible that with nuclear weapons there can be some use of them in a limited, or in connection with what is up to that time, a war solely within the European theatre' (*Daily Telegraph*, 28 October 1981).

4 Discrepancies between Ends and Means

There is very little disagreement about the aims of policy where war and peace are at issue. Everyone desires peace. Everyone professes to hate war. The hard problems arise when we try to see what *means* will lead to the desired *ends*. There is debate as to (i) whether a proposed set of actions will in fact lead to the envisaged objectives. And there is the more fundamental debate as to (ii) whether certain actions in themselves are so objectionable that they cannot be compatible with noble objectives.

(i) The theory held to justify nuclear deterrent weapons is based on
    (a) certain questionable interpretations of the historical record, such as that strategic weapons have prevented war in Europe for thirty years;
    (b) guesswork as to the results of deploying various weapons;
    (c) guesswork as to how the antagonist will speculate on the potential results of *his* deployment of various weapons.

It is important for us to recognize the great uncertainties which are inherent in these three points of argument.

(ii) That certain actions are ethically unjustifiable in personal relationships is universally agreed – murder, victimization of the innocent, lying for personal advantage, and so on, are condemned. The accepted code between groups of people is more controversial. Nevertheless, the human conscience revolts against massacre of innocent people, no matter what the circumstances. Thus, a huge question-mark overshadows all use – and hence logically possession in which there is the faintest chance of use, i.e. all possession – of nuclear weapons.

The problem of choice of means is closely related to that of assessment of risk. Risk is inherent in every policy. In particular, there are risks involved in the possession of nuclear weapons and different risks involved in the renunciation of nuclear weapons. It is our aim to enable the reader to make a clear assessment of these risks. The conclusion to which we ourselves have been driven is that the risks in possession of nuclear weapons outweigh the risks in renunciation.

5 Related Discrepancies

From time to time there emerge discrepant estimates, statements, or opinions which arise from the four types of discrepancy listed above. These are derivative and subsidiary, but they appear in the news and tend to dominate our current discussion. Among these are:

(i) discrepant estimates of military power – in numbers of men, machines, conventional arms, and nuclear weapons.
(ii) discrepant statements on the dangerous effects of atomic energy generation and use, on the relation between civil and military uses of atomic energy, and on the pollution caused by the manufacture of nuclear weapons.

It is natural that people who have already adopted certain interpretations of terms, certain perceptions of threat, and certain judgements on uses and means, will come to different conclusions as to policy and action. We have assumed that the reader comes to this book with an open mind and a desire to evaluate the sources of information, the risks involved, and the policies recommended. We therefore proceed first to a historical account of the origins and development of the dangerous tensions, fears, and threats of the world today.

2   The Trail of Mistrust, 1914–73

1 The First World War and the Russian Revolution

The shadow of war has darkened the continent of Europe not only during the years of combat, 1914–18 and 1939–45, but also long after the conclusion of hostilities. No one can make sense of the development of international politics in this century without recognizing this. The current generation of leaders of the Great Powers came of age during the Second World War just as their fathers had done during the period of the First World War. How they look at the world today is in part a function of their formative experiences, which for them, as for millions of ordinary men and women, were years of war and revolution.

These upheavals were on a scale unmatched in history. A brief glance at some of the causes, conduct, and consequences of the 1914–18 war demonstrates two essential facets of contemporary history. First, we can see the extent to which misconceptions about the intentions of the 'other side' turned a local conflict in 1914 into a global conflagration. Secondly, we can observe the explosive effect of the waging of war on the internal political, economic, and social structure of all major combatant countries.

It was not the purpose of European leaders in late-nineteenth-century Europe to create a rigid alliance system which would polarize the Great Powers into two armed camps. Neither was it the objective of policy-makers to scare the 'other side' into a pre-emptive attack because of the perceived threat of a build-up in arms. And it certainly was not the aim of political leaders of impeccable conservative or reactionary credentials to set in motion a conflict which would threaten their traditional hold on political and economic power. But each of these unintended developments occurred.

Why it all happened remained a mystery to most of the men who made the decisions that brought war to Europe and eventually to the rest of the world. Yet slowly they came to see that the fundamental precipitant of war was a nearly universal tendency to miscalculate the intentions of both allies and adversaries. The steps leading to war in 1914 bear all the marks of forced judgements and casual plots fallen on their inventors' heads. No one planned to make the assassination of the Austrian Crown Prince the occasion for a confrontation between Russia and Austria–Hungary over primacy in south-eastern Europe. No one decided it would be wise to bring about the mobilization of the Russian army as a consequence of a Balkan crisis. No one initially wanted to set in motion the mobilization of the German army which followed or to realize the German plan to eliminate the threat from France before the Russian army was able to swing into operation. No one planned to drag Britain into the conflict through the violation of Belgian neutrality, a step made necessary by the German strategy of a huge flanking arc through Belgium and northern France. And yet all these events happened, primarily because the predictions of military and political leaders about how the 'other side' would behave were hopelessly wrong.

Their views about how the war would be fought and for how long were equally misconceived. All the major armies of the generation of 1914 were trained to fight wars of movement, yet on the Western Front they all fought an almost static war of attrition of a kind unknown even to the most pessimistic military planner in his worst nightmare. Vast artillery barrages promised the obliteration of enemy positions, after which their occupation by the infantry would be a relatively easy operation. Here too the miscalculations were disastrous. Month after month of hopeless frontal assaults on fortifications which withstood everything thrown at them annihilated millions of men on the Western Front alone. No one will ever know how many French and German soldiers fell around the north-eastern French town of Verdun in 1916 or how many British and Germans fell along the river Somme and near Passchendaele later in the same year and in 1917. To this day pieces of artillery shells, bones, and other droppings of war can be seen scattered over a large area of France and Flanders. Verdun and the Somme have entered our vocabulary as monuments, both to the courage and tenacity of the soldiers who served and to the blindness and inhumanity of the men who sent them to their deaths.

To break the ascendancy of the defensive in the war, new weapons and tactics were introduced. But even after the use of flame-throwers, tanks, and poison gas became the rule rather than the exception, still the bloodletting of immobility continued. By 1918 roughly one in every four shells fired on the Western Front contained chlorine, phosgene, or mustard gas. But it was not the use of such vicious tools of war that broke the stalemate on the Western Front in 1918. It was rather the greater economic flexibility of the Allies which won the day. Ultimately, Germany was virtually starved into submission, as news of terrible shortages on the home front broke the morale of the German army in the field. This occurred despite the greater efficiency of German war production. What she lacked was the ability to distribute goods and services effectively as between military and civilian needs.

What the outcome of the First World War demonstrated was the decisive importance in military strategy of the forging of strong links between industry, bureaucracy, and armies. The side that won the war was better able to mobilize mass armies for years, and to equip them, while continuing to fulfil most of the basic needs of the home front. This was not only a question of material and organization. It also involved the willingness of the masses to put up with the restrictions, shortages, and dreariness of ordinary life in wartime. Here the greater social cohesion of Britain and France, compared to Germany, made it possible for the Allies to win the war.

The cost of that victory is incalculable. One price of glory was the end of a long phase of expansion of the European economy. The damage caused by the war must be seen in terms of the diversion of resources away from productive activities and towards war purposes. But it must be measured also in terms of the destabilizing effects of war: inflation, long-term indebtedness, and the loss of markets to the only real victor in the First World War, the United States.

Such consequences of the war in the realm of the balance of economic and political power pale in comparison to the human costs of the conflict. Europeans today, whether they know it or not, walk upon a mound of corpses. To enter any parish graveyard in England or provincial town in France is to see how heavily inscribed are monuments to the fallen. Over seventy million men were mobilized in the 1914–18 war. Over nine million were killed. The indelible imprint the war left on the survivors is no less pervasive. Three million women were widowed and perhaps nine million children orphaned by the First World War. Millions who returned were maimed in body and spirit. Psychiatric records show how widespread was the lingering memory of the dead and how difficult it was for the survivors to rebuild their shattered lives. Even among those who came back without visible signs of damage there is disturbing evidence of a tendency to succumb to illnesses that non-combatants shrugged off. The ordeal of military service may have created a 'burnt-out' generation of men whose lives were shortened by war service, even though they emerged from it without a scratch.[1]

Civilians too bore the costs of war long after the conclusion of peace treaties. How a girl is fed when young is likely a generation later to affect her ability to conceive, to carry a pregnancy to full term, and to give birth to a healthy child.[2] Severe malnutrition in central Europe continued after Armistice Day in 1918, since the Allies maintained their blockade as a form of diplomatic pressure during the Paris Peace Conference. Children born in that period started life with a substantial disadvantage, which showed up a generation later in the diseases and malformations of their offspring. And those children were unlucky enough to come of age during the Second World War and to pass on to a third generation the burdens of malnutrition and deprivation in infancy. Babies born under those conditions are the mothers and fathers of today. Some of the obstacles to improvements in public health today are contemporary phenomena, but others are the legacy of war.

Other costs of the war lingered long after the conclusion of hostilities. The modern precedent of genocide was set by the Turkish massacre of the Armenian people. The use of systematic propaganda, misinformation, and official lies encouraged ordinary people to justify the perpetuation of the war because of the need to extirpate a monstrous enemy. The abuse of science, in which scientists willingly collaborated to produce weapons of appalling cruelty, was a universal phenomenon. The suppression of dissent and free thought as cowardly and subversive reached heights unknown for more than a century. Each of these developments was an outcome of the First World War. Each would return with much greater ferocity a generation later.

However, what made the impact of the 1914–18 war so profound was the fact that the war crisis gave birth to revolution. At the outbreak of hostilities, it seemed to nearly all observers that the threat of revolution had receded in Europe. The rush to the colours was much greater than anyone had anticipated. The adjustment to war conditions initially was relatively smooth. Three years later, war weariness, bereavement, and frustration had drained the enthusiasm of all but the most belligerent sections of the population. Most people still wanted to continue the war, simply to get the job done. But many began to have doubts about a war which seemed to have a life of its own. As the trench poets put it, whoever the loser would be, the only real winner would be the war.

In Russia the strains of the war effort proved too great for the Tsarist regime to support. When a Provisional Government replaced the Tsar in March 1917, it took a fateful and fatal decision to continue the war. This it justified in terms of the principle of revolutionary defensism – that is, the right of the new revolutionary government to throw the German invaders off Russian soil. Within a few months, this position collapsed as the Russian army voted with its feet for an end to the fighting. Still the centrist government of Alexander Kerensky carried on the war effort. This ensured that more and more people would be drawn to the side of Lenin and the Bolsheviks, who promised peace, bread, and land. After the Bolsheviks seized power in November 1918, they did indeed sue for peace. According to the terms of the Treaty of Brest-Litovsk, the Russians ceded to the Germans large parts of the Ukraine. The price of peace was high, but Lenin was right to conclude that the price of continuing the war would be higher still.

Despite the Bolsheviks' belief in the imminent victory of world revolution, it was less their Marxist principles than their abandonment of the war that initially set the Western powers against the Russian Revolution. The collapse of the eastern front and the transfer of German troops to the west inevitably produced a hostile reaction among the Allies. This took the form first of encouraging opponents of the Bolsheviks to revolt against the new Soviet government, and then, with Russia embroiled in a ferocious and bloody civil war, of intervening militarily on the side of the Whites. American, British, French, and Japanese troops landed in Russia; arms were supplied to the White forces. Other countries bordering on Russia, including Finland, Poland, and Romania, meanwhile took the opportunity to deliver further blows to an embattled enemy. In the immediate aftermath of the First World War, it was politically impossible for the Allies to send in sufficient troops to threaten the Soviet regime, and this, combined with the Whites' disunity and the Bolsheviks' superior organization and appeal to the population, ensured the failure of intervention. But it had significantly prolonged the civil war and increased its destructive impact. For the Allies, intervention was a minor episode, soon forgotten. For the Bolsheviks, however, it kindled a deep suspicion of the West and a fear of encirclement which has never died.

2 The Inter-War Years

In retrospect, it is clear that the most important consequences of the First World War for the future of international relations were the greatly enhanced influence of the United States and the formation of the USSR. Only a quarter of a century later these two countries would dominate world politics. But for the two decades following the First World War, the apparent centre of the international system remained in Europe, with

Britain, France, and Germany as the most active participants. Their conflicts culminated in the second phase of the European civil war, in 1939.

The most striking feature of the post-1918 decade in Europe was the emergence of revolutionary mass movements on the *right*. Fervent opposition to international socialism, strident patriotism, and contempt for the supposed decadence of traditional conservative groups were the hallmarks of fascist groups which recruited thousands in the immediate post-war period. Even though Italy was one of the war's victors, her constitution crumbled quickly when Benito Mussolini launched his march on Rome in 1922. As one of the vanquished, and as the scene of an abortive socialist revolution in 1919, Germany's fledgling democracy seemed similarly vulnerable to attacks from the right. But it took another decade and the onset of the Great Depression to provide the conditions for the overthrow of the Weimar Republic. In the event, the Nazi seizure of power in 1933 was perfectly constitutional. Many conservatives went along with Hitler's accession to power as Chancellor of Germany on the grounds that his anti-Communist credentials were excellent and because they believed that the burdens of power would exert a sobering and moderating influence on the Nazi leadership. Nothing could have been further from the truth. Hitler quickly established a ruthless dictatorship and began to give form to his vision of Germany's regaining by any and all means her 'rightful' place in world politics. Admirers and fellow-travellers of the Nazis sprang up in all European countries.

During the same period, for very different reasons and in different ways, the two future superpowers, the Soviet Union and the United States, remained on the sidelines of international affairs. In the Russian case, one reason why she played a peripheral part in world politics was that the First World War continued longer and with more ruinous consequences in Soviet Russia than in any other country. By the time the civil war ended at the beginning of 1921, both the economic and social systems were close to disintegration. Industrial output was only a fifth of the 1913 level, agricultural production less than half. Large areas would soon be ravaged by famine. Millions of people had died or would die as a result of the violence, disease, and famine caused by the World War and civil war: some sixteen million in all between 1914 and 1926, the vast majority of them civilians. Adding two million who had emigrated and another ten million fewer births during the period than would normally have occurred, Russia can be said to have suffered a total population loss of some twenty-eight million. Growing social unrest in the winter of 1920–21 meanwhile threatened to sweep the Bolsheviks from power. Peasant risings, workers' strikes, and, most dramatically of all, the mutiny at the Kronstadt naval base were ruthlessly suppressed. But the material causes of discontent could not be so swiftly removed. The Bolsheviks' response was to introduce the New Economic Policy. The premature and Utopian centralism of War Communism was replaced by economic decentralization, the restoration of the market economy, the encouragement of private agriculture and commerce, even limited denationalization of industry and granting of concessions to foreign companies. The resulting speed of economic recovery took even the regime by surprise. By 1926 pre-war levels of production had been regained in both industry and agriculture.

In its foreign relations, Soviet Russia's total isolation from a hostile world began to be replaced by real though limited contact with its former enemies. Trade agreements were soon followed by the establishment of diplomatic relations with most of the major powers, including Britain, France, Germany, and Japan. With Germany Russia formed a particularly close relationship, the Rapallo Treaty of 1922 providing for both political and military cooperation. The return to diplomatic normalcy, however, was neither uninterrupted nor complete. Diplomatic relations with Britain were broken off between 1927 and 1929 following a British raid on the Soviet trade delegation in London. The Soviet Union refused to join the League of Nations, which it regarded as a capitalist agency. And one great power, the United States, adamantly refused for the first decade and a half of the Soviet Union's existence to extend diplomatic recognition to it. Lenin's government, President Wilson had declared, was 'based upon the negation of every principle of honesty and faith'; it was seen not as a government, but as a group of international revolutionaries using Russia as a base for the overthrow of other governments. Such remained the official American view throughout the 1920s and early 1930s.[3] Communism, it held, was an intrinsically unworkable system, doomed to eventual collapse; recognition would only help to postpone its inevitable demise. Whatever plausibility such an interpretation might have had in the immediate aftermath of the Russian Revolution, it was increasingly divorced from the realities of Soviet policy in and after the civil war. As the prospect of world revolution receded, the Marxist–Leninist belief in the inevitable victory of socialism determined Soviet foreign policy less and less. The activities of the Communist International were strictly subordinated to the national interests of the Soviet Union, seen to lie in coexistence rather than confrontation with the capitalist world. The outcome of the power struggle which followed Lenin's death in 1924 was crucial for Soviet policy. In it Stalin's doctrine of 'socialism in one country', advocating concentration on the tasks of internal development, decisively triumphed over Trotsky's line of encouragement for foreign revolutionary movements or 'permanent revolution'.

The United States had emerged from the First World War as the strongest economic power in the world. While the economies of the European powers, victors and vanquished alike, had suffered decline during the war, the American economy had grown substantially. Post-war Europe was heavily in debt to the United States, and only American financial support maintained the precarious stability of the international economic system. The early 1920s were years of economic hardship and crisis for Europe, prosperity only returning in the second half of the decade. But for the United States, the post-war period until 1929 saw an economic boom of unprecedented proportions.

Economic strength, however, was not reflected in political influence. The year 1920 marked a radical break with the preceding period of decisive intervention in world politics. Disillusionment with Wilsonian internationalism produced a sharp reaction against involvement in political affairs outside the western hemisphere. For most Americans, peace in Europe was the affair of Europeans, not of the United States. In March 1920, the US Senate voted against ratifying the Versailles Treaty. In so doing it also vetoed American membership of the League of Nations, dealing a heavy blow to the League's capacity to maintain world peace by depriving it of an essential part of any potential sanctions against aggression. For the next two decades isolationism was the dominant theme in American foreign policy. In this spirit, the United States in 1923 withdrew its forces from the Rhineland army of occupation, and in 1925 declined to be associated with the Locarno treaties by which France attempted to guarantee stability in central and eastern Europe. The Senate even voted repeatedly against American participation in the International Court of Justice at the Hague.

The force of isolationism reflected in part the nature of native American xenophobia. The 1920s were a period of rabid anti-immigrant and anti-socialist politics, and nothing pleased American audiences more than to hear their leaders proclaim their commitment to keep 'foreign' ideas and nationals out of their country. The sheer vitality of the American economy permitted patriots to look askance at any who doubted the wisdom of what was known as the 'American way of life'.[4]

For both the Soviet Union and the United States, 1929 was a vital turning point. In very different ways, it inaugurated a period of major economic, political, and social change, which saw the evolution of policies of crucial importance for each country's future.

In the Soviet Union, the first five-year plan, approved by the Communist Party in April 1929, launched a still economically backward nation on the path of rapid industrialization. Soviet economic progress over the next decade was astonishing. On the basis of its own resources and with unprecedented speed, the USSR became one of the world's leading industrial powers. Its industrial output as a proportion of that of the United States rose from 7 per cent in 1928 to 45 per cent in 1938. In the process, the face of the country and the composition of its population were transformed. Hundreds of new towns were founded, whole new regions were developed, new industries created. Millions of peasants left the countryside to join the industrial workforce, while hundreds of thousands of ex-peasants and workers (almost all the present leaders of the Soviet Union among them) received higher and specialized education, then being immediately promoted to posts of responsibility and power. The costs as well as the achievements of this transformation were great. In the absence of foreign aid or investment, the capital necessary for investment had to be generated from within an essentially poor society. This meant a drastic fall in living standards – those of urban workers fell by half between 1928 and 1932.[5] To guarantee the supply of food to the towns and to maintain agricultural exports in order to earn foreign currency, as well as to break the richer peasants' capacity to resist government policy, collectivization of agriculture was ruthlessly forced through in the winter of 1929–30. The economic and human consequences were appalling: a catastrophic fall in agricultural production, which led to a famine in the south of the country in 1932–3, and the arrest or exile of huge numbers, perhaps five million, of *kulaks* and their families. Confronted by widespread discontent and opposition within and outside the Party, by severe problems of economic dislocation, and by immense and unforeseen problems arising from a highly mobile population, the regime greatly expanded its apparatus of political control. Within a few years this would be used to carry through the mass repression of real or suspected opponents in all sections of society. The great purges of 1936 to 1939, in which hundreds of thousands of people were executed and several millions dispatched to labour camps, not only caused immense suffering and damage to the Soviet Union's economy, armed forces, and cultural and scientific life, they also destroyed the last remnants of the democratic and humanitarian ideals which had inspired the Revolution of 1917. Despite these colossal self-inflicted wounds, however, the Soviet Union's dynamic economic growth continued and was consolidated. For good and for bad, this was the decisive period in the evolution of modern Soviet society.[6]

There can be no doubt that awareness of the USSR's strategic and military weakness was a prime motive in the Soviet leadership's decision in favour of rapid industrialization. Because the contrast with later Soviet power is so great, it is worth stressing the decidedly second-class status of the Soviet Union in military terms at the end of the 1920s. The Soviet armed forces then were generally considered inferior to those of Poland, let alone to those of the major world powers. In this situation, renewed intervention by the capitalist powers was a real possibility. Nothing better illustrates the connection between economic and military factors in Soviet policy at the time of the first five-year plan than Stalin's famous declaration of February 1931. 'Old Russia was ceaselessly beaten for her backwardness. For military backwardness, for cultural backwardness, for political backwardness, for industrial backwardness, for agricultural backwardness ... We are fifty or a hundred years behind the advanced countries. We must make good this lag in ten years. Either we do it or they crush us.'[7]

Yet the dangers facing the USSR did not diminish, but increased. The Japanese invasion and conquest of Manchuria in 1931 brought an openly expansionist and militarist power to the Soviet Union's own borders. In Europe the threat was more serious still. With Hitler's accession to power in Germany in 1933, war in the not-distant future became a probability rather than a possibility for the Soviet regime. The Nazis' anti-Bolshevik crusade combined with Hitler's proclaimed goal of German expansion eastwards into the Ukraine and European Russia presented a greater menace to Soviet security than anything since 1920. Germany's repudiation of the Rapallo Treaty in 1934 removed any doubt as to the future direction of German–Soviet relations. Fundamental changes in Soviet foreign policy resulted. In 1934 the USSR joined the League of Nations, becoming over the next four years the leading advocate of collective security against aggression. A series of alliances was concluded with neighbouring countries in Eastern Europe. In 1935 the Communist International changed course, directing its members to form a united front with other socialist parties, and later a popular front with all anti-fascist forces. Above all, Stalin attempted to form a bloc with Britain and France against the fascist powers, but unsuccessfully. The West in general, and Britain in particular, were fearful of Communism, repelled by the Soviet regime's violence against its own population, and sceptical of the USSR's military potential. Many right-wing politicians were also inclined to sympathize with Hitler's anti-Bolshevism and to appease German demands, and so did not have a serious interest in allying with the Soviet Union. Indeed, many people in official circles hoped that Germany would turn eastwards and weaken or destroy Soviet Communism. The Western powers' ineffective response to fascist expansionism – to German militarization of the Rhineland and annexation of Austria, to Italy's invasion of Abyssinia, and to German and Italian intervention in the Spanish civil war – culminated in the surrender of Czechoslovakia to Germany at Munich in 1938, at a conference to which the USSR, though an ally of Czechoslovakia, was not invited. It is hardly surprising that when in spring 1939 negotiations about a mutual assistance pact at last got under way, Britain's and France's half-heartedness should have been matched by Soviet scepticism about the Western democracies' intentions. The outcome was a crucial volte-face on Stalin's part, and the signing of the German–Soviet non-aggression treaty of August 1939. Two decades of mutual fear and distrust had thus produced a fateful diplomatic realignment. And so while Germany invaded Poland, precipitating war with Britain and France, the USSR adopted a position of benevolent neutrality towards Germany, moved into eastern Poland, went to war with Finland in 1939 to strengthen its northern defences, and in 1940 annexed the Baltic states of Latvia, Lithuania, and Estonia, as well as Bessarabia (which was Romanian between the wars, annexed by the Soviet Union in 1940, returned to Romania from 1940 to 1944, and taken back into the Soviet Union in 1945, has a non-Romanian population, and is now part of the Ukraine).

For the United States, the 1930s were hardly less traumatic than for the USSR if lacking violence and suffering on the same scale, they also lacked the dynamism and achievement of the Soviet Union. In October 1929 the economic boom collapsed. The Wall Street crash precipitated the greatest crisis American capitalism had experienced. Not only were innumerable personal fortunes destroyed overnight, so also was confidence in the financial system. The consequences went far beyond the USA. In one country after another creditors sought to collect and could not. Over the next two years panic and, in its wake, depression and mass unemployment spread from Austria to Germany to Britain to the rest of Europe and eventually back to the United States itself. Industrial output there had slumped to barely half of the 1929 level by 1931, while the number of unemployed soared to twelve million by 1932.[8]

The eventual response to this crisis laid down the basic lines of economic and social policy for the next four decades. Roosevelt's New Deal, launched in 1933, comprised a series of measures of government intervention designed both to pull the American economy out of the slump and to implement concepts of social justice. In these respects it represented a drastic break with traditional political attitudes and values, based on belief in the merits of self-sufficiency and unrestrained private enterprise; and to a degree it arrested and alleviated the effects of the Depression. But the New Deal had both limitations and costs. It proved incapable of either ending the slump or preventing a worsening of the recession in 1937 and 1938. (There were still ten and a half million unemployed in 1938.) Only rearmament from 1939 onwards would bring the Depression to an end.[9] It must not be forgotten, also, that Franklin D. Roosevelt's Democratic Party was a coalition of Northern liberals and Southern reactionaries, many of the most powerful of whom were unreconstructed racialists. The New Deal did provide remedies for some of the difficulties faced by the American economy, but it did not (and was not intended to) change fundamentally the anti-Communist, anti-black, and insular nature of American politics. The achievement of civil rights for blacks was still a generation away. Much more had been gained by organized labour, which limited its objectives to securing its rightful place in industrial relations. Some dissident voices could be heard in the newly formed Congress of Industrial Organizations, but these were ultimately silenced in an alliance with the older American Federation of Labour, which became (and remains) a bastion of anti-Communism.[10]

In its foreign policy, the Roosevelt administration also stood for a new approach, though the practical effects were relatively small. Pressure from business circles and a belief that cooperation with the USSR might be useful in dealing with problems in Europe and the Far East led to diplomatic recognition in November 1933. But in fact little changed in Soviet–American relations. After a brief honeymoon, official opinion became as anti-Soviet as before. To long-drawn-out disputes about Soviet responsibility for the Provisional Government's debts was added an understandable reaction against the purges of the late 1930s. The conclusion drawn by the United States' Soviet specialists at this time laid the foundation for later attitudes and policies in the Cold War: namely that a totalitarian internal system must mean a foreign policy of unlimited expansionism and unprincipled aggression.[11] Normal diplomatic relations with such a state were either dangerous or impossible; the only appropriate response was toughness and hard bargaining. Soviet behaviour at the end of the decade, with the annexations of 1939 and 1940, and the simultaneous war against Finland, only seemed to confirm this judgement.

Although by the time he became president, Roosevelt had abandoned his earlier commitment to the League of Nations, he retained President

Wilson's belief in the need for international cooperation to preserve peace. And he increasingly came to see Germany and Japan as the main threats to American interests and international stability. But isolationism was deeply entrenched in American political attitudes. The administration's ability to exercise influence on the developing conflicts in Europe and Asia was significantly reduced by a series of 'Neutrality Acts' passed by Congress between 1933 and 1936. These sought to isolate the United States from foreign conflicts by placing an embargo on trade in munitions and weapons with all belligerent countries, including the victims of aggression. Not until well after the outbreak of the Second World War did Roosevelt succeed in amending these laws in order to provide Britain with the possibility of buying war supplies.[12]

3 The Second World War

Although the Second World War is conventionally dated from 1939, the war for the first two years was almost exclusively fought in Europe and on its periphery by European powers, Britain and France, Germany and Italy. The United States and the Soviet Union in this period were neutral, each hoping to avoid entanglement in the European war. American opinion increasingly moved in an anti-German direction, and by 1940 the United States was supplying armaments and credits on a large scale to Britain and France, but still the majority of Americans wanted to stay out of the war. For the Soviet leaders, the war was one between imperialist powers, in which its initial sympathy was on Germany's side. Though German–Soviet relations steadily deteriorated and though Soviet military preparations accelerated, it seemed inconceivable to Stalin that Germany would attack the USSR while Britain was still undefeated.

In the event, both the Soviet Union and the United States were precipitated into war suddenly and unexpectedly. On 22 June 1941 Hitler unleashed an unprovoked and undeclared war on the USSR, while on 7 December 1941 Japan destroyed the American Pacific fleet at Pearl Harbor. These events brought the two countries into a grand alliance with Britain against the Axis powers.

The Soviet Union paid an enormous price for being caught by surprise – a fact of great significance in understanding the attitudes of present Soviet leaders (who in 1941 were already in important posts) towards their country's defence. In the space of a few weeks, the hard-won achievements of Soviet power came close to being entirely wiped out. Vast areas of the USSR were occupied by the enemy: the Baltic republics, Belorussia, the

Ukraine, much of European Russia. A large part of the Soviet air force was destroyed in the first hours of the war. Huge numbers of prisoners were taken by the Germans, over a million in the first six months. The German armies soon reached Moscow and Leningrad. The latter was to be besieged for the next three years. In October 1941, at the battle of Moscow, Soviet troops inflicted the first defeat on German forces in the war and checked their advance. But it resumed in 1942 and by late in the year the Germans had reached Stalingrad on the Volga. There, in one of the most decisive battles of modern history, the Soviet army crushed the Germans and turned the tide. However, it would still take another year and a half of fighting, including the greatest tank battle that the world has ever seen, at Kursk in July 1943, before Soviet territory had been fully liberated, and a further eight months after that before Germany surrendered.

No other experience has made so deep an impression on the outlook of the Soviet population, leaders and masses alike, as the Second World War. Three points are particularly important. First, the fighting on the Eastern front was more protracted and on a larger scale than in any other theatre of war. German military power was in effect destroyed by the Soviet army. From 1941 to 1945 the great majority of German army divisions were in the East. In the winter of 1942–3, at the time of the battles of Stalingrad and El Alamein, fifteen Axis divisions were in North Africa and 240 in the USSR. Even after D-Day in June 1944 the proportion of the German army on the Western front was never more than a third. The losses of the Soviet armed forces were gigantic: some seven to eight million dead. Second, nearly four years of occupation and warfare caused enormous civilian casualties and material damage. Around twelve million civilians died, including over a million during the siege of Leningrad. Many of the dead were victims of deliberate extermination or reprisals for partisan activity. Material destruction included 1,710 towns and 70,000 villages destroyed, and 65,000 kilometres of railway track ruined. By the end of the war half the urban housing in the formerly occupied zones had been destroyed, and twenty-five million people were homeless.[13] Third, the Soviet war effort was primarily a nationalist response to foreign invasion. 'The Great Patriotic War' is the name officially given to the Second World War in the Soviet Union. The regime appealed to the population to defend the motherland and the population responded. Mobilization of the country's resources, human, economic, military, was greater than in any of the other belligerent nations, including Germany or the United States. (Thanks to this, Soviet industrial output, despite the widespread destruction of plant in the occupied areas, actually rose between 1940 and 1945.)

Ironically the Nazi attempt to destroy Soviet Communism produced national unity, a bond between regime and people far greater than had existed before. In the severest possible test of a government's basic duty – to protect its country's population and territory from foreign aggression – the Soviet regime had been victorious.

While the role of the United States in the war was equally decisive, its experience in the war was considerably less traumatic.[14] The fighting took place thousands of miles from the American continent, a fact of considerable economic significance, for while all the European and Asian belligerents suffered extensive material destruction, the American economy boomed: gross national product doubled in the course of the war. For the population, wartime prosperity replaced pre-war depression as unemployment fell and real wages rose. Civilian casualties in the USA were zero, while total military deaths, in Europe, Africa, and the Far East, were 405,000. The United States' massive economic strength gave it for the first time great diplomatic influence as well as military power. From its entry into the war, the USA was the dominant partner in Anglo-American relations, and, moreover, its interests and actions were those of a global power. In the military defeat of the Axis powers, American forces played a major part, in the Pacific, in North Africa and in southern and western Europe. And in the last days of the war, American military strength was vastly increased by possession of the atomic bomb. Debate still continues as to whether dropping the bomb on the Japanese cities of Hiroshima and Nagasaki was justified as the only means of shortening the war and avoiding even more casualties. What is certain is that the use of the bomb fundamentally changed the nature of military conflict.[15]

Table 1. Soldiers Killed in the Two World Wars as a Proportion of Total Populations[16]

Country	First World War		Second World War	
	Total killed (approx.)	Proportion of total population in 1911–14	Total killed (approx.)	Proportion of total population in 1940
France	1,327,000	1/29	211,000	1/200
Germany	2,037,000	1/33	2,850,000	1/25
Great Britain	723,000	1/62	398,000	1/150
Russia/ Soviet Union	1,811,000	1/99	7,500,000	1/22
United States	114,000	1/870	405,000	1/325

Victory in the Second World War was won by an alliance of the United States, the Soviet Union, and Britain. The long years of subsequent conflict have tended to obscure the significance of the wartime alliance, but its contribution to the defeat of fascism was crucial. It was, moreover, more than a simple marriage of convenience among individual countries each pursuing separate national interests, since fascism represented a deadly threat both to Western democracy and to Soviet Communism. Like all alliances, it suffered from clashes of opinion and interests. Hostility to different ideologies and social-political systems, suspicion of intentions to conclude a separate peace with Germany, resentment over the Western Allies' slowness in opening a second front in Europe (originally promised for 1942, but achieved only in June 1944), fears of Soviet hegemony in post-war Eastern Europe, disagreement over the future of Germany: all featured prominently in relations between the Allies. None the less, the alliance held and provided the basis for victory. Substantial economic assistance for the British and Soviet war effort was provided by the United States; the goal of unconditional surrender was firmly adhered to; military strategy was coordinated and agreement on the handling of post-war issues was reached. The Yalta Conference of February 1945, though subsequently denounced by many Western commentators as a capitulation to Soviet expansionism, was seen at the time as embodying genuine compromise by all sides and as laying the foundation for post-war cooperation.[17] Most important of all, despite the strains in the alliance which characterized the closing stages of the war, the Allies – unlike the victors of the First World War – succeeded in hammering out a real framework for future international security, in the form of the United Nations Organization. An essential factor in this achievement was a change in American public opinion and government policy away from isolationism towards recognition that it was in the interests of the United States to take a leading role in international relations. Equally important was the acceptance by the American government that the Soviet Union could no longer be relegated to the periphery of world politics, but that it also had a central role to play, as well as legitimate interests to defend.

As the war ended, differences between the Allies were increasingly becoming evident. At the same time, the potential for cooperation in the task of post-war reconstruction existed. As Roosevelt wrote concerning one dispute only hours before his sudden death in April 1945:

> I would minimize the general Soviet problem as much as possible because these problems, in one form or another, seem to arise every day, and most of them straighten out ... We must be firm, however, and our course thus far is correct.[18]

To most Europeans, the difficulties the Allies had in living with each other paled into insignificance compared with the terrible problems and conflicts posed by the Nazi occupation of almost the entire continent of Europe. Whatever their subsequent behaviour, Russian, British, and American troops were rightly welcomed as liberators who freed Europeans from a regime of appalling brutality. When the Russian army reached Auschwitz and the British and Americans reached Dachau and Buchenwald, they uncovered some of the terrible machinery of murder which the Nazis had used to rid their 'New Order' of political opponents, 'undesirables', and Jews. Even when most of the German General Staff realized that the war against the Allies was lost in late 1944, still the war against the Jews went inexorably on. The great majority of the victims fell into the hands of the Nazis after the invasion of Poland in 1939 and of the Soviet Union in 1941. Enormous numbers were either shot on the spot or concentrated in ghettoes, deported, and exterminated in a network of camps. In contrast to the 1914–18 war, gas was employed by the Nazis not in combat but rather in pursuit of the 'Final Solution of the Jewish Problem', in the course of which approximately six million Jews perished. Among the dead whose ashes were scattered throughout eastern Europe were over one million children.[19]

Yet it would be a mistake to assume that during the war Europeans saw the persecution of European Jewry as the worst part of the Nazi reign of terror. Most Europeans treated the disappearance of entire Jewish communities as an unavoidable part of the upheaval of war. Many chose not to know what was going on in concentration camps, some of which, like Dachau, were located very close to large urban centres.

What was more difficult to turn away from outside Germany was the phenomenon of collaboration. The outsiders of the interwar years, extreme right-wing politicians, romantic intellectuals, and petty criminals, had come to power in the wake of German military victory. Their abject servility to the Nazis, their eager compliance in the theft of property and in the use of slave labour in German factories, and their exploitation of accidental prominence for personal gain and to settle old scores turned most Europeans against collaborators. But as long as the German occupation continued the sad fact is that resignation rather than resistance was the rule. Even though many collaborators paid for their crimes with their lives at the end of the war, many others slipped back into the anonymity of peacetime life.[20] Their presence (and that of many of their Nazi superiors) in Europe today is a lingering reminder of the war of debasement, humiliation, and fear which the Nazis brought to the world and which only the combined weight of the United States, Britain, and the Soviet Union ultimately ended.

4 The Post-War Generation

The decades of prosperity between 1950 and 1973 separate us from the darker years of the two world wars. The insecurity Germans or Italians feel today about their prosperity is in part a function of their memory of war-related deprivation. Many Europeans today have much more to lose by war or revolution than their fathers had. It is this combination of early memories of the material and human costs of war and later experiences of the material gains of peace and stability which informs the political thinking of most Western European leaders. To such men and women, Communism symbolizes the potential loss of what they put together with difficulty after the calamitous years between 1914 and 1945.

The sheer speed of the rebuilding of Europe after 1945 was astounding. In part economic reconstruction was a result of the injection of huge amounts of American capital in the late 1940s when the German economy was still prostrate. In part it was a reflection of the vast store of human capital in Europe, the knowledge, skills, and services of millions of people who were set to constructive tasks after the war. Of equal importance was the creation of a set of economic and political arrangements which brought a kind of stability essential to the revival of manufacture, finance, and commerce. The International Monetary Fund was set up to act as a lender of last resort in international trade. American-sponsored moves towards the political integration of Europe were rejected by European leaders, who instead fashioned a framework for economic cooperation along the lines of the Monnet plan of 1956. Out of these initiatives the Common Market was born.[21]

Europe's post-war recovery took place against a background of worsening relations between the Soviet Union and the Western powers. Wartime cooperation gave way to conflict, confrontation, and Cold War. Where responsibility for this deterioration lies is probably the most controversial issue in modern history.[22] But it is not difficult to identify the factors which made the dissolution of the wartime alliance possible: the legacy of mutual fear and suspicion which had existed from 1917; the Soviet Union's determination to guarantee its Western borders by means of a buffer zone of friendly states between itself and a potentially hostile Western Europe; its resolve to prevent the possibility of any resurgence of German militarism, together with an intention of exacting reparations from defeated enemies to help rebuild its own shattered economy; a strong and confident United States's refusal to accept Soviet hegemony over half of Europe or to see its populations forced to adopt Soviet-style political and economic systems. Out of these conflicting elements arose the events which divided Europe into two hostile camps: the cessation of American aid to the USSR in 1945; the Greek civil war of 1946–7; the establishment of Communist-dominated regimes throughout Eastern Europe between 1946 and 1948; the enunciation of the Truman Doctrine of US support for 'free peoples who are resisting attempted subjugation by armed minorities or by outside pressures' in 1947; the division of Germany into two distinct parts, each with its own administrative and economic systems, in 1948. By the late 1940s economic growth itself was being fostered in Western Europe as an effective bulwark against Communism. It is no surprise, therefore, that the name of the American Secretary of State, George C. Marshall, is associated both with the economic reconstruction of Europe and with the establishment of the American–European military pact, the North Atlantic Treaty Organization, founded in 1949.

In the late 1940s, three events occurred which set the Cold War into the rigid mould in which it rested for a generation. The first was a Russian attempt in 1948 to block ground traffic and supplies to Berlin, which was occupied by all four major powers. A successful Western airlift kept Berlin alive and served as a symbol of resistance to Communism. That victory was soon overshadowed by the explosion of an atomic device by the Soviet Union. This denied the United States its unrivalled position as prime arbiter of international affairs. It also convinced many in the West of the danger of subversive elements who, it was believed, played a key role in the 'theft' by the Soviets of atomic secrets. In America, the witch-hunt that followed was of a force and pervasiveness which terrified virtually all opposition into submission. Lesser waves of anti-Communist fervour also swept over Europe, especially following the third major development of 1949 – the outbreak of the Korean war in the wake of the final victory of the Chinese Communist revolution. To stop a supposedly expansionist China, the United Nations voted, in the absence of the Soviet Union, to engage in a 'police action' in Korea. Some aggressive cold warriors, like General Douglas MacArthur, wanted to use the occasion to invade China herself. For pressing this objective, which was contrary to American policy, he was sacked by President Truman. In 1953 an armistice was agreed, which divided Korea into a Communist north and a non-Communist south.

At the end of the Korean war, the armed truce between East and West began, and there it has continued more or less to this day. As weapons systems became more complex and as logistical lines grew longer and more involved, an additional element was added to the equation of international politics. Since the 1950s, the network of linkages between soldiers, scientists, businessmen, labour leaders, and civil servants has proliferated as the need to devise, develop, and deploy new weapons systems has grown. In his now famous farewell address in 1960, President Dwight Eisenhower warned of the dangers of the further expansion of a 'military-industrial' complex. In Europe as in the United States, such groups have influenced political developments throughout this century (and in the case of Germany, even before 1900). Warfare and preparation for warfare have always been the midwives of bureaucracy. But the crystallization of the alliance system after 1945 into Warsaw Pact (Soviet Union plus satellites) versus NATO (United States plus satellites) brought the process of bureaucratization to a new and higher level. It has become increasingly difficult to tell whether elected officials or career civil servants or arms manufacturers are the prime formulators of defence policy.[23]

The trail of mistrust in this century has thus been extended in part by bureaucratic developments which tend to have a momentum of their own. It is certainly true that the armed stalemate in Europe grew out of the decision taken during the Second World War by the Allied leaders, Churchill, Roosevelt, and Stalin, to divide the continent into spheres of Western and Soviet control. But nearly forty years later, thousands of soldiers manning expensive and sophisticated weapons still sit staring at each other 'over the Iron Curtain'. That they do so is in part a function of a real political conflict, but the stalemate continues also because it is in the interests of bureaucrats on both sides of the great divide.

The inertia of the Cold War has been maintained in defence policy despite the fact that the two opposing sides today bear little resemblance to their counterparts of the late 1940s. The fragmentation and transformation of both Communism and conservatism are among the most important historical developments of this century, and yet strategic issues on both sides are still discussed as if adversaries were trapped in amber forty years ago.

If we can be grateful to Hitler for anything, it is for having unintentionally discredited the ideas of European conservatives who frame political fears in biological terms. The Second World War thus separates two phases in the history of conservatism. Before 1939, many conservatives spoke in the language of race, blood, and breeding. They feared being swamped by the more prolific non-white peoples or the more prolific working-class strata within their own borders. People who voiced such ideas were bound to find in the Russian Revolution evidence of the precipitous decline of the 'civilized' world. In its extreme form anti-Communism thus became a crusade against a biological and racial wave of pollution. We should not forget how widespread were such racialist assumptions on the right (and not only on the right) before 1939.

After 1945, Christian Democracy was born. It was committed to a form of the American concept of free opportunity for all, according to which it was the duty of the state to permit individual talent to win out in free and open competition. A much greater degree of intervention in the economy by the state was accepted by conservatives after 1945, but this action was justified first to revive the European economy and then to permit the market to do its necessary work of regulating relative prices. Racialism was outlawed. When it reared its head, as in Enoch Powell's warnings of rivers of blood flowing in the wake of black immigration to Britain, it was disowned and condemned by conservatives whose predecessors were guilty of much more extreme forms of prejudice.[24]

There are, of course, significant differences among European conservative groups. Some parties, such as Strauss's Bavarian conservatives, are stridently anti-Communist. Some have strong links, both officially and unofficially, with military cliques, whose interest in increasing armaments expenditure is obvious. As the difficult negotiations within the European community show, the objectives of different conservative groups have diverged sharply, both among themselves and between themselves and the United States. European foreign policy has become gradually less and less a form of genuflection to whatever line the State Department has adopted. The success of the Gaullist strategy of partial withdrawal from the American camp plus the failure of the American war effort in Vietnam have meant that the anti-Communist front of the late 1940s and 1950s has ceased to exist as a common political force.

The same fragmentation of ideology and policy has taken place on the other side of the ideological divide. Even before the Second World War, during the worst years of Stalin's bloody dictatorship, the ground was being prepared for the emergence of national forms of Communist politics, some of which are now known as Eurocommunism. In part this phenomenon was the product of men like Antonio Gramsci, who emphasized the need for Communists to draw their political beliefs from the language and historical experience of their own countries. To adopt a strict Russocentrism, as Stalin insisted, would be no gain at all. In part Eurocommunism was born out of the prominent role played by Communists in the resistance to fascism. Such men created mass political parties committed to national and nationalist objectives and organizationally similar to other parties of the left. In France and Italy these parties have taken root and have worked hard to demonstrate their respectability, especially in the field of municipal administration and local government.[25]

In Eastern Europe, the presence of Soviet troops has obscured the growth of similarly centrifugal forces within the Communist movement. The departure of Tito's Yugoslavia from the Soviet camp in 1948, the uprisings of 1956 in Poland and Hungary, the Prague 'spring' of 1968, and the emergence of Solidarity, the free trade union organization in Poland, in 1980, cannot be attributed to anti-Communist or subversive agents, as Radio Moscow has claimed consistently. What the Czech leader Alexander Dubcek called 'socialism with a human face' has had numerous counterparts elsewhere in Eastern Europe.[26] This will remain a contradiction in terms only in the minds of those committed to a demonology in the first place.

Even in the USSR itself, Communism has undergone substantial changes since the death of Stalin in 1953. Although Khrushchev's reforms were limited in their scope and impact, they still caused a dismantling of the Stalinist system. The end of mass repression and terror, the curbing of the authority of the secret police, the loosening of censorship and relaxation of ideological controls over science and culture, the greater role allotted to specialists in the running of society, and the opening up of contact with the non-Communist world have all introduced significant elements of diversity and pluralism into Soviet life. The contemporary Soviet Union is a highly centralized and controlled society compared with its capitalist counterparts and may still be a long way from Western ideals of democracy; but it is equally far removed from the totalitarian state of a quarter of a century ago.[27]

If propagandists in the West in the 1940s and 1950s were convinced that Communism was a unified political force in the world directed by the Kremlin, they had much more trouble in the last decade and a half with the emergence of the Sino-Soviet dispute. What the Chinese and Russians had to quarrel about was no doubt a mystery to those who saw the world in the simple terms of 'communism' versus the 'free world'.[28] By the late 1960s, though, even the American State Department began to advertise the merits of a multipolar strategic outlook, which lasted until the 1980 American election.

The advocates of bipolarity have a difficult time coming to terms with the variations within the centre and left-centre parties which form the heart of the non-Communist opposition to conservatism. A productive, efficient, and roughly egalitarian mixed economy is what some socialists aim to achieve. The West German Social Democratic Party is a case in point. Others believe that a mixed economy is a step on the way to socialism, which requires a fully collectivist economy. People on the left of the British Labour Party are advocates of this latter position. This has offended moderates sufficiently to cause them to form a new 'radical' party, the (British) Social Democratic Party. Whether or not this party will grow is less important than the fact that it is a good illustration of the increasing complexity of the political world of the left and centre-left parties at a time of deepening economic recession.

The mistrust between East and West, which is so deeply ingrained in strategic thinking and propaganda, requires the denial of the extent to which both European and world politics have changed in the years since the end of the Second World War. In Africa and Asia the emergence of the non-aligned movement in the 1950s and 1960s added a further centrifugal force to international affairs. The outlook of leaders such as Nehru of India, Nasser of Egypt, Peron of Argentina, or Gaddafi of Libya cannot be fitted easily into the categories of East versus West. Their power grew in part out of their prominence in pre-liberation struggles against colonialism, the recrudescence of which either in Western or Communist forms they and their successors have strenuously resisted.[29]

Since the onset of the worst economic crisis in forty years, which followed departure from the post-war international financial system, the 1973 Arab–Israeli war, and the steep rise in the price of oil, it has become even more important to revise outdated strategic concepts. Non-European oil producers have been the prime beneficiaries of the greatest capital outflow from Europe since the First World War. The full repercussions of this change in the balance of world financial power have yet to be felt. However, to assume that the nature of the East–West conflict in the 1980s is roughly the same as it was two, three, or four decades ago is to risk concocting the same dangerous mixture of miscalculation and mutual incomprehension which led inexorably to war earlier this century.

Therefore even a very cursory view of trends in European and world history over the last seventy years can show that many of the dominant themes in the strategic thinking and propaganda of the Cold War distort the past and the present political configuration of the world. What Europeans have in common is not so much participation in a single ideological crusade, either against capitalism or against Communism, as the legacy, both human and material, of earlier 'crusades'. It is on collective memory as well as on collective hope that a new approach to strategic thinking in a politically diverse world must rest.

3 'An Extremely Efficient Explosive':
the Early History,
1939–56

In this chapter the early history of strategic thinking about nuclear weapons is told. It shows how and where the theory of 'deterrence' came to be associated with them, and also tells the history of the two occasions when there have been real opportunities to prohibit nuclear weapons and how those opportunites were lost. Both these histories had ended by the mid-1950s.

1 Birth of the Nuclear Age, 1939–45

Winston Churchill, looking back at the first months of the Second World War, described them as 'the Twilight War': the dark night of the evacuation from Dunkirk, the Battle of Britain, and the Blitz lay ahead. But these were portentous times, because the outbreak of war in the autumn of 1939 had caught in England the Austrian physicist Otto Frisch. Frisch stayed in Birmingham with another refugee physicist, Rudolf Peierls, and there, during the months of the 'Twilight War', Frisch continued to work on the question of uranium fission – that is, splitting apart the nucleus (hence 'nuclear') of the atom (hence 'atomic'). Until that moment informed opinion, including Frisch himself, believed that an effective atomic bomb could not be made. But now further work

... gave me a figure for the required amount of uranium 235. To my amazement it was very much smaller than I had expected; it was not a matter of tons, but something like a pound or two.

Of course I discussed that result with Peierls at once ... we stared at each other and realized that an atomic bomb might after all be possible.

I have often been asked why I didn't abandon the project there and then, saying nothing to anybody ... The answer is very simple. We were at war, and the idea was reasonably obvious; very probably some German scientists had had the same idea and were working on it.[1]

So Frisch and Peierls together wrote a memorandum which, more than any other single document, helped to usher in the nuclear age. The memorandum consisted of two parts. One described how a 'super-bomb' based on a chain reaction in uranium might be made. The other reflected on the strategic and moral implications of such a weapon (see box).

EXTRACT FROM THE FRISCH—PEIERLS MEMORANDUM, 1940
Part I, 'On the construction of a "super-bomb" based on a nuclear chain reaction in uranium' [2]

'The possible construction of "super-bombs" based on a nuclear chain reaction in uranium has been discussed a great deal and arguments have been brought forward which seem to exclude this possibility. We wish here to point out and discuss a possibility which seems to have been overlooked in these earlier discussions.

'Uranium consists essentially of two isotopes, U 238 (99.3 per cent) and U 235 (0.7 per cent) . . . Bohr has put forward strong arguments for the suggestion that the fission observed with slow neutrons is to be ascribed to the rare isotope U 235, and that this isotope has, on the whole, a much greater fission probability than the common isotope U 238. Effective methods for the separation of isotopes have been developed recently . . . This permits, in principle, the use of nearly pure U 235 in such a bomb, a possibility which apparently has not so far been seriously considered. We have discussed this possibility and come to the conclusion that a moderate amount of U 235 would indeed constitute an extremely efficient explosive.'

The crucial thing which Frisch and Peierls did was to ask the right question and, from theory alone, to propose answers which showed that an atomic bomb was practicable. German research concentrated on heavy water moderated reactor technology, work that was fatally disrupted by the courageous British commando raid on the Norsk Hydro power station where heavy water was made, and then by the sinking of a ferry with heavy water aboard it by the Norwegian underground. But although the appearance of the V-2 ballistic missile convinced some British defence scientists that this could only mean that the Germans had, or were on the point of obtaining, an atomic weapon (why go to such expense to deliver a ton of TNT?), in fact they never did develop the atomic bomb because their leading scientists, Heisenberg and von Weizsäcker, appear never to have asked the question about U 235, although about this there is still debate:

Professor Peierls has since found detailed accounts of a meeting at which Heisenberg is reported to have quoted the critical size of light uranium isotope to be 'about the size of a football' which, while too large, is not excessively so, and seems to be on the right track. Some commentators have suggested that the German scientists did indeed see the way to proceed, but chose not to tell their national authorities. About this there is much debate also.[3]

In March 1940 the memorandum was shown to Sir Henry Tizard, the senior government scientific adviser. It led directly to the establishment of the MAUD committee, which guided British research on atomic energy in 1940 and 1941. The report of the MAUD committee in the summer of 1941 was instrumental in spurring forward American research in the famous Manhattan Project which eventually produced atomic weapons just in time for them to be used on the Japanese cities of Hiroshima and Nagasaki in August 1945, five and a half years after Frisch and Peierls so lucidly explained that such bombs could, in fact, be made.

Throughout the wartime atomic project, the bombs were regarded primarily as an 'extremely efficient explosive': a much bigger bang than one bomber aircraft had ever been able to deliver before. There was good reason for this. Not until the test of a U 235 bomb at Alamogordo, New Mexico, on 16 July 1945, by which time the decision had been long fixed to use the bomb against Japan, did anyone know how big it would be. The scientists held a sweepstake before the test and estimates ranged from zero to 20,000 tons of TNT. Major-General Leslie Groves, in charge of the Manhattan Project, recalled that, 'as I lay there, in the final seconds, I thought only of what I would do if, when the countdown got to zero, nothing happened. I was spared this embarrassment . . .'[4] The yield of the 'Trinity' test, as it was called, was close to 20,000 tons (20 kilotons). But in total destructiveness, the atomic bombs did not outclass the Allied area-bombing of German and Japanese cities. At Hiroshima probably 140,000 people died within four months. In Hamburg, in one week in 1943, 43,000 were killed; at Dresden, 135,000 are thought to have perished in 1945, while in one incendiary raid on Tokyo six months before the atomic raids, the American air force of Curtis Le May killed 83,000, injured 102,000, and obliterated sixteen square miles of the city.[5]

But atomic bombs were radically different. In contrast to a thousand bombers over a period of hours the psychological effect of a single bomber, a single bomb in a single moment, with such utter devastation as a consequence, was, as one of the Los Alamos scientists later testified, 'unendurable'.[6] And there was something else: radioactivity.

The Frisch–Peierls memorandum had to be kept in deepest secrecy, as the authors themselves wrote, for any rumour connecting isotope separation and a bomb might set a German scientist thinking on the right lines. So very few copies were made, and eventually not even the authors possessed copies of their memorandum. In the second part of the Memorandum, 'On the properties of a radioactive "super-bomb"', Frisch and Peierls pointed out that

in addition, some part of the energy set free by the bomb goes to produce radioactive substances, and these will emit very powerful and dangerous radiations. The effect of these radiations is greatest immediately after the explosion, but it decays only gradually ...

Later in the memorandum they observed that

it must be realized that no shelters are available that would be effective and could be used on a large scale ...[7]

They had also correctly guessed that the blast from a uranium bomb explosion would destroy life in a wide area, they thought perhaps the size of the centre of a large city. At Hiroshima, it was a lucky minority of the total casualties who died instantly. Many of the 'short-term' victims perished from horrific burns, but the 'longer-term' victims died of radiation-induced diseases: cancers, leukemia, general physical degeneration. The final toll in Hiroshima alone may be close to 200,000.[8] This other, special, quality of the atomic bomb led Frisch and Peierls to conclude that it would have no military value:

Owing to the spread of radioactive substances with the wind, the bomb could probably not be used without killing large numbers of civilians, *and this may make it unsuitable as a weapon for use by this country* [our emphasis].

Here is a faith in standards of civilized behaviour, even in war, which is very distant from us in the 1980s. The scientists were writing before the area-bombing of Germany and Japan, the gas chambers and medical 'experiments' of the concentration camps, the Japanese experiments in germ warfare using PoW guinea pigs and their death camps, the slaughter of Hitler's Russian campaign, and the other obscenities of total war were known. We cannot have the luxury of that ignorance. Yet we know what they did not: that the Germans were not to develop a successful atomic weapon. After all, as Frisch and Peierls pointed out in the Memorandum, all the relevant theoretical data were published, and furthermore, much of the seminal work on nuclear physics in the 1930s had been done in

Germany. So it was with excellent cause that, in 1940, they wrote that one might reasonably assume

that Germany is, or will be, in possession of this weapon . . . The most effective reply would be a counter-threat with a similar bomb. Therefore it seems to us important to start production as soon and as rapidly as possible, *even if it is not intended to use the bomb as a means of attack* [our emphasis].

One of those working on atomic research in Liverpool in 1939 was Joseph Rotblat, who at that time also subscribed to this view. However, subsequently he has observed that had it been put to the test, it might not have worked. Hitler in his bunker might have fired the bomb to make a complete *Götterdammerung*.[9] Yet at its very inception we find the atomic bomb accommodated within the theory which, the governments of the nuclear powers today suggest, has been since August 1945 the controlling philosophy of the nuclear age: the theory of 'nuclear deterrence'.

We know that in the war years the prospect of genetic damage and slow death through radiation sickness did not deter the scientists. And the bomb was made to be used. 'There was never a moment's discussion as to whether the atomic bomb should be used or not,' wrote Churchill[10] who, as Prime Minister, was asked to approve the American decision to use the weapon. And that approval, by a President who had only learned of the Manhattan Project on the day of his predecessor's death, would have been immensely difficult to withhold. By the time of Truman's assumption of the presidency two billion dollars and four years' research had been expended. Major-General Groves later commented that 'the President never had an opportunity to say "we *will* drop the bomb". All he could do was say "No".'[11] And, in the circumstances, that was the least likely response. One of the British scientists later reflected that:

Perhaps we should have studied the moral and political implications of the bomb and thought about its use. Perhaps, too, we should have considered whether radioactivity was a poison outlawed in spirit by the Geneva Convention. But we didn't.[12]

One of the Los Alamos scientists, the same Joseph Rotblat, ceased to work on the bomb when it was clear that there was no German threat. He left the project in January 1945 and, despite strenuous objections from the security services, returned to Liverpool University; but his action was unusual. However, after the end of the war with Germany, there was an increasingly vocal concern among the atomic scientists to resist the use of 'their' bomb in the tactical, military way which Frisch and Peierls had dismissed out of hand as inconceivable so short a time before. But the Franck Memorandum in June 1945, in which seven leading scientists in the Manhattan Project urged that the bomb should be revealed in an open demonstration only was swept aside; their pleas were repeated after the Alamogordo test, but to no avail. The scientific director of the Manhattan Project, J. Robert Oppenheimer, had argued against the making of a political appeal by scientists on the grounds that the decision about the use of their weapon properly lay with democratically elected politicians. One of the scientists whom he dissuaded from signing the second appeal was Dr Edward Teller. This action of Oppenheimer's may have had much more far-reaching effects for the future than he intended, as we shall see. A moving force in both appeals was Leo Szilard who had, in 1939, stimulated Einstein to write to President Roosevelt to warn of the danger that Germany could soon be in a position to make a bomb. But now things were different: Germany was defeated and the atomic project was both more terrible in its success than Szilard had thought, and also beyond the scientists' control. As Oppenheimer watched the first fireball rise into the pre-dawn desert sky

... we knew the world could not be the same. A few people laughed, a few people cried. Most people were silent. I remembered the line from the Hindu scripture, the *Bhagavad Gita*: ... 'Now I am become death, destroyer of worlds.'[13]

Oppenheimer had argued in June 1945 against those colleagues who favoured a demonstration only for another reason also. In his opinion, the bomb had to be dropped without warning on an enemy target because there was a risk that it might not work. But the pictures of Hiroshima transformed him. 'The physicists have known sin; and this is a knowledge which they cannot lose,' he later said.

HIROSHIMA: THE FIRST ATOMIC BOMB[14]
More than half the people alive today were born after 6 August 1945, the day when an atomic bomb was first used against people. It seems long ago and it is easy to forget. The city of Hiroshima is again a bustling industrial centre. The Peace Park, where annually, on 6 August, the attack is recalled, and the strong abiding adherence of the Japanese people as a whole to a national policy of non-nuclear self-defence alone seem to stand as public reminders. More privately, in special sanatoria, the radiation damaged 'survivors' – if such a living death can be described by that word – the *hibakusha*, are still living.

'Little Boy', the U 235 bomb which annihilated Hiroshima, was small by modern standards: its yield was about 13 kt. By contrast, a modern Polaris missile has a yield of 660 kt, the cruise missile of 200 kt. So it is well to remember that when governments and soldiers describe fighting limited nuclear wars with 'small' bombs, the very least that means is to repeat Hiroshima. What happened there?

'Little Boy' was dropped at 8.15 am. Immediately, a huge mushroom cloud was seen over the city of Hiroshima. The blast blew many people against buildings, while others, trying to flee,

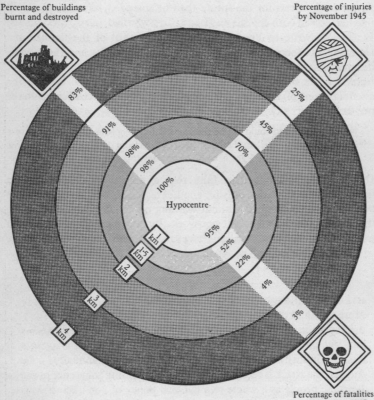

Percentage of buildings burnt and destroyed

Percentage of injuries by November 1945

Percentage of fatalities by November 1945

Figure 1. Fatalities, injuries and damage to buildings caused by the atomic bomb at Hiroshima, August 1945

were crushed beneath falling stone. Half an hour later, a fire storm began to blow, and by late morning a tornado had developed. Over an area of some 400 km² a 'black rain' fell, a sticky, heavy rain which left indelible stains where it fell. The temperature dropped dramatically, so that many people shivered although it was midsummer. Fish died in the river upon which the black rain fell, and even at the extreme edges of the affected area, diarrhoea was noted among animals.

The extent of destruction is difficult to imagine, let alone measure. Figures can only partly express the effects of the bombing. Figure 1 tries to show just how complete was the physical devastation of Hiroshima: the overall casualty rate was 56 per cent dead and injured.

Japanese sources now suggest that this casualty rate represents the deaths of 140,000 people by December 1945. Earlier, in the 1950s, the Americans put the figure at 68,000, but they believed the pre-bombing population to have been smaller.

It is likely that half of all casualties were caused by burns of one type or another. Most of those who died in this excruciating way did so only after a few days, deprived of medical care. Others were roasted alive or died of asphyxiation in the firestorm.

But death from an atomic bomb was not 'clean'. What made the experience of Hiroshima and Nagasaki different, in aspects other than size, from the experience of the blitz in Europe were the delayed effects of the bombings, both physical and psychological. Both are difficult to measure, but the recent comprehensive study by the Committee for the Compilation of Materials on the Damage of the Atomic Bombs in Hiroshima and Nagasaki is an appalling catalogue of a 'society laid waste'. The survivors, the *hibakusha*, live distorted and broken lives. They have proved more prone to cancers and leukemia than the rest of the Japanese population, so that even those who appeared to have survived the bombings themselves are truly victims.

Perhaps equally disturbing are the medical reports on those who, unborn at the time of the bombing, were exposed in the womb. Studies of a group of seventeen-year-olds in 1962 suggest that those whose mothers were exposed to the radiation within a mile during pregnancy were on average 2 cm shorter, 3 kg lighter, and had chest measurements 1 cm less than a group whose mothers, while still exposed to the radiation, were between one and two miles away. The presence of microcephaly – a condition

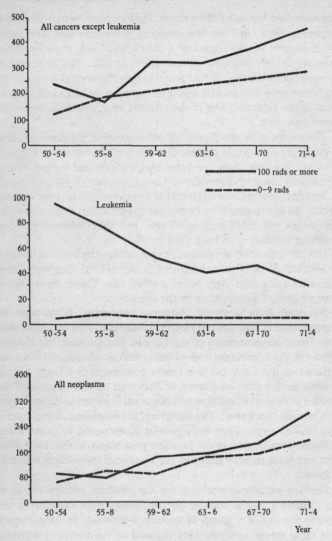

Figure 2. Deaths per 100,000 per year by cause of death, Hiroshima and Nagasaki, 1950-74 (from Committee for the Compilation of Materials on the Damage of the Atomic Bombs in Hiroshima and Nagasaki, *Hiroshima and Nagasaki*, New York, Basic Books, 1981, p. 240); rad is a unit of absorbed dose of radiation

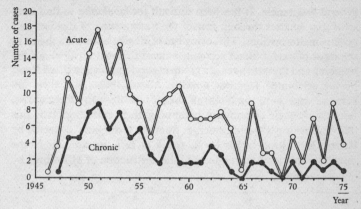

Figure 3. Number of leukemia cases among Hiroshima survivors exposed within 2,000 metres of the hypocentre, according to year of onset (from Committee for the Compilation of Materials on the Damage of the Atomic Bombs in Hiroshima and Nagasaki, *Hiroshima and Nagasaki*, New York, Basic Books, 1981, p. 263)

indicating a head circumference less than two standard deviations below an age- and sex-specific mean head size, and which is often associated with mental retardation – is a further index of the effect of the bomb on unborn children. Fifty per cent of those whose mothers were within a kilometre of the bomb exhibited microcephaly, as did 22 per cent of those whose mothers were between 1 and 1.5 kilometres away. A 'normal' level was found to be 2.7 per cent. In addition, myopia, strabismus, mongolism, liver cirrhosis, hepatitis, and tuberculosis are prevalent among the children of survivors.

In 1979–80, thirty-five years after the bombing, 2,279 names were added to the list of deaths *officially* attributed to the delayed radiation effects on victims of 'Little Boy'. Today this list totals 97,964, so that well over 200,000 people have died as a result of the single atomic bomb dropped on Hiroshima. This compares with a total of 290,000 American direct battle casualties in the entire Second World War.

As well as the catalogue of deaths and injuries, there is a final twist to the story of 'Little Boy' and Hiroshima: the continuing plight of those psychologically scarred by their experience. Their plight takes many forms, difficult to describe precisely. In some ways it is social: employers have been reluctant to employ *hibakusha* because of their tendency to lose time and to develop unexpected illnesses, and their general listlessness. It has been difficult for *hibakusha* to find non-*hibakusha* spouses through fear of the transmission of diseases and genetic malformations. This ostracism of *hibakusha* forms a theme in the most powerful direct account, a quasi-fictional novel about the bombing and the later lives of a group of survivors, called *Black Rain*, by the celebrated Japanese novelist, Masuji Ibuse. But there are personal aspects to the plight of the *hibakusha*; many feel outcast, rejected by their community because of their suffering. It is this 'A-bomb neurosis' which emerges from the testimonial collected by Robert Jay Lifton in his book, *Death in Life*, an account of the unmeasurable long-term effects of the destruction of Hiroshima by atomic bombing.

2 The Defeat of Disarmament, 1945–55

On 26 June 1945 the statesmen of the world, gathered in San Francisco, signed a charter to establish an organization whose prime purpose, expressed in that charter, was 'to save succeeding generations from the scourge of war'. With hindsight we know that it was almost exactly at the same time – late June – that the decision to atom-bomb Japan without warning was conclusively re-confirmed by Secretary of War Stimson's special 'Interim Committee'. The British government was consulted and its agreement noted on 4 July. Despite the private advice of Stimson and Churchill, the Potsdam Proclamation of 26 July did not relent from the demand for unconditional Japanese surrender (there was already strong evidence that a negotiated surrender could have been achieved). So it was not only Hiroshima and Nagasaki, but also in a real sense the newly created United Nations Charter, that was attacked in August.[15]

When the first General Assembly met, in London, on 24 January 1946, the very first resolution, numbered 1(I), was to set up an Atomic Energy Commission charged to produce proposals 'for the elimination from national armaments of atomic weapons ...' The resolution was *unanimously* accepted by all fifty-one member states. It should have been the moment of decision, for only three devices – Alamogordo, Hiroshima, and Nagasaki – had so far been exploded. Henry Stimson, the Secretary of War, who more than any politician was continuously associated with the Manhattan Project, noted on 21 September that American relations with Russia

> may be perhaps irretrievably embittered by the way in which we approach the solution of the bomb with Russia. For if we fail to approach them now and merely continue to negotiate with them, having this weapon rather ostentatiously on our hip, their suspicions and their distrust of our purposes and motives will increase.[16]

In Chapter 2 we have seen that such an observation is fully justified by the historical background.

Others in the United States took a similar view, among them Robert Oppenheimer. He contributed to a plan for the control of atomic weapons called the Acheson–Lilienthal Report. It called for the UN Atomic Energy Commission to have real power and recommended unconditional American cooperation, for, as was prophetically stated when the plan was presented,

> ... the extremely favoured position with regard to atomic devices which the US at present enjoys, is *only temporary. It will not last.* We must use that advantage now to promote international security.[17]

President Truman was getting into his stride, and a financier, Bernard Baruch, was chosen to translate the proposals into terms more favourable to the USA. In them, control preceded prohibition of atomic weapons. The Baruch Plan was presented to the first meeting of the UNAEC on 14 June 1946, but both the underlying principle and the reservations – threats of punishment, demands for inspections – associated with control raised Russian suspicions and they refused to agree and exercised the veto. However, the Soviet delegate Andrei Gromyko countered with a proposal to destroy all weapons in existence and to cease all production. But for prohibition to precede control has never been acceptable to the Western nations, and especially not to the United States at the time when it still possessed a monopoly. It countered the Russian proposal with the world's fourth nuclear explosion, a test over Bikini Atoll on 1 July 1946, even before the UNAEC technical committees had begun work. Bikini may have been called a test, but in truth it blew up one of the only two serious opportunities to bring nuclear weapons under international control.[18]

On 29 August 1949, the Soviet Union ended America's brief monopoly of atomic weapons by exploding its own bomb. The 'Cold War' was by that time intensifying. Stalin's obsessive suspicions of the West had been hugely stimulated by American conduct over the bomb and over the European cease-fire lines. Anti-Communism in the United States verged upon the borders of paranoia, and indeed sometimes crossed them, as in the case of the unfortunate Secretary of Defense, J. V. Forrestal, who eventually committed suicide. This hysterical anti-Communism cannot be ignored, for it was also a time when politicians of the Nixon and Reagan vintage received their formative political lessons. Furthermore, in such a political climate, there were strident demands for a reply in kind to the explosion by the Soviet Union in order to keep America 'ahead' of the Russians.

That reply was to begin to develop a new and far more potent sort of nuclear weapon. Among the strongest and most influential proponents of the H-bomb was the scientist who did much of the basic theoretical research which suggested its feasibility. He was one of Oppenheimer's Manhattan Project team, Hungarian-born Edward Teller. Oppenheimer himself opposed the project, although he continued to believe that, however distasteful, an arsenal of atomic fission bombs should be prepared to deter the Russians. He was chairman of the influential General Advisory Committee of the Atomic Energy Commission which, in October 1949, reported against the H-bomb, arguing that its development was not essential to the national security of the USA and, furthermore, that to develop such a powerful and destructive weapon, which was militarily of little use, would be also morally wrong.

Oppenheimer's position was significantly different from that of June

EXTRACT FROM AMERICAN ATOMIC ENERGY COMMISSION'S
GENERAL ADVISORY COMMITTEE'S OCTOBER 1949 REPORT[19]
'We all hope that by one means or another, the development of these weapons can be avoided. We are all reluctant to see the United States take the initiative in precipitating this development . . .

'We base our recommendation on our belief that the extreme dangers to mankind inherent in the proposal wholly outweigh any military advantage . . . reasonable people the world over would realize that the existence of a weapon of this type whose power of destruction is essentially unlimited represents a threat to the future of the human race which is intolerable . . .

'We believe a super bomb should never be produced . . .

'To the argument that the Russians may succeed in developing this weapon, we would reply that our undertaking it will not prove a deterrent to them.'

1945. But the advocates of the H-bomb won the day, and Oppenheimer was subsequently hounded by the 'Red-baiting' witch-hunters of the House of UnAmerican Activities Committee, and accused of Communistic leanings and implicit treachery.[20]

On 31 January 1951 President Truman announced that research should continue. The first, small, thermonuclear explosion (kindled by a very large fission explosion) occurred in 'George' shot of the 'Greenhouse' series on Eniwetok Atoll in the Pacific on 8 May 1951. It showed that fusion was possible. It was followed on 1 November 1952 by 'Mike' shot, a full-scale experimental device yielding 10 megatons – 10 million tons of TNT, roughly 800 Hiroshimas.[21]

FUSION

The H-bomb would use a limited fission explosion of U 235 to trigger a *fusion* explosion in 'heavy hydrogen', (today it is usually a mixture of the commoner isotope with atomic weight 2 (deuterium) and the rarer hydrogen 3 (tritium)), thus releasing very many times – perhaps a thousand times – the energy of a simple fission A-bomb. The two-stage fission-to-fusion explosion is often called a 'thermonuclear' explosion.

The essential feature of fusion reactions is that atomic nuclei (of the heavy isotopes of hydrogen, deuterium, and tritium) are fused together rather than split as in fission reactions. The fusion involves a small decrease in total mass, and the matter lost appears as an enormous quantity of energy. But to bring about fusion requires the heating of deuterium and tritium to extremely high temperatures, and this is achieved by the small fission explosion. The 'thermo' part of 'thermonuclear' refers to that.

While it was represented to the public as an 'H-Bomb', 'Mike' shot was not, nor was ever intended to be, a usable weapon. It had required many tons of refrigeration equipment to keep the thermonuclear fuel – liquid deuterium – at a temperature below minus 250 °C. But on the sole basis of 'Mike' shot the US Air Force began to develop an inter-continental ballistic missile (ICBM) – the Atlas – to deliver an H-bomb. A usable H-bomb was to be the goal of the 'Castle' test series, planned to follow the 'Ivy' series within a year. Several techniques were to be tested, but the AEC gambled on finding quickly one that worked. The most promising idea employed lithium deuteride – a compound that could be packed like rock salt. The common intellect behind both test series was that of Edward Teller.[22]

While American research for the 'Castle' series was in progress, on 12 August 1953, in Siberia, the Soviet Union exploded what appeared to be an H-bomb. American radiation detection aircraft collected particle samples which revealed traces of lithium. The immediate conclusion drawn was that the Russians might have beaten the USA to the detonation of a usable H-bomb. Subsequent review of circumstantial evidence now suggests that this may only have been a 'boosted' atomic bomb, not an H-bomb at all, which the Russians may not have perfected until 1955.[23] In fact we may never know for certain. But what we do know is that whether or not the belief was well founded at the time, it helped to spur on the 'Castle' programme. On 1 March 1954, at Bikini Atoll, 'Bravo' shot, the first of the 'Castle' series and constructed on the lithium deuteride design, was fired. The test exceeded by far all expectations: its yield was well over a thousand times the Hiroshima bomb (14.8 Mt) – twice what had been expected from calculation.

> Roy Reider, the safety director with the scientific team, had been seeing atomic explosions since 1946. He is a plump, cheery and usually matter-of-fact individual. But when, watching from Parry Island in the pre-dawn darkness, he saw that gigantic fireball balloon out in the shape of a flattened sphere, larger than any fireball he had ever seen, and then grow larger still, the terrifying thought flashed into his mind that it might swallow up the whole world, and he asked himself, 'Isn't that fireball ever going to stop?' Then, he recalls, he performed an act of imagination which surprised him. As he tells it, 'I had been to planetariums in New York and Philadelphia. And you know how you look all around you at the horizon, and there's the outline of a city, in silhouette? I sketched in my mind the outline of a city against that fireball, in silhouette. And I thought, "Oh my God!"'[24]

But not everything went 'well' with the 'Bravo' test. Just after the firing, the wind veered and blew radioactive debris eastwards over an American destroyer, whose crew sealed it up and sustained no ill effects, and over three of the Marshall Islands, whose populations did not know about radioactivity, and who thus became the world's first known victims of fall-out. Later it was learned that they were not alone in this dubious honour, for a small Japanese trawler, the *Fukuryu Maru* – the *Lucky Dragon* – was fishing for tuna east of Bikini before dawn on 1 March.

Shinzo Suzuki was unable to sleep and was standing on deck when suddenly the western sky erupted with a flare of whitish-yellow light, before changing to a yellow red, and finally a flaming orange ball. Suzuki rushed into the cabin, and blurted out to his cabin-mate, 'The sun rises in the west!' The other sailors gathered, and some soon realized that what they had seen was a *pika-don* – a thunder-flash (the word created at Hiroshima to describe the A-bomb).

The crew hauled in their nets and began to sail north-east. Although the night had been clear, about two hours later a light drizzle began to fall on the *Lucky Dragon*, but not of rain. It was a strange sandy ash. The puzzled sailors rubbed it between their fingers; some tasted it. It stopped falling later during the day. By evening, some of the men complained of loss of appetite. Low on fuel, the *Lucky Dragon* turned for home. As the voyage proceeded, the men became listless, and suffered nausea and weakness. The engineer Shinzo Suzuki was confined to his bunk on 2 March. Before long open sores appeared, and some men began to lose their hair. The *Lucky Dragon* tied up in her home port of Yaizu early on 14 March.[25]

'It would be desirable if sites could be found which are so remote from populous areas that the tests could be conducted without regard to the direction of the winds. Unfortunately the bombs are too big and the planet is too small.'

(E. Teller and A. L. Latter, 1958)[26]

After much delay, the sailors found their way to hospital and were found to be radioactive two weeks after exposure. This was puzzling to Japanese doctors, for there had been no appreciable fall-out associated with the air-burst Hiroshima and Nagasaki bombs. The illnesses and subsequent death of one among the crew of the *Lucky Dragon* made headlines in Japan, severely straining relations with the USA. But the little fishing-boat sailed into the world's press also, bringing the question of radioactive fall-out to popular attention for the first time, and with important consequences.

The fall-out from the Bikini bomb collected from the decks of the *Lucky Dragon* puzzled nuclear scientists not involved with the test in a different way from the Japanese doctors. Fusion does not create radioactive isotopes: the 'Bravo' fall-out was much 'dirtier' than it should have been and, significantly, was found to contain U 237. Professor Rotblat, who had left the Manhattan Project to specialize in radiation medicine, heard of the finding of $U\,237$ – which indicated that natural uranium ($U\,238$) was somehow present. He was the first to deduce that 'Bravo' shot had, in fact, been not a two-stage, but a *three*-stage bomb: fission to fusion, then fission again in a coating of natural uranium – plentiful and cheap. This third stage had added the large amount of radioactivity to the fall-out.[27]

'... we need weapons which will do their job against an aggressor and will do the least possible damage to the innocent bystander.

In this last respect, in particular, notable progress has been made. We are developing clean weapons which are effective by their blast and heat, but which produce little radioactivity.'

(E. Teller and A. L. Latter, 1958)[28]

Secondly, the voyage of the *Lucky Dragon* served to focus the efforts of those opposed to nuclear weapons, which led in the late 1950s to the creation of the Campaign for Nuclear Disarmament in Britain and of similar movements elsewhere in Europe. In the United States, Adlai Stevenson pressed for an atmospheric test ban in his unsuccessful presidential campaign of 1956. But by this time, the last chance for general and complete disarmament (GCD) had passed. That had occurred in 1955, as will now be told.

The race to develop the H-bomb, the anti-Communist witch-hunting of McCarthyism, the depth of the Cold War during Stalin's final years and the Korean war had combined to strangle even those modest United Nations initiatives of the Atomic Energy Commission and the Disarmament Commission. But three months after the *Lucky Dragon* encountered the fall-out from Bikini, France and Britain tried again, and submitted to a Five-Power Sub-committee of the Disarmament Commission a comprehensive proposal for GCD.[29] It combined the Western preference for control measures with a proposal for prohibition of the manufacture of nuclear weapons close to the Soviet position. The initial response of the Soviet delegate, Mr Malik, was cool, but the Sub-committee met frequently over the next months. Then, at the UN General Assembly in September 1954, Russia delivered a surprise by accepting the Anglo-French plan in principle as a basis for negotiation. The USA reciprocated, proposing specific force levels and control and verification mechanisms in association with the proposal for prohibition of nuclear weapons when 75 per cent of conventional troop reductions were achieved. What was it that caused this dramatic change in the Soviet position? An immediate trigger may have been a hope that negotiation might prevent the remilitarization of West Germany and its accession to NATO, but there were much deeper currents stirring within the Soviet Union which meant that in 1955, real action was on the cards.

Between the death of Stalin in 1953 and 1956 both the composition of the Soviet leadership and the direction of Soviet policy were undergoing major changes. Stalin's successor, Malenkov, had been forced by his colleagues to surrender the post of First Secretary of the Communist Party in March 1953, retaining the apparently more powerful position of Prime Minister. But over the next two years, the new First Secretary, Nikita Khrushchev, worked to restore the Party's role in decision-making, to establish its control over the state apparatus, and to undermine Malenkov's position. From August 1954, foreign policy was again being directed by the Party, and it was in September that the UN announcement came, while in December, Malenkov was forced to resign as Prime Minister, although the change was not made official until February 1955. His successor was Marshal Nikolai Bulganin, a supporter of Khrushchev. However, the latter's influence was not yet total, and would not be until 1958. Malenkov was still a member of the leadership, as were other leading Stalinists: Kaganovich, Molotov, and Voroshilov.

Meanwhile policy was rapidly changing. On the domestic front, more investment was being devoted to consumer goods industries; and agriculture, after a quarter of a century's neglect, was now a priority. Information was beginning to come out about the scale of Stalin's repression of opponents and in 1955 a special commission of the Party Central Committee was set up to investigate the purges. Its findings would provide the basis for Khrushchev's secret speech denouncing Stalin at the 20th Party Congress in February 1956.

No less radical were the changes in foreign policy, as Stalin's isolationist policies were reversed one after another, especially in the months following Malenkov's removal from office.

May 1955 was a significant month: on the 9th, West Germany formally entered NATO, but nevertheless, on 10 May, the Soviet Union responded to the American proposals of the previous autumn, accepting the force levels and the programme for linked conventional/nuclear disarmament, accepting for the first time the principle of an international control and verification agency and proposing in response the most detailed scheme yet for its implementation, favouring a wide network of land-based UN observer posts. The Soviet Union also proposed an immediate ban upon testing of any nuclear weapons, and suggested that a UN agency should oversee compliance. A detailed timetable of implementation during 1956 and 1957 was set out: the first step, a 50 per cent reduction of forces in 1956, should be accompanied by solemn undertakings not to use nuclear weapons between the stages, and their prohibition, at step two, should be completed by the end of 1957.[30] Lord Noel-Baker, the experienced British disarmament negotiator, called this, in a chapter title of his book, *The Arms Race*, 'The moment of hope . . .' That same month the Soviet Union signed a peace treaty with Austria and withdrew its troops from that country. Also during May 1955, a Soviet delegation headed by Khrushchev flew to Belgrade to effect a rapprochement with Yugoslavia.

Disarmament negotiations now rested until the Geneva Summit of August 1955; but meanwhile, in June, in response to the extension of NATO the previous month by ratification of the Paris Agreements whereby West Germany entered the Alliance, eight East European countries signed a treaty of mutual assistance in Warsaw, thus setting up the Warsaw Pact.[31] At the Conference Marshal Bulganin repeated the Soviet proposals for disarmament, suggesting that the solution to the nine-year-old disagreement over control procedures was to have land-based control posts, many of them, to observe all strategic transport.

When the world leaders converged on Geneva that summer, Eisenhower's contribution was to propose, without prior consultation, his 'Open Skies' plan – to facilitate control by reciprocal aerial photography, and on 30 August, the USA proposed a hybrid control structure, combining the American-favoured aerial surveillance and Russian-favoured land-based control posts. But this suited no one. After the conference ended, other statesmen, notably Jules Moch of France, tried to make more acceptable syntheses, but the moment had passed, primarily as a result of the hardening of the American position at Geneva, where Harold Stassen, the US representative, vetoed the process by announcing that his country 'placed a reservation on all of its pre-Geneva substantive positions'.[32] One cannot give a definitive explanation of this American action. However, it is worth recalling two things. First, this was precisely the time when US intelligence agencies were coming to conclude, as it happens quite incorrectly, that the USSR was constructing a massive fleet of bombers, a story told in Chapter 4. Secondly, only a short time before, the USA had experienced what was widely perceived as a defeat in Korea at the hands of Soviet 'proxy' forces; many in the USA had sympathized with General MacArthur, who had wished to prosecute the war far more vigorously. His recall had given rise to the same explanation that was to be used later in

Vietnam: that victory was denied because the hands of the Army were tied. This experience had left a bitter memory, still alive in 1955.

But this American refusal did not stop the process of the new Soviet foreign policy. Immediately after the Summit, the Soviet Union unilaterally reduced its armed forces by 640,000 men 'in recognition of a lessening in international tension', as it was officially described. This was the first reduction in eight years. In September 1955, the Soviet Union removed its troops from Finland, and also recognized West Germany. In November, Khrushchev and Bulganin visited India. While there, in late November, the largest-yet Soviet nuclear weapons test took place. Moscow Radio announced that so long as there was no Western agreement to suspend tests, Soviet tests would have to continue. The juxtaposition of these events revealed that there were clashes between 'hawks' and 'doves' in the Kremlin, as in Washington, and indeed, not only between individuals, but within Khrushchev's mind.

The new diplomacy had its critics, prominent among them Molotov, Stalin's Foreign Minister. But his influence was waning and in July 1955 he had been sharply criticized. The dominant group in the Soviet leadership was set on a new course in its foreign policy, reaching a new stage of doctrinal entrenchment at the 20th Party Congress in February 1956 in the policy of 'peaceful coexistence', which superseded the doctrine of the inevitable war between capitalism and Communism (see box).

At Geneva and subsequently the Western nations refused to give the unqualified 'No first use' undertaking to which the Soviet Union attached such importance. Eisenhower and Bulganin exchanged letters of increasing coolness during the autumn of 1955, revealing that the control issue

---

'When we say that the socialist system will win in the competition between the two systems, the capitalist and the socialist, this by no means signifies that its victory will be achieved through armed interference by the socialist countries in the internal affairs of the capitalist countries ... The principle of peaceful coexistence is gaining ever wider international recognition ... And this is natural, for in present-day conditions there is no other way out. Indeed there are only two ways: either peaceful coexistence or the most destructive war in history. There is no third way.'

(N. Khrushchev, speech before XXth Party Congress, 14 February 1956)[33]

had again been instrumental in wrecking hopes,[34] so it was no surprise that when the Disarmament Sub-committee resumed at Lancaster House, London, in March 1956, it ended with suspension of discussion and no agreement. On 4 May 1956, both sides issued final statements. In his, Andrei Gromyko observed that 'Actually, the position now is either that there will be an agreement on part of the problem, with a view to facilitating later agreement on the disarmament problem as a whole, or there will be no agreement...'[35]

During 1956, things became rapidly worse. This was an American presidential election year, and the Republican Eisenhower had to begin to look to his conservative supporters. The Secretary of State, John Foster Dulles, precipitated the Middle East crisis by unilateral American withdrawal from the Aswan High Dam project in Egypt on 19 July (followed by Britain on the 20th). Of subsequent American conduct over Suez, one British MP was drawn to comment, during the stormy debates in the House of Commons, that he did not know whether Dulles's mind was more on the 'expansion of oil in the Middle East, or of his vote in the Middle West'. President Nasser responded on 26 July by nationalizing the Suez Canal, arguing that with its revenues, the High Dam would be built independently of any Western aid. In fact, the Soviet Union provided the necessary backing.

Nasser's action led finally to the ill-fated Anglo-French Suez invasion of 31 October to 6 November. This operation was passionately supported by the 'Old Empire' right wing of the Conservative Party, passionately and openly opposed by wide sections of liberal British public opinion, and, as was much later revealed, passionately and privately opposed by the Chief of Staff instructed to carry out the scheme, Admiral of the Fleet Lord Mountbatten. For different reasons, the American administration was hostile to it also. Opposition by Eisenhower was muted in the weeks before the presidential election in November, in order not to lose conservative Republican voters (in the event, he was returned to the White House). However, means other than words were employed to force Britain to halt the Suez operation. First they engineered a run on the pound in the international money markets of such proportions that the government was compelled to approach the International Monetary Fund for a loan. The IMF is officially an independent body, but the USA has always had great influence over it – to put it charitably. The IMF refused the loan unless the British government agreed to an immediate cease-fire. The Chancellor of the Exchequer, Harold Macmillan, one of the earliest supporters of the military intervention, now became prominent in the Cabinet calling for its immediate termination. He threatened resignation unless the IMF loan could be obtained. Ground operations were proceeding well when, to the great annoyance of the soldiers, a cease-fire was ordered for midnight on 5–6 November.

While events in the Middle East developed, in Eastern Europe, nationalist and anti-Communist opposition to the Communist regime and Soviet presence in Hungary boiled over into open conflict. Mass demonstrations by workers, students, and soldiers on 22–3 October demanded the withdrawal of Soviet troops, democratization of government, the release of Cardinal Mindszenty, and the return to power of the former Prime Minister, Imre Nagy. Heavy fighting in Budapest on 23–4 October was followed by the formation of a Democratic National Government by Nagy, which requested the withdrawal of Soviet troops. The USSR said that it would comply. On 31 October, Nagy declared that Hungary wished to leave the Warsaw Pact and pursue an independent and neutral course.

In the House of Commons the day before, Hugh Gaitskell, Leader of the Opposition, demanded that the Prime Minister, Sir Anthony Eden, state upon what authority he was proceeding with his Suez operation. 'There is nothing in the [UN] Charter that justifies any nation appointing itself as world policeman,' he said. 'The great danger of the situation is that if we can do this, so can anyone else.' His words were only too accurate.

At dawn on 4 November, as the Suez war was in full spate, massed Soviet tank and infantry formations attacked Budapest. At 8 am, after playing the Hungarian National Anthem, Budapest Radio went off the air, its last words being, 'Help Hungary! . . . help us! . . . help us! . . .' But the Suez operation had given the Soviet Union both precedent and cover. In Belgrade wounded Soviet troops were heard by a Hungarian doctor tending them to ask 'Where is the canal?'; in Port Said, Egyptian troops resisting the Allied landings were told that Russian reinforcements would come and that the Third World War had begun. Addressing the British nation on television on the evening of 4 November, Gaitskell lamented that, at a time when all should be united in condemnation of the Soviet attack, 'we by our criminal folly should have lost the moral leadership of which we were once so proud'.

It is believed that fifty thousand Hungarians died in the initial assault. A grim and bloody repression of the Hungarian uprising followed. By mid-November, the truth of Gromyko's prediction in May concerning disarmament was dismally apparent.[36]

At no time since the summer of 1955 has the world been anywhere as close to the realization of general and complete disarmament. It is facile to attribute blame for this in one quarter only; it is a shared tragedy. From the late 1950s onwards, proponents of disarmament have devoted their energies to attempts to secure arms control and peripheral treaties; and here the reward has been bitter. The failure of arms control is reviewed in the final section of Chapter 4.

Meanwhile, the main efforts of soldiers and politicians continued to pour into the expansion of military might of all types in the belief that in the absence of trust, threats could serve to produce security. In one of his last speeches as Prime Minister, Winston Churchill gave his vision of this logic:

> ... a curious paradox has emerged. Let me put it simply. After a certain point has been passed, it may be said, 'The worse things get the better.' The broad effect of the latest developments [the H-bomb] is to spread almost indefinitely and at least to a vast extent the area of mortal danger ... Then it may well be that we shall by a process of sublime irony have reached a stage in this story where safety will be the sturdy child of terror, and survival the twin brother of annihilation.[37]

Like Churchill, others involved with nuclear weapons comforted themselves that they would never be used, that the memory of Hiroshima would serve as a constant reminder of the consequences of any use, that the policy which controlled their creation and deployment was deterrence. 'Peace is our profession' was the motto chosen for the Strategic Air Command. But how far was that true at any time? How true is it now?

4 Changing Nuclear Policies: the Quest for Flexibility since the Late 1950s

In this chapter it is shown how the United States raced ahead in the development of both strategies and weapons. At first, the accumulation of numbers of weapons was an extension of the deterrent threat of massive destruction, but soon it became a race to match the real or imagined capabilities of the Soviets. It was then not a difficult step to consider strategies for this new and huge arsenal which could render it flexible and therefore politically useful, a process which continues with increasing vigour today.

This chapter tells mainly the narrative history; it does not explain in detail why the quest for flexibility results in bad (i.e. untenable) war plans and is therefore so immensely dangerous; nor does it explain how the rest of American society was able to respond so warmly and productively to the speculations of strategists and soldiers. That is done in Chapter 5, 'The Steel Triangle'.

From 1945 to 1955, the competition between the superpowers centred upon acquisition first of the atomic, then of the thermonuclear, bomb, a competition in which the subsequent usual pattern of the nuclear arms race was set: the USA leading and the USSR following with a time-lag of some years in both research and deployment. Only in the later 1950s did attention come to focus on the question of numbers of these weapons and their delivery systems (see box).

When it did so, the gulf between 'deterrence' and this changing reality rapidly widened. This was principally because, in arguing that deterrence (i.e. the threat of certain and horrendous retaliation) was still the correct description of the new situation, both in popular understanding and in much military and political calculation, two mistakes became pervasive (and remain so today).

The first mistake is that the essence of deterrence is maintenance of a balance of force interpreted as a balance of numbers. It is not. This mistake confuses the *means* (a body of force) with the *end*: deterrence calls for a *sufficient threat of unacceptable damage*. In pre-nuclear times, the means to

'Our unilateral decisions have set the rate and scale for most of the individual steps in the strategic arms race. In many cases we started development before they did and we easily established a large and long-lasting lead in terms of deployed numbers and types. Examples include the A-bomb itself, intercontinental bombers, submarine-launched ballistic missiles, and MIRV [multiple independently targeted re-entry vehicles: several warheads dispersed on descent from one missile carrier]. In other instances, the first development steps were taken by the two sides at about the same time, but immediately afterward our program ran well ahead of theirs in the development of further types and applications in the deployment of large numbers. Such cases include the mighty H-bomb and, very probably, military space applications. In some cases, to be sure, they started development work ahead of us and arrived first at the stage where they were able to commence deployment. But we usually reacted so strongly that our deployments and capabilities soon ran far ahead of theirs and we, in effect, even here, determined the final size of the operation. Such cases include the intercontinental ballistic missile and, though it is not strictly a military matter, manned space flight.'

(H. F. York,[1] First Director of the Lawrence Livermore Laboratory, America's thermonuclear weapons research establishment, 1952–8; First Director of Defense Engineering and Research at the Pentagon, 1958–61)

'In each case it seems to me that the Soviet Union is following the US lead and that the US is not reacting to Soviet action. Our current effort to get a MIRV capability on our missiles is not reacting to a Soviet capability so much as it is moving ahead to make sure that, whatever they do of the possible things that we imagine they might do, we will be prepared.'

(Paul Warnke, Chief US negotiator in the SALT II process)[2]

'. . . a strategic planner . . . must prepare for the worst plausible case and not be content to hope and prepare for the most probable.'

(Robert McNamara, US Secretary of Defense, 1961–8, 18 September 1967)[3] effect such a threat was composed of many units. For example, during the 'battleship race' which preceded the First World War, the national fleets of Britain and Germany each consisted of a mixture of vessels of different types and quality. One Dreadnought alone did not make a 'credible' threat, but one nuclear weapon is a different question. This leads to the second mistake: that more nuclear weapons mean, just like more battleships, that you are stronger, therefore that your security has been enhanced and your defence improved. In 1964 the true relationship between numbers of nuclear weapons and security was neatly expressed in an article by Jerome B. Wiesner, President Kennedy's chief science adviser, and Herbert York, who has already been quoted in this chapter:

> Ever since shortly after the Second World War the military power of the United States has been steadily increasing. Throughout this same period, the national security of the US has been rapidly and inexorably diminishing . . . From the Soviet point of view the picture is similar but much worse. The military power of the USSR has been steadily increasing since it became an atomic power in 1949. Soviet national security, however, has been steadily decreasing . . . Both sides in the arms race are thus confronted by the dilemma of steadily increasing military power and steadily decreasing national security . . . *It is our considered professional judgment that this dilemma has no technical solution.*[4]

The pervasiveness of these mistakes had several effects. By concentrating attention and effort upon technical questions of numbers, it drastically narrowed the perspectives of politicians. By equating this complex 'bean counting' with deterrence, the inherent unrealism of nuclear deterrence as a pure theory, explained in Chapter 6 below, continued to be ignored. Finally and crucially, it made accurate, detailed assessment of the adversary's capabilities of central importance: analysis on the assumption of the 'worst case' weakened the incentive to understand Soviet intentions, and in the situation of the Cold War it was not difficult to assume that these were as horrendous as required. 'Intentions' were conflated with 'capabilities' and were taken for all practical purposes to be the same. Furthermore, 'capabilities' were demonstrated by 'hard' data from U-2 spy-planes and later satellites, whereas 'intentions' were always 'soft' data; and common sense suggested to intelligence analysts that 'hard' data was to be preferred. Things were not as simple as that.

This chapter is concerned with the way in which American, not Russian, nuclear policy has changed. The reason for this is self-evident from the words of York and Warnke: economy of space directs us to the leading, not the trailing, edge of the process, and that leading edge was American. By the same token, NATO's strategies for the defence of Europe warrant little analysis, since they have always been dependent upon the central course of American strategy.

1 The Arsenal Expands

During most of the history of the American republic, professional soldiers have not commanded high status. The War of Independence was fought against King George III's Redcoats, a standing army seen as the servile prop of an anti-democratic regime. The Founding Fathers of the Republic expressed openly their distrust of standing armies, arguing that they had a predisposition to foster or to acquiesce to tyrants. They felt that the surest defence of a state against enemies without and erosion from within lay in an army of its citizens who would band together when danger threatened and return to their normal lives when it had passed. Such a citizens' army had fought the British. At a moment's notice, men could leave their occupations, take down their muskets from the living-room wall and go to war; hence their name, the 'Minutemen'. Belief in the importance of this type of defence was expressed in the Second Amendment to the Constitution.

> 'A well regulated Militia, being necessary to the security of a free state, the right of the people to keep and bear Arms, shall not be infringed.'
> (Article II, 15 December 1791)[5]

Nowadays the gun lobby in the USA usually cites only the second clause, separating the right from the obligation; but for the founders of the Republic, the right to bear arms was expressly in order to facilitate a form of defence which would not, in their opinion, erode those freedoms which it was intended to defend.

While such principles may not have been the cause, nevertheless after both the Civil War and the First World War, huge conscript armies were dissolved and war industries converted back to peacetime activities; and there was no military clique, no equivalent to the Prussian officer-caste in American society. But after the Second World War, things were different.

Major-General Leslie Groves, who supervised the Manhattan Project to build the bomb, came to that work from a building scheme – construction of a military headquarters for the USA from which the unprecedented war effort could be directed. Because of its shape, it was called the Pentagon. The Pentagon is entered up gently sloping ramps. They were constructed in this way to allow stretcher trolleys to be wheeled in with ease, not in the event of attack, but because it was intended to turn the building into a hospital when the war ended and it was no longer required for a military purpose. The ramps of the Pentagon serve to remind us that the present American military machine is the institutionalization of a temporary need and is aberrant in the history and principles of the republic.

Nevertheless, since 1945, the American armed forces have come to possess enormous power. It is a consequence of the world leadership which the United States assumed during the Second World War, of the possession by the military of vastly powerful nuclear weapons, and of the extent to which the Pentagon increased its political influence during the war and during the Cold War years. As a consequence, for the first time, military men defined the questions whose answers, while formally technical, had great political importance.

To answer these questions – about the weapons which the US could and should build, and about Russian capabilities – the US government has acquired a vast train of research and intelligence organizations. In addition to the Central Intelligence Agency (CIA), the Defense Intelligence Agency (DIA) and the National Security Agency (NSA), the State Department and each of the three services have their own intelligence offices, all created in their present forms since the Second World War.

The historian of American intelligence operations, Lawrence Freedman, suggests that the pressures upon any intelligence analyst to conform to the views and assumptions of his peers are great; and that without some fairly clear idea of what he is looking for, the analyst would drown in the sea of information presented to him. By a reasonable extension, he suggests that officers in military intelligence, themselves serving officers fixed in a conspicuous and formal hierarchy of ranks, are, for that reason, under an extra pressure to cast their often flimsy data in a way which appears to support authoritatively the point of view known to be held by superior officers. And the record of the military intelligence services supports this.[6] This is not just of academic interest, because inter-service rivalry, associated with quite astonishing misinterpretation of 'hard' data, or simple blind guessing, about Soviet capabilities in the 1950s and 1960s were instrumental in creating that wider political frame of mind in which American legislators procured huge numbers of strategic bombers and missiles.

'The thing that rather chills one's blood is to observe what is nothing less than lack of integrity in the way the intelligence agencies deal with the meager stuff they have. It is chiefly a matter of reasoning from our own American experience, guessing from that how much longer it will take Russia using our methods and based upon our problems of achieving weapons. But when this is put into a report, the reader, e.g. Congressional committee, is given the impression, and deliberately, that behind the estimates lies specific knowledge, knowledge so important and delicate that its nature and sources cannot be disclosed or hinted at.'

(David Lilienthal, Chairman, Atomic Energy Commission, 1948)[7]

In the 1950s four circumstances conspired to encourage U S intelligence agencies to expect the worst of the Russians. First, many analysts had been confidently predicting that the Russians would not perfect atomic weapons, let alone a hydrogen bomb, for very many years. The tests of 1949 and 1953 caught them by surprise and they were therefore inclined to be wary. Secondly, the agencies were still close to the painful experience of the gross errors of judgement that had been made in assessing the Korean situation. They had thought that the war would be a quick, easy, and limited operation; they had been proved completely wrong, and the dispute over what tactics should then be pursued had produced deep and bitter divisions between the civilian government and the US military, culminating in the humiliating recall from Korea of General MacArthur.[8] The Korean fiasco had been an important contributing factor in stirring up the waves of hysterical nationalism of the McCarthy years, which in turn had helped to create the Cold War climate. And thirdly, that climate hugely stimulated suspicions of the Soviet Union in the nuclear field. Finally, before overhead reconnaissance became available, any 'hard' data were sparse. The eye-witness accounts of military attachés attending parades, for example, were very important.

At the 1954 May Day parade in Moscow, the first long-range Soviet bomber was seen and the intelligence agencies began to calculate and extrapolate. Further examples of the M-4 Bison were spotted in 1955, and at the Aviation Day parade that year it was believed that about thirty flew past (although it later emerged that the Russians only had ten, but created the illusion by flying them past several times). On this basis US Air Force Intelligence credited the Russians with eighty aircraft and estimated a force of six to seven hundred by mid-1959. Army, navy and CIA were more sceptical but the official estimate in the National Intelligence Estimate (NIE) was around five hundred. News of a 'bomber gap' became public. Although by mid-1956 the first U-2 spy-plane photographs had begun to revise estimates downwards, on the basis of the 'bomber gap' the US Air Force procured 538 B-52 heavy bombers – the backbone of the Strategic Air Command – and also a massive air defence system for the continental United States. By July 1961, 67 active Air Force and 55 Air National Guard squadrons of interceptors were stationed at 42 bases across the country, backed by 7 anti-aircraft missile squadrons and Nike-Ajax point-defence missile batteries at 30 cities, supplemented by nuclear-capable Nike-Hercules missiles in the early 1960s. (These systems were all cut back in the 1970s.) By the start of 1961, in fact, the Russians had built only 190 long-range bombers, and at maximum deployment in 1966 had only 210 heavy bombers.[9]

But when the estimates of Russian bombers began to fall, the intelligence services did not take this as a warning about the dangers of over-estimation. Instead, they asked why the Russians were building fewer bombers than they had anticipated – an estimate extrapolated from American experience with their strategic bomber programme. The United States was then currently engaged in an intensive programme to develop intercontinental ballistic missiles (ICBMs). So the search was on for the Russian ICBM because the intelligence community could not conceive that the Russians would not be doing the same as the USA, and therefore concluded that the shortfall in perceived bomber production from their American-based estimates was because resources had been massively switched to ICBM production. On 4 October 1957, the Soviets launched the first earth satellite, Sputnik I. The fact of the launch seemed to confirm suspicions, and within informed circles in the military, the success of the launch and the size of the payload appeared even more ominous in the light of continuing American failures with their programme. This had been dogged by inter-service rivalry. The Navy had been charged with the task of putting an American satellite into orbit for International Geophysical Year 1957, but their Vanguard booster experienced continual failures. The

Army had meanwhile quietly developed the Jupiter-C rocket from their Redstone IRBM (intermediate range ballistic missile), itself a development of the German V–2 rocket, but in the face of official disapproval, since the Navy was not to be embarrassed publicly. But once the Sputnik was launched, success overrode propriety as main priority. Werner von Braun, Hitler's ballistic missile expert, was called in and told to put a satellite into space by all means and as soon as possible. He and his team launched the tiny Explorer satellite with a Jupiter booster in January 1959.[10] The Sputnik story created consternation in the American media and helped to prepare public opinion to receive and to respond hawkishly to the news that the 'bomber gap' was now followed by a far more dangerous 'missile gap'.

Intermittent Russian test firings of ICBMs between 1957 and 1959 had been observed by American radar in Turkey and Iran, and while the CIA tended to regard the evidence as indicative of technical problems, the Air Force took the opposite view. Again Air Force Intelligence made the pace, scrutinizing U–2 film. 'To the American Air Force every flyspeck on a film was a missile,' one analyst complained. At various times ammunition storage sheds, a Crimean War monument, and a medieval tower were identified as the elusive ICBM. In the end satellite photographs of the missile complex at Plesetsk found the missile, the SS–6. Further information caused earlier official estimates to be scaled down, eventually to a tiny fraction of the earlier, politically important, hypothetical projections.[11] In fact only four SS–6 were ever deployed. At that time, such effort in missile development as the Russians were making was concentrated in the IRBM area, in which, since the Americans were not pressing forward, the Russians had numerical superiority. Some analysts viewed this as a sinister development. But with hindsight it seems more likely that the Soviets just did what they were technically able to do, which was less than the Americans could do. This also fitted in with the intense counter-European emphasis in Soviet strategy in the 1950s, a strategy stimulated by the Soviet experiences of European aggression that were discussed in Chapter 2.

But this was all of little importance. During the summer and autumn of 1960 the Air Force view held sway and at that time, in his presidential campaign, J. F. Kennedy had used the 'missile gap' as a stick with which to berate the incumbent, Eisenhower, as a way of attacking his opponent, Richard Nixon, and it was politically impossible to admit that it was a myth. The table shows, A, the figures put out by the Pentagon and, B, the best estimates, with hindsight, of the true situation.

Table 2. The Missile Gap: ICBMs[12]

Date	United States	Soviet Union	Balance + = US superiority − = Soviet superiority
(a) Missile gap projection			
1960	30	100	− 70
1961	70	500	− 430
1962	130	1,000	− 870
1963	130	1,500	− 1,370
1964	130	2,000	− 1,870
(b) 'Actual figures'			
1960	18	4	+ 14
1961	63	20	+ 43
1962	294	75	+ 219
1963	424	100	+ 324
1964	834	200	+ 634

When the Kennedy administration came to power in 1960, the new Secretary of Defense, Robert McNamara, soon saw from intelligence sources that the 'gap' had little substance, but none the less, under his control, in 1962 the US Air Force deployed the first of a force of 1,000 'Minuteman' land-based ICBMs (a use of their name which must make the true Minutemen turn in their graves).[13]

What were the reasons that caused McNamara to continue with the Minuteman and Polaris programmes even after he knew that the 'missile gap' was a myth? He gave them in a public defence of his actions in a speech in 1967, towards the end of his period of office. Fifteen years later, while advocating the abandonment of a fundamental principle of the NATO nuclear doctrine which he had been prominent in fashioning (the NATO intention to be the first to employ nuclear weapons in a conflict if it considered that circumstances so demanded) McNamara spelt out his view, only hinted at in 1967, of what had been the effect of the Minuteman and Polaris programmes of the early 1960s upon subsequent Soviet views and actions in the nuclear arms race. Both testimonies are of the greatest interest because of the centrality of McNamara in any history of the nuclear arms race and therefore extracts are given in the accompanying box.

ROBERT McNAMARA'S EXPLANATIONS OF THE REASONS FOR
AND CONSEQUENCES OF THE MINUTEMAN AND POLARIS
PROGRAMMES OF THE EARLY 1960s[14]

1967

'In 1961, when I became Secretary of Defense, the Soviet Union possessed a very small operational arsenal of intercontinental missiles. However, they did possess the technological and industrial capacity to enlarge the arsenal very substantially over the succeeding several years. Now, we had no evidence that the Soviets did in fact plan to fully use that capability . . .

'Thus, in the course of hedging against what was then only a theoretically possible Soviet build-up, we took decisions which have resulted in our current superiority in numbers of warheads and deliverable megatons. But the blunt fact remains that if we had more accurate information about planned Soviet strategic forces, we simply would not have needed to build as large a nuclear arsenal as we have today.

'Now let me be absolutely clear. I am not saying that our decision in 1961 was unjustified. I am simply saying that it was necessitated by the lack of accurate information.

'Furthermore, that decision in itself – as justified as it was – in the end, could not possibly have left unaffected the Soviet Union's future nuclear plans.'

1982

'. . . [by 1962] the advantage in the US warhead inventory was so great *vis-à-vis* the Soviets that the Air Force was saying that they felt we had a first-strike capability and could, and should, continue to have one. If the Air Force thought that, imagine what the Soviets thought . . .

'The point on the Soviet concern about our first strike is an important one. This is a highly classified memorandum from me to President Kennedy dated 21 November 1962 [released to the public under the Freedom of Information Act – Ed.]. In the memorandum I state:

It has become clear to me the Air Force proposals are based on the objective of achieving a first-strike capability. In the words of the Air Force report to me "The Air Force has rather supported the development of forces which provide the United States with a first-strike capability credible to the Soviet Union by virtue of our ability to limit damage to the United States and our allies to levels acceptable in light of the circumstances and the alternatives available" [i.e. the

Air Force regarded 50 million direct American fatalities as a consequence of a Soviet second strike to be "acceptable" – Ed.] . . . I reaffirm now my belief that the full first-strike capability – and I now include the Air Force's variant of it – should be rejected as a US policy objective.

'. . . The Soviets didn't have this document, at least I hope they didn't. But they may have heard talk that we were trying to achieve a first-strike capability and, in any case, they saw the size force we had.

'. . . I have no doubt but that the Soviets thought we were trying to achieve a first-strike capability. We were not. We did not have it; we could not attain it; we didn't have any thought of attaining it. But they probably thought we did.

'. . . If I had been the Soviet Secretary of Defense, I'd have been worried as hell at the imbalance of force. And I would have been concerned that the United States was trying to build a first-strike capability. I would have been concerned simply because I would have had knowledge of what the nuclear strength was of the United States and I would have heard rumours that the Air Force was recommending achievement of such a capability.

'. . . Read again my memo to President Kennedy. It scares me today to even read the damn thing. What that means is the Air Force supported the development of US forces sufficiently large to destroy so much of the Soviet nuclear force, by a first strike, that there would not be enough left to cause us any concern if they shot at us. My God! If the Soviets thought that was our objective, how would you expect them to react? The way they reacted was by substantially expanding their strategic nuclear weapons programme.

'. . . So you have an action–reaction phenomenon. And the result is that during the last twenty-five years, and particularly during the last fifteen, there has been a huge build-up, much more than people realize, in the nuclear strength of these two forces. That has changed the nature of the problem and increased the risk greatly.'

In the public arena, the 'bomber gap' and the 'missile gap' had different and distinct effects, serving to hasten or to facilitate decisions on deployment and numbers of weapons. But behind closed doors, their effect on the fundamental decisions to proceed with research was merged; for it was at the height of the *bomber* scare, in February 1955, that the National Security Council stressed the urgency of the ballistic missile programme, and in the summer of that year that the Killian Report recommended, and the NSC approved, that part of the rocket force should go to sea.

The original idea was to fit a version of the Army's massive (162,000 lb) Jupiter IRBM into a submarine; then in the late summer of 1956, the ubiquitous and indispensable Dr Edward Teller from the Atomic Energy Commission asked a simple and vital question, 'Why are you designing a 1965 weapon system with 1958 technology?' He predicted dramatic reductions in warhead weight for an 'acceptable yield'. The answer to Dr Teller was the much smaller (30,000 lb) Polaris missile, sixteen of which could fit into a submarine, and the Polaris programme sped from initial authorization on 8 December 1956 to the first successful under-water firings from the USS *George Washington* on 20 July 1960. As the president of Lockheed Missiles put it, 'with these two "shots heard around the world" the Navy resoundingly entered the Strategic Age',[15] so for the first time acquiring a substantial nuclear role.

In response to the new weapons systems created in this way, the different experts began to develop new strategies and to provide new justifications. In fact changes were gradual and rather muddled: there was no clean-cut division between policies in thought or in time.

The idea of massive retaliation was the logical extension of the defensive deterrent view of nuclear weapons. But as numbers of weapons increased, so, along with that, the justification was modified in the form of the annual estimates of what constituted a 'credible' deterrent in Russian eyes.

But what constitutes a 'credible' nuclear deterrent? For Oppenheimer in 1949, it was an arsenal of air-dropped fission bombs. He found this conclusion distasteful but essential. His view was in effect to say that since we have 'known sin', and have nuclear weapons, we should accept as justified the lesser horror of threatening civilian populations with A-bombs, while rejecting the greater horror of threatening similar targets with vastly bigger H-bombs. Fermi and Rabi, two members of the General Advisory Committee of the Atomic Energy Commission, which was asked to assess the need for thermonuclear weapons in 1949, saw the H-bomb issue in more starkly ethical terms than their colleagues:

> Necessarily such a weapon goes far beyond any military objective and enters the range of very great natural catastrophes. [It] becomes a weapon which in practical effect is almost one of genocide. It is clear that the use of such a weapon cannot be justified on any ethical ground which gives a human being a certain individuality and dignity . . .[16]

Thus before we attempt to quantify further a 'minimum nuclear deterrent', a contradiction appears: it is deeply morally repugnant; such means deny and pollute the very things which they purport to defend. The veteran American diplomat George Kennan described nuclear deterrence in any form as 'a concept which attributes to others – to others who, like ourselves, were born of women, walk on two legs and love their children, to human beings in short – the most fiendish and inhuman of tendencies'.[17] In making its threat, a nuclear deterrent raises the issue from military calculations about relative sacrifices of conventional armed forces to assessments of the adversary's willingness to expose his territory and people to indiscriminate attack.

> 'It may be possible to have a just war, but there can be no such thing as just mutual obliteration . . . It is vital that we see modern weapons of war for what they are – evidence of madness. Our Lord said "love your enemies, do good to those who persecute you". This saying is still offensive and obscure to many, but "love your enemies" is a credible peace strategy and the only one the Church as such is authorized to pursue.'
>
> (The Archbishop of Canterbury, Rt Rev. Robert Runcie, 1981)

Thus, ignoring the laws of war, or any moral consideration, on the wholly expedient ground that you must attack what hurts the opponent most, given that Oppenheimer and his committee were defeated and the H-bomb was made, what, in the H-bomb world, constituted an adequate deterrent? The only military aspect of the answer was that sufficient destructive capacity should be able to survive a first strike by the enemy to be fired in retaliation from invulnerable sites.

A further contradiction in nuclear deterrence then appears: deterrence is vulnerable to destabilization by technological advance in weapons systems. This point was carefully made in the late 1950s by a senior American strategist in an article entitled 'The delicate balance of terror'.[18] So estimates constantly varied – always upwards – of the weapons required. But to what end? How many bombs or megatons are enough? No better answer has been given than that by McGeorge Bundy shortly after he left his post as President Kennedy's special assistant for national security affairs:

In the real world of real political leaders – whether here or in the Soviet Union – a decision that would bring even one hydrogen bomb on one city of one's own country would be recognized in advance as a catastrophic blunder; ten bombs on ten cities would be a disaster beyond history; and a hundred bombs on a hundred cities are unthinkable.[19]

THE RADIATION EFFECT OF A NUCLEAR EXPLOSION
IN GREAT BRITAIN[20]

The map shows the pattern of radiation one month after the explosions. The prevailing wind is south-westerly and brisk, at about 15 mph. The plumes are idealized and take no account of shear: reality would not be as neat as this. The contours show the *dose* accumulated during the first year, measured from one month after the explosion, in rads, for levels of 100, 50, and 10 rads respectively. (For comparison, the average dose of background radiation is 0.1 rad, although in industrial countries, man-made radiation may increase this by 30 to 70 per cent, through medical examinations or treatment; and there is still a significant contribution from past atmospheric weapons tests.)

In a nuclear attack, most casualties would occur within the first weeks as a result of the prompt effects of blast, heat, acute radiation exposure and associated infection and disease. During this period external doses of gamma radiation would be dominant and it has been calculated that, with an average European population density of about 100/km², about 230,000 people would receive swiftly lethal doses from a single 1 Mt bomb without 'enhancement' from other radioactive products. However, since death from infection would probably come to those with lower, yet appreciable levels of acute dose (100 rad and over), this figure would – at this population density – be nearer to a million. These figures would be slightly reduced by people remaining indoors. But what would short-term 'survival' be for? Radioactivity would persist and as the map and graph show, especially if nuclear installations were breached, this would affect even wider areas for longer periods than in the event of 'ordinary' nuclear explosions. Furthermore, the map shows only *external* radiation levels and takes no account of the α- and β-emitting radio-isotopes that would be unavoidably ingested from fall-out, contaminated food and water (see Chapter 9 and Appendix B). Some of these isotopes are selectively absorbed and retained by specific organs of the body. Local irradiation by α and β emitters may become the dominant problem for the 'survivors', leading to increasing morbidity and mortality from cancer and other causes after a few years. McGeorge Bundy's estimate (and, incidentally, official assurances about the efficacy of 'shelter') should be read in the light of such evidence.

However, were the explosion to be part of a general release of nuclear weapons, mainly in the northern hemisphere, as is most probable, then other important but unquantified effects might overshadow those already mentioned. Vast quantities of particulate matter and of hydrocarbon gases would create severe smog, loading the atmosphere with light-absorbing matter that would cause darkness in daytime. Photosynthesis would be disrupted in those plants not already killed by radiation or fire, and effective agriculture would cease. Survivors of the immediate effects in the rich world of the northern hemisphere would probably die of starvation in great numbers; loss of northern hemisphere food production would lead also to mass starvation in the poor world of the south.

Injection by high-yield explosions of huge quantities of nitrous oxides into the upper atmosphere, where it would become nitric oxide, would deplete the protective ozone layer and expose the earth to increased amounts of ultraviolet radiation from the sun. These would kill or variously injure humans, animals, plants, and micro-organisms and could therefore severely unbalance terrestrial and oceanic ecosystems.

These insults to the biosphere might all work synergistically and lead to perhaps catastrophic but at present unknown effects greater than a simple addition would suggest.

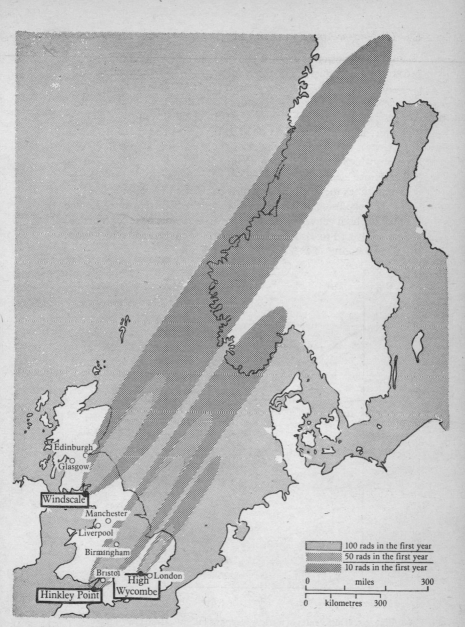

Figure 4. Radiation effects of nuclear attacks on Britain (for explanation see overleaf)

—— The explosion at *High Wycombe* is a 1 Mt ground-burst at the command headquarters of the R A F.

——. The explosion at *Hinkley Point* is a 1 Mt ground-burst on the nuclear power station. The contours are taken from Professor Rotblat's calculation of the release of a fifth of the inventory of a Gw(e) reactor. Hinkley Point A is rated at 0.5 Gw(e) and the B reactor at 1.3 Gw(e). No account is taken of the spent fuel stored in cooling ponds, which would be drawn up into the fireball also. Therefore the figures are deliberately conservative, and may underestimate by several times the likely real pattern of released radiation.

—— The explosion at *Windscale* assumes the involvement of storage tanks for high active waste. The calculations for these contours are derived using Professor Rotblat's figures for a 3,000 m³ tank, scaled for the 1,000 m³ of H A W held at Windscale.

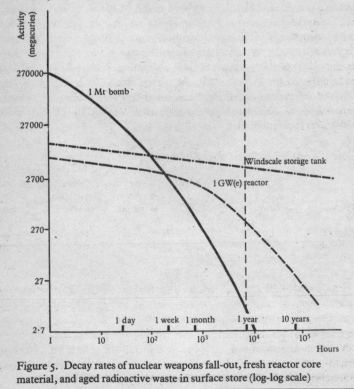

Figure 5. Decay rates of nuclear weapons fall-out, fresh reactor core material, and aged radioactive waste in surface store (log-log scale)

Because of the power of even a single nuclear weapon, the matter can with some justice be considered in absolute terms. Since there is an excellent and expanding literature on the effects of nuclear explosions this book does not examine them at length. But, to help British readers to decide for themselves the 'adequacy' of a minimum deterrent, the map and explanation on pages 96–8 situate the problem in familiar terms.

Starting in the early 1950s from an idea close to McGeorge Bundy's definition of the minimum deterrent, chiefs of staff and intelligence analysts year by year built up an amazing catalogue of the destruction deemed essential to 'deter' Russia.

By the later 1960s, this process had acquired a spuriously scientific air, and in 1968 Secretary of Defense McNamara told the Senate Armed Services Committee that the ability to destroy one-fifth to one-quarter of Russia's people and half her industry 'would serve as an effective deterrent'. To achieve this goal, the Secretary of Defense explained that the US had to dispose of four hundred 'equivalent megatons' (defined in Appendix A1) and, for safety, that that strength had to be independently available on each 'leg' of the 'Strategic Triad' of bombers, ICBMs, and SLBMs (Submarine-Launched Ballistic Missiles). And as it happens, four hundred equivalent megatons represented just about what the administration had, or planned to procure, on each 'leg' of the 'Triad' in the mid-1960s (see Table 3).[21]

Table 3. The Strategic Triad in the Mid-1960s

Weapon	Number	Warheads per vehicle	Equivalent Mt per warhead	Availability/ reliability (out of 1.0)	Total EMt
Polaris	41	16	1	.60	= 400
Minuteman I	450	1	1	.90	= 400
B–52	300	4	1.3	.25	= 400

But this calculation seems to have little to do with thinking the situation through from a Soviet point of view, as the pure theory of deterrence requires. In fact after 400 equivalent Mt, the 'pay-off' of increased megatonnage falls away sharply (see Table 4 and Figure 6).

A similar history of changing the tune to suit the pipe is seen when we turn to modifications in strategy. Here the issue was clouded by the intense inter-service rivalry between Air Force, Navy and Army.

Table 4. Soviet Population and Industry Destroyed[22]
(assumed 1972 total population of 247 million; urban population of 116 million)

1 Mt equivalent delivered warheads	Total population fatalities		Industrial capacity destroyed (percentage)
	Millions	Percentage	
100	37	15	59
200	52	21	72
400	74	30	76
800	96	39	77
1,200	109	44	77
1,600	116	47	77

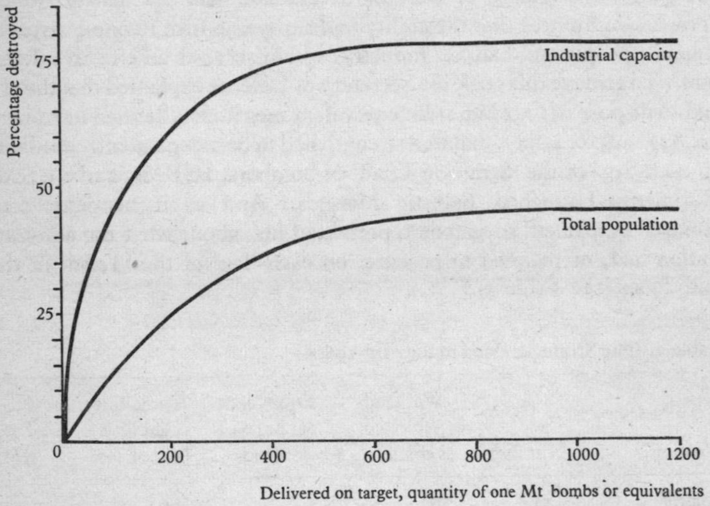

Figure 6. Soviet population and industrial capacity destroyed

In the 1950s, the Strategic Air Command of the Air Force carried the American nuclear capability. B–52s could bomb large targets best, with large bombs. So SAC officers believed in massive retaliation, because that was what they could do. During this period, the Navy had no major nuclear role, and argued that it was immoral to plan for the genocidal sort of assault contemplated by the Air Force. Meanwhile, in 1956, Secretary of Defense Charles 'Engine Charlie' Wilson had ruled that the US Army's nuclear role should be restricted to short-range systems, and accordingly the Army had begun to acquire small 'tactical' nuclear weapons, some of which it began to deploy in West Germany in 1956, the year after that country entered NATO. Army strategists proposed ways of fighting limited nuclear war, although the Army was never quite reconciled to being excluded from the 'big time' of offensive strategic warfare; and indeed as we shall see, it will succeed in overturning 'Engine Charlie's' ruling in the 1980s, unless it is prevented.[23]

With the prospect of Polaris, the navy suddenly changed its tune and argued that it should take the pre-eminent deterrent role, using its invulnerable submarines to threaten a far more terrible and sure destruction than could ever be done with bombers. Indeed, to some Navy officers it appeared that the Strategic Air Command had now outlived its usefulness. True to form, the Air Force counter-attack was massive, rebutting the claim, and indeed asserting that the Air Force should have tighter control over all US nuclear forces – including the Navy's new submarines![24] Furthermore, the secret memorandum from McNamara to Kennedy – declassified in 1982 and quoted in the box above – reveals that Air Force ambitions at this time were greater even than this, and that it wanted a full first-strike capacity against the USSR, which Kennedy and McNamara vetoed. In its new stance, the Navy found a happy coincidence of interest with the Army, for together they could argue for a 'balanced deterrent' which would restore to military force the flexibility which the advent of nuclear weapons had taken away: the Russians would be deterred from using their big nuclear bombs in any circumstances by the Navy and, under this shield, the Army and the Navy's Marines could get on with fighting limited wars, including limited nuclear wars.[25] 'Balanced deterrence' tried to get back to the nineteenth century by nullifying thermonuclear weapons. In this way the ideas of 'mutually assured destruction' (MAD) and 'flexible response' (i.e. the ability to respond to an attack with force graded according to the scale of the attack) coexisted for a time, and naturally became NATO policy in Europe also.[26]

While the danger of escalation was obvious from the start, it grew steadily worse with technical developments and the deployment of 'small' atomic weapons in Europe in Army hands. 'Flexible response' had another consequence also. Hitherto there had been a 'firebreak', which experienced soldiers regarded as essential, between all other types of weapons and nuclear weapons. But this was now destroyed, thus lowering the nuclear threshold.

In 1958, the 'bomber gap' faced Air Force strategists with a new

'It was not long, however, before smaller nuclear weapons of various designs were produced and deployed for use in what was assumed to be a tactical or theatre war. The belief was that were hostilities ever to break out in Western Europe, such weapons could be used in field warfare without triggering an all-out nuclear exchange leading to the final holocaust.

'I have never found this idea credible. I have never been able to accept the reasons for the belief that any class of nuclear weapons can be categorized in terms of their tactical or strategic purposes.'

(Earl Mountbatten of Burma)[27]

problem. 'Massive retaliation' was itself deterred by the prospect of Soviet H-bombs, bombers, and perhaps missiles. But rather than conclude that this made thermonuclear war too dangerous to consider, Air Force officers, some academics on contract to the Air Force from the RAND Corporation,[28] and some officials in Air Force related industries worked out a refinement to make thermonuclear war thinkable, rational, flexible, and therefore possible. They proposed to use their weapons against enemy military, not civilian targets; in short, to believe that nuclear war could (and therefore would) be amenable to pre-nuclear rules of war. This they called 'counter-force' strategy.[29] It is the subject of the next section.

2 Counterforce

In that same sort of closed circle just seen operating in the last section – a circle which blurs the relationship of cause and effect between strategies and weapons systems – 'counterforce' is the nuclear strategy which today is said to determine the nature of modern nuclear weapons and the direction in which the world's nuclear arsenal is moving (led by the United States), and at the same time is itself justified by the weapons in the eyes of strategists and military men. Counterforce is the theory of introducing precision and the controlled and limited use of force into fighting a war with nuclear weapons. Only recently has a wide public awareness of counterforce been awakened, and the suggestion has been made that this is a new and exceedingly dangerous strategy. Government and military spokesmen have replied that that is not so, that counterforce is not at all new, that we are 'steady as we go'; and by indicating that their critics are ignorant, they have tried to discredit and thus to sweep aside their concerns.[30]

The history of counterforce shows that both critics and governments are correct, but in different ways: governments are correct to say that counterforce is not a new idea. However, their critics are correct also, and in a more important, material sense, in that it has indeed only been in the last few years that technology has succeeded in perfecting counterforce weapons and deploying them in large numbers: from 1970 the Minuteman III and from the mid-1970s, the SS–17, SS–18 and SS–19 ICBMs, from 1971 the Poseidon C–3 and from 1979 the Trident I SLBMs.[31] It is this fact, and the threat of a new and enormously more 'efficient' generation of advanced American weapons in the 1980s (the missile experimental [MX] ICBM, the Trident II SLBM, the Pershing II IRBM and the cruise missile) that combine with the dangerously lowered nuclear threshold and huge quantities of short-range nuclear explosives to make the possibility of nuclear war far greater now than it has ever been before.

Counterforce strategy is the clearest expression of exasperation with the contradiction that the most powerful weapons ever invented seem to be unable to contribute to the utility of military power as an instrument of policy. We saw, at the end of the last section, that it was in the late 1950s that counterforce first appeared openly in Air Force circles as a 'solution' to the threat of the illusory Russian heavy bomber force. The development of weapons with a counterforce potential was hastened in the United States by another scare – the third – generated in the intelligence community, a scare which, like the bomber and missile 'gaps' also turned out to be an illusion: the anti-ballistic-missile (ABM) 'gap'.

Immediately after the development of the first American ICBM, the Atlas, began, the Bell Telephone Laboratory (which does not only design telephones, as one might think) was asked to consider the feasibility of a defensive anti-ballistic missile (the Nike-Zeus).[32] Knowing what was being done at home, US intelligence was on the lookout for Soviet ABM development. In 1960, photographs were obtained of radars which might, perhaps, have an ABM role, and in the early 1960s, there was good evidence of ABM complexes around Moscow and Leningrad. Then in 1961, reports began to circulate of a string of sites from Archangel to Riga, across the path of incoming American ICBMs. It was named the 'Tallinn Line' after the Estonian capital. By the mid-1960s more construction work was observed and a high-altitude defensive rocket identified. To Secretary of Defense McNamara, knowing that the USA had just completed deployment of the Minuteman and Polaris missiles, it seemed most likely that the Tallinn Line was a massive ABM system, designed to neutralize the American force: to deter the deterrent.

By 1967, it was widely accepted that in fact the Tallinn Line was no such thing, but consisted of anti-aircraft emplacements: a response to the vast fleet of American B–52 intercontinental bombers. But in 1964, the USA was fully committed to a programme to put multiple warheads, or 're-entry vehicles' (MRV), and, in 1965, multiple independently targeted warheads (MIRV), on to its strategic missiles, ostensibly to saturate the ABM defences. But the Tallinn Line ABM theory was by no means dead; 'worst case' assumptions breathed life into it still. In 1968 the Air Force was prominent in arguing that even if the Tallinn Line was *not* an ABM system, one day it could be 'upgraded' to become one: so best MIRV and be prepared![33]

The development of MIRV during the 1960s and its deployment during the 1970s represented the single most important and dangerous move in the nuclear arms race since the creation of the H-bomb. By permitting a vast increase in numbers of warheads on the same number of delivery systems, MIRV made effective arms control far more difficult and greatly increased the physical capacity to pursue counterforce strategies. The story of MIRV also illustrates well other aspects of the arms race and it is offered as a case-study of these at the end of Chapter 5.

MIRV's contribution to counterforce depended not only upon the proliferation of warheads, but also upon technical developments in the guidance systems of missiles, on the terminal guidance on to their targets of the warheads, and, if the missiles were launched from submarines, on their navigation systems too, since you cannot aim a ballistic missile accurately unless you know exactly where you launch it from. In these fields, the USA has had a consistent and commanding superiority.[34] Knowing this, in late 1969 and early 1970, when a ban on MIRV technology was discussed informally before and formally at the outset of the Strategic Arms Limitation Talks (SALT), President Nixon and Henry Kissinger, in his role as national security adviser, took a conscious decision to outrace the Russians on the technology. They therefore refused to contemplate banning MIRV.[35] This was also the time when the reality of defeat in Vietnam was staring the administration in the face, and while the evidence for it cannot be more than circumstantial, it is reasonable to think that the decision to press on in one field where the USA *could* be seen to be winning was not unrelated.

Accuracy is at the heart of counterforce.[36] Put quite simply, making a missile twice as accurate improves its lethality as much as an eightfold increase in explosive yield. It was advances in American missile guidance that in 1962 encouraged Secretary of Defense McNamara to make public for the first time the inclusion of counterforce in America's plan for general warfare, although at that time it is most doubtful that the plans could have been carried out. This followed a year of work which in January 1962 had resulted in approval by the Joint Chiefs of Staff of a dramatic revision of the first single integrated operational plan (SIOP) which had proposed massive retaliation. The new SIOP included 'nuclear threat' and 'other military' designations for targets as well as 'urban-industrial' ones.[37] McNamara explained this in a speech which became known as the 'No cities' speech. In it he made plain the intention to ignore the special nature of the nuclear age. The Air Force was lobbying for a first-strike policy and capability; Kennedy and McNamara gave it 'flexible response' with counterforce.

> 'The US has come to the conclusion that to the extent feasible, basic military strategy in a possible general nuclear war should be approached in much the same way that more conventional military operations have been regarded in the past. That is to say, principal military objectives, in the event of a nuclear war stemming from a major attack on the Alliance, should be the destruction of the enemy's military forces, not of his civilian population.'
>
> (R. McNamara, Ann Arbor, 16 June 1962)[38]

Counterforce, as presented then, dovetailed with the already well-established plans for limited nuclear war in Europe which were a legacy both of the Army/Navy 'balanced deterrent' idea and of the NATO belief that nuclear weapons would be a cheap and therefore politically more palatable way of preparing to stop a conventional Russian invasion of Western Europe. Counterforce was, it was suggested, more humane because strikes could be precise and therefore restricted, and subsequently the policy as advocated in the West has been based upon the assumption, shared by the NATO plan for limited nuclear war, that such war *can* be limited – plainly contrary to Clausewitz's view (*On War*, 1832) that war consists of reciprocal actions that tend to escalate and have no logical limit.

Soviet spokesmen also have stated that to them the ideas of limitation, of graduated escalation, and of crisis bargaining, which figure so prominently in these 'games-theory' scenarios of Western strategists, seem quite unconvincing. 'Nuclear war would be a universal disaster ... It may lead to the destruction of all humankind. There may be no victor in such a war and it can solve no political problems,' has been their consistent message. But such statements are rejected as mere propaganda by British and American government agencies, who point instead to military theorists like Marshal V. D. Sokolovskii, who in his classic work *Military Strategy* states that

strategic operation of a future nuclear war will consist of coordinated operation of the services of the armed forces . . . The main forces of such an operation will be the strategic nuclear weapons . . . the basic aim of this [nuclear missile] type of operation is to undermine the military power of the enemy by eliminating the nuclear means of fighting and formations of armed forces, and eliminating the military-economic potential by destroying the economic foundations for war . . .[39]

The dispositions and training practices of the Red Army also support the view that they are prepared to use nuclear weapons for war-fighting. Thus it is suggested that it is self-evident that the Soviets too believe in and prepare for limited nuclear war – and have done so for longer than the West. It would be as wrong to think otherwise as it would be to believe that Earl Mountbatten's views accurately described NATO doctrine, deployments, or training practices. However, this interpretation is incorrect.

It is true that the military ('counterforce') use of nuclear weapons has *always* been part of Soviet strategy: short-range nuclear missiles are viewed as an extension of the artillery. But this does not mean that the Soviets share the Western belief in limited nuclear war – because the Soviets do not share the Western concept of nuclear deterrence; they even lack a proper term for it. The Western theory of 'minimum deterrence', explained earlier in this chapter, with its emphasis on holding cities hostage and so preventing war through fear is distinct from 'defence'. In the West it is conventional to assert that 'the nuclear deterrent has failed if it is used'. Soviet military doctrine has no equivalent for this, and does not separate the idea of 'deterrence' from that of general defence. It uses 'deterrence' in its old sense: defence of the Soviet Union depends on the ability to repel (or absorb) an attack *and then go on* and win the war. Clearly, as their spokesmen have repeatedly stated, the Soviets hope that their total defensive capability will be sufficient to discourage or hold back (*sderzhivat*) an aggressor – they are not looking to be attacked or hoping for war – but if war with the West does come, it will be *mirovaya voyna*, a global conflict started by the West (Marxist–Leninist theory conceives of no other way that it can begin); it will be general war, a fight to the finish and Soviet defence will only have failed if their armed forces are unable to recover from the initial attack and go on to 'victory'. 'Defence through war-fighting' is the Soviet concept equivalent to 'nuclear deterrence' in the West. But it is a different idea and so it calls for a different range of weapons and military practices. It is therefore a simple, very common, and dangerous category of mistake to interpret Soviet capabilities in terms of the Western theories – or indeed, *vice versa*, to see Western forces and practices in Soviet terms.

Should nuclear war come, both sides would share responsibility: the West for clinging to the belief that nuclear war can be graduated and limited, the East for failing to make a 'firebreak' between nuclear and other weapons. Yet the two sides do differ, in that while Western soldiers and politicians adamantly refuse to renounce the intention to be the first to use nuclear weapons in war (and indeed, some argue that this firm intention is a good 'stabilizing' factor in the confrontation), the USSR has, in accordance with its policy of old-fashioned deterrence ('defence through war-fighting'), consistently stated that they will not be the first to employ nuclear weapons, and have repeatedly offered the chance to make a mutual agreement to renounce first use, which the West has always refused, but which would be an obvious first step away from the present hair-trigger posture.[40]

Knowledge of these fundamental differences in Soviet and Western strategy may help to explain otherwise puzzling things. For example, it becomes clear why, after the USA began to deploy Polaris submarines in 1961, the USSR responded in the 1960s and 1970s by constructing a new, forward-deployed navy with the primary mission of trying to destroy American missile-carrying submarines in order to deny the West the possibility of an invulnerable 'second-strike' force: the 'blue water' Navy was part of homeland defence, responding to a new threat. Similarly, the 'defence through war-fighting' policy may help explain why the USSR concentrated first on medium- and intermediate-range missiles, appropriate to this policy, and has only much more recently tried to obtain a long-range counterforce capability, although it appears that none of the major Soviet counterforce rockets (SS–17, 18, 19, ICBMs, SS–20 IRBM) attain the accuracies of Western missiles. To take one example, the SS–20 is not, as is often suggested, a particularly accurate weapon. It has a 'circular error probable' (CEP – see Appendix A1 for a definition) of 1,500 feet and a single-shot kill probability (SSKP) of 0.17 against a target like a missile silo, 'hardened' to resist an overpressure of 1,000 psi. By contrast, the new US Army Pershing II is intended to have a CEP of 120 feet and in consequence an SSKP against a 'hard' target of 0.99.[41]

But such accuracies, and therefore effective counterforce weapons, are a recent development. In 1970 General Ryan, Chief of Staff of the US Air Force, was quoted as saying 'we have a programme we are pushing to increase the yield of our warheads and decrease the circle error probable, so that we have what we call a hard-target killer, which we do not have in the inventory at the present time'.[42] The programme was denied at the time by President Nixon, but the figures for the arsenal in 1970 and in 1980 shown in Table 5 confirm that, while the total number of long-range missiles owned by the USA actually decreased during the decade, the number of warheads more than doubled, reflecting the introduction of MIRV, the technology associated with counterforce strategy. Further figures are given in Appendix A1.

Table 5. Strategic Nuclear Forces of the USA and USSR over the Decade 1970–80[43]

	1970	1980
Launch vehicles		
ICBM		
USA	1,054	1,052
USSR	1,487	1,398
SLBM		
USA	656	576
USSR	248	950
Heavy bombers		
USA	512	348
USSR	156	156
Total warheads		
USA	4,000	10,312
USSR	1,800	6,846

Note: the warheads mentioned in this table are long range only. By far the largest proportion of all warheads are in short-range systems.

During the 1970s, officials became less coy about counterforce. In 1974 Secretary of Defense Schlesinger told the Senate Sub-committee on Arms Control that there had been a change in 'targeting doctrine' to one 'which emphasizes flexibility and selectivity'. Pressed by committee members, he admitted that in fact counterforce targeting had already happened. At the same time, Schlesinger stressed that the doctrine was for controlled warfare and denied energetically that it was the same as a first-strike capability.[44] But herein lay the rub: counterforce weapons are indistinguishable from those required for a disarming first strike. Therefore, once the situation has deteriorated to the point where nuclear war threatens, how is the adversary to know what is intended?

> Senator Case: '. . . in fact there isn't anything new because we already have targets. We have weapons targeted, individual targets that can be selected.'
> Schlesinger: 'Yes.'
> Case: 'It is just a matter of thinking about it, isn't it?'
> Schlesinger: 'Right. That is why I referred to it as targeting doctrine rather than the term retargeting that has been employed. It is a question of firing doctrine, and how you view the problem. You are quite right, Senator, to stress that aspect.'
> Senator Humphrey: 'And the indoctrination of our own people, isn't it?'
> Schlesinger: 'That is right.'[45]

By the time that strategic doctrine was again aired before the Senate Foreign Relations Committee in 1980, public awareness about strategic theory was thoroughly aroused. The new refinement to counterforce was Presidential Directive No. 59 (PD59) signed by President Carter on 25 July 1980. Aware of the public controversy aroused by leaks about PD59,

> 'This doctrine, as I emphasized earlier, is *not* a new departure. The US has never had a doctrine based simply and solely on reflexive, massive attacks on Soviet cities. Instead, we have always planned both more selectively (options limiting urban-industrial damage) and more comprehensively (a range of military targets). Previous administrations, going back well into the 1960s, recognized the inadequacy of a strategic doctrine that would give us too narrow a range of options. The fundamental premises of our countervailing strategy are a natural evolution of the conceptual foundations built over the course of a generation by, for example, Secretaries McNamara and Schlesinger, to name only two of my predecessors who have been most identified with development of our nuclear doctrine.'
>
> (Secretary of Defense, Harold Brown, August 1980)[46]

Secretary of Defense Harold Brown went to such great lengths to explain what PD59 was *not* (not new; not assuming that one could win a limited nuclear war; not a military-target-only policy; not a first-strike policy, etc.) that the Chairman, Senator Frank Church of Idaho, was drawn to ask precisely what PD59 *was*. The answers were extended but limp. It was, said Brown, all about being flexible so that, in Soviet eyes, the American will to resist would be credible (see boxes).[47]

> Senator Glenn: 'I get lost in what is credible and not credible. This whole thing gets so incredible when you consider wiping out whole nations, it is difficult to establish credibility.'
>   Secretary Brown: 'That is why we sound a little crazy when we talk about it.'[48]

Like Schlesinger in 1974, Brown was asked if he believed that there could be limited nuclear warfare; unlike Schlesinger, he claimed to believe not. Like Schlesinger he was asked if counterforce was not a first-strike doctrine; like Schlesinger he replied by distinguishing between 'first strike' (strategic) and 'first use' (tactical), and while agreeing that first use was policy, stated that first strike was not. And significantly, like Schlesinger, under cross-questioning, he admitted that PD59 was a consequence of, not a cause of, the new weapons procurement, in this case Trident, MX, Pershing II, and cruise: both Secretaries of Defense therefore agreed that counterforce was reacting to rather than directing events, although Brown's position was more confused, even if more realistic, since belief in the possibility of limitation is logically essential to the counterforce posture.

In 1966, having deployed the first generation of American ICBMs and SLBMs and having urged forward research into MIRV technology, Robert McNamara, the most important Secretary of Defense of recent years, initiated the strategic exercise (Strat-X) study to define the successor generation of delivery systems. Top priority was given to a new SLBM – the under-sea long-range missile system (ULMS) of sufficient range that its submarines could patrol worldwide from American ports only, so that forward Polaris bases at Holy Loch (Scotland), Rota (Spain), and Guam could be phased out. No doubt it was recalled that on occasion there had been some local trouble over one of these. This missile has become the Trident. But encouragement was also there for a new ICBM to keep the Air Force happy. This has become the MX.[49]

The Pershing II and cruise missiles, third and fourth members of the new 'counterforce' generation, were not an outcome of Strat-X. The Pershing II is not a 'battlefield' weapon. It is a straightforward, offensive, strategic ballistic missile. When finally proven, it promises to be almost instantaneously ready, requiring no count-down procedure, fast, and phenomenally accurate thanks to on-board radar terminal guidance of the warhead. The Pershing II was first presented in 1970–71 as an 'evolutionary' modification of the Pershing IA, to have approximately the same 100–400 mile range, consistent with the 1956 ruling restricting army weapons to short-range systems. But when the Pershing II went into full-scale development in February 1979, the FY 1980 Arms Control Impact Statement for long-range theatre nuclear missile programmes revealed that not only the re-entry vehicle, but the whole rocket would be new. The range was censored. However, at the time of the December 1979 'modernization' decision, NATO officials stated that the range would be 1,800 kilometres. European aerospace industry sources also heard of a proposed 4,000 km version. From West Germany the 1,800 km version could strike Leningrad or Kiev; a 4,000 km version, beyond Moscow.[50]

The cruise missile, unlike Pershing II, has never had a clearly defined military role, since as a counterforce weapon it is flawed. It is said to possess the accuracy and ability to penetrate enemy territory (although at present both are highly questionable), but no one has ever suggested that it possesses the speed to 'kill' 'time-urgent' targets. This is not surprising, given its history which, since much controversy surrounds this weapon, needs to be told.[51]

It was originally conceived in 1967 as an electronic decoy to help saturate the Soviet air defences and jam the radars of the Tallinn Line in its 'downgraded' image and so to protect the B–52 bombers of the Strategic Air Command. Faced with Russian high-altitude surface-to-air missiles (SAMs), which successfully shot down Francis Gary Powers in a high-flying U–2 spy-plane in 1960, SAC was forced to abandon the original high-flying mission for the B–52s and to reassign them to a low-level penetration of Russian airspace. At the same time, the Air Force began studies for a new manned penetrating bomber (which has become the B–1), to replace the B–52; so the new, low-level B–52 mission was seen as a temporary expedient. It is important to realize that the USAF (and, in its much smaller way, the RAF) – the two Air Forces which pioneered and were the major exponents of mass area bombing during the Second World War – identify the long-range manned nuclear-capable bomber mission as the essence of being a 'proper' air force, which explains the tenacity with which the USAF has fought for the B–1 and why the RAF has insisted that the new Tornado multi-role combat aircraft should also have this capability, whether or not it has military rationale.[52] The B–52 had, before the U–2 incident, a decoy missile (the Quail) and an air-to-surface 'stand-off' 'defence-suppression' missile (i.e. an anti-anti-aircraft-missile-battery missile) (the Hound Dog). But neither worked best at low altitude. So a new, specialist low-level decoy and a new defence-suppression missile were seen as urgent requirements. From the outset, they were intended for the new B–52 replacement (the B–1).

The Hound Dog was swiftly and successfully turned into SRAM (short-range attack missile). The Air Force welcomed it especially because it was *short range* (100 miles): the constant fear – to be realized later – was that *too* successful a stand-off missile could threaten the whole rationale of the manned bomber itself. But the new decoy *had* to have greater range to be any use at all, and therefore was potentially even more of a threat to the B–1. It was called SCUD (subsonic cruise unarmed decoy) and was the air-launched cruise missile in all but warhead. A warhead was soon proposed, to ensure that the Russians would have to attack it even if they recognized it as a decoy, and SCUD became SCAD. ('Unarmed' becomes 'armed'.) Throughout, the Air Force insisted firmly that this was a decoy and not a stand-off – let alone a long-range – cruise missile.[53]

But other people had other ideas. In June 1972, Secretary of Defense Melvin Laird began to look around for a 'SALT-free' weapons system – that is a new strategic weapon which could be built without violating the terms, even when it was intended to violate the spirit, of the newly signed Strategic Arms Limitation Treaty (SALT I). He heard that the *Navy* was toying with the idea of a 'strategic cruise missile'. This was not far advanced for two reasons: Navy experience with earlier cruise missiles in the 1950s (Regulus and Snark) had been unhappy – they didn't work well – one Snark missile disappeared into the wrong hemisphere, and got lost up the Amazon. And secondly, only one of the three 'branches' of the Navy wanted such a weapon.

On 22 October 1967 the Egyptians had sunk the Israeli destroyer *Elath* with Soviet surface-to-surface Styx anti-ship missiles and this had much impressed the *surface* fleet admirals. But the influential *carrier* admirals were hostile to a long-range anti-ship missile because it threatened the ship-attacking role of their sea-based aircraft; and the *submariners* were quite content with a mixture of fleet ballistic missile and attack submarines, and could see no role for cruise missiles in submarines.

Laird's intention seems to have been to promote the Navy cruise pro-gramme in order to force the Air Force into eventual cooperation to produce a strategic nuclear long-range land-attack cruise missile that neither service wanted. And indeed it was Congress that forced the pro-gramme down the throats of the military. The Navy's interest in an anti-ship missile was, to its displeasure, subordinated by Congress to a sea-launched cruise missile (the Tomahawk) which the submariners, who would have to deploy it, actively did not want. The worst dreams of the SAC generals in the Air Force were realized and the Air Force decoy was cancelled in 1973. SCAD became the air-launched cruise missile (ALCM) that was to be used during President Carter's presidency as the argument to cancel the B–1 bomber. The Air Force began to campaign for a B–1 successor, the so-called Stealth bomber, as the best tactic for protecting its manned bomber role. However, Mr Reagan's arrival in Washington created a new climate, and in 1981, the Senate voted by a large margin for construction of 100 B–1s. As this is written it seems possible that no choices will be made and all weapons systems constructed.

Meanwhile, congressional and executive pressure had from the mid-1970s forced development of a ground-launched version of the cruise missile (GLCM). Its main virtues were always political: it was to be a SALT II 'bargaining chip' and a highly visible symbol of American commitment to Chancellor Schmidt's vision of Europe. It is worth stress-ing that the very visibility which stirred the peoples of Europe was seen initially as desirable by NATO decision-makers. The Army successfully resisted being lumbered with the GLCM, and so in 1979 it was a bitter pill for the Air Force that it was compelled to embrace the overgrown decoy which seemed to have killed its cherished bomber; and it didn't even have a pilot!

Thus the cruise missile programme has reached its present stage by a mixture of political 'pull', prolonged inter- and intra-service skirmishing, and the momentum generated by manufacturers' 'push'. As a result, the missile has at various times been all things to all men: a low-level decoy, an anti-ship missile, a long-range air-, sea- or ground-launched strategic nuclear missile, a tactical weapon. So it is not surprising that it has continued to encounter severe technical problems, especially with its terrain-following navigation system (TERCOM). In 1973, the air force thought that SCAD might hit 'undefended urban-industrial targets' (i.e. large targets), but since decoys need to be seen and do not require accuracy

– the opposite of missiles – that did not seem to matter. Originally invented in the 1950s, the cruise missile TERCOM works by matching radar altitude readings to a special electronic map. It has been tested in well-mapped, undulating country in southern California. Recently, journalists and the US Government General Accounting Office have wondered seriously whether it will work at all in the featureless, tree-covered, snow-and-ice-enveloped environment of the Russian steppes.[54] One response, which informed sources suggest may be being followed, is to scrap TERCOM and install satellite guidance in cruise missiles, using the new NAVSTAR satellite system like the D–5 Trident SLBM.[55] 'Worst case' assumptions are in order; somehow or other, cruise will be made to work.

But now we come to the most extraordinary part of the cruise missile story. It and the Pershing II are being presented to the European public as an 'answer' to the Soviet SS–20 IRBM.[56] This is the oddest justification of all. We have seen that in so far as the Russians have figured in the story so far at all, which is little, it is as the providers of incidental stimuli. These were the shooting down of the U–2 in 1960, and the use by Egypt of Soviet Styx missiles to sink the *Elath* in 1967. Beyond this, it was the existence of their anti-aircraft defences against the very real and visible threat of the SAC fleet of B–52s in the late 1960s which propelled the SCAD programme. The Pershing II developed independently of any particular Russian stimulus, beyond appeal to the all-purpose bogeyman picture of the 'Russian threat'. So what role did the SS–20 play?

After development in the mid-1970s this missile was first deployed in 1977 to replace the ageing SS–4 and SS–5 IRBMs.[57] It is neither new nor revolutionary, being the top two stages of the SS–X–16 ICBM which was first flight-tested in March 1972 but not developed under the terms of the SALT treaty. As the Pentagon publication, *Soviet Military Power*, graphically reveals, the SS–20 is not particularly mobile, nor, as has been already mentioned, is it very accurate compared to Western systems, although it is considerably more capable than the SS–4s and SS–5s which it replaced. None of this makes it nice. Its three warheads, each with a yield ten times that of the Hiroshima bomb, can devastate the European cities against which they are aimed and they are in a real sense the 'Soviet threat' which we face. But why are they there at all?

There has been a constant superiority and, in the 1970s, increasing margin in total numbers of warheads capable of striking Eastern Europe possessed by NATO in comparison to Soviet systems aimed at Western Europe. In particular, in 1971–2 the USA, which has since 1961 assigned

a small number (five) of Polaris ballistic missile submarines to the command of S A C E U R (Supreme Allied Commander, Europe), replaced the
Polaris missiles with Poseidon C–3 missiles. These placed 400 MIRV
warheads under S A C E U R's control for use as Euro-strategic weapons.
These S L B Ms are counted as central strategic systems under the S A L T
II protocol, which the U S Senate has refused to ratify. On the grounds that
they are 'S A L T-counted', it is now argued that they are not to be included
in European 'theatre' counting. This is just pedantic and perverse. It has
led to the American insistence in the 1981–2 arms control talks that a
settlement of land-based systems must precede inclusion of sea-based and
aircraft systems. Yet in the F Y 1982 Arms Control Impact Statement, our
assertion – that all systems, regardless of basing mode, must be considered
if like is to balance like – is conceded. In that document, the list of current
long-range theatre nuclear forces includes the American/N A T O Poseidon
and the British/N A T O Polaris S L B Ms. Different ways of counting the
European 'balance' are set out in Appendix A2.[58] But this lunatic
mathematics of warhead balancing must not be taken within its own terms.
It commits both the errors pointed out at the beginning of this chapter. It
has nothing to do with deterrence strictly defined and can only result in
increasing the probability of nuclear war.

Counterforce strategy appears to have become more convoluted and less
logically coherent, culminating in PD59, as improvements in missile
accuracy and increase in numbers of weapons have made the 'posture'
seem increasingly attractive. And it is, of course, a posture only. Counterforce is entirely hypothetical, based on no good empirical evidence. The
General Accounting Office has concluded that the U S arsenal is technically quite unlikely to be able to execute a 'countervailing strategy': that
means that if it were used, the result would be most unlikely to be swift,
surgical, or humane – and certainly not controlled or limited.[59] For
instance, mercifully, so far no I C B M has ever flown the route it would fly
in war over the Pole. Given the earth's gravitational field no one knows for
sure what that would do to its accuracy. The attraction of counterforce is
that it appears to make military might politically usable again. But it, like
the theory of nuclear deterrence, is riddled with defects. Yet unlike the
position of minimal deterrence, counterforce actively encourages 'games
players' in the Pentagon and (in their October 1981 statements) President
Reagan and Secretary of Defense Weinberger, to treat nuclear war like any
other war – to share the Soviet failure to keep a 'firebreak', but in the
context of an adventurist and not a defensive military tradition. Together,
the technical and numerical superiority of Western nuclear forces, the

defects in the theory governing them, and the shared Eastern and Western delusion that nuclear war is amenable to conventional planning constitute our present mortal peril.

This chapter has dealt almost exclusively with the United States, for the reason given at the beginning: that we should attend to the leading edge of the process. This is not to imply that in the Soviet Union there is not also a story to be told. There is. Its characters are not McNamara and the Joint Chiefs of Staff, Minuteman and cruise; they are Ustinov, Gorshkov, and Ogarkov, SS–9 and SS–18. In place of the Iron and Steel Triangles which propel Western nuclear arms development and which are the subject of the next chapter, there is a much more tightly controlled Party and military grip upon decisions and procurement of weapons by those within the ruling hierarchy, whom Khrushchev called the 'metal eaters'. These forces are now knit deeply into the fabric of society in the East as well as in the West. Had this apparatus been the one that blazed the trail, it would have been our subject, although given the inveterate secrecy of Soviet officialdom, it would have been much more difficult to portray it with the detail and precision possible in the Western case.[60] But it was not the leading force, as the evidence in Appendices A1 and A2 clearly shows.

COUNTERFORCE IN BRIEF

Claims

1. It is to be treated like any other pre-nuclear war.

2. It is humane and 'surgical'.

3. It offers military and political flexibility.

4. It is 'credible'.

Defects in counterforce

1. Its weapons are indistinguishable from those required for a first strike. Therefore it increases that temptation and in equal proportion raises suspicion.

2. Its claim to be 'controlled' depends upon fanciful beliefs in the limitation of nuclear war, which the Soviets have consistently rejected.

3. It assumes superb performance by the weapons while all evidence suggests that such an assumption is hopelessly unrealistic.

4. The entire posture is built on weapons and theories that have never been empirically verified. Nor can there be any trial and error. Only error.

3 The Failure of Arms Control

Since the late 1950s, the dominant aspects of the nuclear arms race have been the quantitative expansion and qualitative improvement of the arsenals. However, since the early 1960s there has been a minor aspect which, paradoxically, has received consistently more exposure in the public media. Arms-control measures have been the only sort of agreements made between the superpowers since the failure to agree on disarmament proposals at Geneva in the summer of 1955. Arms control has for twenty years occupied the energies of many who desire eventual disarmament because it was believed that if limited agreements on tightly demarcated issues could be achieved, they would form a basis for future transition to disarmament. This was President Kennedy's wish when, in presenting the Partial Test Ban Treaty to the American public in 1963, he borrowed a Chinese proverb, and described it as the first step on a journey of a thousand miles. It also underlay a heated debate during his presidency about the name of the newly created Arms Control and Disarmament Agency (ACDA): should 'Disarmament' or 'Arms Control' come first? It was because of the hope that arms control would lead to disarmament that 'Arms Control' was given precedence. But has that hope and that order of precedence proved to be well founded?

The evidence of arms control agreements over the last twenty years does not suggest so. Their net effect has been, if anything, quite the contrary: they have failed to curb significantly the numerical growth of the superpower arsenals and the improvement in deadliness of nuclear weapons. They have failed to halt nuclear proliferation. But also, and of greater consequence, the assertion, expressed repeatedly in the preambles to arms control treaties, that the road of arms control would lead eventually to general and complete disarmament has helped to derail the attempts, principally of non-aligned countries like Sweden, to promote actual disarmament through international agencies like the UN: the Undén plan of October 1961 to stop nuclear tests, halt proliferation, and to create nuclear-free zones was shipwrecked by Western obduracy, as also was the similar 1957 plan of Polish Foreign Minister Rapacki, upon which the Undén plan drew. Likewise, a Swedish plan of April 1969 to prohibit underground nuclear tests was blocked by technical objections from the USA, UK, and, to a lesser extent, the USSR.[61] However, arguably the worst consequence of the twenty-year history of arms control has been to give ordinary people the impression that governments were taking action over nuclear arms, and thus to deflate the strong pressures which demanded disarmament in the European public at large. Instrumental in producing these effects and in setting that trend was the Partial Test Ban Treaty in 1963.

John F. Kennedy laid stress during his election campaign on the question of America's alleged military weakness compared to the alleged strength of the USSR. The existence of a 'missile gap' figured prominently. By the narrowest margin of votes in any presidential election this century (119,450), Kennedy defeated the Republican candidate Richard Nixon in November 1960. He was therefore very conscious of the need to consolidate his position. During 1961 he learned that the 'missile gap' did not exist, but none the less allowed the Minuteman and Polaris missile programmes, both already far advanced, to continue. It seemed that the tide flowed for rearmament.

From June to September, Soviet Deputy Foreign Minister Valerian Zorin and Kennedy's special disarmament adviser John J. McCloy met regularly to discuss procedural matters relating to possible future resumption of discussions on disarmament; but their deliberations were ultimately of little consequence, failing to agree on the perennial problem of verification and inspection, and being quite overshadowed by the Berlin crisis which dominated the summer months of 1961. Soviet threats to end Western access to the city prompted Kennedy to announce $3.25 billion of additional defence appropriations in July, including substantial additional procurement of Minuteman and Polaris missiles. On 13 August, East German forces sealed the boundaries of Berlin, leaving only thirteen official crossing points; during the night of 17–18 August the first sections of the Berlin Wall appeared. The West reacted by sending formal notes of protest on 26 August, by reinforcement of the Berlin garrison, and by wider troop mobilizations. About the only hopeful sign in the deteriorating relations between East and West was that both superpowers continued to observe an informal moratorium on the testing of nuclear weapons that had held since 1958.

In reply to the Western protests of 26 August about Berlin, the USSR announced that it intended to break the moratorium on nuclear tests and, between 1 September and 4 November, did so with a series of about fifty explosions, the largest of which, on 30 October, was the biggest explosion that man has ever made, estimated to have had a force of fifty-seven megatons. President Kennedy was unable any longer to resist demands from the Joint Chiefs of Staff and scientists like Dr Edward Teller to recommence testing by the USA. It began again with underground explosions in September 1961, and atmospheric tests in April 1962. Observing that nuclear testing was the 1962 fashion for showing that one was a Great Power, Britain dutifully began tests again with underground explosions at the Nevada range in March 1962.[62]

The UN General Assembly was in session when the Soviets broke the moratorium and, amid general condemnation and anxiety, it was resolved that the eighteen-nation Geneva talks to end nuclear tests should be resumed in March 1962 (France later declined to join in). The General Assembly also adopted a proposal from the Swedish Prime Minister, Östen Undén to create a 'non-nuclear' club of nations who would undertake not to manufacture or obtain nuclear weapons, or permit to be deployed on their territory those of any other power. This scheme thus combined the control of nuclear proliferation with the beginnings of concrete movement from regional nuclear disarmament to general nuclear disarmament. The Undén scheme was supported by the USSR, the Warsaw Pact nations, most non-aligned nations, four NATO members (Canada, Denmark, Norway, and Iceland), and was opposed by twelve nations, ten of whom were the other NATO countries.[63]

The worldwide revulsion at resumption of nuclear testing found public expression mainly in fears about the effects of fall-out (about which there was great divergence of opinions then and still some doubt now),[64] and it caused eight of the non-aligned delegations, led by Sweden, to propose within a month of reconvening at Geneva a new, simple, and verifiable scheme for a comprehensive test ban using existing observation stations, and thus cutting through earlier problems raised by the superpowers about the need for special new monitoring facilities. An American proposal, put forward at the autumn 1961 General Assembly, had foundered precisely because of the US demand for on-site verification of doubtful earth tremors. Kennedy welcomed the non-aligned proposals. As the summer wore on, both the USSR and the USA seemed, to a prominent Swedish delegate, to be serious about negotiating a comprehensive test ban; the verification of underground tests soon remained the only main matter of contention.[65] To circumvent this, the US proposed a 'Three Environment' ban, excluding underground tests, yet banning all tests in air, above the atmosphere, or in the seas. While failing to find favour then, the idea was to return in 1963.

In October 1962, both superpowers received a frightening reminder of the need to reach some sort of mutual understanding on nuclear weapons. On the morning of 16 October, Kennedy was informed that Soviet technicians were engaged in the installation of medium-range ballistic missiles

(SS–4s and SS–5s) in western Cuba on America's doorstep: missiles that would be able to strike the United States within minutes of launching. The President decided that they had to be removed and, in announcing the Cuban missile crisis to the American public on television on 22 October, warned that 'I have directed the armed forces to prepare for any eventualities.' A naval blockade of Cuba was imposed, 200,000 troops were assembled in Florida, squadrons of tactical fighters were moved within striking distance of the island; there is some evidence that US warships in the Caribbean began the very dangerous exercise of forcing Soviet submarines to the surface. But still aerial reconnaissance showed work continuing on the missile emplacements. By Saturday 27 October, the Attorney-General, Robert Kennedy, recorded that his brother was resigned to military confrontation within a few days. Then, suddenly, on Sunday 28th, the threat of war was lifted.[66]

On 17 April 1961 a force of Cuban exiles (who, it was subsequently revealed, had been encouraged, trained, and equipped by the CIA) had landed on Cuba at the Bay of Pigs in an attempt to overthrow the regime of Fidel Castro. The invasion had gone disastrously wrong and, although the American administration stoutly denied any complicity in the affair, American involvement was vigorously asserted in Khrushchev's condemnation of the bungled operation. During and after the October missile crisis, Khrushchev consistently asserted that the rockets were intended solely for the defence of Cuba from any future invasion (for which the Bay of Pigs was presumed to be proof of intent). Thus, when Kennedy agreed to give firm guarantees of American resolve never to invade Cuba in reply to a request for such guarantees from the USSR, Khrushchev promised in his message of Sunday 28th 'in return' to withdraw the Soviet weapons. Thus he was able in his speech to the Supreme Soviet on 12 December to represent his retreat from the prospect of a conflict which, if it had begun, threatened to have escalated to a general nuclear exchange, as an action made possible by an American concession.[67] In just the same way, American retreat from the same ghastly possibility was made possible by Khrushchev's act, which was represented as a climb-down in the face of American military might and political resolve.

Whereas before the missile crisis, neither superpower appeared to have sufficient political will to conclude any agreement, the shock of the confrontation seemed to generate it. Throughout the Geneva negotiations and before, the issue of on-site inspection of suspect seismic tremors had impeded progress towards a comprehensive test ban. The Soviet Union had refused to contemplate such visits until, on 19 December 1962, barely a week after he had defended his conduct over Cuba, Khrushchev announced that he would agree to two or three on-site inspections per year, and to the siting of three automatic recording stations in seismic zones of the USSR.[68] It was not enough. The USA continued to insist on a minimum of eight to ten inspections and the locations proposed for the unmanned sensors were said to be unacceptable. Neither side would move to close the final gap between them, and so the possibility of a comprehensive test ban, so nearly in the grasp of the world community, was permitted to slip slowly away.

President Kennedy resolved to try to obtain a partial agreement. On 10 June 1963, at the American University, he delivered the most important speech of his presidency. In it he spoke of peace: 'I speak of peace because of the new face of war. Total war makes no sense ... I speak of peace, therefore, as the necessary rational end of rational men.' He spoke of the need to recognize that peace had to be practical and attainable, based '... on a series of concrete actions and effective agreements'. He called for a re-examination of American attitudes towards the Soviet Union, for an ending of the hostile suspicions of the 'Cold War' mentality, for mutual tolerance, for a recognition both of the achievements of the Soviet people and of their terrible sufferings during the Second World War. He urged also that while American repugnance for Communism was profound, '... in the final analysis, our most basic common link is that we all inhabit this small planet. We all breathe the same air. We all cherish our children's future. And we are all mortal.' At the end of the speech he announced that high-level negotiations 'towards early agreement on a comprehensive test ban treaty' would begin shortly in Moscow, to break the deadlock of the multilateral Geneva negotiations. By virtue of its independent nuclear capability, Britain was also to be represented at these 'top table' talks, but, as in the other bilateral negotiations which followed, the British presence was of negligible importance. However, to play the self-important retainer to an indulgent American potentate satisfied the delusions of grandeur still entertained by sections of the British political community.

PRESIDENT KENNEDY'S SPEECH
ABOUT PEACE AND THE COLD WAR[69]
'What kind of peace do I mean? What kind of peace do we seek? Not a Pax Americana enforced in the world by American weapons of war. Not the peace of the grave or the security of the slave. I am talking about genuine peace, the kind of peace that makes life on earth worth living, the kind that enables men and nations to grow and to hope and

to build a better life for their children – not merely peace for Americans but peace for all men and women – not merely peace in our time but peace in all time.

'I speak of peace because of the new face of war. Total war makes no sense in an age where great powers can maintain large and relatively invulnerable nuclear forces and refuse to surrender without resort to those forces. It makes no sense in an age when a single nuclear weapon contains almost ten times the explosive force delivered by all the Allied air forces in the Second World War. It makes no sense in an age when the deadly poisons produced by a nuclear exchange would be carried by wind and water and soil and seed to the far corners of the globe and to generations yet unborn . . .

'I speak of peace, therefore, as the necessary rational end of rational men . . . Some say that it is useless to speak of peace or world law or world disarmament – and that it will be useless until the leaders of the Soviet Union adopt a more enlightened attitude. I hope they do. I believe we can help them do it. 'But I also believe that we must re-examine our own attitude – as individuals and as a Nation – for our attitude is as essential as theirs. And . . . every thoughtful citizen who despairs of war and wishes to bring peace, should begin by looking inward – by examining his own attitude toward the possibilities of peace, toward the Soviet Union, toward the course of the cold war and toward freedom and peace here at home.

'First: Let us examine our attitude toward peace itself. Too many of us think it is impossible. Too many think it is unreal. But that is a dangerous, defeatist belief. It leads to the conclusion that war is inevitable – that mankind is doomed – that we are gripped by forces we cannot control.

'We need not accept that view. Our problems are manmade – therefore they can be solved by man . . . No problem of human destiny is beyond human beings. Man's reason and spirit have often solved the seemingly unsolvable – and we believe they can do it again . . .

'. . . history teaches us that enmities between nations, as between individuals, do not last forever. However fixed our likes and dislikes may seem, the tide of time and events will often bring surprising changes in the relations between nations and neighbors.

'So let us persevere. Peace need not be impracticable, and war need not be inevitable. By defining our goal more clearly, by making it seem more manageable and less remote, we can help all peoples to see it, to draw hope from it, and to move irresistibly toward it.

'Second: Let us reexamine our attitude toward the Soviet Union. It is discouraging to think that their leaders may actually believe what their propagandists write. It is discouraging to read a recent authoritative Soviet text on *Military Strategy* and find, on page after page, wholly baseless and incredible claims ...

'... it is sad to read these Soviet statements – to realize the extent of the gulf between us. But it is also a warning – a warning to the American people not to fall into the same trap as the Soviets, not to see only a distorted and desperate view of the other side, not to see conflict as inevitable, accommodation as impossible, and communication as nothing more than an exchange of threats.

'No government or social system is so evil that its people must be considered as lacking in virtue. As Americans, we find communism profoundly repugnant as a negation of personal freedom and dignity. But we can still hail the Russian people for their many achievements – in science and space, in economic and industrial growth, in culture and in acts of courage.

'Among the many traits the peoples of our two countries have in common, none is stronger than our mutual abhorrence of war. Almost unique among the major world powers, we have never been at war with each other. And no nation in the history of battle ever suffered more than the Soviet Union suffered in the course of the Second World War. At least 20 million lost their lives. Countless millions of homes and farms were burned or sacked. A third of the nation's territory, including two thirds of its industrial base, was turned into a wasteland – a loss equivalent to the devastation of this country east of Chicago.

'... both the United States and its allies, and the Soviet Union and its allies, have a mutually deep interest in a just and genuine peace and in halting the arms race. Agreements to this end are in the interests of the Soviet Union as well as ours – and even the most hostile nations can be relied upon to accept and keep those treaty obligations, and only those treaty delegations, which are in their own interest.

'So let us not be blind to our differences – but let us also direct attention to our common interests and the means by which those differences can be resolved. And if we cannot end now our differences, at least we can help make the world safe for diversity. For, in the final analysis, our most basic common link is that we all inhabit this small planet. We all breathe the same air. We all cherish our children's future. And we are all mortal.'

The American University speech (see box) was received with unprecedented enthusiasm in the USSR. It was given extensive news coverage, and on 2 July Khrushchev praised it publicly and offered a limited test ban to be agreed with the British and American representatives. Kennedy sent America's most experienced negotiator, Averell Harriman; Macmillan sent Lord Hailsham. Within the space of ten days (15–25 July) the 'Three Environment' Test Ban was resurrected, agreed, and signed.

What could be wrong with this? The indications were already present: what had happened was that the two superpowers had decided between themselves to set out ground rules for their nuclear competition and to exclude the rest of the world community from negotiations, thus also removing the possibility of effective disarmament measures being inserted by the politically influential (i.e. non-aligned and non-nuclear) middle-ranking states, like Sweden. The preamble of the Moscow accord indeed spoke fulsomely of the desirability of proceeding to a comprehensive test ban and, as Alva Myrdal, one of the Swedish delegation, wrote afterwards, for the other negotiators at Geneva (whose position had now been undermined) at first these words were taken at face value, and the abrupt switch from comprehensive to partial agreement was seen as a temporary concession to political expediency.[70] But there was no timetable suggested for proceeding to the next step, and there has been no next step. Instead there was in 1974 the Threshold Test Ban Treaty which limited the yield of underground tests to 150 kt and in 1976 a Treaty on Underground Explosions for Peaceful Purposes. These were measures which enabled the superpowers to achieve the 'benefits' of limited testing without commitment to a comprehensive ban. Both treaties were submitted to the US Senate in July 1977 and to date neither has been ratified.[71] Furthermore, written into the Partial Test Ban Treaty (at British suggestion) was an escape clause (Clause 4), permitting abrogation of even its limited provisions if the 'supreme interest' of a country were felt to be jeopardized.

That there was no intention of proceeding to a comprehensive ban became clear when, in order to win Senate ratification, Kennedy was obliged to permit the Joint Chiefs of Staff a lavish shopping-list of weapons, a virtually free hand to conduct underground tests, and retention intact of the atmospheric testing site at Johnson Atoll, should need for it arise.[72] If the politics of the test ban treaty marked a return, for reasons of political expediency, to traditional pragmatism in diplomacy, it also marked the abandonment of disarmament as the goal of that diplomacy. Sixty per cent of all the nuclear explosions that have occurred since 1945 have taken place underground since the Partial Test Ban was concluded (783 of 1,271).[73]

The Partial Test Ban Treaty may be welcomed as a public health measure, reducing the rate of increase of atmospheric fall-out, but it has had no significant effect upon the development of new nuclear weapons. What it did stem successfully for many years (by giving the erroneous impression that action by governments to control the arms race was in hand) were the widespread movements of popular opposition to nuclear weapons, and for this it is greatly to be regretted. The way in which the Partial Test Ban was negotiated also provided the model for the way in which the superpowers have conducted their bilateral arms-control negotiations since then: it was the first and therefore the most important act institutionalizing the nuclear arms race.

Since 1963, disarmament measures have been continuously discussed in the forum of the United Nations. Where agreements have been signed, they have been of two sorts: first, there have been *agreements not to do things which it was unlikely that anybody would wish to do*. Examples of this are the Sea-bed Treaty, in force since 1972, which agreed not to place nuclear weapons on the sea-bed, and the Antarctic Treaty, in force since 1961. But, as the Chinese pointed out in objecting to the Sea-bed Treaty at the time of its negotiation, the problem in the sea is not on the sea bed, it is mobile – the missile-carrying submarine.[74] And – before 1982 – no power had shown serious interest in militarizing penguins. Then there have been *agreements not to do what cannot be done* at the time that the agreement is made. The major example of this is the Outer Space Treaty, in force since 1967, which pledges that space shall not be militarized. However, both the USA and the USSR now appear to be proceeding rapidly with pro-grammes to do this: the USA with the Space Shuttle and space-based laser weapons, and the USSR principally with anti-satellite weapons. This Treaty is simply breached secretly, or under a thin 'civilian' disguise. A similar fate seems to be in store for the spirit of the Treaty of Tlateloko, in force since 1967, which prohibits nuclear weapons from Latin America. Both Argentina and Brazil are thought to be well advanced in weapons research.

The Non-Proliferation Treaty is an example of a measure which, like the Partial Test Ban, is self-defeating in its own drafting. In the first place, the Treaty institutionalized the situation existing in 1967 by defining different conditions to apply to 'nuclear weapons states' and 'non-nuclear weapons states'. Article I then embodied the compromise between the USA and USSR which made the Treaty possible (and lack of which had caused the

NATO countries to object to the Undén scheme): nuclear-weapons states should agree not to 'transfer' nuclear weapons to any non-nuclear state. 'Transfer' was the pivotal word, interpreted strictly to refer to ownership. Under this legalistic reading US- or Soviet-owned weapons could be stationed in non-weapons countries, since they were still 'owned', even if physically transferred. Then the clause bound nuclear states not to assist non-nuclear states to obtain nuclear weapons (but of course cooperation between existing nuclear states on nuclear research, such as British use of the Nevada Test Range, could continue). Clause II was the reciprocal agreement by non-nuclear states to comply with these terms. But the intention of Clauses I and II was vitiated by Clause IV which guaranteed the right to pursue peaceful nuclear applications and encouraged full exchange of nuclear information and equipment for 'peaceful' purposes (the reasons why this clause undermined the treaty are explored in Chapters 8 and 9). Signatory non-nuclear states undertook to submit installations to inspection by the International Atomic Energy Commission, but for technical reasons confidence in such measures could never be high and in volatile political regions was clearly even lower. The treaty came into force in 1970, and, like the Partial Test Ban, was produced by the governments of the USA and the USSR (not forgetting the British government), committed them to no major sacrifice, and was then offered to the rest of the world community for signature.[75] States that did not like even these provisions, like Argentina, Brazil, China, France, India, Israel, Pakistan, South Africa, or – interestingly – Saudi Arabia, simply have not signed. Most of these states are already nuclear states or are thought to be engaged actively in nuclear weapons programmes.

Defenders of the value of these peripheral treaties, mostly negotiated during the decade 1963–73, today tend to argue that they have at least had a demonstration value, keeping the issue of nuclear weapons in the public eye. But this must be set against the cost of concealing from full public awareness the fact that not one of these treaties has succeeded in stopping any part of the mainstream of the superpower arms race or of the proliferation of weapons.

However, the peripheral treaties are much less well known to the public than the two series of bilateral arms control negotiations between the superpowers which since 1969 have carried most hopes of curbing the arms race. The Strategic Arms Limitations Talks (SALT) have been represented to the public as extraordinarily complex and therefore lengthy discussions of highly technical matters. This is true. Negotiations for SALT I began in Helsinki during the winter of 1969 and ended with the

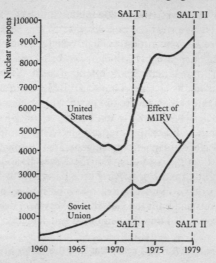

Figure 7. The strategic nuclear weapons race, 1960–79 (*source*: CDI)

signing of various agreements in late 1972; negotiations for SALT II began seriously after President Ford met Secretary Brezhnev at Vladivostok in November 1974 and ended with the signature of a treaty by President Carter and Secretary Brezhnev in Vienna in June 1979, a treaty hitherto not ratified by the US Senate. The SALT treaties have also been represented as being very important. In terms of stopping – or even slowing to any significant degree – the growth of the world's nuclear arsenal, this is not true, as can be seen from the rising curves in the graph of warhead numbers. Neither SALT I nor SALT II committed either superpower to surrender any weapon that it really wished to keep. In each case, the political price demanded by the respective military establishments and their political lobbies had the net effect of stimulating a further new twist in the upwards spiral of the arms race. These costs must be set against the international political benefit deemed to derive from the simple fact that the superpowers were at least talking to each other.

The SALT I negotiations produced a treaty which restricted each side to two sites for the deployment of anti-ballistic missile (ABM) systems; it was ratified and put into force on 3 October 1972. SALT I also produced an interim agreement limiting numbers of launchers and delivery systems to those currently deployed, which was intended to lead to a comprehensive treaty on offensive weapons at SALT II.[77]

The ABM Treaty is regarded as highly significant by many arms-control experts. In one sense it was like the Sea-bed Treaty in that it was an agreement not to do what neither side intended to do. At the time that the treaty was concluded, the USA had built an ABM system and had realized that while it was unlikely to succeed in destroying attacking missiles, the detonation of nuclear warheads by its 'defensive' missiles would wreak havoc with modern, solid-state American electronic equipment through the action of the electromagnetic pulse generated by nuclear explosions (see box on EMP on pp. 140–41). For these reasons the sole American ABM site, built at Grand Forks Air Force base, North Dakota, for $7 billion, was shut down hurriedly just one month after becoming operational. The Soviets had built the Galosh ABM system near Moscow, but seemed to have concluded that the command and detection problems were insuperable.

In another sense, the ABM Treaty was like the Outer Space Treaty, for it included a clause (V (1))[78] prohibiting future ballistic missile defence systems that might operate in different environments. Indeed, it is the fact that the Treaty prohibits the 'mission' of ballistic missile defence that commends it to some analysts as an example for future arms-control measures.[79] However, both the USA and USSR have invested heavily in exotic ABM technology: there are high-energy lasers and technology for what the Pentagon coyly calls 'national security space missions', and the USA has tested and is continuing to develop a totally new ballistic missile defence system (BMD is the acronym replacing ABM) using infra-red space telescopes and non-nuclear interceptors. It seems increasingly likely that both treaties are currently being broken.[80] But future developments apart, in the late 1960s the challenge perceived in an 'ABM gap' had already drawn forth a potent response: the development and placing of multiple independently targeted warheads on a single rocket (MIRV).

The account of the SALT I negotiations by the chief US negotiator, Gerard Smith, is unequivocal in its judgement: 'In retrospect, the weak effort to ban MIRVs was a key aspect of SALT. It was considered by some knowledgeable people as the leading lost opportunity of the negotiation.'[81] Smith favoured a real ban on MIRV, believing – quite correctly, as the 1970s have shown – that to 'protect' America's MIRV monopoly in 1972 was in fact to opt for a less – not more – secure future in a world of many-headed missiles. But this view did not prevail. When President Nixon eventually permitted an American proposal to be made, it was tied to other conditions (to do with dismantling Soviet radars, on-site inspections, etc.) so that it was highly unpalatable to the Soviets, and Gerard Smith was not surprised when it was rejected.

Certainly there is evidence that any effective arms control would have been resisted by Nixon.[82] In July 1969 113 members of Congress sponsored a call for a moratorium on MIRV development. To this the Joint Chiefs of Staff were adamantly and vociferously opposed, as was Nixon, who made his view on a MIRV moratorium clear to Gerard Smith in characteristically rough language: 'Any, repeat any, individual who gives any, repeat any, encouragement to this kind of speculation should be first reprimanded and then discharged.'[83]

There are persistent rumours that the Soviets offered a MIRV ban informally in October 1969, just before the official Helsinki sessions began, and that the American administration rebuffed them. Although Paul Warnke, the SALT II negotiator, has no privileged knowledge of that period, he is of the opinion that in the circumstances of a decisive US lead in MIRV technology, it would have been surprising had the Soviets *not* made such an approach; and, on the other side, there is ample reason to suspect that any offer would have been rejected. But the rumour cannot be conclusively confirmed. Instead, different participants in the negotiations independently used the same phrase several times: to try to obtain an ABM ban and a MIRV ban would 'overload the circuits';[84] Congress would not consent to both. As a result, an agreement not to develop what then seemed to be a bankrupt technology (and thus to save both sides money) and a freeze at existing levels on the numbers of launchers was obtained at the expense of letting MIRV – the qualitative improvement that revolutionized the arms race – roar ahead, with the Americans leading and the Soviets following on behind.

Despite the fact that the US superiority in nuclear warheads was untouched, the fact that SALT I permitted the Soviets to have numerically more launchers than the USA was viewed as a 'sell-out' by conservative opponents of the SALT process, led by Senator Henry Jackson and by Paul Nitze, then chairman of the privately funded right-wing lobbying group, the Committee on the Present Danger, and now the US negotiator at the 1982 Geneva arms-control talks. Thus when in 1977 President Carter presented the liberal lawyer Paul Warnke for congressional approval as the US negotiator for SALT II (which was hoped to produce binding limits and perhaps reductions in numbers of launchers and even of warheads) the fact that the Senate confirmed his appointment on 9 March by a vote of 58–40 was an early warning of Senate resistance to any treaty that Warnke might negotiate – for the margin was less than the two-thirds majority required for Senate ratification of the treaty.[85]

The day after his confirmation by the Senate Warnke spoke of the prospects for SALT II. Looking at the way in which the exclusion of MIRV from SALT I had produced not security, but instead, with Soviet MIRVs now appearing, terrible uncertainty, he warned that unless the lesson was learned, and the next major new technology – the cruise missile – was controlled, the results would be yet further destabilization.[86] It was just such an attitude – warning about the dangers of American weapons still under development rather than the 'present danger' of existing Soviet weapons – that enraged conservative critics of SALT, and their hostility to SALT II, combined with effective and well-financed lobbying, succeeded in representing to the American public the terms finally agreed by Warnke's successor as grossly weighted in favour of the Soviets. (Warnke had returned to his private law practice before the end of the negotiations.)

In fact the SALT II accord merely regulated the superpower competition. It set limits on numbers of launchers and sub-limits on the numbers of MIRVed launchers, which would oblige each side to dismantle a token number of operational systems (33 US, 254 USSR). For this, obsolete systems that were due to be retired could be chosen.[87] It imposed a limit below the maximum technically possible on the numbers of warheads permitted for existing MIRV launchers, and of cruise missiles per heavy bomber (fixed at the maximum load of a B–52). In addition, each side would be permitted one new ICBM system. Ceilings would be imposed on the 'throw-weight' of missiles (see Appendix A1 for why this is valueless) and on certain other offensive weapons not yet developed (the 'Outer Space' syndrome). So congenial are these terms to the respective military establishments that even without Senate ratification, they appear to be being observed anyway.

As with each of the previous arms-control agreements, there was a price to be paid, and given American leadership in the arms race, the American price mattered most: for the Partial Test Ban the Joint Chiefs of Staff demanded underground tests; for SALT I they demanded MIRV; for SALT II, they demanded the unfettered, and indeed accelerated, development of the new generation of counterforce missiles: MX, Trident, cruise, and Pershing II. They have got their price and the world has not got a treaty, adroitly scuttled by 'linkage' of ratification to the next convenient Soviet action of which the West disapproved, which happened to be the occupation of Afghanistan in December 1979.

However, the SALT process had obvious values to the governments of the USA and USSR, too useful to throw away with an unratified treaty, and which guaranteed the resumption of talks sooner or later; as it happened, the Geneva talks began sooner than might otherwise have been the case, in an attempt to quench the great flames of popular demand for disarmament that have engulfed Europe since 1979. These virtues are that the SALT process, and its successor, constantly and conspicuously underline the special status of the superpowers in the eyes of the rest of the world community; they keep open a useful channel of communication, legitimize new weapons systems, and, by pre-empting the nascent political pressures for disarmament, neatly bottle them and render them ineffective.

In terms of stopping the arms race, the demise of SALT II was immaterial. For opponents of the arms race, its only values were at best dubious: by setting ceilings, any ceilings, on aspects of the nuclear arsenal it gave each side enough information – and principally the Americans of the Soviets – not to need to resort to 'worst-case' guesses about each other (though in fact they still do). Secondly, the SALT process at least kept the issue of nuclear weapons on the international agenda.

Against this must be placed the fact that negotiations that were primarily about numbers of launchers misled the public about the nature of the nuclear weapon problem by focusing on meaningless numerical comparisons, and by giving the impression that action to limit weapons and to proceed eventually to nuclear disarmament was in hand. Thus the existence of SALT made it easier for nuclear-weapon-state governments to resist pressures to engage in real disarmament, whether proposed diplomatically by states like Sweden or democratically by protest among their own people.

An especially heavy price has been paid by the many active, intelligent, and persistent opponents of the arms race who have, over the last twenty years, committed themselves to the SALT process as the best hope for some movement, however slight, towards disarmament. The SALT process has failed entirely in that respect. Furthermore, in their attempt to slow down the pace of the competition, arms controllers have been compelled to accept the basic axioms of the arms race, and have therefore been unable to maintain a logically consistent case for nuclear disarmament. In particular they have had to depend on the shaky concept of 'stable deterrence': accepting that some nuclear weapons are stabilizing in order to argue that others are not. 'Deterrence' is examined further in Chapter 6. They have also been obliged to accept three other axioms, each equally insecure: the axiom that the confrontation between the USA and the

USSR is the prime feature of the world international order in the 1980s was attacked in Chapter 2, and will be again from a different direction in the final section of Chapter 5; the axiom that military power is essential to the pursuit of national interests is demonstrably challenged by the post-war successes of non-aligned countries like Finland, Yugoslavia, or Sweden, or of Japan and West Germany, who for many years were forbidden to engage in extensive military spending; the axiom that nuclear weapons are useful instruments of rational military policies has been continually questioned earlier in this chapter and is the first subject of the next.[88] In short, the experience of attempted arms control has been an extended illustration of the dangers of compromising the pragmatic and the moral case for nuclear disarmament.

5 The Steel Triangle

From the history of weapons development set out in the previous two chapters, it seems that the nature and volume of nuclear weapons are no longer determined by military 'needs'; nor is military strategy any longer under the control of political policies. Rather, like Frankenstein's monster, the weapons have acquired the power to dictate to their political masters. How has this come about?

The role of exaggerated or faulty intelligence in the relationships between soldiers and politicians described above is a necessary but not alone a sufficient answer. In this chapter we suggest the nature of other forces that seem to play a part in translating the thoughts of strategists and policy-makers into tangible weapons. We are presenting a hypothesis which we believe represents the most convincing explanation at present available, and we invite readers to test it against their own evidence and experience.

The accurate but inelegant phrase 'military–industrial complex' was coined by General Eisenhower, the Supreme Allied Commander at the end of the Second World War, who became President of the United States. In 1946, he spoke warmly of the successful cooperation which had helped so materially to win the war (see box).

'The armed forces could not have won the war alone. Scientists and business men contributed techniques and weapons which enabled us to outwit and overwhelm the enemy . . . In the interests of cultivating to the utmost the integration of civilian and military resources, and of securing the most effective unified direction of our research and development activities, this responsibility is being consolidated in a separate section on the highest War Department level.'[1]

But his experiences of the ensuing years, during many of which he was President, wrought a significant change in his outlook. His farewell speech (see box overleaf) was cast in a more sombre tone. The things which he described are the subject of this chapter.

PRESIDENT EISENHOWER'S FAREWELL SPEECH ABOUT THE
MILITARY–INDUSTRIAL COMPLEX

'Until the latest of our world conflicts, the United States had no
armaments industry. American makers of ploughshares could, with
time and as required, make swords as well. But now we can no longer
risk emergency improvisation of national defence; we have been
compelled to create a permanent armaments industry of vast proportions ...

'This conjunction of an immense military establishment and a large
arms industry is new in the American experience. The total influence
– economic, political, even spiritual – is felt in every city, every
statehouse, every office of the federal government. We recognize the
imperative need for this development. Yet we must not fail to com-
prehend its grave implications. Our toil, resources, and livelihood are
all involved; so is the very structure of our society.

'In the councils of government we must guard against the acquisition of unwarranted influence, whether sought or unsought, by the
military–industrial complex. The potential for the disastrous rise of
misplaced power exists and will persist.

'We must never let the weight of this combination endanger our
liberties or democratic processes.'[2]

We do not see the operation of the 'military–industrial complex' – or,
more accurately, the three-pointed 'military–academic–industrial complex' – which we represent by the image of the Steel Triangle, as involving
conspiracy, although there is clear evidence of collusion between people in
its different component parts, which undoubtedly helps to propel the
whole process. Nor do we wholly subscribe to the fatalistic belief that the
operation of the Steel Triangle is the result of vast, impersonal forces
which are variously out of control, although, again, we have seen convincing evidence of the existence of gigantic momentum in technological
development and industrial production at different times and places. We
have been drawn to conclude that it is precisely the combination of the
different dynamics which are found at each point of the Steel Triangle
which imparts momentum to the Triangle and, in turn to the nuclear arms
race. This view is represented visually in the figure opposite.

The chapter proceeds by examining in turn and briefly each point of the
Steel Triangle. We use this image deliberately to represent its relationship

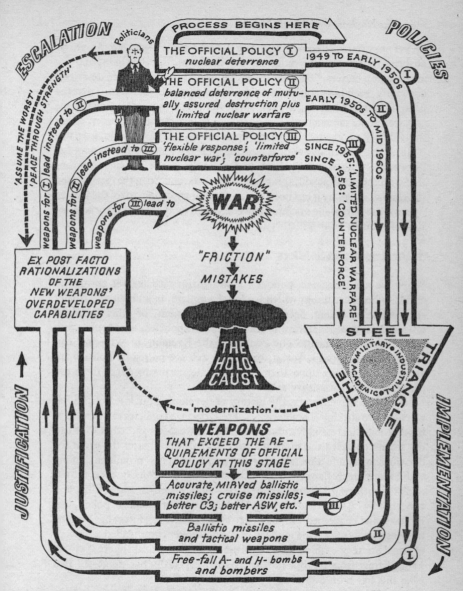

Figure 8. The frictionless spiralling of nuclear arms development in the West since 1949

to, yet important difference from, the 'Iron Triangle', which in American analyses represents the vertices of the Congress, the Pentagon, and the arms manufacturers.[3] Then the chapter illustrates what has been described abstractly, seen in operation in a significant case study. It argues that the powerful forces favouring a 'permanent war economy' can be seen to have acquired some momentum. But equally it shows that these forces, either individually or together, do not represent an unstoppable juggernaut. Neither the American political tradition nor the American economy has been entirely taken over by them. This is an optimistic message: it means that with the political will, things could be different. So in the final section the chapter asks why it has been that in the late 1970s and 1980s the United States – the hub of the system – has embarked on the most costly acquisition of arms in human history.

1 Strategies and Soldiers

When we ask 'what is a policy?', a straightforward answer springs to mind: policies are things which leaders formulate, talk about and finally encapsulate in orders, decrees, Acts of Parliament, or other forms of official document; therefore to find out about policies, we should go to those official documents. The Pentagon, the Kremlin, or Whitehall can tell us what American, Soviet, or British defence policy is. Policies are *declared* and, acting upon them, appropriate means to effect them are procured. But is it as easy as that?

In the last two chapters, the history of developing nuclear policies has revealed two striking characteristics. First, declared policies can be seen to have become increasingly subordinate to the weapons and what they can do, taking on more and more the role of justification after the event for decisions to manufacture taken for quite other reasons – prominent among which were deeply flawed intelligence estimates. As a consequence, the old and straightforward distinction between 'policy' (which was civilian and concerned with ends) and 'strategy' (which was subordinate to policy, was military, and concerned with means to effect policies by force) has become hopelessly confused. One modern military thinker commended a concept of 'total strategy', which took cognizance of the political sphere, yet was kept distinct from it;[4] but the last chapter especially has suggested that even this has been overtaken by events.

A second characteristic of the history of nuclear policies was the fertility of imagination demonstrated in discovering threats, in proposing specifications for weapons to counter those threats, and in generating strategies to contain the weapons. This owed a great deal to the competitive vigour of inter-service rivalry.

At the beginning of Chapter 4, it was noted that the power which came to be held by the US military establishment after 1945 was both exceptional in America's history and vast. The Air Force's rivalry with the Army/Navy axis in the late 1950s was extremely fruitful in terms of the phoney intelligence, the weapons systems, and the excessively complicated strategies which it stimulated. In the 1960s, once ways had been found to marry up flexible response in limited warfare (Army) with controlled counterforce (originally Air Force, but increasingly Navy also), inter-service rivalry took a different form: all now pursued the goal of making nuclear war thinkable. Navy and Air Force vied with each other to develop and deploy their own strategic counterforce weapons.

Official policy was committed to maintaining the 'Strategic Triad'. But since any one weapons programme was becoming ever more costly, the Air Force and Navy began to fear that they might lose their 'leg' of the triad because the country could not afford all; and the Army continued to hanker after a strategic role. Therefore each set out to make its strategic nuclear force appear to be indispensable. Once it had deployed the first – revolutionary – Polaris (A–1) missiles in November 1960, the Navy pressed ahead with improved variants: the slightly longer-range A–2 in June 1962 and the even longer-range (2,500 nautical miles) multiple warhead A–3 in September 1964, an 85 per cent new missile, as soon as deployment of the predecessor was complete. The Poseidon C–3 counterforce SLBM (1971 onwards) was followed by the 4,000 nautical miles range Trident I C–4, a missile which pioneered further technological developments with stellar-inertial guidance and miniaturized electronics; and soon the Trident 2 D–5 with the Mark 500 manoeuvrable advanced re-entry vehicle (MARV) programmes will follow on inexorably. Similarly the Air Force missiles Minuteman I (from 1961), II (from 1964), III (from 1969), the Mark 12A MIRVed warhead and NS–20 guidance system (1979 onwards), improved command, control and communication (C^3), rapid re-targeting through the Command Data Buffer computer, and the missile experimental (MX) seem to have the same unstoppable momentum.[5] Nor has the Army been left out. In the late 1960s, it had a share in the Sentinel/Safeguard American ABM programme which was President Nixon's equivalent to Kennedy's response to the 'missile gap' of a decade before, although Safeguard ended in technical failure.[6] In addition the Army had a huge increase in its inventory of 'tactical' nuclear weapons and now, in Pershing II, a strategic ballistic missile, although during the 1960s its main efforts related to the war in Vietnam.

So the basic intoxication with hardware was further assisted by the invigorating air of friendly rivalry. There was little restraint upon the resulting proposals for action for two reasons. The first, by now familiar, was that use of 'worst case' assumptions about the enemy's intentions provided a rationale for basing policy on assessment of capabilities alone; and we have seen in the history of the bomber, missile, and ABM 'gaps' the quality of such assessment. Secondly, since there was no hard evidence from experience against which to measure and assess the burgeoning plans for controlled nuclear war, there was no constraint from that source upon the speculations of the strategists. Why there was no constraint upon the translation of those military desires into real bombs, planes, and rockets we consider in the other sections of this chapter. But even if counterforce policies could not be tested against the realities of nuclear war, there were centuries of pre-nuclear conflicts; and since the principal virtue of counterforce is supposed to be the restoration of the 'normal' rules of warfare to nuclear conflict, one might have expected someone to see how the strategy scored in comparison with others. What would happen if they did?

To find out, let us first take the extreme situation: deterrence has failed, armies are mobilized, war – any sort of war – has begun. What generals *say* they will do in a war plan (an official document and an essential part of any defence policy) turns out to be not necessarily the same as what their armed

---

FRICTION IN WAR – C. VON CLAUSEWITZ[7]

'If one has never personally experienced war, one cannot understand in what the difficulties constantly mentioned really consist . . . Everything looks simple; the knowledge required does not look remarkable, the strategic options are so obvious that by comparison the simplest problem of higher mathematics has an impressive scientific dignity. Once war has actually been seen the difficulties become clear; but it is still extremely hard to describe the unseen, all-pervading element that brings about this change of perspective.

'Everything in war is very simple, but the simplest thing is difficult. The difficulties accumulate and end by producing a kind of friction that is inconceivable unless one has experienced war . . . Countless minor incidents – the kind you can never really foresee – combine to lower the general level of performance, so that one always falls far short of the intended goal. Iron will-power can overcome this friction;

it pulverizes every obstacle, but of course it wears down the machine as well . . .

'Friction is the only concept that more or less corresponds to the factors that distinguish real war from war on paper. The military machine – the army and everything related to it – is basically very simple and therefore seems easy to manage . . . In fact, it is different, and every fault and exaggeration of the theory is instantly exposed in war . . .

'This tremendous friction, which cannot, as in mechanics, be reduced to a few points, is everywhere in contact with chance, and brings about effects that cannot be measured, just because they are largely due to chance . . . Action in war is like movement in a resistant element. Just as the simplest and most natural of movements, walking, cannot easily be performed in water, so in war it is difficult for normal efforts to achieve even moderate results . . . The good general must know friction in order to overcome it whenever possible, and in order not to expect a standard of achievement in his operations which this very friction makes impossible. Incidentally, it is a force that theory can never quite define . . . only the experienced officer will make the right decisions in major and minor matters – at every pulsebeat of war. Practice and experience dictate the answer: "this is possible, that is not".'

forces do in action in attempting to follow that plan. Something odd seems to happen when the clear, conscious policy is channelled through the soldiers and their equipment into the real world. What that odd thing is has never been better described than by the great strategic theorist Clausewitz more than a century and a half ago (see box).

Although simple, 'friction' as Clausewitz called it, is pervasive whenever the strategy of war has to become the reality of war. Its message is blunt: assume that nothing will work as you intend and plan for that eventuality. It is the natural and true home of the 'worst case' assumptions. Its truth was illustrated at the beginning of Chapter 2 in the ghastly fiasco of strategy and the First World War.

On War must be one of the texts most frequently prescribed to be read by officers at staff colleges throughout the world. Yet the soldiers and strategists who made counterforce strategies, and who press them today, appear to have ignored or forgotten this section of Clausewitz's book. Therefore if 'controlled counterforce' and 'flexible response', as explained for example in Secretary of Defense Harold Brown's Naval War College speech of August 1980, were submitted in staff college as a student's essay, a competent and experienced instructor would give it a very low mark. It is a bad strategy, as a strategy, because it violates the basic requirements of good strategy through its many and over-hopeful assumptions.

Indeed one instructor, one of the most distinguished and experienced of his generation, did submit his report on his subordinates' efforts. He began by repeating the axiom of Clausewitz's 'friction' effect:

> Next month I enter my eightieth year, I am one of the few survivors of the First World War who rose to high command in the Second and I know how impossible it is to pursue military operations in accordance with fixed plans and agreements. In warfare the unexpected is the rule and no one can anticipate what an opponent's reaction will be to the unexpected.

Admiral of the Fleet Earl Mountbatten went on to mention the horror of war as he had seen it, and then added:

> But that was all conventional warfare and, horrible as it was, we all felt we had a 'fighting' chance of survival. In the event of a nuclear war there will be no chances, there will be no survivors – all will be obliterated.

> I am not asserting this without having deeply thought about the matter. When I was Chief of the British Defence Staff I made my views known. I have heard the arguments against this view, but I have never found them convincing. So I repeat in all sincerity as a military man I can see no use for any nuclear weapons which would not end in escalation, with consequences that no one can conceive ... As a military man who has given half a century of active service I say in all sincerity that the nuclear arms race has no military purpose. Wars cannot be fought with nuclear weapons. Their existence only adds to our perils because of the illusions which they have generated.[8]

Nor is there only this plain argument about people, there is also a plain and richly ironic argument about machines which supports the contention that counterforce is a poor and therefore very perilous strategy.

During 1980, the American military and scientific establishment began to be aware of the full extent to which the electronic systems upon which the military rely are vulnerable to, and probably cannot be fully protected from, one of the forms in which energy is released from nuclear explosion: the electromagnetic pulse (see box).

ELECTROMAGNETIC PULSE[9]

The electromagnetic pulse (EMP) from a nuclear explosion was first observed by Western scientists in 1962 in the Pacific, when the Americans detonated a 1 Mt bomb 250 miles above Johnson Island. Street lighting in Hawaii, 800 miles away, failed as a high-energy electromagnetic field caused huge current surges in the power cables.

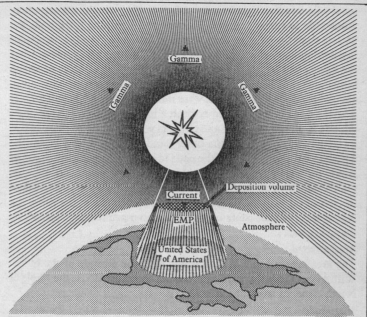

Figure 9. Electromagnetic pulse

EMP mechanism

A nuclear explosion results in a large, sudden burst of gamma-radiation, which propagates outwards carrying away between 0.1 and 1 per cent of the total energy. These gamma rays interact with the atoms of the atmosphere by a process known as Compton scattering, within a region many miles across known as the 'deposition volume'. Energy is transferred to the electrons orbiting the air atoms, by collision, and an instantaneous electrical current is created, resulting in a large electromagnetic field. The whole process happens extremely quickly, the pulse building up in a hundred-millionth (10^{-8}) of a second. For an explosion high in the atmosphere the earth's magnetic field magnifies the effect by coordinating the motions of the scattered electrons.

Effects of EMP

In that region of the earth's surface exposed to the EMP large currents will be induced in any electrical conductor, and particularly in long conductors such as power cables, telephone lines, or transmitter aerials. Modern transistor and microelectric circuits are extremely vulnerable to current surges. Normal anti-lightning safeguards are useless since the onset of the pulse is so fast, and despite attempts to 'harden' military electronics against EMP no one really knows what the effects will be, since the miniaturization of electronics occurred after the Partial Test Ban Treaty of 1963, banning atmospheric tests, and the previous valve circuits were millions of times less vulnerable. The US Air Force has recently built a huge wooden structure upon which a B–52 can be placed and charged with a simulated pulse to test its response to EMP. On the other hand, there is evidence that the Russians have been aware of the need to protect avionics, etc., against EMP for much longer. The MIG 25 Foxbat, examined after its pilot's defection to Japan in 1969, contained tiny vacuum valves instead of transistors. While this puzzled scientists at the time, the replacement of transistors by valves is under active consideration by the USA today.

Area affected

The area exposed to EMP increases with the altitude of the burst. With a large (10 Mt) explosion 200 miles above the USA, the whole of North America would be affected.

Magnitude

Maximum electric field = 50,000 volts/meter. In the explosion described above, the energy collected by a radio aerial 1 cm × 1 m would be sufficient, were it in the form of mechanical energy, to lift it several feet into the air.

The irony is that EMP destroys precisely the advanced transistorized, microchip electronics which make possible the small yet powerful computers of missile guidance systems and the highly automatic and capable C³I (command, control, communication, and intelligence) technology which makes counterforce appear such a tempting strategy.

Predictably, the response of the Steel Triangle to the 'EMP threat' has been to spend vast amounts of money to try and find a technical 'fix', to protect or to render safe from EMP the electrical brains of the military machine. But much of this equipment cannot be both EMP-proof and perform to the standards required by a counterforce strategy. Strenuous efforts are being made to replace transmission of data via electrical impulses in cables by light signals through fibre-optic conduits. But such substitution cannot offer universal applications. The essence of C³I for counterforce is speed; and filters and screens for sensors and computers

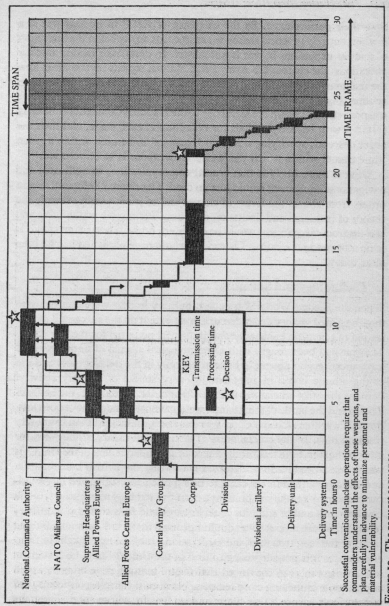

Figure 10. The request sequence

slow their performance. So the existence of EMP in nuclear war is a further, entirely practical reason to assume that any belief in the limitation of nuclear explosions in war is unrealistic. In describing tactical nuclear operations, the current US Army Field Manual repeats several times how the maintenance of swift and reliable communication is essential for such actions. Figure 10 shows how, in theory, the request to employ nuclear weapons should rise up the hierarchy to the National Command Authority (NCA), with leisurely periods for reflection at each stage, and then the order descend, specifying a nuclear 'package' to be used within a given 'time frame' within which the 'pulse' of weapons is to be released.[10]

What is more likely is that crucial communication, surveillance, and navigational equipment would just go dead. Deprived of information and orders from above, the forces of chance and of panic would overrule the theory of precision and limitation of action. Permissive action links and self-destruct mechanisms would be operated, broken, or circumvented. It is no more and no less than Clausewitz would have predicted had he been alive today.

2 Technology and Scientists

When the Second World War ended, military leaders were clearly aware that the Allied victory depended to a great extent on the successful mobilization of scientific knowledge and industrial potential for the war effort. The war had been fought with a technological arsenal of unprecedented sophistication and power, to be seen not only in the development and use of the atomic bomb in 1945 but in every sphere of military activity. Perhaps the most crucial was in the field of radar. Without it, the battle of Britain and the battle of the Atlantic would almost certainly have been lost. But this wartime research effort was less institutionalized than is military research now. In the crucial areas of aircraft and radar, Britain was, for most of the war, both technically ahead of and independent of the USA. (It was in mass-produced standardized goods that the British home market and Britain's armed forces came to be supplied and supported by American industry.) Yet the war brought a period of strongly rising wages, of full employment, and of stimulus to technology and science-based industries (even if the pure research was not indigenous) to the US economy, pulling it out of the long trough of the Depression years. So in the light of these experiences it is not surprising to find in the United States both soldiers and civilians in 1946 convinced that future military development would depend on maintaining close relations between the army, politicians, and industry and science. (This contrasts with Britain, where, for example, the radar team dissolved and returned to industry, the universities, the BBC, etc.) Eisenhower's memorandum as United States Chief of Staff, quoted at the beginning of this chapter, expressed both the debt which was felt for past services and the prospect of a continuing partnership.

The memorandum is an important document for understanding the shape and the dynamics of the Steel Triangle, because it illustrates the way in which the inception of what has come to be called the 'military–industrial complex' was recognized and instigated by the conscious actions of policy-makers. Furthermore, it clearly suggests that there was to be an institutionalization of the military and civilian scientists and industrialists in peacetime domestic America. Eisenhower – and many others – did not envisage a significant scaling down of American military effort.[11] We now know that defence spending has come to dominate the institutional structure of American life to a greater extent than ever before.

Since 1945, the growing sophistication of weaponry and research technology has given rise to a view of the arms race which attributes its course and pace to the 'pull' of technological advance rather than the 'push' of political initiative. This argument has various forms and proponents, but it probably commands most respect when advanced by men whose experiences as science advisers to government has given them an inside knowledge of the workings of government. We have made extensive use of such commentators already, because their experience and knowledge makes them authoritative observers of the arms race: they include Herbert York, first Director of the American thermonuclear research laboratory, the Lawrence Livermore, then first Director of Defense Research and Engineering, one of the most powerful jobs in the Pentagon; Jerome B. Wiesner, President Kennedy's science adviser; and Lord Zuckerman, science adviser to a succession of British governments in the 1960s.

'The scientists and technologists were themselves the ones who initiated ... new demands; who warned the public about new hazards. They were the ones who, at base, were determining the social, economic, and political future of the world. Without any badge of authority conferred on them either by democratic decision or autocratic *diktat*, without any coherent concern for political values or goals, scientists and engineers had become the begetters of new social demand and the architects of new economic and social situations, over which those who exercised political power then had to rule.'

(Lord Zuckerman)[12]

The argument which they advance has three stages. First, the peculiar sophistication of science in the modern world leads governments to employ science advisers, whose knowledge gives them particular power, as a tool of policy advice. Secondly, and in spite of this, science itself proceeds without any coherently defined set of political or social principles, so that government harnessing of science is at best partial. Thirdly, and as a consequence, policy becomes increasingly a matter of responding to technical change. In terms of the arms race, this argument suggests that strategic planning is a matter of an out-of-control science. As Zuckerman observes, all American science advisers were agreed that 'once the threshold of mutual deterrence has been crossed, there is no technical sense in the further elaboration or multiplication of nuclear-weapons systems', but the pressures generated by previous weapons development produced a continued spate of technological advance.

The views of men like Zuckerman and York are obviously important, and this argument has several convenient aspects. The first, and clearest, is that it fits our normal view of science as a disinterested and value-free pursuit of knowledge at the same time as identifying the relationship between the scientific and political spheres. Zuckerman traces the rise of the science adviser very much in these terms. There are other, more sinister attractions of the argument. It absolves politicians from blame. The arms race itself is allowed to become 'inevitable', a consequence of 'progress' to which we have to adapt: in short, it is an inescapable feature of the modern world. Political action and military planning are then merely an attempt to master new situations. In addition, those who oppose the arms race can be portrayed as Luddites who would like to switch off 'progress'. But the notion that 'progress cannot stop' is often simply a mask for the belief that 'we do not want it to stop'. The apparent continuity of the process of weapons research and development and then of procurement is adduced as proof of the argument that 'science can't be stopped', as if the process were a natural one rather than a politically organized and complex set of relationships within the Steel Triangle.[13]

Compelling and useful though it may seem, the argument for the propulsive role of technology is not the whole story. Science cannot be viewed as independent or untrammelled. In 1980 203 higher education institutions in America were Department of Defense contractors receiving contracts worth $652 million.[14] Effectively, the Eisenhower memorandum was transformed into practical control of many university research facilities. One documented example is the US Navy's domination of the applied physics laboratory at the University of Washington, where anti-submarine warfare research has prevented the laboratory's facilities being used for other purposes. In 1969 Secretary of the Air Force Robert C. Seamans, a former MIT professor, made the point that 'we cannot provide the necessary weapons for defense without the aid of university research laboratories'.[15] There was a period at the height of opposition to the Vietnam war a decade ago when there was open opposition to the involvement of universities in military research, including the destruction by a bomb of the Army Mathematics Research Center in the University of Wisconsin, Madison, in 1970. But as the economic climate for universities has grown more chill, the volume of Pentagon-funded research has increased significantly and has received a warm welcome from university

Table 6. Top Twenty Universities in the USA in Military Research for Fiscal Years 1979 and 1980[16]

University or university-affiliated institution	Fiscal year 1979	Fiscal year 1980	Percentage change
1 Johns Hopkins University	$155,801,000	$163,327,000	+4
2 Massachusetts Institute of Technology	123,724,000	154,564,000	+25
3 University of California (system)	24,159,000	29,679,000	+22
4 Illinois Institute of Technology	23,442,000	26,319,000	+12
5 Stanford University	10,694,000	18,068,000	+69
6 University of Texas	15,072,000	15,772,000	+4
7 University of Rochester	12,848,000	15,480,000	+20
8 Georgia Technology Research Institute	8,360,000	14,758,000	+76
9 University of Dayton	13,564,000	13,859,000	+2
10 Pennsylvania State University	14,562,000	12,226,000	−16
11 University of Southern California	11,872,000	10,260,000	−16
12 University of Washington	8,717,000	10,069,000	+16
13 University of Alaska	9,338,000	8,119,000	−13
14 Carnegie Mellon University	4,536,000	7,335,000	+62
15 University of Illinois	3,727,000	6,797,000	+82
16 University of New Mexico	5,428,000	6,472,000	+1
17 California Institute of Technology	3,309,000	5,428,000	+64
18 Harvard University	1,421,000	4,902,000	+245
19 University of Pennsylvania	3,132,000	4,900,000	+56
20 Columbia University	4,052,000	4,848,000	+20

administration. In the period 1978–81, military research on American campuses has increased 70 per cent in dollar volume and has become the most reliable and fastest growing source of external finance for many distinguished institutions.[17]

In short, then, the technical progress of the last thirty-five years was at first *directed* along certain lines by the immediate post-war defence planning, and there has been an ever more tangled and tight knitting together of politics and technical effort ever since. This is not the same as the converse of the science advisers' case. It is to suggest that politics *does* have a role; one of agreeing to general trends in strategic policies, often, but not always, in response to situations shaped by autonomous technological initiatives. As we saw, in the early 1950s ICBMs became technically feasible at the same time that 'countervalue' or MAD (Mutually Assured Destruction) deterrence theorizing appeared. But in contrast, in 1957 the Gaither Committee report stressed the need for ABMs before they became technically feasible (in fact they never became available, because they don't work). More recently, as we also saw, MIRV planning was a response to a perceived (if greatly exaggerated) Soviet ABM capability. It was not the choice of politicians imprisoned in a world of easily available gadgetry. But again, the converse can also be seen. The formal decisions to *deploy* the new generation of American missiles – cruise, MX, and Trident – are fairly recent and reflect the decisions to *develop* them made in the later 1960s. It is confusing, but from the history of weapons procurement it appears that while politics does not dictate every step of technological and scientific research it does, in the first instance, prescribe the goals to which science should work.

Yet even this is not the whole story. After receiving initial encouragement from politicians, the subsequent step has always been of vital significance. At every stage of the arms race since 1946 scientists have *over-achieved*. They have consistently delivered more than requested of them. The case study of MIRV in Section 4 illustrates this point as well as many others, and its importance cannot be stressed too strongly. Growing out of an immediate perceived threat – the Soviet ABMs – to American missiles, MIRV developed *pari passu* with the doctrine of 'counterforce'; and the realization of multiple *independently* targetable warheads made possible the further refinement of counterforce, most recently in PD59. Another example is that of the cruise missile which, originating as a decoy device, has changed its character several times in the process of development as a result of both changing political needs and technical possibilities. In essence then, the relationship between the soldiers and politicians promotes an in-built tendency for the arms race to escalate. Political guidelines and requirements, based on existing scientific potential, initiate a process of technical research and development. We have already seen that this elementary stage frequently rises out of inter-service rivalry, so that 'policy' is less firm than might be thought. It is at this point, however, that scientific initiative takes over, for technology produces more than is required. Policy then adapts to, and even overtakes, this over-achievement, so setting off the process once more, one twist further up the spiral. (See figure, p. 135.)

If this relationship explained all, then spiralling within the Western arms procurement might be prevented by a stronger political will or by fixing ceilings upon technical achievement. However, there is a third point in the Steel Triangle of the military, the scientists, and industry, and it is to the role of industry that we now turn. But before doing so it must be said that the distinction between the research and production sectors is by no means clear cut. All the prime defence contractors maintain their own large R and D sections. Lockheed has large research and development projects for, amongst others, the cruise missile carriers, the Trident I and II missiles, the NASA space telescope and the Space Shuttle retractable wing, while McDonnell Douglas have similar projects for work on cruise missile guidance, the advanced manoeuvrable re-entry vehicle (MARV) and a more general project for the Defense Department on military space systems.[18] However, the distinction justifies itself in that the forces which radiate from the presence of a manufacturing industry into the fabric of the society in which it is situated are different from those generated by technology and science; and such industries are driven in a different way.

3 Industry and Industrialists

Military planning and scientific development create the framework of the arms race, but its realization depends ultimately upon the ability of the economy to meet demands made on it. Economically, however, the choice of certain products and methods of production excludes other possible courses of action. In this section we examine the extent to which defence contracting distorts the functioning of the economy, and argue that this distortion has now created a positive feedback in which the defence industry is not simply a supplier of arms in a competitive market but demands the extension and continuation of contracts. Furthermore, the peculiar nature of the final product dictates a closed structure for the industry which tends to restrict alternative economic choices.

The demands of strategic planning for new weapons systems place defence contractors in a strong bargaining position. The vast cost and lengthy lead times for new weapons mean that once a contract is granted, the government cannot afford to allow the contract to fail. There are, in consequence, exceptionally attractive clauses in many military contracts. Special clauses are included which make it impossible for firms to lose money; the Department of Defense frequently provides working capital for projects so that larger firms do not have to borrow on the open market. These are so-called GOCO (government-owned, contractor-operated) plants. The Douglas plant at Tulsa, Oklahoma, was 99.9 per cent government financed.[19] In spite of these terms, delivery dates are rarely achieved (the Polaris programme was exceptional in beating its deadlines), but financial commitment and 'national security' leave the government no effective recourse. Thus, for example, the Air Force anticipated the first test flight of the cruise decoy in September 1974, and in 1982 what is basically the same weapon still does not work properly.[20] The converse of this process is that some firms come to depend almost entirely on Department of Defense contracts. Eighty-eight per cent of total Lockheed business in aerospace (as compared to all areas of activity, as given in the table below) comes from military contracts, and for Newport News Shipbuilding, which constructs warships for the Navy, the figure is over 90 per cent.[21] In both America and Great Britain, the aerospace industry is effectively a war producer.[22]

In the long run, two trends may be discerned. On the one hand,

Table 7. Contractor Dependency on the Department of Defense, 1975–9[23] (five-year average for top companies); constant (1980) prices

	Percentage	$ millions
Fairchild Industries	87	559
Grumman	85	1,322
Hughes Aircraft*	76	1,819
General Dynamics	67	3,518
McDonnell Douglas	63	3,247
Northrop	63	1,227
Lockheed	52	2,037
Raytheon	34	1,745
Boeing	31	2,385
United Technologies	31	3,109

*Data for two years only disclosed.

important defence contractors come to depend on the continuation of the arms race for their very existence and, at the same time, competition for defence contracts is limited to those firms already in the select club of defence contractors.

In 1972, Lockheed was awarded the prime contract to develop the first generation Trident missile without any competitive tenders. In 1975, the Air Force requested competitive tenders on the precision guided re-entry vehicles project, but there were only two competitors, McDonnell Douglas and General Electric, both of whom had previously tested earlier flight-manoeuvring concepts. They alone had the expertise to be able to tender. In addition, General Electric were sub-contractors on the Lockheed Trident contract.[24] In fact, it is the general experience that despite American law, which requires defence procurement to be sited in 'low-cost plants', once the research grant is awarded, the corporations carrying out research will be given the contract to produce. In all, 88.5 per cent of DoD contracts are granted without competitive bidding.[25]

The oligopolistic stability of the defence industry has been frequently criticized in Congress, but entry to and exit from the industry is difficult.[26] Entry of new firms tends to occur when technical innovation shifts the focus of the industry. Missiles contractors proliferated in the 1950s, but by the 1960s the prohibitive development costs of new systems – Poseidon cost $10 billion – shut off further entry. By the later 1960s the 'big league' of contractors was immovable.

This dependence by firms on the arms race creates a tendency to accelerate the arms race. Lockheed's contract on the Polaris A–3 missile programme illustrates this last point well. In 1964, the programme was coming to an end, and Stanley Buriss, then president of Lockheed's missile system division, made it clear that the B–3 development was necessary to bring new business to Lockheed.[27] B–3 was a wider diameter version of A–3, but with a single warhead, and was in fact never produced, being swiftly superseded by the C–3 model, which is also called Poseidon.

In 1970, Rockwell International began a campaign for the contract for the development and production of the new manned bomber, the B–1, which the Air Force had wanted for several years. At the time of the contract for development, the chairman suggested that without the contract, Rockwell would collapse. Then in the early 1970s, with cost estimates on the aircraft rising, Rockwell became anxious about the contract for production, and, as the decision date on production approached, their efforts became frantic. Between 1975 and 1977 Rockwell spent an estimated $1.3m on financing grassroots support for the B–1 and entertained over ninety Defense Department officials. In spite of all this, in June 1977 President Carter cancelled the B–1. But by this time Rockwell were on a surer footing. Their efforts on the B–1, in addition to the spending of an estimated $40m, earned them the prime contract on the main engine of the Space Shuttle, and in 1980 they were the largest single corporate contractor on the MX missile.[28] Then in December 1981 the jackpot was increased, when Congress voted for construction of 100 B–1 bombers at a cost of $30–40 billion.

Table 8. Research and Development Funding in the USA, 1973–8[29]

	DoD and NASA contracts R & D ($m)	Independent R & D investment ($m)	Percentage independent R & D later reimbursed by DoD
Boeing	3,692.6	1,183.8	17.5
General Dynamics	2,507.3	159.8	43.9
Grumman	704.4	237.7	78.1
Lockheed	3,723.5	299.6	50.1
McDonnell Douglas	3,714.5	812.8	15.2
Northrop	569.5	173.1	65.0
Rockwell	7,115.2	486.3	31.7
United Technologies	1,224.7	2,030.6	14.5

On a much smaller scale, the same tendencies have been seen in the British arms industry among companies producing the increasingly baroque delivery systems desired by the British armed forces. The government purchases over 70 per cent of output, and the resulting dependence has been formalized in the nationalization of British Aerospace, British Shipbuilders, Rolls Royce Ltd, and of course the Royal Dockyards and Royal Ordnance Factories. This sector has experienced remarkable stability. The names of companies may have changed, but the physical plants remain the same as they were twenty-five years ago.[30] Under the British system, the promotion of job-saving projects can be achieved much more decorously than in the USA, under the veil of secrecy, without commercial pressures. The recently revealed 'Chevaline' project to build a British MIRV is a good example of expensive job-creation using public money without public decision or public accountability.

The comfortable self-perpetuation of the defence industry has wide ramifications for the rest of the economy. Warning about the dangers of the military–industrial complex at the end of his presidency, Eisenhower's emphasis was very different from his memorandum as Chief of Staff in 1946. There was now an ominous ring when he noted that its influence was 'felt in every city, every state house, every office of federal government', whereas his earlier statement had been more like an optimistic prophecy. As the Second World War drew to a close, the chairman of General Electric, Charles E. Wilson, declared that what was needed was a 'permanent war economy', so that military preparedness might be 'a continuing programme, and not the creature of an emergency'. All Congress would have to do would be to vote the funds; together the military and industry would run the show.[31] Nor were these mere words; Wilson matched them with action and between 1953 and 1957 he was Eisenhower's Secretary of Defense.

The effects of the military–industrial complex on the rest of the American economy, if not dominant, have been pervasive. Bruce Russett's study of the opportunity cost of defence spending suggests that each dollar increase in defence expenditure reduced personal consumption by 42 cents and fixed investment by 29 cents.[32] The effects spread as widely as Eisenhower implied.

In a study of Iowa, the state ranking thirty-fourth in terms of Department of Defense contracting, it was suggested that 8.8 per cent of the gross state product, amounting to $732 million, derived from such contracts, and this in a state normally described as being overwhelmingly agricultural. It led Alvin Sunseri to argue not for the term 'military–industrial complex' but, as a way of expressing the true extent of Iowa's dependence, for a 'military–industrial technological–labour academic–managerial–political complex', MITLAMP for short: a 'Steel Heptagon'.[33] Table 9 gives simple contract figures for thirteen of the most dependent states.

All of this suggests a lack of political alternatives, that industrial 'pull' replaces a technological 'pull' as a driving force of the arms race. But there are points of contact which suggest, once more, that the spiralling of the arms race is to be explained in the *relationship* between politics, research, and industry rather than in any one of them. In 1969, 2,062 former high-ranking military officers were employed by 100 companies, who between them accounted for 66 per cent of Department of Defense work (Lockheed employed 210, Boeing 169, and McDonnell Douglas 110), and between 1970 and 1979 over 1,500 former Department of Defense military employees moved into industry, including 316 to Boeing, 284 to Northrop, and 240 to Lockheed.[34]

Table 9. Geographical Pervasiveness of Prime Defence Contracts in the USA, four periods 1941–68[35]
(figures are a percentage of the national total)

		Second World War 1941–5	Korean war 1950–56	Missile age 1959–60	Vietnam war 1967–8	Reagan re-armament from 1981	Column 6[†]
1	New York	11.0	14.6	11.4	9.1	7.7	10.3
2	Michigan	10.9	6.4	3.3	2.5	2.4	13.8
3	California	8.7	16.4	24.0	17.7	19.4	40.0
4	Ohio	8.4	6.1	4.4	4.4	2.8	17.5
5	New Jersey	6.8	5.3	5.0	3.2	2.2	14.1
6	Pennsylvania	6.6	4.3	3.2	4.5	3.9	18.4
7	Illinois	6.1	4.8	2.1	2.6	1.5	9.7
8	Indiana	4.5	*	1.7	2.4	1.2	22.9
9	Connecticut	4.1	*	4.2	5.9	5.2	36.5
10	Massachusetts	3.4	2.7	5.3	4.1	5.1	25.9
11	Texas	3.1	3.8	5.8	10.3	8.0	33.6
12	Washington	2.3	*	4.0	1.5	3.4	34.8
13	Missouri	1.8	2.3	2.2	4.9	4.4	34.9
	Mean	5.98	6.67	5.89	5.62	5.16	24.03

*Not among top states for this period.
†Column 6 shows the defence expenditure as a percentage of federal tax expenditure in each state.

By 1973 the number of retired officers on the payrolls had risen to 3,233.[36] And there is evidence that the traffic is two-way: in 1973 275 former defence industry managers held ranks in the top three echelons (GS13 or higher) of government service in the Defense Department. This traffic in personnel may even contravene US law. The 'criminal selling law' states that 'nothing herein shall be construed to allow any retired officer to represent any person in the sale of anything to the government through the department in whose service he holds a retired status'. This law is being fought in the courts on behalf of retired officers whom the government has prosecuted under it.[37]

The most important invasion of the government service and Pentagon from industry and the academic world came in the 1960s with the appointment of Robert McNamara to the Department of Defense. He came from being president of the Ford Motor Company and as a condition insisted that he be able to choose his own staff.

Table 10. The Twenty Largest Companies by 1968 Value of Prime Military Contracts and the Number of Retired Colonels or Navy Captains and Above Employed by Them, February 1969[38]

1	General Dynamics Corp.	113
2	Lockheed Aircraft Corp.	210
3	General Electric Co.	89
4	United Aircraft Corp.	48
5	McDonnell Douglas Corp.	141
6	American Telephone & Telegraph	9
7	Boeing Corp.	169
8	Ling–Temco–Vought, Inc.	69
9	North American Rockwell Corp.	104
10	General Motors Corp.	17
11	Grumman Aircraft Engineering Corp.	31
12	AVCO Corp.	23
13	Textron, Inc.	28
14	Litton Industries, Inc.	49
15	Raytheon Co.	37
16	Sperry Rand Corp.	36
17	Martin Marietta Corp.	40
18	Kaiser Industries Corp.	11
19	Ford Motor Co.	43
20	Honeywell, Inc.	26

McNamara was a systems analyst and he soon gathered around him men who had his cast of mind. There was, for example, Charles Hitch from the RAND corporation, whose stringent insistence on cost-effectiveness and cost analysis was soon known as 'Hitch-craft', and a bevy of similar men who soon began to make military decisions on strategy and procurement. This was deeply resented by the traditional military elite. But the McNamara Pentagon was one of the clearest examples of the extent to which the Steel Triangle operates as an integrated whole.

4 A Case Study: MIRV

The development of MIRV (multiple independently targetable re-entry vehicles) provides a telling example of the ways in which the three points of the Steel Triangle combine to promote nuclear weapons in America. The installation of MIRV warheads on ICBMs constituted a crucial step up in the arms race, and its development provides a well-documented case study of complicated relationships between strategic planning, industry, and technological breakthrough.

By the late 1950s, culminating in the Report of the Re-entry Body Identification Group, deterrence theorists had come to argue in favour of the primacy of attack over defence,[39] so that 'credible deterrence' depended on being able to penetrate Soviet defences against ICBMs. The ballistic flight-path of ICBMs took them out of the earth's atmosphere before the delivery vehicle launched its warhead back towards its target on the earth's surface. Advances in ABM technology made this an increasingly uncertain method of attack. In 1959, the Gaither Committee was satisfied that the most effective way of penetrating ABM defence – should these ever be built – was by using decoy warheads, which would draw much of the Soviet fire.[40] Two sets of developments undermined their initial certainty about the need for decoys. American intelligence reports, which we have seen to have been exaggerated, began to suggest that construction had indeed begun, with photographs of ABM systems around Moscow and Leningrad, and then (after 1961) on a larger scale, along the 'Tallinn Line'. The best National Intelligence Estimates suggested, throughout the 1960s, that large-scale Soviet ABM capability might be achieved by 1966–7, and phoney as many projections were, the reports provided a powerful stimulus to American anxiety.[41] The Americans felt perhaps more threatened by Russian achievements in space. The launching of Sputnik in 1957 and Khrushchev's famous boast that Russian anti-missile rockets could 'hit a fly in outer space' elicited a political and a technical response from the Americans.[42] Kennedy replied:

He might hit a fly but whether he could hit a thousand flies, with decoys you see, every missile that comes might have four or five missiles in it, or would appear to be missiles, and the radar screen has to pick those out and hit them going thousands of miles an hour and select which one is the real missile and which are the decoys.[43]

The way in which American perceptions were translated into practical action is more complicated. By 1961 the Navy was seeking to develop a primitive response to the problem of ABM defences in the Polaris A–3 multiple re-entry vehicle (MRV). Deployed first in 1964, Polaris A–3 launched a missile with three warheads, which descended on their target in triangular formation. The intention was that the points of the triangle would be sufficiently far apart to make a single ABM attack on one warhead ineffective on the other two, but close enough together to knock out the target. This tactic would clearly be threatened either by massive

Soviet ABM deployments or by an American choice of smaller targets.[44] The Navy feared that its role would be replaced by that of the Air Force, which in the early 1960s took the decision to switch from the Minuteman I (LGM–30A) which had a single warhead and no penetration aids, to the Minuteman I (LGM–30B) with two warheads and, subsequently, to the Minuteman II with eight warheads and the penetration packages MK–I and MK–IA.[45] The Navy therefore began research into the possibility of adding independently targetable warheads to their ICBMs – in short, to achieve the flexibility which Air Force decisions looked like achieving. These developments actually came to constitute an over-achievement, because the actual MIRVed capacity that was produced enabled not only ABM penetration, but a targeting policy of far greater precision: it became possible to manoeuvre the re-entry vehicle not just backwards and forwards but sideways too, so that re-targeting was feasible.[46]

On the technical and industrial points of the Steel Triangle there were two further developments which spurred on MIRV. Developments in US space technology made possible the design of 'space bus' delivery warhead launch systems. The prime contractors for the space programme – RAND, Aerospace Corporation, Lockheed, and Lincoln Laboratories were also the prime contractors on the technology for MIRV.[47] All had available and unused expertise. Finally, there was clear pressure from Lockheed by 1963 for a defence programme to replace the Polaris A–3, which by then was coming to the end of its development cycle.[48]

Throughout this process of inter-service rivalry and research and development there were shifts in the attitude of the Department of Defense and politicians which reflected and encouraged the development of MIRV. The origin of explicit 'counterforce' theory dates from McNamara's speech at Ann Arbor in 1962.[49] At this time America did not have effective counterforce capability, although improved missile guidance pointed the way to it, and it is likely that McNamara chose to express ideas which were circulating in the Defense Department. The decision to develop MIRV was finally taken as a result of two political stimuli. First, it was attractive to the cost-obsessed systems theorists on McNamara's staff. As John Foster, York's successor as Pentagon Director of Defense Research and Engineering, argued,

We could increase the Polaris force by a factor of five or ten . . . But we can get the same equivalent military capability against the Soviet Union by taking the existing boats and changing . . . to the Poseidon warheads.[50]

By 1963, it was clear that the United States would get most 'bang for its buck'[51] through MIRV, which expanded fire-power by proliferating the number of warheads but not increasing the number of missiles. This was also an attractive way to subvert arms control.[52] Secondly, in the 1964 presidential election, Barry Goldwater repeatedly accused Johnson of neglecting national defence and in particular that during his presidency he had not deployed a single major new weapons system. Johnson's reply was to accelerate the Polaris A–3 programme and, in early 1965, to announce the development of Poseidon C–3. In 1967, at the height of another Soviet ABM scare, McNamara announced publicly that Minuteman III and Poseidon missiles would have a MIRV capacity.

The decision to *deploy* MIRV was still not made. From 1965 American intelligence suggested a Soviet MIRV programme, and in 1969 its imminent operational deployment was predicted. It was based upon over-optimistic assessment of Russian estimates of lead times and in spite of America's own tortuous experience. In fact, the first ICBM with a MIRVed warhead, the SS–9 'triplet', was tested in 1969. But it was too crude a device to meet the requirements of counterforce, and was in any case not deployed in number because of technical deficiency. The first more or less efficient Russian MIRVs (the SS–18) were not deployed until the late 1970s.[53] Yet pressure built up on the Nixon administration of 1968 to 1972 to deploy MIRVs, and in 1970 Nixon and Kissinger authorized their deployment. In this way, after twelve years of planning and preparation, a new missile system emerged from the Steel Triangle.

By 1970, the spiral had started to twist upwards once more. Research had begun on the Strat-X study of 1966, which proposed Trident and MX, the systems to be deployed in the 1980s. This arsenal will supersede currently deployed MIRVs. In 1968 Lockheed began work on the man-oeuvrable advanced re-entry vehicle – MARV – the Mark 500 Evader, a multiple warhead launcher which has 'terminal guidance' permitting extraordinary accuracy. It is intended for the Trident 2 SLBM. When he realized that MARV capacity would give a sudden and massive increase in aggressive nuclear capability to the US, the engineering group leader of the advanced design team for the Mark 500, Robert Aldridge, resigned his position as a senior engineer at Lockheed in protest, and has since provided us with an account of the early developments of counterforce technology in his book, *The Counterforce Syndrome*.[54]

5 The Build-up in Military Spending

So far we have examined the different driving forces to be found at each point of the Steel Triangle, which together give it such strong momentum. But it is important to realize that the recent renewal of commitment by both superpowers to 'keep up' with, or surpass, the strategic arsenal of the other is not just the consequence of those pressures, powerful as they are.

In Chapter 2 we described how, since the Russian Revolution, West and East have been locked in mutual suspicion, which today colours the perception and explanation of the adversary's arsenal by the leaders of America and the Soviet Union alike. There is no reason to doubt that Mr Reagan believes in the conspiratorial and expansionist character of Soviet Communism or that Mr Brezhnev believes in a cynical Western plot to detach the satellite states of Eastern Europe, as opportunity presents, and thus to breach the Soviet '*cordon sanitaire*'. However outrageous or misconceived they may appear to be, it is unwise to neglect beliefs in a study of the arms race, because they matter in the conduct of international affairs.

Critics have sometimes suggested that military spending on the scale proposed and undertaken by the Reagan administration has a more sinister intention than merely to provide forces for self-defence: that the spending itself has the conscious aim of defeating the USSR by bankrupting it. The logic of this – hitherto inferred – argument is that the Soviet economy is half the size of America's, that if America can force the USSR into a military competition which it cannot win, and has not the resources to win, the distorting strains imposed by playing this global poker game will so disrupt the Soviet economy that ferocious internal social unrest will occur. The USSR will then lose political control of the East European satellite countries; finally, the Soviet government will lose control of its own peoples. In this way, the argument concludes, 'capitalism' will have defeated 'communism' without a shot being fired. These intentions have now been explicitly endorsed by a new five-year defence plan entitled 'Fiscal 1984–1988 Defense Guidance' prepared by senior Pentagon officials, knowledge of which became public in May 1982.

The document instructs the American armed forces to be prepared to defeat the USSR at every level from guerrilla insurgency in third countries to a general nuclear war, which the Pentagon believes can be controlled, can be limited, can be won, and therefore may be protracted. Accordingly, it emphasizes the need for research into and procurement of nuclear resistant communications equipment. But it believes that war should not wait on the soldiers. Now, in 'peacetime', the USA and its allies should wage economic and technical war on the USSR as part of a determined crusade to destroy it. First, Western trade policies should be designed to deny the USSR access to technology and to impose maximum pressure on the Soviet economy; second, American arms procurement should favour weapons 'that are difficult for the Soviets to counter, impose dispro- portionate costs, open up new areas of major military competition, and render the accumulated Soviet equipment stocks obsolescent'. A prime region for this is space, where the document proposes the 'prototype development of space-based weapons systems'. Lastly, the West should redouble its efforts to foment unrest in Eastern Europe and to that end the USA should expand its 'special operations' forces 'to project United States power where the use of conventional force would be premature [*sic*], inappropriate, or infeasible'.[55]

These views are quite consistent with the publicly expressed desire of President Reagan to wage a holy war against an enemy which he sees as the embodiment of Evil. However, fortunately, in American politics there is frequently a wide gap between radical rhetoric, such as the strident hostil- ity to the USSR in this report, and eventual action. This document represents the thinking of Secretary of Defense Weinberger, his assistant Frank Carlucci, of the Joint Chiefs of Staff, and other senior military and civilian planners; but it has to pass through the Congress, and is only one factor among many that combine to determine what is actually done. While it is important to attend carefully to what such senior Pentagon figures say, in the past Europeans have often been misled by believing too literally the extravagant language which is a feature of the internal struggle for power within the American political system. Therefore, as well as noting statements such as this, we must equally consider other factors in the situation, especially economic matters, which are of particular importance in current debate about the costs and benefits of military preparation. To this aspect of the question we now turn.

Those pressing for high military expenditure in both the West and the East have had to compete in the political arena with others urging that resources be used in other ways. In the United States, between the early 1950s and 1980, military expenditure has tended to fall as a proportion of US federal government spending and as a proportion of US national income – although the US has nevertheless devoted a much higher pro- portion of its (much larger) national income to military expenditure than any of the other advanced Western industrial nations.[56] In view of the pressing need everywhere to devote resources to socially useful purposes, needs which in all societies are expressed in one way or another through political processes, it is perhaps not surprising that the Steel Triangle has failed to get its own way all the time. It is also worth noting that US military expenditure has been very volatile – the volume of expenditure was absolutely higher in the early to mid-1950s and during the Vietnam war – and this volatility introduced an element of instability for both the domestic US economy and the world economy as a whole.

Table 11. American Military Expenditure, 1950–80

	US military expenditure excluding veterans' benefits US $b (at constant [1972] prices)	As a percentage	
		of federal outlays	of GDP
1950	29.4	29.1	4.7
1955	75.8	58.1	10.5
average 1962–4	77.0	44.8	8.7
average 1965–70	87.9	41.9	8.4
average 1971–9	70.1	27.8	5.8

These data are consistent over time; they are adjusted for changes in presentation of budget information, introduced in 1969. American 'billions' (1,000 million) are used.

Source: US Department of Commerce, *Statistical Abstract of the U.S.*, 1980.

In November 1981, Secretary of Defense Weinberger testified before the Senate Foreign Relations Committee on these data and argued that 'Since the mid-1960s the Soviets have been engaged in their own private arms race while the United States spending on strategic forces actually has declined.'[57] Some, most notably the 1981 Reith Lecturer, Professor Martin, have gone further and argued that the concept of an arms race is disproven by the figures above,[58] which show a long-term decline in the post-Second-World-War period of the share of US military expenditure in national income. This is doubly misleading. Economic growth worldwide has been especially rapid since 1950, and it is this phenomenon which has permitted the *relative* burden of military expenditure in most advanced capitalist countries to decline – despite the fact that the *absolute* volume of resources devoted to military spending remains huge. Furthermore, the figures are strictly irrelevant to the existence or non-existence of an arms race, because the true measure of an arms race is warheads; and the 1960s saw, with the introduction by the USA of MIRV technology, a means of massively accelerating the strategic competition while at the same time fulfilling the demand of the McNamara Pentagon for cost effectiveness: MIRVed missiles give a lot more 'bang for the buck'. Secretary Weinberger's observation cannot obscure the fact that the Reagan administration has been planning and is now beginning to implement an increase in US military expenditure whose magnitude is without parallel under 'peace-time' conditions.

We begin by outlining what the Reagan administration has proposed. We then go on to argue that, against the background of a world economic crisis characterized by a series of acute conflicts of interest between the advanced industrial countries, the magnification by American leaders of the Soviet military threat and the associated US arms build-up can be seen as part of the attempt to re-assert US political leadership within the industrialized world. Finally, since purely economic factors have been advanced as one of the principal explanations for the military build-up, we examine its potentially disruptive effects on the US economy, and on that of the Western world as a whole.

Reagan's initial budgetary proposals have been somewhat modified as a result of deliberations inside the administration and in their passage through Congress, but the proposals for increased military expenditure remain unchanged in their essential features. The *volume* of US military expenditure is planned to rise by 55 per cent between 1981 and 1986 – an increase which is almost three times as large as the *volume* increase in military spending incurred during the five-year period 1965–70 of the Vietnam war.[59] It is proposed that military expenditure should increase from 24.7 per cent of the US federal budget in 1981 to 37.6 per cent by 1986, by which time US military expenditure will be US $343 billion.[60]

How is the federal government planning to finance this huge additional outlay? In part, it is to be achieved by a cut in welfare spending (planned to fall in *volume* terms by an estimated 16 per cent between 1981 and 1986); in part, by an increase in federal revenue generated by the higher level of economic activity which Reagan's tax reductions for middle-income and higher-income families are intended to induce. By handing out carrots to the well-off and urging self-help on the poor, Reagan hoped to convince everyone that the arms build-up could be paid for, that US economic activity would recover, and the federal budget could also be balanced. Increasingly fewer people believe that these sums add up. Even Reagan's Budget Director, Mr David Stockman, has admitted that the administration's prospectus as a whole is unconvincing.

Is there any purely economic rationale for this huge escalation of military expenditure? One interpretation is that its fundamental aim is to alleviate some of the central problems of the US economy in its international setting. This view is controversial, but worth considering. We doubt that this objective will be realized in this way, as a (necessarily) brief sketch of recent economic and political developments will suggest.

The US is currently experiencing its highest rates of unemployment since the 1930s. Profitability and investment generally are depressed. American firms have been failing to compete successfully with European and Japanese firms in the production of many kinds of standardized manufactured products, and the US economy, having failed to achieve any worthwhile energy savings, has become increasingly dependent on imported oil.[61]

The downturn in the US national economy has also been a major contributory factor in the current world economic crisis. Its competitive weakness, as reflected in the deficit in the US balance of payments, the huge outflow of dollars required to finance the economy's imports, and the lack of confidence in the dollar, have been a source of instability in the international financial system throughout the 1970s.[62] The view is widespread that the current economic crisis stems entirely from actions of the OPEC oil cartel in 1973 and subsequently. However, though exacerbated by the action of OPEC, the origins of the crisis in fact lie elsewhere. These must be examined briefly.

Towards the end of the 1960s, the post-war Western economy entered a period of prolonged crisis, from which there currently seems no clear way forward to general economic recovery. The crucial factors sparking off this crisis in the early 1970s were the erosion of America's technological lead in many areas of manufacturing industry and the effects on US aggregate demand of expenditure related to the Vietnam war: these factors led to the disappearance of the US surplus of trade in manufactures during the early 1970s, which was accompanied by a prolonged crisis of confidence in the dollar.[63] In turn, this led to a series of unilateral measures by the Nixon administration, which, though addressed to the specific problems of the American domestic economy, can be seen to have failed to take account of the needs of the international economy as a whole. These included the suspension of convertibility of the dollar into gold on

15 August 1971 and a successful attempt to force revaluation of European and Japanese currencies relative to the dollar in order to diminish the relative competitive strength of their manufactured exports. OPEC's decision to raise oil prices in 1973 represented in many ways a *response* to the economic crisis. Their ability to do so was also a reflection of the growing discord between the major industrial nations over economic issues. It became increasingly clear to the oil-producing countries that they had for many years received an unequal share of the benefits which accrued from the rapid growth of the post-war boom. Furthermore, to the Arab oil-producers, it was apparent that the US was using some of the benefits of rapid economic growth to sustain their arch-enemy, Israel. Their real returns from oil production were eroded by the worldwide acceleration in inflation accompanying the Vietnam war, by the effective dollar devaluation, and, particularly, by the rise in grain prices associated with massive American sales of grain to the USSR. It is in this sense that, while the oil price rise was an additional source of pressure on the international financial community, it was essentially a response to a crisis not of its own creation.

We cannot hope to provide here a full account of subsequent international economic developments during the 1970s; for one thing, these developments are as yet only partially understood. But in attempting to account for recent developments in the US, it is important to note that, as a result of a series of unilateral actions by US governments in the sphere of international economic relations in the 1970s – actions which (to Europeans at least) amounted to a set of rather insular solutions to international problems and which failed to take account of the general requirements of the Western economy – the 1970s have witnessed a growing challenge to US leadership of the international economy. So far, partly because of the evident lack of political unity within Europe, it can probably be said that the US has had its own way on a series of issues. But all the important problems remain, many important disputed questions persist, and failure to reach agreement on these issues has deepened the world recession. There are four main areas of conflict.

The first concerns the role of the dollar as an international reserve currency. When Nixon cut the convertibility of the dollar into gold, he in effect allowed the US to continue financing its overseas investment, military expenditures, and oil purchases by printing dollars. The determination and ability of the US to do this represents an enormous asymmetry in the international economy and is resented by many Europeans. At the same time, the dollar 'overhang' remains a source of instability in international currency markets. The second area of conflict concerns the sharing of costs of adjustment to the relative decline of US national economic competitiveness. By forcing the Europeans and Japanese to revalue their currencies relative to the dollar, painful restructuring has been imposed on the successful export-oriented sectors of these countries, which, unlike the UK, have to generate a surplus on trade in manufactures to finance their oil imports. A third area of conflict concerns international trade: intense competition over markets in *third* countries has been accompanied by increasingly severe disputes at governmental level between the US, EEC, and Japan over access to each other's markets across a broad range of commodities. A fourth area of dispute concerns the absence of controls on international capital movements, which makes European monetary and interest rate policies peculiarly vulnerable to the actions of the US authorities.

While the US has managed to turn its considerable bargaining power in international economic negotiations to its own advantage in many of these areas, due to fundamental conflicts of interest, the failure to reach an agreed solution to these problems and to devise a coordinated strategy for world economic recovery runs the grave risk, from the point of view of the US, that the Europeans may develop their own solutions to these problems, solutions which work against what are perceived to be US interests.

The sort of development in Europe which clearly worries the current political leadership in the US has been the growth of trade and financial relations between Western Europe and Comecon. By 1979, Comecon markets absorbed 16 per cent of Western European manufactured exports (*excluding* trade in manufactures amongst themselves), whereas the proportion for the US was only 1.2 per cent. A recent example of the growth of these economic ties is the German–Soviet natural gas pipeline, an agreement which has been bitterly resisted by the US administration. In the global struggle for markets during the 1970s, not only were European firms more successful at exploiting the economic opportunities created by the improved political climate of detente, but, in the long run, it is clear that enormous advantages could accrue from a natural international division of labour spanning the 'Iron Curtain' in which Western Europe would gain increasing access to the abundant Soviet supplies of raw materials, energy, and cheap manufactures, while Comecon would benefit from Western European advanced technology. The difference of strategy towards the USSR between President Reagan and several European countries was made highly visible by the American administration's failure to obtain European cooperation in a trade boycott of the USSR in the wake of the imposition of military law in Poland. The West German government made it plain that it believed that greater security lay in involving the USSR in as much trade and economic interdependence as possible, rather than in trying to drive them into isolation, which would serve only to stimulate further historic Soviet fears of the West.

But, for better or worse, the USA is not following the West German course, and is instead engaging in an arms build-up. The arms build-up will certainly lead to increased activity, profitability, and investment in certain sectors of the US economy and thereby to a reduction in unemployment. In principle, also, increased military spending may improve the competitive position of some sectors of the US national economy. Since military research and development is the principal form of state aid to technological progress in the US, heavy military expenditure on research and development might help US firms close part of the technological gap which has opened up between American and Japanese firms in certain areas of advanced technology. These are the beneficial so-called 'spin-off' effects for civilian production. Also, the heightening of Cold War tensions which has legitimized the increase in military spending and the development of new weapons systems may boost US arms sales abroad and thereby strengthen the US balance of payments. Certainly, military technology is the one area where US firms maintain a considerable lead over their rivals in other advanced capitalist countries. However, one problem here is that the new weapons systems are so expensive that few countries outside the oil-rich Arab states are actually in a position to be able to afford them.

Specific defence contractors on the west coast of the US, the region which has for so long helped foster President Reagan's political ambitions, will certainly benefit from the arms build-up. But Reagan's military, economic, and social policies taken together fail to address the underlying problems of the US national economy, may well be socially disruptive in the US, and are likely to be highly destabilizing for the world economy as a whole – quite apart from the real risk of producing a nuclear holocaust.

We have already experienced some of the disruptive effects of these policies, both on the US economy and on the world economy. Since Reagan's claim that the arms build-up could be financed without incurring a massive federal budget deficit has not gained acceptance in US financial circles, US interest rates have soared to record levels – against a background of restrictive financial policies. In the US, this is already (1982) having the effect of deepening the recession. In the other advanced industrial countries, high US interest rates have forced competitive rises in interest rates in order to stem destabilizing capital outflows and so to stabilize exchange rates. High interest rates have similarly exacerbated recessionary tendencies elsewhere. In the Third World and the East European countries high interest rates have increased the cost of servicing their huge foreign currency debts, leading governments to squeeze domestic consumption and contract economic activity further, and therefore tending to exacerbate domestic social conflict.

Within the US, the positive benefits of increased military spending in terms of activity and employment are likely to be concentrated in certain regions only – principally the south-west and the west – thereby further accentuating regional differentials with respect to the deindustrializing north-east and its decaying inner city areas.

If the planned arms build-up does continue, its net impact is likely to worsen the underlying problems of the US economy and hence further weaken the world economy. First, the size and tempo of the arms build-up are likely to divert resources, especially of skilled manpower, from the urgent task of restructuring US domestic industry in a form appropriate to the late twentieth century – to meet tough overseas competition in civilian production and to develop energy-saving technologies and products. Second, US military procurement will have a high import-content in terms of certain strategic raw materials, many manufactured components, and even complete weapons systems. This is partly because of the bottlenecks and supply problems that US defence contractors will face in adjusting to such a rapid increase in military procurement. The further weakening of the competitive position of the US national economy and of its balance of payments, with the associated prolongation of the dollar crisis, will probably be far more destabilizing for the world economy than any positive economic stimulus which other countries can expect from US arms procurements (for example, the much vaunted recent US purchase from British Aerospace of the Hawk trainer for the US Navy). In the same way in which the Vietnam war helped sow the seeds of the international economic crisis of the 1970s, the US arms programme of the 1980s is likely to worsen the economic difficulties facing the Western world as a whole.

It is, therefore, difficult to accept the view that the proposed escalation in US military spending is in the best general interests of the US national economy. Considered from the point of view of world economic recovery, it is thoroughly risky – an opinion held by an increasing number of European leaders.

In European eyes, it is perfectly possible to see the breakdown of detente and the associated weapons programmes as misguided and economically perilous attempts by the US to reassert American political pre-eminence throughout the world, especially in relation to the other advanced countries, and thereby to try and re-create the world order of the years of the 'Long Boom' which ended in 1971–3. Current political leaders in Washington, whose attitudes were shaped by the experience of the Depression of the 1930s, its ending with the Second World War, and the spectacular affluence of the following twenty years, may find it hard to adjust to changed times. But their attempt to force back the hands of the clock by accelerated arms expenditure may lead us all on to a path which is fraught with danger.

Part Two
The Nuclear Arms Race:
Where to Next?

So far in this book, we have sought to provide a sustained account of the arms race. We have situated it within the discrepancies of interpretation that surround it. We have shown that an understanding of the present requires an understanding of a long trail of mistrust between East and West. We have given a narrative that tells the story of the nuclear age from its birth to the present. We have provided a tentative explanation of the forces that drive the Steel Triangle.

Now we shall change our line of approach. In the light of the knowledge accumulated so far, we shall address the debate about a nuclear defence policy for the future. First, we shall engage closely the formal arguments in favour of such a policy in their most comprehensive and coherent form, as they are presented by the British government. Then we shall indicate the wide range of other, converging arguments against the official position, in addition to those which emerge from explaining its inconsistencies and lack of realism. Finally, we shall offer a detailed view of how we may take the first step towards a defence policy for Great Britain and its allies that would promise 'defence' and not, as at present, the prospect of eventual incineration.

6 The Case for and against a Nuclear Defence Policy

1 The British Government's Case

The bases of the government's policy are set out each year in a *Statement on the Defence Estimates*. These are introduced by the Secretary of State for Defence and accepted by Parliament. The 1981 *Statement* included a special effort to meet criticism, consisting of eleven points under the heading 'Nuclear Weapons and Preventing War', subsequently republished as an attractive leaflet. We shall use these points as a framework for presenting, as faithfully as we can, the overall principles guiding the government's policy, supplementing them from elsewhere as necessary with more details about the actions taken. This does not imply that we agree with that policy – our own views follow – but we feel it proper to present the official view first. It is this:

1. Nuclear war would be terrible, and we must make realistic plans to prevent it.

2. Nuclear weapons cannot be dis-invented; we must ensure that they are never used.

3. Even non-nuclear war would be fought with weapons much more powerful than those used between 1939 and 1945. Action to prevent nuclear war and still permit 'conventional war' could also be calamitous.

4. Non-nuclear war is the likeliest road to nuclear war.

5. It is essential for us to have nuclear arms for two reasons. First, because of its geography and the totalitarian direction of its resources, the Soviet Union has a massive preponderance of military power in Europe. For the West to attempt to match this with conventional forces would entail huge social and other costs. Nuclear arms are thus necessary to deter a Soviet thrust. Second, no amount of effort not involving nuclear weapons would make us safe against the Soviets' nuclear force.

'... Deterrence means transmitting a basically simple message: if you attack me, I will resist; I will go on resisting until you stop or until my strength fails; and, if it is the latter, my strength will not fail before I have inflicted on you damage so heavy that you will be much worse off at the end than if you had never started; so do not start.'

(M. Quinlan, Ministry of Defence nuclear deterrence theorist)[1]

6. A policy of deterrence in the nuclear age requires clear thought. Its primary aim must be to influence the calculations of anyone who might consider aggression before they actually undertake it. In addition, if war were to start, there must be plans to bring it to an end before it escalates to a global catastrophe. Escalation, once war has begun, is not inevitable, and carefully prepared plans to stop it could work. But the only safe course is outright prevention.

7. For such plans to be effective, we must attempt to perceive the situation as it would seem to a potential adversary. In effect this means ensuring that a future Soviet leader could never foresee a situation in which the West would be left with no reasonable alternative but to surrender.

8. Thus the basis of deterrence is to provide for a variety of possible courses of action in any nuclear war, which, like a chess-master's strategy, would block off a variety of possible moves in the opponent's mind, and to plan to reduce its devastation by modest civil-defence measures. (The nature of these possible courses of action is outlined elsewhere in the *Statement*, and is summarized below.)

9. The UK helped to develop NATO's nuclear strategy and fully endorses it. We share in the protection it gives. We cooperate by making bases available to the USA and by providing delivery systems for US warheads. And we commit to NATO nuclear forces (strategic and theatre) under our independent control.

The *Statement* argues that any suggestion that we should shed our nuclear arms while continuing to enjoy US nuclear protection as a member of NATO would offer neither moral merit nor greater safety. Whether or not nuclear weapons are located here, our size and location make us crucial to NATO and thus an inevitable target. A nuclear-free Britain would mean a weaker NATO, weaker deterrence, and thus more risk of war; and if war started we would be even more likely to be attacked.

10. In spite of the ideological conflict, the East–West peace has lasted for thirty-five years, and common sense suggests that this is a consequence of deterrence centred upon nuclear weapons. Deterrence can continue to hold.

11. This does not mean that deterrence should be the last word. The readiness to use nuclear weapons is terrible. We must seek unremittingly, through arms control and otherwise, for better ways of ordering the world. But the search may be a very long one. No safer system than deterrence is yet in view, and it would be immensely irresponsible and dangerous to destroy the present system before a better one is firmly within our grasp.

We must now outline the 'possible courses of action' referred to above. They involve the adoption by N A T O of 'a strategy of forward defence and flexible response'.[2] The former implies 'a defence robust enough to deny an aggressor easy or rapid capture of territory or other major assets',[3] and involves defence forces stationed near the eastern boundaries of the N A T O area, ready to meet any attack. 'Flexible response' strategy implies an ability to respond to an attack with appropriately graded counter-measures, at every level from conventional forces, through the use of tactical or theatre nuclear arms (i.e. everything from nuclear shells to medium-range missiles), to very-long-range (e.g. intercontinental) nuclear missiles. Thus it is argued that, while we must aim, by a show of strength, to prevent war, we must also, if that fails, have ready alternative courses of practical action. Without giving in, we must be prepared for further shows of strength at successively higher levels, in the hope that the adversary will think better and pull back.

This flexible response strategy replaced the earlier 'trip-wire' strategy of massive nuclear retaliation to any aggressive act,[4] a strategy now regarded as neither appropriate nor credible in any but the most extreme circum-stances.[5] For example, if N A T O had only strategic nuclear weapons, the U S S R might think it could launch an attack on Europe with conventional weapons without fear of nuclear reprisals; they would expect the U S A to hesitate to use its strategic weapons since such a course would invite devastating reprisals against its own homeland. However, they might be deterred from a conventional attack by N A T O's possession of tactical nuclear weapons, since use of the latter would not necessarily precipitate the ultimate holocaust.

In practice there could be many steps between conventional war and an all-out nuclear exchange, so that capacity for an even more finely tuned response than the above implies is required. Thus, the use of tactical nuclear weapons by NATO to halt a conventional attack might conceivably cause the aggressor to back off rather than to take the risks of going on. But if it induced the USSR to consider response in kind, no advantage would be gained unless NATO were seen to be prepared to deliver an even more severe blow with theatre or even strategic nuclear weapons. In the same way, long-range theatre weapons, such as cruise missiles, are seen to be essential: without them the USSR might feel able to launch long-range nuclear strikes from inside their own territory against European targets, with NATO's only option a strategic attack which would invite reprisals of a similar kind. Some people claim that the increased proportion of military targets for strategic missiles, as set out in Presidential Directive 59 (see pp. 109–10) involves a continuation of the same line of thought: it is said to provide opportunity for selective and stepped response to an attack, rather than the stark choice between all-out massed attack, with the inevitable counter-attack, or nothing.

Thus at each stage NATO policy requires a *capacity* for a *graded* increase in response, in the hope that an adversary will be deterred from taking a step that would lead to further escalation and thus even more unacceptable damage than that already sustained. The intermediate stages are necessary because the enemy would not believe that NATO would use a strategic deterrent in the knowledge that such a move would invite a strategic reply.

Some critics of Western policy represent such plans, and the instigation of civil-defence measures, as involving a 'war-fighting strategy', with nuclear war perceived as something expected and survivable. Such views (the *Statement* asserts) fail to recognize that the policy of deterrence demands that an adversary must perceive all possible moves to be blocked off in advance: only thus can we render nuclear war as improbable as we humanly can.

All this applies to NATO as a whole. The UK independent deterrent is seen as providing additional flexibility. It involves the maintenance, under our own control, of a strategic nuclear capability – the Polaris submarine force, to be replaced in due course by the Trident system. Although this represents only a very small proportion of the strategic deterrent force available to the West, the UK government lays great stress on the fact that it is *ours* and, ostensibly at least, independent of the USA. This is held to be important because, it is suggested, in an escalating conflict US resolution might waver, or be misperceived by the Soviet Union to waver. In those circumstances the Soviet Union might be deterred by a nuclear deterrent in the hands of one or more stalwart European powers. In addition, it is held that the Western alliance would be less predictable, and thus more difficult to assail, if there were two independent sources of nuclear decision-making.[6]

That, then, is the government's case. It will be apparent that it rests on two crucial assumptions: that the Soviet Union is aggressive and expansionist by nature, eager to invade Western Europe the moment it gets the chance, and secondly that, although imperfect, deterrence is a practical, realistic sort of policy, the best that we have at present, and that it accurately describes the posture in which we hold nuclear weapons. We shall have a good deal to say about the assumption of Soviet aggression in Chapter 7. First, however, we must consider the internal logic of the government's policy.

2 The Government's Case Dissected Point by Point

1–2. We agree wholeheartedly with the views that nuclear war would be terrible and that we must do all we can to prevent it.

3. We also agree that conventional war, though a lesser evil, would be a catastrophe and must never again be permitted. We would add the necessity for thinking in global terms; conventional wars bring untold suffering wherever they happen, and we must seek to prevent them anywhere, not only on our own doorstep.

4. It is indeed the case that nuclear war is most likely to occur as a result of conventional war, but NATO must bear its full share of responsibility for that fact. It is NATO policy to be ready to use nuclear weapons to meet a conventional attack. In a section entitled 'Conventional attack', at Paragraph 326, the *Statement on the Defence Estimates* gives a hypothetical scenario for such use: RAF (Germany) Jaguar and Buccaneer aircraft would make nuclear strikes against 'specific targets' to 'demonstrate political will'. The transition to nuclear war is unremarked. The current US Army Field Manual, in use with commanders and in military training establishments, is even more explicit. Chapter 10 of the Manual describes tactical nuclear operations: 'In any battle', it says, 'we must have the capability to use nuclear weapons effectively, along with our conventional weapons [*sic*], in support of the land battle.' It then goes on to detail procedures for field commanders to specify and request nuclear 'packages', and urges them to submit such requests in plenty of time. Logical targets, it suggests, are: committed enemy forces; reserves; second echelon forces; enemy nuclear, artillery, and anti-aircraft systems; command

and control facilities and logistics trains; i.e. virtually anything of a military nature.[7] The responsibility for initiating the escalation would be ours.

> 'The NATO aim is to deter attack by possessing nuclear weapons; should deterrence fail and an attack occur which conventional forces alone could not contain, NATO could threaten to use – and, if necessary, actually use – nuclear weapons to cause the aggressor to abandon his attack.'
>
> (*Statement on the Defence Estimates*, 1980, §124)
>
> '. . . it [present NATO policy regarding nuclear conflict] is illogical, because whether or not we could limit it, and I do not believe that we could, in any scenario of nuclear war the West would come off worse than the East. It is impractical because you cannot fight a controlled nuclear war, and it is immoral because the total results of it in terms of destruction, the misery and the after-effects could not in any conceivable sense of the word be called defence.'
>
> (Field-Marshal Lord Carver, Chief of the Defence Staff 1973–6, House of Lords, 20 July 1981)[8]

An agreement by both sides not to be the first to use nuclear weapons would go some way towards lessening this danger. But we must note that NATO's intention to meet a conventional attack with nuclear weapons has been for years a major stumbling block in disarmament negotiations. All offers of an agreement to renounce first use have been rebuffed by the West. This is sometimes denied but, as we saw in Chapter 4, the denial comes down to a play on words between 'first strike' and 'first use'.

Abandonment of the NATO first-use doctrine would be the most profound change in its direction since the foundation of the Alliance. But continued adherence to that doctrine, especially in the face of growing public awareness and abhorrence, is seen by increasing numbers of senior NATO politicians and military men as likely to destroy the Alliance from within. Accordingly, in April 1982, McGeorge Bundy, George Kennan, Robert McNamara, and Gerard Smith, four senior figures in the American political establishment who have all been deeply involved with nuclear policies, and who have all already appeared in this book for that reason, took an unprecedented step. Together they published an article which noted that the transformations during the 1960s and 1970s in the world's nuclear arsenal and in Western nuclear strategies had greatly increased the risk of nuclear war; that strategies first developed in the 1950s were now dangerously anachronistic and that therefore renunciation of first use was the obvious first step to reduce that risk (see box).

THE ARGUMENT FOR NO FIRST USE

'It is time to recognize that no one has ever succeeded in advancing any persuasive reason to believe that any use of nuclear weapons, even on the smallest scale, could reliably be expected to remain limited. Every serious analysis and every military exercise for over twenty-five years, has demonstrated that even the most restrained battlefield use would be enormously destructive to civilian life and property . . .

'The one clearly definable firebreak against the world-wide disaster of general nuclear war is the one that stands between all other kinds of conflict and any use whatsoever of nuclear weapons. To keep that firebreak wide and strong is in the deepest interest of all mankind. In retrospect, indeed, it is remarkable that this country has not responded to this reality more quickly . . .

'. . . the basic argument for a no-first-use policy can be stated in strictly military terms: that any other course involves unacceptable risks to the national life that military forces exist to defend. The military officers of the Alliance can be expected to understand the force of this proposition, even if many of them do not initially agree with it.'

Bundy, Kennan, McNamara, and Smith also suggested in their article that renunciation of first use of nuclear weapons would make it important to 'strengthen' NATO's non-nuclear forces to provide credible deterrence, although they did not spell out what 'strengthen' implied in their view. We discuss in detail the changes in nature and disposition of non-nuclear forces in Chapter 10, and under Point 5 of the government's case, we examine how one should – and how one should not – go about trying to compare the relative strengths of NATO and the Warsaw Pact.

Sensing the threat posed by this proposal coming from such distinguished authors, Secretary of State Alexander Haig was quick to reject their case totally, even before it had appeared in print, by suggesting that in his judgement, 'strengthening' the non-nuclear forces would involve reintroduction of the draft, a *tripling* of the size of the United States armed forces and putting the economy on a 'wartime footing'. This is simply nonsense. It is hard to make progress when senior politicians behave so wildly.[9]

5. While the government claims that the Warsaw Pact forces are much stronger than NATO's, it must be remembered that each side in the arms race has constantly emphasized the superiority of the other in order to justify its own arms programme. As we have seen in the cases of the supposed bomber and missile 'gaps' of the fifties and sixties, the myth of Russian superiority was used by the US government to justify its own substantial increase in arms expenditure. In practice, the estimated balance of power depends very much on how the sums are calculated. This can be well illustrated in terms of a basic index – manpower.

First, we beg the question of how NATO and the Warsaw Pact *use* soldiers – Western soldiers being more professional – by giving them equivalence. Then we add up. The total depends on how we count the forces of France and the forces of the non-Soviet Eastern European nations. But even if the latter are added to the Soviet forces, the Eastern total does not exceed that of the Western countries. The IISS *Military Balance 1981–2*, a normally conservative source when estimating Western capabilities, gives the following figures for total manpower in uniform: NATO, 4,933,000; Warsaw Pact, 4,788,000, a marginal NATO advantage of 1.03:1. If, instead, total ground forces in Europe are taken, then the figures are NATO, 2,123,000; Warsaw Pact, 1,669,000, a NATO advantage of 1.27:1. Strategists normally reckon, as a rule of thumb, that a 3:1 advantage in number is necessary before it is safe to contemplate a surprise attack of the sort that the Warsaw Pact is supposed to envisage; and of course, this does not account for the higher proportion of skilled soldiers in the West, nor does it embrace the fact that the USSR would also bring its *eastern* front into the calculation. Include China (3,900,000), and the USSR is outnumbered by 1.84:1. However, if one continues to look at the European front alone, the figures are still not quite clear. Can the satellite troops be relied on? Soviet contingency plans suggest not: they keep the nuclear forces out of satellite troops' hands, and station these troops in 'sandwich' battle formations, between reliable units, a tactic which would be familiar to any commander of British Empire native troops in the past. Furthermore, some of the Soviet forces in its satellite countries could more properly be seen as armies of occupation. So most of the national armies, and also an element of Soviet troops, should not be added to the Warsaw Pact total of battle-ready troops opposing NATO. In fact the Eastern bloc may rely as much upon a myth of NATO aggressive intentions to justify the scale and deployment of Soviet troops in satellite countries as the West depends upon a myth of Soviet aggressive intentions to justify its military establishment.

Comparisons are complicated by two further issues. First, quality is important as well as quantity: this is true of soldiers; it is more visibly so of equipment. Many of the Warsaw Pact tanks would be counted as obsolete for modern battle by NATO, although they still remain excellent for intimidating civilian populations, as in 1956 and 1968. Second, to 'match' conventional forces it is not necessary to compare the numbers of each type of weapon, although this is the way in which the evidence is usually presented to the public. A force whose aims are purely defensive does not need numerical parity (or superiority) in every type of weapon, as the government sometimes admits, although continuing to issue misleading ratios and histograms. This is because a defensive force which wishes to prevail should not compare the number of its tanks with those of the enemy, or its aircraft with theirs, but rather its anti-tank forces with their tanks and its anti-aircraft defences with the attack aircraft. Thus, whereas the West has a 1:2.5 inferiority in main battle tanks in the Ministry of Defence's much reproduced histogram, by 1978 NATO had in place 200,000 precision-guided munitions and 17,000 launchers, which gives better than a 10:1 superiority in precision-guided anti-tank weapons over Warsaw Pact tanks. This is a less well publicized ratio.[10]

Point 5 has two other related propositions. First is the argument that the West could not hope to match the military power of the Soviet forces by conventional means without enormous social costs. This is open to question, since it assumes a 'one for one' balance, which is not required; and furthermore, in recent years, advantages both in cost and effectiveness have moved decisively from the offensive force to the defence. This question, and alternative methods of defence, are discussed in Chapter 10.

Second, the *Statement* argues that non-nuclear forces can never make us safe against nuclear attack. In the operational sense this is quite true. But then neither can nuclear forces: during the 1960s both superpowers engaged in expensive experiments with anti-ballistic missile systems, only to discover that they did not work. There is no defence against a ballistic missile. Once launched, it has a free ride. There is no defence against the mad dictator or group of soldiers, or accident, or chance, launching such a missile except to remove the missile beforehand. As has been argued in Chapter 4, congruence between weapons systems and the strategy of nuclear deterrence has been long since left behind: current nuclear forces and postures are increasingly likely to precipitate the holocaust rather than to deter it and, as we shall shortly argue, even the 'pure' form of deterrence as envisaged in the early 1950s is badly defective.

Since the most likely reason for a nuclear attack is to try to pre-empt a feared attack from the victim country, it is clear that removal of targets (i.e. nuclear weapons) *reduces* that risk. Of course it does not remove all risk of attack, nor of being affected by fall-out from nuclear conflict elsewhere; that can only happen several steps further down the road to survival, and until that time the European country with non-nuclear defence forces, like Sweden or Switzerland, is prudent to undertake provision of shelter from fall-out for its people. But such provision should not for a moment be compared with, let alone equated with, 'civil defence' in a potential target country: they serve quite different functions and face quite different requirements. Swiss and Swedish shelter programmes are designed on the assumption that there is no protection from direct attack, and that the bombs will drop elsewhere; they are intended to protect people from the side-effects which, in a fashion, may be survivable. The *Statement* mentions only nuclear forces of the adversary, and so we leave until Chapter 10 the question of defence against invasion and occupation.

6. Point 6 has three component ideas which we take in reverse order. First, we entirely agree that the permanent prevention of nuclear war is the only safe course and, as we shall argue under Points 7 and 8 below, the *Statement*'s prescription to achieve that is most unlikely to succeed. Secondly, in Chapter 5 we have already shown in detail why the *Statement*'s confidence in the possibility of limiting nuclear war is misplaced. Thirdly, we agree that the present situation demands clear thought. But that must embrace three issues neglected by the defence strategists. First, we must examine carefully the probable effects of our moves on the Soviet planners. Arms acquired in the name of deterrence, and perhaps genuinely intended to ensure that the Soviet Union should see all possible moves blocked in advance, may nevertheless be perceived by the other side as preparations for an aggressive strike.

To take a current example, American medium-range land-based nuclear weapons based in Europe are supposed to be a response to medium-range Soviet nuclear weapons. There are two fundamental problems with this view. The first concerns the belief that comparisons must be between 'systems of similar capability'. The difficulty here is that much depends on how rigidly 'similar capability' is interpreted. The Ministry of Defence and the Pentagon apply a rigid criterion, comparing long-range land-based with long-range land-based, sea-based with sea-based, short-range with short-range, etc., apparently because they assume that in some vague way this tidiness of the 'war-gaming' exercise corresponds to the real world. Of course, by greater and yet greater circumscription, eventually reduced to the absurd (almost to the level of 'long-range land-based theatre air-breathing missiles with red ribbons tied to the left tailplane', etc.) 'gaps' can be found and a Soviet 'advantage' revealed. The way that this numbers game has been played is taken up in Appendix A2. How might the Soviet General Staff view the same missiles? The new generation NATO systems and the SS–20 are of approximately similar range (hence 'broadly similar' in the Western view). But such weapons are incorrectly compared on the basis of range alone. Because of the facts of geography American weapons based in western Europe can strike deep into Soviet territory, and therefore it is quite reasonable for the USSR to regard these as forward-based American strategic systems with five, instead of thirty, minutes' warning time. In contrast the SS–4, 5, and 20 cannot reach the USA, and thus, although of similar range to Pershing and the cruise missile, are in no other sense comparable. The closest analogy to the present NATO plan is the emplacement of Soviet IRBMs ninety miles from the continental United States – on the island of Cuba – in the autumn of 1962. At that time Paul Nitze, Assistant Secretary of Defense for International Affairs, a consistently gloomy hawk, stated that the south-eastern United States would be open to sudden attack; 'The warning time would be cut from fifteen minutes to two or three minutes.' The US government regarded this position as intolerable.[11] This time the roles are reversed and the incident takes place against a background of changed nuclear strategies, of greatly augmented nuclear stockpiles, and of less agile statesmen than were Kennedy and Khrushchev. Paul Nitze is the senior American negotiator at the 1981–2 Geneva Arms Control Talks. A full circle indeed.

> '. . . it is inconsequential whether NATO is actually planning a first strike or not. The decisive factor is simply whether this potential leads to fear on the part of the adversary that this could be the case . . . It is . . . unrealistic to believe that the placement of the planned land-based mid-range systems in Europe would be perceived by the Soviet Union as simply response to the SS–20, just because the West justifies its plans in this way. It is more reasonable to assume that the Soviet Union will see in NATO's rearmament a sign of a definite change in the West's nuclear war planning, and therefore resolve to engage in the same sort of re-thinking of the Warsaw Pact's military strategy.'
>
> (Major-General Gert Bastian, West German Army, retired, during the seminar on 'Nuclear War in Europe' at Groningen University, the Netherlands)[12]

Second, the clear thinking must be concerned with *all* the consequences of the arms race. The logic developed in the official statements is trapped by the constraints of the war games on which official policy appears to rest – the alternative scenarios of move and counter-move distract attention from the presumptions on which the whole argument rests, and from the many effects which the arms race has even in the absence of war. The latter are discussed in Chapters 8 and 9. But clear thinking is required in a third area: the real nature and operation of 'deterrence theory' must be opened up for view. In this, we may embrace aspects of points 7 and 8.   ·

7–8. Point 7 makes a fundamental demand for accurate perception of the adversary, including understanding of his perception of us, as well as sharing with Point 8 a 'war-games' approach to action consequent upon that perception. Elsewhere throughout this book we question whether these two either can be in theory, or have been in practice, compatible. But here we address the theory of deterrence employed by the Ministry in its 'pure' form which, the *Statement* reveals, is believed to correspond to reality, a proposition which in earlier chapters we have consistently questioned.

Deterrence is a concept central to discussion of strategic theory today, yet it is as old as conflict itself. The intention of deterrence is to prevent conflict for as long as possible. This is done by threatening the adversary that, in the event of aggression, greater violence will be done to him than the potential gains from aggression could, in his own judgement, possibly justify.[13] In the pre-nuclear age the threat to wreak unacceptable damage was not necessarily all-or-nothing. Instead it involved a continuum of graduated threats, capable of being matched closely to the aggressive act. Means – in the form of sufficient and appropriate arms and men – had to be available for each graduated step to make each threat 'credible'. But history has repeatedly shown that confrontations tend to escalate up the scale of destructive power, so that in fact deterrence usually resides in the most powerful weapons available. Thus deterrence is a policy of bluff; it hangs less upon what you do than upon what the enemy thinks you might do.

Predicting what the other side will do is no easy matter, and the deterrence theorist plays safe by assuming the worst about man – that he is greedy and aggressive, and that his aggression can be inhibited only by fear. That this binds the theory to a narrow, inflexible view of mankind is acceptable to the theorist because of its simplicity. Although this view of mankind is claimed to be 'realistic', it clearly is not. Man and society are more subtle than that.

Before the invention of nuclear weapons the absolute destructive power of any individual weapon was limited and known, so that it was relatively easy to translate the deterrent threat into precise yet flexible military terms. And just as the numbers and nature of men and armaments necessary to pose a 'credible' threat could be finely calculated, so also could the strength and intentions of an enemy – intentions latent in the composition of his armed forces – be guessed with some precision. In this way the two could be matched, so that the leashed menace of the deterring force could just balance that of the aggressor. This flexibility, consequent upon the relative weakness of the weapons systems, provided military strength which could either, as an extension of politics, *coerce* action, or be used as a *defensive* threat, with no demand on the adversary other than the threat of retribution in the event of invasion. Of course the calculations sometimes went wrong: the deterrent might not be 'credible', or the enemy might calculate that the potential gain did outweigh the probable cost. Deterrence involved a 'profit and loss account' logic, with the adversaries constantly comparing and sometimes testing their relative strengths. It was this that caused Carl von Clausewitz, in the most influential treatise on strategy in modern history, to suggest that among other human activities, the closest parallel to war is in the transactions of the market-place.[14]

Now for a deterrent threat to work, three conditions must always be fulfilled.

● (a) The 'adversary' (meaning whoever sits at the top of the pyramid of power in the enemy state) must be assumed to *behave rationally*, or else, obviously, all threats are vain. But in times of crisis, national leaders are inevitably under great strain, tired, and easily susceptible to errors of judgement. Or they may not be rational at all, as the pioneer atomic scientist Professor Rotblat suspects could have been the case had Hitler had an atomic bomb in 1945. Proliferation in the present puts nuclear arms into ever more hands, increasing the chance that eventually a 'bandit state' led by a fanatic or madman will control a nuclear device. Thus this condition may well not be met.

● (b) The leader, or leaders, must be assumed to see the world in ways which, while not necessarily the same as our own, are at least *systematically and reliably comprehensible* to us. Only in that way can our estimate of 'unacceptable damage' be so also in his eyes. Quoting the ancient Chinese strategist Sun Tzu, Mao Tsetung put the importance of doing this crisply: 'Know the enemy and know yourself; in a hundred battles you will never be in peril.' The Ministry of Defence deterrence theorist Mr Michael Quinlan echoes Mao more prosaically: 'Planning deterrence means thinking through the possible reasoning of an adversary and the way in which alternative courses of action might appear to him in advance. It means doing this in his terms, not in ours . . .'[15] Now 'assuming the worst' is one way, in practice the commonest way, to meet this requirement, but it is not at all the same as comprehending the enemy. It is to caricature him in a dangerously inflexible way. It is doubly dangerous if the caricature is confused with comprehension. Using the lowest common denominator assumption instead of seeking comprehension makes it difficult to resist escalation of threat and counter-threat, and inevitably militates against any controlled process of flexible response such as the theory advocates.

• (c) He must be assumed to be able to *translate his judgement*, arising from assessment of our threat, *into real action*: to have, responsive to his will, an integrated system of command, control and communication with his armed forces. The chaos inevitable in time of crisis or war will involve a breakdown in communication, with units of the armed forces taking on some degree of autonomy. Thus condition (c) also may not be met.

So it is not surprising to see that history abounds with examples of the failure of deterrence as long-term policy to prevent war; at best, deterrence *defers* war. It scarcely recommends itself on past performance as the policy of choice in the nuclear age when circumstances conspire even more towards the failure of the three essential conditions and when war would not be simply unfortunate, resulting in a minor scuffle (in relative terms) like the First World War, after which the world picked up the pieces and began again, but would be final and irretrievable. In this context it is a strictly hope-less policy, offering no pathway towards a stable future.

9. The ninth point in the essay on *Nuclear Weapons and Preventing War* concerns British involvement with NATO and thus with the USA. Two interrelated aspects of this – the question of how far the so-called 'independent deterrent' really merits the term, and the encroachment on our sovereignty implied by the presence of so many American bases in our country and by the imposition of American policies – are considered elsewhere, the first later in this chapter, the other in Chapter 8. Here we would question the view that we should still be as likely a target for nuclear attack if we divested ourselves of nuclear arms, both British and American. In such a case, we might or might not wish to remain a member of NATO as it is at present constituted. Let us be very clear what we mean by that.

The North Atlantic Treaty, as distinct from the Organization set up to implement it, makes no mention of command structures or the necessity of nuclear weapons to fulfil its ends. It merely details those ends: mutual security of signatory states. If, therefore, NATO could be realigned to

---

DISARMAMENT: THE PROBLEM OF ORGANIZING THE WORLD COMMUNITY

'. . . We are a member of a regional defensive alliance that includes three of the five nuclear-weapon states. We are, nonetheless, a country that has renounced the production of nuclear weapons or the acquisition of such weapons under our control.

'We have withdrawn from any nuclear role by Canada's Armed Forces in Europe and are now in the process of replacing with conventionally armed aircraft the nuclear-capable planes assigned to our forces in North America. We were thus not only the first country in the world with the capacity to produce nuclear weapons that chose not to do so; we are also the first nuclear-armed country to have chosen to divest itself of nuclear weapons.

'. . . It has been an assumption of our policy that countries like Canada can do something to slow down the arms race. But obviously, we can do a great deal more if we act together. That is why a great responsibility rests upon this special session.

'. . . It is hardly credible that nations that have learnt that their destinies are linked, that national aims can no longer be wholly realized within national boundaries, that beggaring our neighbours is the surest way of beggaring ourselves, should have discovered no better alternative to assuring their security than an escalating balance of terror. And it is even less credible that, in a world of finite resources, in so many parts of which basic human needs remain unsatisfied, nearly $400 billion in resources should have to be spent year by year for purposes of security.

'Security, even absolute security, is not an end in itself. It is only the setting that permits us to pursue our real ends: economic well-being, cultural attainment, the fulfilment of the human personality. But those ends are all incompatible with a world of neighbours armed to the teeth.'

(Speech by Prime Minister Pierre Trudeau to the United Nations General Assembly Special Session on Disarmament, New York, 26 May 1978)[16]

PREAMBLE TO THE NORTH ATLANTIC TREATY, 4 APRIL 1949
'The Parties to this Treaty reaffirm their faith in the purposes and principles of the Charter of the United Nations and their desire to live in peace with all peoples and all Governments.

'They are determined to safeguard the freedom, common heritage and civilization of their peoples, founded on the principles of democracy, individual liberty and the rule of law.

'They seek to promote stability and well-being in the North Atlantic area.

'They are resolved to unite their efforts for collective defence and for the preservation of peace and security.'

---

fulfil the aims of the Treaty, instead of, as at present, threatening them, it is difficult to see why Britain would not wish to be a member.

In such circumstances it is difficult to see why we should ever be the object of a nuclear attack. But pulling NATO back from the drift towards becoming a suicide pact cannot be achieved overnight. How to begin? Should Britain act alone? If so, what action should be taken? The question is sometimes put as one of agonizing newness, as if it involved Britain taking unprecedented steps to lead the world. Had action been taken in the 1960s, we would have been in the forefront, but now we have been overtaken. In fact, our friends and allies have shown the way.

As a result of intensive public debate outside and within Parliament during the late 1950s and early 1960s at the time when nuclear issues were last prominent in British politics also, Sweden decided not to become a nuclear-weapons state, concluding that this would not enhance her security as a neutral country. Within NATO, Norway and Denmark have never possessed nuclear weapons either. More recently, on 26 May 1978 at the United Nations General Assembly Special Session on Disarmament, Canada, another of our NATO partners, renounced the possession or use of nuclear weapons, or the stationing of American weapons on their soil. In the final chapter, we discuss in more detail the practical steps towards survival that we might take. But here a common anxiety about the first of those steps – that of following Canada – must be relieved.

Britain's geographical position, the fact that we manufacture our own nuclear weapons, and the extent to which our country is filled with American military facilities of every sort make us different from Canada: in present circumstances this first step of renouncing possession, stationing, or use of nuclear weapons in Britain would not detach us absolutely from the American nuclear force. The presence of submarine detection facilities and the use of the UK as a supply base might cause us to remain a nuclear target, though one to be attacked on a much smaller scale. But such a move would be a first move in the right direction and would take us on a much safer course than the US Senate's failure to ratify the SALT II treaty coupled with the stationing of mobile ground-launched cruise missiles in eastern England. The Soviet Union has stated that its likely military response to such installation would be to redeploy the 25 Mt (*megaton* – not kiloton) warheads of the now withdrawn SS–9 heavy ICBMs for pattern-bombardment (i.e. total obliteration) of cruise missile dispersal areas.

However, the Soviet Union has given an undertaking that it would not use nuclear weapons against states that do not produce or acquire such weapons and do not have them on their territory.[17] Some may argue that this is bluff, remembering that Hitler made – and broke – non-aggression pacts, but there are obvious reasons for thinking that, however distasteful the regime that gives such an undertaking in a nuclear world, it is not bluff. A country that has been subjected to nuclear attack is of little use to an aggressor; and fall-out does not respect national frontiers, it comes back home eventually. An aggressor therefore has a strong incentive *not* to launch a nuclear attack unless it is really necessary, and necessity relates directly and solely to fear on behalf of the attacker that unless he strikes first, he will himself be attacked.

'We must not forget that by creating the American atomic base in East Anglia, we have made ourselves the target and perhaps the bull's-eye of a Soviet attack.'

(Winston Churchill, commenting on the Attlee government's decision to give the US Air Force facilities in Britain, 15 February 1951)[18]

The ninth point also raises another aspect of the first step to survival: what the *Statement* calls the 'moral issue' of whether we should wish to accept US nuclear protection (and here the *Statement* implicitly censures Norway, Denmark, and Canada, our non-nuclear NATO allies) without bearing our share of the burden and risk. The arms race poses many moral problems, and this is surely one of the most trivial. We might equally invert the proposition and raise the question of the morality of President Reagan envisaging a limited nuclear exchange in which Europe was destroyed but the United States was spared. But neither question drives to the heart of the moral issues of nuclear arms. This is that the very possession of nuclear arms implies the intention, in certain circumstances, of obliterating millions of fellow human beings. Any government which trains men to fire such weapons is training them for mass murder. Surely these are more important moral issues?

Many distinguished senior officers have taken the same course as Admiral of the Fleet Earl Mountbatten both in expressing their deep disquiet about the present course of events and in some cases translating that disquiet, after retirement, into action. Several have already appeared in the pages of this book: Admirals La Rocque and Carroll from the United States, Field-Marshal Lord Carver in this country, Major-General Bastian in West Germany: and the testimony of the late General of the Army Omar Bradley who was, at the time of his death, the only five-star general in the US Army and thus its highest ranking officer, in the conclusion of this book. On 25 November 1981, six retired generals and a retired admiral from seven of the NATO states (West Germany, Norway, Portugal, Greece, the Netherlands, Italy, and France) presented an alternative to the official view on military strategy and political detente in a memorandum for the NATO winter session, an unprecedented move by such senior military men. It is already clear that they do not stand as isolated figures. Among the lower ranks of serving officers and men, their disquiet is shared.

The demands of nuclear war put any thinking soldier in an impossible situation. That is true even of the 'second strike' strategy. What does it mean? That an officer shall sit and watch his equipment, men, home, and family be destroyed, and then shall gather together whatever weapons are left and send them off to wreak a similar havoc upon as many unarmed and defenceless civilians as possible in the assailant's land? Such a policy, the Stockholm International Peace Research Institute observed in its 1981 *Yearbook*, the good officers will refuse to carry out and the bad and unprincipled ones will do badly.

In the Netherlands a Peace and Security Council has been established in the armed forces, and among serving officers there has been active discussion of a question raised at the outset of the nuclear age – raised then but not pursued: Are not nuclear weapons in contravention of the Geneva Conventions?[19] May not their use in any form constitute a war crime under the terms first defined in the Nuremberg International Military Tribunal of 1946, affirmed unanimously by the UN General Assembly in 1946, and finally reformulated in 1950 by the International Law Commission, which, among other things, established the responsibility of the individual soldier for his actions? Is a country able to require its soldiers to break such international codes for which it has voted in the UN and to which it is a signatory? What should a soldier do when, having joined the armed forces to defend his country, that country orders him to undertake actions which are, in his view, both grossly immoral and futile – likely to result in the destruction of his country, not in its defence? One Dutch air force captain has announced that he will not fly nuclear armed missions, and among the lower ranks there have been and continue to be many cases of soldiers in the Dutch army refusing to guard US nuclear arms depots. The Dutch Army Conscripts Union opposes the new generation of long-range theatre weapons and demands nuclear disarmament. More than five hundred soldiers marched in uniform in the ranks of one of the largest demonstrations in post-war European history, in Amsterdam on 21 November 1981. Such soldiers are usually punished by being confined to barracks. There are some who might consider such treatment lenient. On the other hand, is it right that soldiers should be expected to assist in preparations for nuclear action when the use of nuclear weapons clearly contravenes international law? The defence of one's country should be an honourable profession.

10. Next the *Statement* offers a historical judgement: that the absence of war in Europe since 1945 has been due to nuclear weapons. Whether or not deterrence has been instrumental in preventing war is open to question. There has certainly been a correlation between the accumulation of nuclear arms by the superpowers and the absence of overt conflict *between them*. But it is a simple mistake to confuse *correlation* with *cause*. There are other, more convincing, reasons to explain why there has been no war in Europe since 1945. Foremost is the silent and massive economic integration of Europe, on both sides of and across the 'Iron Curtain', the fruit of the years of post-war economic expansion. For those who would discount this view and cling to the 'deterrence' explanation another question must then be answered. What indigenous points of conflict persist in Europe that would burst into flames, the flashpoint for war, without nuclear deterrence? Northern Ireland? Basque nationalism? (The Berlin situation, of course, was not made in Europe; it is a superpower creation.) This is not to underrate the local tragedy of local conflicts such as those of various ethnic or religious minorities, it is simply to point out that they *are* local. The

absence of any large-scale *casus belli* combines with the positive argument from economic integration to discount the *Statement*'s historical judgement about European history.

If one looks globally, the judgement lacks any substance, for nuclear deterrence has certainly not been effective in preventing the 130 or so wars which have broken out in one part of the world or another in the last thirty years. Some at least of them have been precipitated or exacerbated by the continuing mistrust between the superpowers, which the arms race both feeds upon and engenders.

Furthermore, as we have argued earlier, technical advances threaten the current precarious stability of the confrontation between the superpowers in a very serious way: the diminishing flight time of super-accurate missiles like the German-based Pershing IIs may tempt a 'launch-on-warning' policy; for either side, believing the other to have launched missiles towards as yet unknown targets, might strive to send its own on their way before the incoming missiles land and destroy the silos. Similarly, the development of counterforce strategies and weapons carries the temptation to launch a pre-emptive strike. The very fact that each side perceives new technological advances by the other as destabilizing the present situation argues against the government's comfortable view that we have a system that works. And in any case its costs in absolute terms of lost alternatives are enormous.

11. We agree with the UK government that nuclear deterrence is not a desirable way of maintaining peace and that we must seek unremittingly to find a better way of ordering our affairs. Where we differ is on the urgency of the task. We contend that when the unrealism of the strategy, the fact that it has been in any case superseded in practice, and the full costs of the arms race are taken into account, finding another course becomes an immediate imperative.

But these policies are not only deficient in general, they are also flawed in the particulars of their execution, so we must take up briefly a few points about the specific courses of action they involve.

The first concerns the *numbers and nature of nuclear arms*. Although the need for nuclear forces 'strong' enough to deter an attacker is emphasized in the *Statement on the Defence Estimates*, the actual numbers of weapons deployed far exceed that, and are more in keeping with a policy of 'balance' (see Chapter 3). Even a policy of 'flexible response' does not demand parity at every level, but only a capacity to inflict unacceptable damage at each level. Mr Quinlan (of the British Ministry of Defence) has attempted to justify the numbers and nature of our weapons on the view that the deterrent effects of weapons and plans is closely linked to their capability for actual use, arguing that 'people who recoil from more accurate weapons and less widespread targeting plans are in fact proposing less credible deterrence and therefore more risk of war'.[20] But he misses the point, which we explained in Chapter 4, that such weapons are not necessary for deterrence: if deterrence were a proper aim, a far smaller and less expensive force would be adequate. To operate deterrence in the nuclear age, your weapons do not have to be as numerous as those of your enemy – you need only sufficient for a few of your missiles to survive a first strike. Building up weapons of great accuracy on the present scale is bound to suggest to the adversary an attempt to build up a first-strike capacity, and thus to promote escalation. Robert McNamara believes now that that was the effect of his programmes in the early 1960s and it is even more likely to be so today. We find the government's arguments that the numbers and characteristics of modern strategic weapons are a natural consequence of the policy of flexible response less convincing than the view, advanced in Chapter 5, that their characteristics arise from the nature of the Steel Triangle.

A second point attaches to the question of numbers. It is really fairly trivial, but it is one to which the British government's policy attaches great importance: it is the question of *Britain's 'independent deterrent'* – the Polaris or projected Trident submarine systems. We use inverted commas advisedly, because it is extremely doubtful whether any so-called independent deterrent would really be independent at all, since it requires technical and intelligence assistance from the USA. It normally uses American LORAN (long range navigation) satellite data and American communications; the missiles need constant maintenance and spares.[21] If the government really purchases Trident D5 missiles, independence will be a technical impossibility, since this system only works accurately through satellite guidance from US NAVSTAR satellites; and the radar terminal guidance of the warheads requires target map images – again only obtainable through American satellites. But more important is Russian perception. It is difficult to believe that the Soviet Union would invade Western Europe in the hope that the USA would not intervene; or that, if the Soviet Union did think seriously of doing so, it would be deterred by our submarines. And as Lord Carver, former Chief of the Defence Staff, has argued, any situation in which a sane British Prime Minister would initiate a strategic attack on the Soviet Union, thereby inviting untold devastation of the UK, is impossible to conceive. The argument for an independent deterrent thus seems to imply a mistrust of the USA, *misrepresented* as a possible misperception of the USA by the USSR: by firing British missiles, we would draw a reluctant USA into the holocaust. This is the only realistic meaning of the *Statement*'s argument for a 'second centre of decision-making', a view of quite stunning irresponsibility, implying not only this, but also, by suggesting that it is a better thing to have a British nuclear trigger-finger than not to have it, making it logically impossible for Britain to argue against proliferation of nuclear weapons. But, more probably, Britain's continued possession of nuclear weapons is something not consciously thought out at all, more a rather pathetic harking back to the days when the UK really was a world force translated into the woolly feeling that a 'top country' must have some at least of the most destructive weapons available. Exactly the same interpretation holds for General de Gaulle's *'force de frappe'*. Like Britain, France also first obtained and continues to possess nuclear weapons without any hard thinking or public decision.[22]

'A limited nuclear war, as conceived by the Americans in, say, Europe, would from the outset mean certain destruction of European civilization.'

(President Brezhnev)[23]

'Our fine great buildings, our homes will exist no more. The thousands of years it took to develop our civilization will have been in vain. ... there will be no help, there will be no hope.'

(Earl Mountbatten)

The third point concerns the effects on Europe of virtually all the scenarios envisaged. It is easy to be carried away by plans to eliminate this or that city, to respond to an attack here with a counter-blast there, and so on. The fact is that the use of even tactical nuclear weapons in Europe would lead to immense damage and enormous loss of life. Europe is so densely populated that any nuclear attack, even though aimed at military forces, would certainly also affect cities. A policy which embraces the possibility that nuclear conflict could be confined to Europe might seem to be in the interests of the USA (at least until the fall-out arrived), but is nothing but folly for Europeans.

The fourth issue follows from the third and concerns civil defence. It was recognized in the Defence White Paper of 1957 that civil defence would be virtually useless against nuclear attack, and the same is even more true now.[24] The devastation would affect inhabitants and rescue services alike: in any case radiation would make it impossible for rescue teams to enter the affected areas until it was too late.[25] Civil defence precautions serve only to make nuclear war appear survivable and thus acceptable.

Finally, although we have felt it necessary to point to these inherent inconsistencies in the government's policy, above all we wish to reject the whole way of thinking that it represents. This is symbolized by the prominence given to the chess-playing analogy in the Ministry's publicity. That the Ministry uses and obviously believes in the correctness of this analogy is disturbing. Games require the players to be bound by rules that are detached from, and irrelevant to, the real world. Games like chess formalize conflict and that conflict assumes intense aggression in the opponent. Perhaps for this reason, and also perhaps because of the prestigious intellectual reputation of chess, the Ministry strategists find it an appealing analogy for thinking about nuclear weapons and preventing war. They would presumably argue that such thinking is related to diplomacy – the most rule-bound and detached aspect of international relations – and hence that the chess analogy is apposite: that deterrence is the continuation of diplomacy by other means. And so it was, before the nuclear age, when it was possible to think of battleships as bishops and regiments as rooks, to be moved in complicated and fluid patterns of threat, deferring and then fighting wars. Some strategists believe that nuclear missiles are also pawns in this same game and therefore that if, for example, public resistance prevents NATO deploying the new generation of cruise and Pershing II missiles in Europe, then the European public will have weakened their generals' and diplomats' position in the great chess game by depriving them of pieces. It has been a major task so far in this book to argue in detail that to believe that pre-nuclear concepts of military strength and security apply in the nuclear age is a tragic and fundamental misunderstanding of that age's nature. Albert Einstein's observation, quoted already, bears repetition: 'With the nuclear age everything changes – except the way that men think.' More missiles mean less security and a greater chance of their being used.

Consequently, the application of chess-like rules to thinking about deterrence and the prospect of conflict in the nuclear age is not only misleading but also, through the imposition of blinkered vision which blocks out most of human nature and all of human history, it is positively dangerous. It is doubly dangerous because each side recognizes different rules. The Russian language has no direct equivalent for the English verb 'to deter', with its two meanings of 'inspiring fear' and 'holding back an aggressor'. For years, the Soviet Ministry of Defence dictionary had no entry at all for 'deterrence' and under 'nuclear deterrence' gave, not a translation, but an explanatory sentence. More recently the Soviet military have created a special word (*yadernoye* (nuclear) *sderzhivanie*) which represents the Western concept of nuclear deterrence and is used only for that purpose.[26] However, seduced by the games-playing analogy, assuming, against the evidence, that both sides play by the same rules, and unrestrained by concrete evidence, the Ministry has moved away from the only safe assumption about nuclear war, which is that the smallest use of nuclear weapons will initiate an irresistible escalation to catastrophe. That assumption is the modern extrapolation of Clausewitz's inflexible expectation of 'friction'.

But, it might be objected, we are guilty of a deceitful logic, for Clausewitz wrote of war, and deterrence is precisely about the prevention of war; therefore Clausewitz's notion does not apply and games theory does. If only that were true. But, as we have argued earlier in this chapter, 'pure' deterrence only *defers* war, and in any case in earlier chapters we showed how 'pure' deterrence was not the correct description of the present-day Western nuclear posture. Thus the particular danger arises from belief in that incorrect objection. The 'war games' mentality ignores or makes naïve assumptions about the world of real people and, because of its lack of realism, threatens to create a version of its 'war game' in that real world. What is left out of the Ministry's misapplied chess analogy is that reality can break into the complicated manoeuvring of chess pieces, especially if each player follows different rules; it can overturn the chessboard. Nuclear missiles are not pawns, they are nuclear missiles.

We saw the chessboard overturned in Chapter 2. As if in a nightmare, under the influence of Clausewitz's 'friction', the detailed chess-like plans for mobile war made by war ministries and generals before 1914 turned into the static carnage of the trenches. Their present-day successors appear to have learned absolutely nothing from that experience. And today's chess-like plans will not degrade into the mud and blood of Flanders but into something unimaginably worse.

7 The Soviet Threat

The basic assumption on which U K defence policy rests is the existence of a major Soviet threat to Britain's security. The government concedes that there appears to be no immediate Soviet intention to invade Western Europe. But it believes that Soviet military strength is greater than is necessary for defence alone, and that Soviet actions past and present indicate that this strength would be used if the Soviet government believed that by so doing it could gain an advantage. In the words of Mr Quinlan, the spokesman referred to on p. 184, the government 'does not, of course, assume a constant and implacable hostile desire to attack us; it simply judges, in the light perhaps of history, that we cannot prudently assume that we would never be attacked if attack on us were a soft option'.[1] In other words, it is best to assume the worst, so that we are prepared to meet an attack whenever and wherever it might come.

It must be said that this assumption is widely held in Britain. Most people know little about the Soviet Union and still less about its government's policies; none the less, many feel that it poses the chief external threat to their lives and well-being. Ideas about the specific forms hostile action by the USSR might take – military conquest, political subjugation, nuclear obliteration, and so on – vary. The general sense of danger, which is continuously and powerfully reinforced by the media, is so strong, however, that in the minds of many people the words 'Soviet' or 'Russian' are virtually synonymous with threat, expansion, or aggression. But what exactly is the nature of this threat? What is the evidence for it? Since the consequences of actions based on assumptions about its existence may be so serious, this question must be examined in some detail.

It is necessary at the outset to maintain a clear distinction between *fear of Soviet expansionism* and *dislike of the Soviet system*. There is certainly much that is undesirable about the latter. The restrictions on individual liberty, the treatment of political dissidents, the absence of a right to strike, the limitations on citizens' ability to travel abroad, censorship and controls on political discussion, official secrecy, and lack of public accountability – many such features are totally unacceptable to those with Western democratic values. They are excusable neither on the grounds that comparable conditions were endemic in the Russian system long before the 1917 Revolution, nor on the grounds that they occur in other countries, including some whose regimes are heavily supported by the USA – though such facts do add a salient perspective. Similarly, the inefficiency and bureaucracy of the Soviet system and the one-party political system would be quite alien in the West. But these issues are not to be confused with the presumption of Soviet expansionism. That there are ideological differences between the USSR and the West is beyond dispute. That such differences will continue for the present is equally clear. But the ideological debate will never be settled by force of arms.

Belief in a Soviet threat depends ultimately on our assessment of Soviet aims and intentions. There are basically three sorts of general aim with which Soviet leaders are credited by those who claim that their actions reveal hostile intentions.

(a) *The aim of world Communist domination.* As head of the world's first and most powerful Marxist state, the Soviet government is seen as having the prime objective of spreading Marxist theory and practice throughout the world and establishing Communist regimes in all countries. It heads, in this view, an international crusade or conspiracy designed to secure the destruction of capitalism and the victory of Communism everywhere. This view was illustrated from an American history book in Chapter 1.

(b) *The aim of Russian expansion.* This approach maintains that ideology is only a cloak for traditional objectives. The USSR is a thinly disguised version of the Russian Empire, and continues the latter's inexorable growth. Whether for reasons of security, political influence, or economic advantage, it is set on unlimited territorial expansion.

(c) *The aim of superpower hegemony.* While not seeking direct control over other areas of the globe, the USSR seeks an unlimited capacity to promote its own interests wherever it wishes.

There is no shortage of evidence which can be used in support of one or other of these interpretations. The most obvious is the official ideology to which the Soviet government subscribes. According to Marxism–Leninism, capitalism is historically doomed and its final twentieth-century form, imperialism, must eventually disappear. The victory of Communism throughout the world is regarded as inevitable. As Khrushchev once declared to the Americans, 'We shall bury you.' Then there is the fact that the Soviet Union has expanded territorially since 1917. Latvia, Lithuania, Estonia, western Ukraine, western Belorussia, and Bessarabia have all been added to the area originally ruled by the Soviet government. Furthermore, Soviet dominance over neighbouring countries in Eastern Europe, made possible by the Soviet army's victories in the Second World War, has extended the effective frontier of Soviet rule further westwards than the Tsars ever dreamed of. From Poland on the Baltic to Bulgaria on the Black Sea, the Soviet Union in effect controls all the countries across its western borders. To this must be added a whole list of countries where, though not by direct force of Soviet arms, Marxist–Leninist regimes have been established, from China, North Korea, and Vietnam in the Far East, to Angola and Mozambique in Africa, South Yemen and Ethiopia in the Middle East, and Cuba in the western hemisphere. Besides these, there exists a worldwide network of Communist parties, sharing the same Marxist–Leninist goals as the Soviet government and to a greater or lesser degree appearing to accept its leadership. More alarmingly for proponents of this theory, the Soviet Union has on a number of occasions used military force to achieve political ends beyond its own borders, most notably in Hungary (1956), Czechoslovakia (1968), and Afghanistan (1979 to the present). Finally, the Soviet Union has over the past two decades moved from a position of military inferiority compared with the United States to one of parity or even, some would say, superiority. This has been achieved by means of the rapid build-up of both its nuclear and conventional forces.

Many of our politicians and journalists believe that these are 'facts' which speak for themselves and confirm beyond dispute the correctness of Mr Quinlan's view, mentioned above. Yet they do not. The significance of these events has to be established by assessing the purposes and intentions which lie behind them; the judgement of relative military 'strength' depends on a critical reading of difficult sources. Not least because of the relative absence of open discussion and debate about Soviet policy in the USSR itself, this is no simple matter.

Take Soviet ideological pronouncements about the victory of Communism. Is this an aim which really influences Soviet actions, or merely a long-term prediction, an article of faith to which Soviet leaders formally subscribe? The length of time seen as necessary for the realization of this goal is very relevant to assessing, for example, the meaning of Khrushchev's remark. His words could amount to a chilling threat or an abstract generalization, depending on whether the time-span envisaged was a few years or a century. Judging by their behaviour as well as by their state-ments, since the early 1920s Soviet leaders have apparently believed that capitalism's collapse and the victory of the world revolution were far off. At various times, they have even acknowledged capitalism's real if 'temporary' recoveries. As a result, they have generally been reluctant to risk forfeiting the Soviet Union's achievements by embarking on an adventurist foreign policy. Better to concentrate on exploiting its vast but underdeveloped resources. This approach was behind Stalin's policy of 'socialism in one country', for which he was bitterly denounced by Trotsky – just as Khrushchev and Brezhnev have been denounced by Trotskyists, Maoists, and other 'revolutionary' Marxist–Leninists for insufficiently supporting revolutionary movements around the world. The corollary of this line was the policy of 'peaceful coexistence' between states with different social systems, first proclaimed by Lenin in the early 1920s, revived by Khrushchev after Stalin's death, and continued in the pro-detente diplomacy of Brezhnev. Now such pronouncements *may* be mere camouflage for aggressive designs as 'worst case' analysts would argue. But in the light of the historical record, an alternative interpretation deserves to be given at least as much attention as the more ostensibly threatening aspects of Soviet ideology.

If the evidence for a practical commitment to world revolution on the part of the Soviet leadership is not very strong, that for an attachment to nationalist values is greater. They are the most obvious motive behind the territorial expansion of the USSR since 1917: the areas subsequently incorporated in the Soviet Union were former provinces of the Russian empire lost during the First World War. This may or may not justify their re-acquisition, but it does indicate a significant limitation to Soviet ter-ritorial ambitions. It is perhaps worth noting as collateral support for this view that the USSR made no attempt to re-annex two major former parts of the Russian empire, Poland and Finland, when it could easily have done so in 1945. The maintenance of an East European buffer zone between the USSR and Western Europe certainly indicates that the Soviet Union gives its own defence needs priority over its neighbours' independence; a policy which is understandable, if not pardonable, given the catastrophic costs of invasion in two world wars. It is still, however, not evidence of expansion-ism, let alone of a Communist crusade. In any case, Soviet policy towards Eastern Europe is not indiscriminately aimed at control. Finland, though a defeated ally of Nazi Germany, was permitted virtually complete auton-omy. Austria, another former enemy, after ten years of occupation saw Soviet troops withdraw. And no attempt was made to reincorporate

Yugoslavia and Albania into the Soviet bloc after their defections in 1948 and 1961 respectively.

But the USSR did send troops into Hungary in 1956 and into Czechoslovakia in 1968 to maintain the *status quo*, against the wishes of the majority of their populations. In Hungary, the Nagy government which the Soviet troops suppressed had declared its intention of leaving the Warsaw Pact. In Czechoslovakia, Dubcek's government seemed to have lost control of the reform movement, which was pressing for fundamental changes in the country's economic and political institutions. Military intervention was a crude way of reversing these developments and preserving the stability of an area seen as vital to the Soviet Union's defence against the West. In the case of Czechoslovakia, it was probably not even the most effective way of achieving Soviet objectives. By contrast, a marked reluctance to become involved directly in crushing internal opposition to the Communist regime marked Soviet policy towards events in Poland in 1980 and 1981 – though pressure from the Soviet government may have been the main factor determining the Polish authorities' resort to military rule in December 1981 to combat the free trade union, Solidarity. The Soviet interventions of 1956 and 1968 were ruthless actions, with tragic consequences for many people. Unfortunately, they, like the probable indirect involvement in Poland, were not exceptional by the standards of modern international relations. Like American interventions to suppress radical and revolutionary movements in Latin America and south-east Asia, or to arm and support a military dictatorship in Turkey, they reflected a superpower's determination to use force if necessary in defence of its strategic interests within its own sphere of influence. In the Soviet case, its sphere of influence is very sharply defined and these different actions were not proof of an intention to act aggressively outside it.

However, Soviet intervention in Afghanistan in December 1979 has been interpreted by some Western politicians as providing precisely such proof. How independent Afghanistan was prior to Soviet intervention is a matter for debate. It was not part of the Soviet bloc in the sense that Bulgaria or Hungary are; it was not a member of the Warsaw Pact or Comecon. On the other hand, it had a pro-Soviet and Marxist government which had been brought to power three years earlier by a Communist-led revolution. Moreover there was no sign from the West that it considered Afghanistan as other than a dependent state bordering on the USSR. Intervention in aid of the Communist regime was presented by the Soviet government with some plausibility as a legitimate act of support for a neighbouring Marxist government. It was also probably seen as a means of guarding against the spread of Islamic unrest into predominantly Muslim areas of the USSR. What is dubious is whether it was undertaken with any major strategic purpose in mind. The House of Commons Foreign Affairs Committee, after taking evidence on the intervention for eleven days, concluded that 'the Committee heard no evidence that the invasion of Afghanistan was part of a Soviet grand strategy to extend its influence to the full and threaten Western oil supplies'.[2]

It is also relevant to note that the Soviet intervention in Afghanistan took place against a background of worsening East–West relations, closer American and West European military and industrial contacts with China, the Chinese incursion into Vietnam, the US Senate's failure to ratify the SALT II treaty after it had been signed by Carter and Brezhnev, and the NATO decision to deploy Pershing II and cruise missiles in Europe. It was less a cause than a consequence of the demise of detente.

Involvement in Afghanistan may not be aimed at bringing the USSR closer to Middle Eastern oil; but the fear is often expressed that there is a Soviet threat to the oil supplies vital to the economies of Western nations. Whether the USSR is perceived as entertaining such an objective for strategic reasons depends on a general assessment of Soviet policy towards the West. But might there, in fact, be an economic motive? In a world increasingly aware of the limited size of its energy reserves, might the Soviet Union at some future time be driven by economic necessity to use its great military power to gain control of oil-producing regions? A CIA forecast, published in 1977, predicted that Soviet oil production would peak in the 1980s and then decline to a point where the Soviet Union and Eastern Europe would have to become net importers of oil. It certainly reinforces such a fear. However, three points should be borne in mind.

First, it is a matter of considerable debate whether the Soviet Union is facing an impending energy crisis at all. The CIA forecasts have been hotly disputed by numerous Western economists, who argue that the Soviet bloc will not become an oil importer in the next decade.[3] In response to criticism, the CIA postponed the estimated date of Soviet oil shortfalls in its 1980 follow-up report. Second, pessimistic projections of future Soviet oil needs assume an unchanging pattern of energy use, which is at present more wasteful even than in the West; a failure to discover substantial new oil reserves or to utilize effectively other forms of energy (for example, the USSR has the largest proven gas reserves in the world – more in western Siberia alone than in the whole of North America); and an inability to develop or acquire the technology needed to exploit those resources.

Whether such assumptions are reasonable is open to some doubt. Third, even if the most pessimistic predictions were to prove accurate, the USSR would still face less of a problem with respect to energy supply than the USA, West Germany, France, or Japan. It is worth recalling that at present the USSR is the only major industrialized country in the world, other than the UK, to be self-sufficient in energy. Why should the Soviet response to a common problem, although on a considerably smaller scale, be so much more threatening to world peace than that of Western nations?

What of the indirect expansion of Soviet power through the establishment of Communist or at least pro-Soviet regimes and the activities of Communist parties outside Eastern Europe? Three points need mentioning here. First, some of the main examples of Communist revolutions occurred with little or no Soviet support (and sometimes even despite Soviet advice), as in China, Vietnam, and Cuba. Second, the relative extent of Soviet influences is not very impressive. Of 155 countries in the world, the USSR has significant influence in nineteen. Outside Eastern Europe, most are very poor countries in dire need of aid and of little military significance. Afghanistan, Angola, Cambodia, Congo, Laos, Mozambique, and South Yemen hardly make a major addition to the USSR's strategic capacity or economic strength. And the support of a handful of less destitute countries (such as Cuba, Ethiopia, Libya and Syria) is greatly outweighed by the fact that all the world's major military powers and advanced economies outside Eastern Europe are either allied to the USA or closely tied to it economically. Third, the USSR has been conspicuously unsuccessful in maintaining its influence. Soviet influence in the world is *less* now than it was two decades ago. In 1958, on one calculation, pro-Soviet countries accounted for 31 per cent of the world's population and 9 per cent of the world's GNP, excluding the Soviet Union. In 1979, the corresponding figures were 6 per cent of population and 6 per cent of GNP.[4] China's bitter hostility over the past two decades is the greatest single failure of Soviet foreign policy in the modern period; but it is not an isolated phenomenon, as the cases of Albania, Egypt, Indonesia, India, Iraq, and Somalia show. Similarly, disunity in the world Communist movement – expressed in many parties' opposition to the invasions of Czechoslovakia and Afghanistan, the treatment of Soviet dissidents, and even fundamental tenets of Marxist–Leninist doctrine such as the dictatorship of the proletariat – has reached the point where the Soviet Union has not been able to summon a world conference of Communist parties for a decade. The limitations of Soviet world influence were put succinctly by Rear-Admiral La Rocque in a recent interview.

It just baffles me how we have developed this paranoia about the Soviets. The Soviets are in six little relatively unimportant countries today. They're in Angola, Mozambique, Ethiopia, Cuba, Afghanistan, and South Yemen, none of which is important, and all of which cost the Soviet Union money and resources every day. Then, take a look at the Soviet Union over the last thirty years and look at the places they've been kicked out of. They've been kicked out of Indonesia, the sixth largest nation in the world, kicked out of China, kicked out of Egypt, and kicked out of Somalia, where they had their only naval base outside of the Soviet Union. I think our fear of the Soviets is based on lack of information and total absence of any factual data. If you look at the success of the Soviets as imperialists, they are flops. They are not strong around the world.[5]

However, it is certainly true that the USSR possesses a vast and rapidly improving armoury of weapons, which seems to many to be in excess of its defensive requirements. The UK government, like other Western governments, draws an unequivocal conclusion: 'There is an explicitly aggressive motive for the Soviet military build-up.'[6] But some scepticism is in order here. Previous estimates of the relative sizes of Western and Soviet forces by Western agencies have proved inaccurate. Some, like the question of numbers of tanks, were found to be based on faulty intelligence assumptions (equating tank sheds with operational vehicles). Some, like the 'missile gap' of the late 1950s, had the effect of massively augmenting American military expenditure. Continuously to the present, misleading comparisons are made by matching classes of weapons (tank versus tank) instead of offensive versus defensive system (tank versus anti-tank weapon). But in any case, it is not difficult to see why Soviet leaders might be prone to acquire a huge military capacity. A tendency to over-insure against surprise attack would not be strange for a nation which suffered as the USSR did as a result of German invasion in June 1941, or for leaders who occupied leading political or military posts during the war. A reliance on quantity of military hardware to compensate for a perceived and real inferiority in the quality of military technology compared with the West would also be likely. And finally, for a government with thousands of miles of vulnerable borders to defend, possession of huge and visible military force obviously acts as a deterrent to outside aggression and as reassurance to its own population. Furthermore, the West's military capacity may equally well be viewed from a Soviet perspective as going far beyond defensive needs, in which case Soviet military expenditure would depend on the West as much as ours does on theirs.

Following the Chinese strategist's advice to try to understand the adversary, it is instructive to try to visualize the threat from the West as seen in Moscow. 'Imagine yourself in our position,' Leonid Brezhnev recently declared to a Western correspondent. 'Could we indifferently regard how they were besieging us on all sides with military bases, how increasing numbers of carriers of nuclear death, irrespective of what form – missiles from the sea or land, air bombs, etc. – were targeted from various areas of Europe on Soviet cities and factories?'[7] Propagandistic rhetoric or a genuine perception of the USSR's position? The fact is that the Soviet Union and its allies confront a Western alliance with far greater economic power, with superior technology, and with a greater and more varied deployment of military force around the world. On many of its borders it faces hostile countries allied or sympathetic to the West. In recent years it has seen the West move steadily closer to an alliance with the People's Republic of China, a major power with a huge population and with nuclear weapons of its own, bitterly opposed to Soviet Communism and Soviet influence in the Far East. In the USA, economically twice its strength, it faces the leading world power of the last four decades, a country which for all its attachment to democratic ideals and humane values, is the only one in the world to have used the atomic bomb against an enemy, which has frequently intervened openly and by subversion to maintain the *status quo* in what it regarded as its sphere of influence, from Iran in the 1950s, to Lebanon, Vietnam, Dominica, Greece, Chile, and El Salvador. So overall the USSR is in competition with a capitalist system which, for all its signs of decay and degeneration, has in the past had gigantic achievements and still displays enormous reserves of strength, dynamism, and creativity; and which, furthermore, according to its own declared theory, simply has to expand in order to survive. Finally, among the leaders of the major Western nations are politicians such as President Reagan and the British Prime Minister, Mrs Thatcher, who are implacable in their hostility to the Soviet Union, firm in their belief that it will eventually disintegrate, and resolute in their determination to use force, if other means fail, to prevent the spread of its influence.

Given all this, does the assumption of aggressive Soviet intentions make sense? Is an expansionist policy in the interests of the USSR? Is it likely that the Soviet Union seeks conflict with an opponent which is in so many respects stronger, or that it wishes to maintain a level of military expenditure which it is less able than the West to bear? How likely is it that it would want to add to the countries it controls (some of which, such as Poland and Romania, are difficult enough to keep in line), others whose populations would be still more likely to resist Soviet domination? Would it be prepared to go to war to acquire new economic resources when so much of its own great natural wealth still remains to be exploited?

Now one consequence of what Admiral La Rocque described as 'this paranoia about the Soviets' is the reflex reaction that if one returns negative answers to the rhetorical questions just listed (as we believe a reflective consideration of the best evidence suggests that we should), then, automatically, one is adopting the equally unreal position that the Soviet Union is in no way responsible for international tension, entirely innocent in its foreign policy, and – by a short extension – entirely praiseworthy and admirable in all respects. Such a reaction must be recognized for what it is and, once understood, put aside.

The alternative is not to assume that the Soviet Union has no interests which conflict with those of Western countries, or that its leaders are motivated purely by altruistic considerations. On the contrary, it is a superpower which aspires to a global role, which like all great powers desires influence and seeks to change the *status quo* in the furtherance of its interests. Inevitably these interests do and will clash with those of other countries. Soviet advocacy of detente has emphasized the desirability of a relaxation of international tension, a lessening of the danger of conflict; but Soviet leaders have never portrayed detente as entailing the end of competition and struggle between different states and different social systems. However, this is a long way from the belief that war, especially nuclear war, is an acceptable or even possible means of pursuing national interests.

This assessment of Soviet aims and intentions suggests that the 'Soviet threat', in the sense of expansion and aggression against Western countries, has far less substance than our policy-makers assert. But there are general threats, including a Soviet threat, as well as American, British, Chinese, and other threats, which arise out of the strategic realities of contemporary international relations. For the inhabitants of this country, the USSR does constitute a danger. It possesses a massive array of weapons. Many nuclear missiles are targeted on our cities. To the populations of some other West European countries – and particularly to the West Germans, much closer to the Warsaw Pact's armoured divisions, occupying the main probable battleground of any future European war, and sharply aware of the precarious position of West Berlin – the Soviet Union inevitably looks more menacing still. There is no reason, moreover, to assume that Soviet politicians and generals are any more immune from irrational and self-destructive urges than those of any other nation. There are certainly hawks as well as doves in the Soviet Politburo just as there are pressures on political leaders from the military establishment and defence industry, although the Communist Party's tight control over all Soviet institutions would appear to prevent the formation of a Western style of military–industrial complex in the USSR. While the Soviet leadership may display a united face to the world, there must be important divisions of interest within it, as in all large-scale bureaucratic regimes. It would be excessively optimistic to expect it to be consistently guided in its policies and actions by totally rational considerations. There is a Soviet threat, and its existence dictates a proper caution in relations with the USSR. But this kind of threat is not inevitably permanent; it is not something which justifies the present politics of nuclear terror. This is a threat which it is in the power of policy-makers in the East and West to diminish and to remove.

8 The Case against a Nuclear Defence Policy

I: Accidents, Proliferation, and the Threat to the Constitution

The nuclear question has been set historically within the confrontation of the superpowers, and in most public consideration so it remains today. For this reason we have addressed it first in that context. Yet the issues involved are far broader than this. In this chapter and the next we shall explore several consequences of the manufacture, possession, and deployment of nuclear weapons, as well as the risk of their explosion by accident, both in peacetime and in a premeditated war between the USA and the Soviet Union.

1 The Danger that Possession will Lead to Use

The governments of both superpowers claim that they are accumulating weapons in order that weapons should not be used. We have already seen that, whether or not this was once the case, the very nature and quantity of the stockpiled arms seem to contradict it. Vast research efforts and resources have been directed towards producing weapons capable of striking the other before he can strike back, and of striking him so hard that he is unable to strike back. To this end President Reagan has announced plans to spend $222 billion in the period 1981–6, to increase the American nuclear stockpile by about 65 per cent (26,000 to 43,000 weapons) by purchasing highly accurate nuclear systems of the sort needed to create a 'war-fighting' capability.

> 'We set out to ... achieve improved capabilities to enhance deterrence and US capabilities to prevail should deterrence fail.'
>
> (Secretary of Defense Caspar Weinberger, 13 November 1981)[1]
>
> 'I think we need to have a counterforce capability. Over and above that, I think we need to have a war-fighting capability.'
>
> (Deputy Secretary of Defense Frank Carlucci, 13 January 1981)

It is easy enough to shrug one's shoulders and be reassured by the thought that no one would be sufficiently unbalanced to unleash such unprecedented devastation on a major portion of the globe, but as General of the Army, Omar Bradley, observed in a speech reproduced at greater length in the Conclusion, 'To those who would take comfort in the likelihood of an atomic peace to be secured solely by rationale and reason, I would recall the lapse of reason in the bunker under the Reich Chancellery in Berlin. It failed before, it can fail again.' Just because the idea of nuclear war is so horrifying, we tend to turn our backs on it and regard the possibility as more remote than it actually is. So long as such weapons exist, they may be used. However improbable nuclear war may *seem* to be, the consequences would be so horrendous that even a slight possibility is of great significance.

A nuclear conflict could start without conscious intent. It might be precipitated by misinformation of an impending attack. In such a situation time would be crucial. Communications would probably be ineffective. Fear would be at its maximum. The balance would be weighed heavily against the making of rational decisions. It has been noticed that skills needed to make decisions are impaired in crises. Under stress, people tend to see situations as black and white, never distinguishing greys. They display deterioration of verbal performance, increased rate of error, diminished tolerance for ambiguity, loss of abstract ability:[a] the temptation to press the button might be extreme.[3]

It is becoming increasingly possible that a war could start as the result of a malfunction of part of the complex warning systems now in use. During recent years the United States North American Aerospace Defense Command (NORAD) has several times alerted American forces around the world that a nuclear attack was in progress. Twice, on 3 June and 6 June 1980, this was because of the failure of a minor part in a computer and on another occasion (9 November 1979) because an operator ran a computer program designed for practice without disconnecting the alert system. Bombers carrying nuclear weapons were prepared for take-off. Alerts caused by system failures occur regularly according to a spokesman for NORAD. Following the June 1980 incidents, extensive actions were undertaken to alter procedures and to improve the computers of the 427 M missile attack warning system. Of course one assumes that the most rigid precautions are taken.[4]

The incident on 3 June 1980 began when the computers showed that the USA was under attack from submarine-launched missiles flying trajectories that would hit the USA with about half the warning time of ICBMs launched from the Soviet Union. Journalists' sources subsequently reported panic and confusion during the emergency as officers broke preordained procedures (the Hart–Goldwater report confirmed this by raising questions about 'an air of confusion'). Fortunately the incident was ended within the hypothetical flight-time of the non-existent missiles. The USA assumes that its command and communication system would be a prime target in a real attack and presumably the Soviet High Command makes the same judgement. So what would be the situation if, for either side, the warning time was reduced from about 30 minutes for ICBMs or 18 minutes for SLBMs to only 5 or 10 minutes – insufficient time to decide whether the information was erroneous or real, insufficient time to use the 'hot line' to the other side but sufficient time to order the launch of weapons *presumed* to be threatened? If stationed in West Germany, the new Pershing II ballistic missiles, the most accurate missiles yet built, will be able to reach the USSR in 4 to 8 minutes. Faced with the prospect of Soviet missiles in Cuba, the USA declared that it would not tolerate such a threat. Would it be surprising if the Soviet leadership took the same attitude towards a much more potent yet comparable threat today? What is to be gained from such dangerous and destabilizing provocation?

Apart from nuclear war developing out of general hostilities or out of misunderstandings between NATO and the Warsaw Pact, war in Europe might also come for reasons that had nothing to do with Europe – except that this is the part of the world where a full-scale nuclear battlefield is laid out, waiting to be activated. War might be *reflexive*. For example, it is known that during periodic crises in the Middle East, American forces in Europe, including nuclear-capable forces, have been put on the alert. This happened during the Iranian hostage crisis also. At present the Reagan administration is pursuing a belligerent policy and so deeply are all military forces now interwoven with nuclear weapons that the spark from any such flashpoint could ignite the powder keg.

It must always be remembered that there are about 3,500 artillery-fired atomic projectiles (AFAPs) of two calibres (155 mm: 2,500; 8 inch: 1,000) in Europe, with a NATO programme in hand to phase out non-nuclear-capable artillery guns in favour of the 155 mm and 8 inch calibre weapons and with new atomic shells of both calibres in production or in development; the Joint Chiefs of Staff were correct to observe that the Warsaw Pact is faced with 'possible nuclear capability in every artillery position across the entire front' and, as was shown in Chapter 6, a clear intention to use that capability.[5]

It has never been clear that physical locks placed on these weapons (or in the case of shells, upon their carrying containers) would actually prevent use if all the relevant field staff were determined to do so. In addition, there is no firm information on the chain of nuclear command on either side. In the West, officially, the President of the USA is alone empowered to authorize the use of nuclear weapons; but we know that a study in 1959–60 of American command and control procedures in the Pacific revealed that President Eisenhower had written letters delegating authority which in practice went via the commander of the Seventh Fleet down to the rank of major. The researcher Dr Daniel Ellsberg, who was then a Pentagon analyst, had the authority of the Commander-in-Chief (Pacific) to discover such information. He found that it was well known within the armed forces, but was contrary to public pronouncements. The danger, as Ellsberg saw it, was less from a crazed soldier, more from highly disciplined officers, trained to use their initiative in the absence of orders from above and, knowing of the chain of delegated authority, believing it to be their patriotic duty to use the nuclear weapons under their command if they believed that this would have been the President's wish, had it been communicated. It is known that Presidents Kennedy and Johnson renewed the delegation procedures. It is believed that they still exist today. This was confirmed unequivocally in the case of submarine commanders during the 1981 CBS television series 'The Defense of the United States'. We know nothing of Soviet procedures and can only hope that they are more centralized; certainly nuclear weapons are less dispersed in peacetime military formations than is the case in NATO. But even that is cold comfort. We must assume that the risks described by Ellsberg are in reality at least twice that size.[6]

2 Accidents

Quite apart from the use of nuclear weapons in war, so long as they are in existence there is an ever-present possibility of a nuclear explosion or of extensive radioactive contamination. Accidents involving nuclear weapons have been frequent: usually they are hushed up, and the information that gets out to the general public is very limited. But in 1980 the Pentagon admitted to thirty-two 'broken arrows' – the euphemism for the most serious class of accidents involving nuclear weapons. This is certainly an underestimate of the total: the Stockholm International Peace Research Institute estimated thirty-three major accidents involving US nuclear weapons before 1968, and a total of about 125 major and minor nuclear accidents between 1945 and 1976 – one accident every two and a half months. In addition there have been British, French, and Soviet accidents for which data are not so readily available, but SIPRI has estimated a minimum of twelve before 1968.[7]

At least two of these accidents were in Britain. On 27 July 1956, a B–47 bomber crashed into a store containing three Mark 6 nuclear bombs at Lakenheath, Suffolk. The fuel caught fire, but fortunately the TNT of the trigger mechanisms did not ignite. Each bomb had about 8,000 lb of TNT within it. 'It is possible that a part of eastern England would have become a desert,' said a now retired Air Force general who was in the UK at the time.[8]

On 2 November 1981, a Poseidon missile being winched between a nuclear submarine and the submarine tender USS *Holland* in the Holy Loch, Scotland, slipped and fell fourteen to seventeen feet. Eye-witnesses have reported that it struck the tender as klaxons sounded alert state 'alpha' and as crewmen dived for cover. The US Navy spokesman was correct that a nuclear explosion could not have occurred. But tests at the Lawrence Livermore Laboratory on the chemical explosive charge LX–09 (used to trigger the primary in most of the Poseidon MIRV W–68 warheads) have shown it to be among the most sensitive of plastic-bonded explosives; the laboratory found that LX–09 exhibited 'low-threshold velocity for reaction and rapid build-up to violent reaction', i.e. it can explode with full force if dropped from as little as fifteen inches. It was an explosion of LX–09 that killed two men at the Pantex warhead assembly facility at Amarillo, Texas, on 30 March 1977. Had detonation occurred in the Holy Loch the likelihood is that all ten warheads would have been involved and that their radioactive materials would have been released into the environment. For most of 2 November the wind was light to moderate, at times gusting to 30 mph, and from the south and west, later backing to the north-east; it became stronger and returned to the south and west on 3 November. This means that debris would have been blown across Kilcreggan, Helensburgh, Loch Lomond, and, ironically, the British naval facility at Faslane, and/or across Sandbank and Dunoon. November 2nd was a day of drizzle and rain around the Holy Loch, which means that debris thrown up by an explosion would have probably been brought back to the ground swiftly.[9]

At least two nuclear weapons accidents have involved widespread contamination of the environment. On 17 January 1966 a B–52 carrying four nuclear weapons believed to be in the 20–25 Mt range was involved in a mid-air collision with a KC–135 tanker while refuelling from it. Both aircraft crashed near Palomares, Spain. The conventional detonating devices of two of the bombs exploded, scattering plutonium across the landscape: approximately 1,400 tons of radioactive soil and vegetation had to be removed. A third bomb fell into the Mediterranean and was recovered from a depth of 2,500 feet only after an extensive operation. Another B–52 which was, like the Palomares plane, on airborne alert with weapons on board, crashed on 21 January 1968 on the sea-ice of North Star bay near Thule, Greenland, while flying in an area in which Denmark had prohibited nuclear weapons. The four bombs were destroyed by fire, and intensive contamination of the environment occurred. Some 237,000 cubic feet of contaminated material were removed. A few days after the crash Secretary of Defense McNamara ordered the removal of nuclear weapons from planes on airborne alert, and shortly after the practice was suspended altogether.[10]

Perhaps the nearest that we have yet been to accidental thermonuclear explosion was on 24 January 1961 when a B–52 on airborne alert over Goldsboro, North Carolina, suffered structural wing failure and broke up. It was carrying two 24 Mt bombs – a combined equivalent of 3,700 Hiroshimas. (All the bombs dropped on Japan and Germany during the Second World War totalled 2.2 Mt.) One of the bombs free-fell to earth and broke up. The other parachuted down, and upon recovery, it was discovered that five of the six safety devices had failed. Official spokesmen have declared that the bomb was not armed – that the 'capsule' was not inserted. But this assurance lacks conviction both because it was not given until long after the accident had become a source of public concern and because commentators with 'inside' knowledge have denied it. This occurred four days after J. F. Kennedy became President.[11] It is worth repeating that, while it is not *likely* that a nuclear bomb will explode, the possibility is there. This possibility is of something infinitely awful happening – not only the accident itself, but the possibility that the accidental explosion would be mistaken for a nuclear attack, with consequent nuclear retaliation. Such a possibility cannot be tolerated.

Yet another possibility is that nuclear weapons will fall into the hands of a terrorist group. As weapons proliferate and as warheads become smaller, this becomes an ever more real danger. Fear of hijacking was one of the prominent reasons in the minds of politicians and strategic planners when they decided against mobile basing for the Minuteman ICBMs. An earlier generation of US army mobile missiles was withdrawn from Europe when it was discovered that security was lax. Furthermore, it is not difficult to find out how to make crude but usable atomic weapons, and although the plutonium or enriched uranium required is usually manufactured in special plants (see Chapter 9), where in theory strict controls are exercised, it would be possible to acquire the materials necessary to make nuclear weapons. Equally, spreading unexploded radioactive materials would be horribly lethal. These possibilities were examined by an Australian government commission, which found them to be serious: 'The risks are presently real and will tend to increase with the further spread of nuclear technology', it concluded. In Britain the Flowers Commission reached similar conclusions (see box).

RISKS OF THE PLUTONIUM ECONOMY[12]

'Another aspect of the problem is the possible effect of such threats [of nuclear terrorism] on society. The security measures that might become necessary to protect society could seriously affect personal liberties. The need for such measures would be affected by increasing tensions between nations. Indeed, the future risks posed by plutonium constitute a world problem that would not be solved by unilateral action by the UK, though the action we take in response to our assessment of these risks could have a substantial impact on world opinion. We emphasize again that our concern here is not with the position at present, or even in the next decade, but with what it might become within the next fifty years. In speculating on developments on such a time scale no one has a prerogative of vision. It appears to us, however, that the dangers of the creation of plutonium in large quantities in conditions of world unrest are genuine and serious.

'For this reason we think it remarkable that none of the official documents we have seen during our study convey any unease on this score. The management and safeguarding of plutonium are regarded as just another problem arising from nuclear development, and as one which can certainly be solved given suitable control arrangements. Nowhere is there any suggestion of apprehension about the possible long-term dangers to the fabric and freedom of our society. Our consideration of these matters, however, has led us to the view that we should not rely for energy supply on a process that produces such a hazardous substance as plutonium unless there is no reasonable alternative.'

(This reasoning led the Commission to view any move towards fast breeders with misgiving and to favour the longest possible delay.)

Pure plutonium is relatively easy to handle, if it is covered with a light shield and not exposed to air: it becomes dangerous only if allowed to oxidize in air, when it forms a fine dust which is readily inhaled. The accuracy of inventories is insufficient to detect small but cumulatively significant thefts, and any accounting system is susceptible to dishonest operators.[13] Numerous cases of inadequacy amongst those responsible for handling nuclear materials, and actual cases of theft, have in fact been reported.[14] Indeed it is suggested that Israel, in the course of several independent and successful operations in the USA and Western Europe, acquired the materials for a small arsenal of nuclear weapons.[15] And the inventory controls are far from being perfectly efficient: for instance in 1978 the Nuclear Regulatory Commission admitted that over a ton of plutonium and four tons of other radioactive materials were unaccounted for.[16] The strikingly sanguine view of such possibilities taken by the British nuclear establishment was both noted and criticized by the Royal Commission on Environmental Pollution.

Maintenance of existing stockpiles of weapons, especially of thermo-nuclear weapons, requires constant traffic between bases, storage areas, and refurbishing laboratories, and operation of nuclear power stations also requires continual movement of ores, fuels, and wastes. In Britain, journalists have recently revealed aspects of this constant traffic and, to make a point of the vulnerability of such deadly cargoes, on one occasion critics carried a replica bazooka on to a railway station platform and pointed it at a cask of radioactive materials sitting at a siding, entirely unchallenged, although observed by British Rail staff. In the United States, concerned citizens have identified the main facilities involved in the nuclear cycle and have pointed out the similar dangers of attack or accident involved in very long haul truck journeys and in air transport of nuclear materials. In the USA, the Energy Research and Development Agency (ERDA) (now called the Department of Energy) transports fissile material in 'Safe Secure Trailers': armour-plated lorries in constant radio communication with the headquarters at Kirtland Air Force Base, Albuquerque, each accompanied by unmarked escort vehicles carrying armed paramilitary guards.[17] In Britain, the Atomic Energy Authority's constabulary, which accompanies fissile shipments, is unlike any other civilian police force in the country, and routinely carries automatic weapons also. But despite all precautions, the more widely dispersed nuclear weapons are, the greater the possibility that one of them, one day, will fall into the hands of men who will use it for their own ends.

3 Proliferation

The major powers continue to build up their nuclear stockpiles, and their spokesmen and apologists continue to use the bizarre question, 'Well, would the USA have attacked Japan had she had nuclear weapons?' as what they see as a glowingly self-evident justification of possession of nuclear arms. They apparently cannot see how this particular argument – quite apart from its irrelevance to the real understanding of the atomic bombings and its historical illegitimacy – both supports the Soviet view that America is the nuclear power that, on past behaviour, most needs to be restrained, and also cuts the legs from under their exhortations that other countries should forgo nuclear weapons, that proliferation is a bad thing. Five countries admit to possessing nuclear weapons – the USA, UK, USSR, France, and China. India conducted a test explosion, but then pledged herself to use nuclear technology only for peaceful purposes. Israel and South Africa have almost certainly acquired nuclear weapons. A number of other countries now have, or nearly have, the ability to make nuclear weapons: Argentina, Brazil, Egypt, Mexico, South Korea, Pakistan, and Spain, and perhaps some of the Eastern European countries. Although many countries have declared their unwillingness to harbour nuclear weapons (see below), there are others who are eager to acquire them – if not for 'defence', then for the prestige brought by membership of the nuclear club.

Attempts have been made to prevent this lateral spread of nuclear weapons. In 1970 the Non-Proliferation Treaty was signed by many nations. However, its effectiveness is limited by four major groups of factors. First, France, China, and a number of other countries with nuclear technology, and many major developing countries, did not sign. Second, the major powers that did sign (USA, USSR, and UK) have not honoured the undertakings they then gave to proceed with disarmament, and have thereby brought the treaty into disrepute elsewhere. Third, the acquisition of nuclear weapons would be regarded by many Third World countries as symbolic of a gradual redressing of the balance between rich and poor nations: the treaty merely stabilizes the existing balance of power in the international system. Fourth, the Treaty stipulates that the safeguards which it advocates should not hamper the flow of nuclear expertise or of nuclear materials designed to serve peaceful ends. As we shall see later (Chapter 9), the materials and technology required for the 'peaceful' use of nuclear power are closely similar to those required for the manufacture of nuclear weapons; once a country can produce nuclear power the capacity to produce nuclear weapons may be only a short step further along the road.[18]

This danger has been recognized since the early days of the atomic era.[19] Nevertheless, over the years countries with nuclear know-how have seen powerful rewards in encouraging the spread of nuclear power. Quite apart from the financial incentive, itself important in helping to offset the development costs involved in designing and building nuclear power stations, nuclear technology has been used by the USA as a pawn in the competition with the USSR for influence and prestige in many parts of the world. Largely under the 'Atoms for Peace' policy, the USA gave, or provided at cut rates, twenty-six research reactors to countries which included Indonesia, Thailand, South Vietnam, and Zaïre.[20]

Such transfers of nuclear expertise, equipment, or materials have usually been accompanied by agreements designed to ensure that they will be used only for peaceful purposes. Furthermore, the International Atomic Energy Agency not only attempts to promote cooperation in the peaceful use of atomic energy but also has responsibility for ensuring that nuclear technology is used only for peaceful purposes. But it would be relatively easy to divert nuclear materials even from closely guarded facilities, and the IAEA might well not even be able to detect their disappearance. As noted earlier in the chapter, considerable quantities of plutonium and highly enriched uranium have been 'lost' by the US Atomic Energy Agency and its successors, and by comparable organizations in other countries.[21] The perfection of laser separation of Pu 239 and Pu 240 makes any reactor waste potential weapons-grade material; and the laser technology will be very hard to control if steps are not taken now.

As a result of the spread of nuclear power technology, around forty countries are likely to have enough separated or separable plutonium to make at least a few bombs by 1985. And since the time required to convert plutonium fuels into materials for bombs may be only a matter of weeks, the detection of the disappearance of nuclear materials by the IAEA is not likely to be of much use. Indeed some of the fuels used – for instance for reactors on nuclear-powered ships and in experiments on fast-breeder reactors – consist of highly enriched uranium or weapons-grade plutonium. It has even been argued that the IAEA has unwittingly exacerbated the situation by making it easier for exporters of nuclear technology to pretend that their practices were safe and to shed responsibility for safeguards on to the IAEA.[22]

The issue of peaceful versus military uses of nuclear energy was brought to public attention by the Israeli raid on the Iraqi nuclear reactor in June

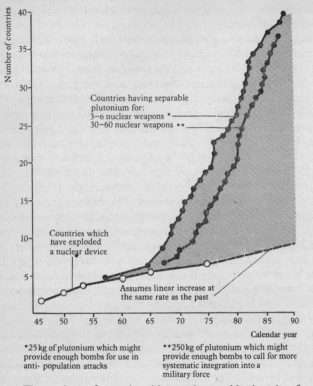

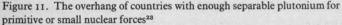

*25 kg of plutonium which might provide enough bombs for use in anti-population attacks

**250 kg of plutonium which might provide enough bombs to call for more systematic integration into a military force

Figure 11. The overhang of countries with enough separable plutonium for primitive or small nuclear forces[23]

1981. Although a signatory of the Non-Proliferation Treaty, and without breaking any of the international rules, Iraq carefully built up a nuclear capability over a number of years. She obtained a reactor first from the USSR, and later concluded a deal with France (a non-signatory of the NPT) by which she received a large research centre with two reactors and fuel in return for assurances on oil supplies and an arms contract. Later Iraq made comparable agreements for other parts of the nuclear cycle with Italy, Brazil, and Portugal, and attempted another with Canada. The French offered the Iraqis a specially formulated reactor fuel called 'caramel' from which it is not easily possible to extract weapons-grade plutonium. This offer was refused. The Iraqis insisted upon ordinary fuel. While there is no evidence that Iraq had already made a bomb or was on the point of doing so, there is overwhelming evidence, both declaratory in the speeches of the leadership and technical in the nature of the nuclear technology purchased, that she intended from the outset to pursue weapons research, and that she had acquired the capability of doing so.

The impotence of the International Atomic Energy Agency and the ease with which the Non-Proliferation Treaty can be ignored are best illustrated in the case of Argentina's nuclear programme, which, like that of Iraq, is hard to see as other than a weapons' procurement programme, despite the protestations of all involved.

At the end of the Second World War, as is well known, many prominent Nazis fled to Argentina from the ruins of the Third Reich. Among them was Hitler's explosives expert, Walter Schnurr. For ten years he worked for Argentina's dictator Perón, establishing an explosives industry, but in 1955 was invited to return to Germany by Franz-Josef Strauss, who was then Germany's Minister for Nuclear Issues, to open a nuclear research facility at Karlsruhe. There the first project was to build a test reactor, the MZFR, which was based upon the natural uranium/heavy water moderated design that had been pursued during the war but failed to give Hitler an atomic bomb. An inefficient producer of electricity, this design optimizes the creation of weapons-grade plutonium in its spent fuel. Even before the MZFR was tested, work began to build another like it at Atucha in Argentina.

However, spent fuel must be reprocessed to extract the Pu 239, and in a second German–Argentine deal of 1968 – secret until 1981 – Germany provided 'hot cells' in which fuel rods can be remotely handled. These were erected at Ezeiza. Under the same deal, Argentine uranium was sent to Karlsruhe and there irradiated in the MZFR, then returned to Ezeiza where together Argentine and German technicians could learn how to extract plutonium. None of this was reported to the IAEA or to Euratom, the EEC nuclear agency. The hot cells operated from 1968 to 1972 and in that time enough plutonium could have been extracted to make nuclear weapons. Walter Schnurr now lives in retirement in Argentina where he made public details of these deals in an interview with two British journalists in 1981.

The same journalists were also able to confirm by filming it that a full-scale reprocessing plant is under construction at Ezeiza. Argentina has no plans for a fast breeder reactor; it is well provided with its own oil and has large reserves of uranium which would be a cheaper way of generating electricity, if that was indeed the aim.[24]

Various means of slowing down proliferation have been suggested.

These include delaying work on fast breeder reactors and greater exploitation of conventional thermal reactors, adaptations of the fuel cycle to reduce proliferation possibilities (for example by 'doctoring' fuel), the outlawing of certain types of research which could facilitate proliferation, and especially the internationalization of those parts of the nuclear fuel cycle – reprocessing above all – which could be used to produce fissile materials for weapons. None of these are yet effective, and it is doubtful if any could be fully effective. Subterfuge would still be possible. The Fox Commission concluded that 'the nuclear power industry is unintentionally contributing to an increased risk of nuclear war. This is the most serious hazard associated with the industry.'[25]

4 The Erosion of Parliamentary Democracy

The report by the Royal Commission on Environmental Pollution mentioned above was unusual among official discussions of nuclear technology in pointing to the damaging effects which nuclear projects can have upon our democratic constitution. A nuclear defence policy is a different but related subject, and in formulating a case against the possession of nuclear weapons it is not surprising that we tend to concentrate first on the practical or tangible consequences of such possession. But it is also important that due regard be paid to less readily quantifiable consequences, particularly the effects on parliamentary democracy and basic civil liberties. The intense secrecy associated with nuclear arms policy has undermined the accountability of successive British governments to both Parliament and the electorate. In addition, in stifling opposition to nuclear defence policy, governments have resorted to a number of dubious practices which strike at fundamental rights and liberties. It is not suggested that the erosion of parliamentary democracy and the denial of basic civil rights can be traced exclusively to a nuclear defence policy, but the existence of such a policy is an important catalyst for many recent departures from our democratic constitution.

It is not denied for a moment that the position in this regard is far worse in the USSR. But that is not an argument for inaction. In fact, on the contrary, awareness of this contrast should make us more jealous to protect our democratic principles and to exercise the privilege of action which they give us for the general good.

The development and implementation of a nuclear defence policy has derogated from parliamentary democracy in a number of significant ways.

One of the most serious consequences has been the relentless diminution of Parliament's power to control executive decisions on nuclear defence. Two related factors have operated to produce this situation: official secrecy and the concentration of decision-making power in the hands of a few individuals.

Secrecy characterizes most aspects of British government, but it has reached obsessional proportions at the Cabinet level of decision-making. Cabinet secrecy is often regarded as an essential aspect of the doctrine of collective ministerial responsibility which requires collective assent for Cabinet decisions once they have been taken. Secrecy is defended because it is supposed to encourage full and candid discussion within Cabinet before formal decisions are taken. It is also argued that the actual processes of Cabinet decision-making must be kept secret in order to preserve the appearance of Cabinet unity. Although membership of the Cabinet is a public matter, the existence, membership, and function of Cabinet committees are not officially announced.

A number of political and legal sanctions operate to preserve Cabinet secrecy. A serving Cabinet minister is required to take an oath of secrecy and he would probably be stripped of his office if it were shown that he divulged details of Cabinet discussions. If a former Cabinet minister should threaten to publish information relating to national security, external relations, or other confidential matters without obtaining the Cabinet Secretary's consent,[26] an injunction might be obtained to prevent publication if the confidentiality of the information could be established to a court's satisfaction.[27] Cabinet documents are protected by the Official Secrets Act and enjoy in principle an immunity from disclosure in legal proceedings. Cabinet papers are also protected from disclosure by the Public Records Acts of 1958 and 1967 which provide that government documents will generally only be made available for public inspection after thirty years. In fact, the Lord Chancellor has a discretion to extend even that basic thirty-year period and this power has been used repeatedly to withhold from public scrutiny in the Public Record Office documents relating to nuclear defence policy. One important example is the minutes of the meeting of the select group of ministers who took the decision to manufacture a British atomic bomb in 1947.[28] Another is that the Ministry of Defence refused to make available a paper by its chief scientific adviser, Sir Henry Tizard, who argued before the Chiefs of Staff Committee in 1949 that Britain should abandon its attempt to become an independent nuclear power. The Reagan administration has also put pressure on the British government to withhold papers prepared in March and April 1950 on the first British atomic bomb.[29] A further example – a matter of considerable contemporary interest – is of files relating to the agreements and conditions governing the use of British military facilities by American nuclear forces in 1951.[30]

The doctrine of collective ministerial responsibility and its corollary, Cabinet secrecy, operate to suppress information which might otherwise be made available to Parliament and to the public. Of course, the veil of secrecy which shrouds Cabinet discussions and documents is not restricted to nuclear defence policy but extends to the whole range of Cabinet decision-making. But there are sound reasons for being especially suspicious of the pervasive nature of Cabinet secrecy in the context of nuclear defence policy. In the first place, there has apparently not been any frank and detailed discussion on nuclear defence policy within the confines of the Cabinet room simply because the most critical decisions have been taken, not by the full Cabinet, but by the Prime Minister and a few select Cabinet members. Decisions which have had a major impact on the national budget and on the lives of all citizens have been taken by a few individuals without discussion by all members of the Cabinet and without any preliminary discussion in Parliament or in the country as a whole. Churchill excluded most members of his Cabinet from discussion about atomic weapons during the Second World War and this practice has continued ever since. The Attlee government, which launched Britain's independent atomic research programme, did so without any Parliamentary debate. The decision to make a British bomb was taken by a Cabinet sub-committee called 'GEN 163' to disguise its real purpose. The decision to modernize the warheads of the missiles carried by Polaris submarines, a decision which was to cost £1,000 million, was taken by Mr Callaghan and three members of his Labour Cabinet. The expenditure of £1,000 million was not mentioned in the defence estimates,[31] and the decision was simply presented in Parliament as a *fait accompli*. In a similar manner, the decision to acquire the Trident submarine system at a cost in excess of £5,000 million, as well as the decision to base cruise missiles in Britain, were taken by Mrs Thatcher and a few of her Conservative colleagues. It is alarming that such important decisions should be taken without informed discussion in the whole Cabinet, let alone in Parliament itself.

The absence of any detailed discussion in the full Cabinet preceding critical policy decisions on nuclear weapons would not be quite so serious if Parliament acted as an effective check on executive decision-making in this area. But government accountability to Parliament for nuclear defence policy is far more apparent than real. Not only are parliamentarians denied an opportunity to participate in the process leading up to the taking of important decisions, but intense secrecy also ensures that they are deprived of basic information which might provide a foundation for challenging government policy. By controlling the flow of information, the government itself determines to what extent it will be answerable to Parliament and ultimately to the public. Parliamentary questions have not proved a fruitful source of information. Embarrassing questions can be avoided altogether by raising the convenient umbrella of national security. Although ministers do occasionally respond more positively to parliamentary questions on aspects of national defence policy, the information contained in their answers is often inconsistent with earlier government statements. In a period of two months, three parliamentary questions on the number of US military bases in the United Kingdom elicited three very different answers (12, 53 and 56 bases, *Hansard*, 18 June 1980, col. 587; 7 July 1980, col. 54; 8 August 1980, col. 481), and even then the accuracy of the final figure was hotly disputed by an independent source which claimed that there were over 100 bases. The 1981 edition of the US *Defense Almanac* gives a figure of 18 (13 Air Force, 4 Navy, and 1 Army). The fuller and more authoritative *Inventory of Military Real Estate Property* gives a total of 52 main sites (excluding housing annexes, waste dumps, etc.): 38 Air Force, 10 Navy, and 4 Army.[32]

There is also some evidence to suggest that governments have manipulated their monopoly on information to influence public opinion in their favour. It is now recognized that the supposed bomber gap of the 1950s and the supposed missile gap of the early 1960s – perhaps based originally on this misinformation – were deliberately exploited by the American government to justify arms expenditure. As an example of such distortions in more recent years, it can be seen how the relative numbers of missiles of East and West were manipulated in the period leading up to the NATO decision to deploy cruise missiles in Europe. The case was made by allowing people to believe that there was a massive build-up of Soviet SS–20 missiles to which NATO had no reply, an assertion which has been demolished in earlier chapters. See also Appendix A2.[33]

Another quite separate effect of nuclear defence policy on Britain's constitutional system of government relates to the threat to national sovereignty of locating US-controlled nuclear missiles on British territory. It is ironic that at a time when there is much public concern about the loss of national sovereignty consequent upon membership of the EEC, little attention has been paid to the important constitutional implications of allowing an independent sovereign state, answerable to another electorate, to operate nuclear weapons from British soil. The actual terms and conditions upon which US military bases operate in this country are closely guarded secrets. Vague suggestions that the British government would be 'consulted' in the event of cruise missiles being used provide scant comfort for Britons facing the prospect of a retaliatory nuclear attack if America decided to launch her British-based missiles against another foreign power. It is scarcely more comfort to have a British 'finger on the trigger' under a 'dual key' arrangement, such as was the case when American Thor medium-range ballistic missiles were stationed here in the early 1960s (the result – incineration – would be the same), although such an arrangement would appear to satisfy Lord Kennet in a pamphlet which in practice advocates slight tinkering with the present situation.[34] In any case, one should not be overawed by 'dual key' or other 'safeguards'. Regardless of how many or how complicated are the codes compared, eventually pulses running round microchips have to come out into the open and operate a relay between two real wires in an arming circuit, i.e. a switch; and there is a risk that these procedures could surreptitiously be circumvented.

5   Effects on Civil Liberties

It is not only the constitutional processes of government which are affected by a nuclear defence policy. Civil liberties may also be threatened in a number of significant ways. Of course, any measure designed to protect national security will invariably conflict to a greater or lesser degree with the rights and freedoms of individual citizens. The central question is fundamentally one of balance or degree and opinions are bound to differ upon what that policy ought to be and how it best can be obtained. It is surely important, however, that we consider whether the pressures of a nuclear defence policy tilt the balance so heavily in favour of national security that such a policy becomes unacceptable in a society which purports to abide by democratic principles and respect the rule of law.

Any defence policy involves some degree of secrecy. This is normally felt to be justified because the cost of this surrender of fundamental civil rights is considered to be outweighed by the benefit of the defence thus obtained. But it is not at all clear that 'defence' is obtained by the manufacture and deployment of nuclear weapons. Since such weapons threaten the population to be defended with the possibility of indiscriminate destruction, authorities who propose the deployment of nuclear weapons cannot reasonably expect to have extended to them the privilege of secrecy by their potential victims.

(A) FREEDOM OF EXPRESSION

It was noted in the Introduction that a Ministry of Defence official, Mr Michael Legge, had encouraged members of the academic community to participate in the debate on nuclear defence policy in order to ensure that 'the debate is conducted on an informed basis'. There is no doubting Mr Legge's sincerity but the overwhelming evidence indicates that the government does not share his concern that the debate should be supplied with clear information. We have already seen in the previous section that Parliament has been effectively excluded from much of the debate and those few members of the Cabinet who have been involved in critical decisions on nuclear defence policy are gagged by the doctrine of collective ministerial responsibility. We also saw how a number of important documents on nuclear defence policy have not been released in accordance with public-records legislation even though the normal thirty-year period has elapsed. The government also has at its disposal a number of other devices for ensuring that information relevant to the debate does not become publicly available.

(i) Official Secrets Acts

The Official Secrets Acts are an important weapon in suppressing the flow of information. Enacted originally in 1889, this legislation was strengthened in 1911, 1920, and 1939. These Acts go far beyond any desire to protect the interests of the state against espionage and spying. Their cumulative effect is to create 'a formidable obstacle to the free communication of information regarding governmental activity and the free expression of opinion therein'.[35] The notorious section 2 of the 1911 Act makes it an offence (punishable by three months' imprisonment and/or a fine of £1,000 on summary conviction) for a civil servant to communicate without authorization any official information which he has obtained in his capacity as a civil servant.[36] It is not necessary that that information relate to national security or that it be of a secret nature or confidential. Indeed, it has even been said that section 2 'makes it a crime, without any possibility of a defence, to report the number of cups of tea consumed per week in a government department'.[37] It is also an offence under section 2 for anyone (not just a civil servant) to receive information knowing that the communication contravenes the Act.

The 1911 Act has the dubious distinction of having passed through all of the stages in the House of Commons within an hour of being introduced. At one time, a member was physically restrained in his seat by other members to prevent him commenting on the measure. The speed with which it was passed is reflected in its vague, nebulous wording. It has been estimated that section 2 actually creates no less than 2,000 differently worded offences relating to the misuse of official information.

It is hardly surprising that section 2 has been trenchantly criticized and there have been frequent calls for its reform. One judge demanded that section 2 be 'pensioned off', and it was stated in a major official report that the 'present law contained in section 2 is notable for its extreme width and for the considerable uncertainty attaching to its interpretation and enforcement. It does not carry public confidence. We propose its replacement by provisions reduced in scope and less uncertain in operation.'[38] That view was expressed nine years ago, yet despite promises from both the last Labour government and the current Conservative government to change section 2, the law remains unchanged today. In fact, there have been several successful section 2 prosecutions in recent years, including the controversial ABC trial in 1978 when the three defendants, Aubrey, Berry, and Campbell, were convicted of offences under section 2 relating to the communication of information about British Signals Intelligence.[39] The ABC trial raised a whole host of issues, including the scope of the Official Secrets Act, the role of the Special Branch, contempt of court, contempt of Parliament, and jury vetting. Of particular interest is the reply given by a Ministry of Defence witness who was accused during the trial of being 'obsessed with secrecy'. He said: 'I am not obsessed with secrecy. Because of my knowledge of the subject I am better aware than many people of the critical need to ensure that some secrets which are more secret than others are kept as secret as possible.'

Since the last war there have been only about forty prosecutions under section 2, even though there must have been countless technical contraventions during that period. One suspects that the factor that will ultimately impel reform of section 2 will be the government's concern to have an even more effective sanction against leaks rather than any concern to remove an unacceptable restriction on freedom of expression. Indeed, the last Labour Home Secretary, Mr Merlyn Rees, made his motives quite plain when he spoke of the need to replace the 'blunderbuss' of section 2 with an 'armalite rifle'. But in the last analysis, the draconian effect of section 2 on freedom of expression cannot be measured in terms of the number of prosecutions brought. It is surely the mere threat of a prosecution which makes section 2 such a powerful weapon in the hands of a government intent upon preserving official secrecy at all costs, not least in relation to nuclear defence policy.

Section 1 of the Official Secrets Act 1911 has also proved a useful instrument in protecting the government's nuclear defence policy from public opposition. This section makes it a felony punishable by up to fourteen years' imprisonment for any person for any purpose prejudicial to the safety or interests of the state to approach or enter any military or naval installation or prohibited place. Section 1 was originally intended to apply only to spying activities but it has subsequently been given a wider interpretation. The House of Lords ruled in 1962 in *DPP* v *Chandler* that five members of the Committee of 100 who planned to enter Wethersfield airfield and prevent American aircraft from taking off by sitting in front of them, were guilty of conspiring to commit a breach of section 1. The defendants were not allowed to give evidence that their purpose was not prejudicial to the safety or interests of the state but was a peaceable protest against nuclear weapons. The House of Lords held that the question of whether it was prejudicial to the interests of the state to possess nuclear weapons was a political question, intrinsically unsuited to resolution in a court of law. Professor Street has rightly condemned this approach as one which upholds the dangerous doctrine that whatever is Crown policy is necessarily in the interests of the state.[40]

(ii) D Notices

The obsession of successive British governments with secrecy is manifest in other ways which operate to stifle information. There is a non-statutory procedure by which newspaper editors are warned not to publish certain material which, in the government's opinion, would be contrary to the public interest. These so-called D Notices are primarily related to defence and they clearly touch on many aspects of nuclear defence policy. D Notices have been issued on such matters as nuclear weapons and equipment, national defence, war precautions and civil defence, and the British Intelligence Service.[41]

A D Notice was issued in 1963 to prevent the press reproducing a pamphlet entitled *Spies for Peace*, which had been distributed among nuclear disarmament supporters. The pamphlet gave details of the location of regional seats of government in the event of a nuclear war. Mr Patrick Gordon Walker asked in the House, 'Is not the purpose of a D Notice to stop enemies of the country from discovering facts? Has not everybody who wants to have the document already got it? Is not the purpose of this D Notice, therefore, to stop the

British public from knowing it, and is not that an abuse of the D Notice?'
The Prime Minister was content to congratulate the press for complying
with the Notice.

It is not an offence in itself to defy a D Notice, but the government has
made it quite clear that defiance could result in a prosecution under the
Official Secrets Acts. The D Notice system is a form of indirect press
censorship and its attractiveness to the government is self-evident. Since
the D Notice system is entirely non-statutory, there is limited opportunity
for challenging the legality of a Notice in a court of law and parliamentary
control is also severely restricted. The government enjoys an absolute and
unreviewable discretion to determine the scope and the meaning of
individual D Notices. The ultimate sanction of a prosecution under the
Official Secrets Act serves as a constant reminder that any editor who
disagrees with the government's view does so at his peril.

(iii) Freedom of information

Considering the lengths to which successive British governments have
gone to create a wall of secrecy around government decision-making, it is
hardly surprising that attempts by individual parliamentarians to introduce a statutory right of access to official information in the spirit of
freedom-of-information legislation in the United States have been firmly
resisted. Although it has been official Labour party policy since 1974 to
support the notion of a positive right of access to official information, it fell
to an individual parliamentarian to introduce a Private Member's Bill on
freedom of information during the last Labour government (Clement
Freud's Official Information Bill 1978). The Bill foundered when it failed
to gain government support. Likewise, a recent attempt to pass another
Private Member's Bill on the same subject (Frank Hooley's Freedom of
Information Bill 1980) met a similar fate when the Conservative government withheld its support. Government objections that freedom-of-
information legislation would undermine ministerial responsibility carry
little weight when it is considered that other countries which have a
Westminster model of government – such as Canada and Australia – have
recently enacted freedom-of-information legislation. The attitude of successive British governments to open government is perhaps best illustrated
by the fact that a recent report on open government by a group of senior
Whitehall officials was itself kept secret when the government refused to
publish it.[42]

Seen in the context of nuclear defence policy, secrecy has attained
paranoic proportions. Take, for instance, the 1956 bomber crash in

Suffolk described earlier in this chapter. On the face of it there was no need for the matter to be hushed up in the manner it was. In fact it was not until 5 November 1979 that a report on the crash appeared in the *Omaha World Herald*. This report was denied by US military sources and the British Defence Ministry would only comment that 'the crash was contained by the emergency services without hazard to the civilian population'. This sort of secrecy can scarcely be justified solely in the interests of national security. Such secrecy appears to be directed more against the citizens of this country than against foreign powers. There is little doubt that had the facts of incidents such as the Suffolk bomber crash been widely known, the Campaign for Nuclear Disarmament in the 1960s would have been greatly strengthened.

(iv) Vetting and surveillance

Obsessional government secrecy is only one aspect of a nuclear defence policy. Such a policy also threatens individual rights and freedoms in more direct ways. Some of the major areas of concern were identified by the Royal Commission on Environmental Pollution in its *Report on Nuclear Power and the Environment* in 1976.[43] Although the Royal Commission was concerned with nuclear energy policy rather than nuclear defence policy, the effects of both on civil liberties are similar. The Royal Commission recognized, first, that such policies have a significant effect on the rights of people who are directly involved with nuclear projects. Not only are such individuals subjected to intense screening and vetting, but the Royal Commission also conceded that they 'may subsequently be subjected to unusual surveillance'. The problem of security risks in the civil service is dealt with by the so-called 'purge procedure' which has been described by Professor Street as a travesty of English justice. He emphasizes that it may afford 'the maximum protection to state security and leave the citizen stripped of any rights which might, even remotely, militate against security'.[44] In brief, if a civil servant is suspected of being a security risk, he may have his case referred to three advisers, none of whom is a lawyer. He is not given any of the particulars which might disclose the sources of the evidence against him; he is not allowed to be represented; he is not entitled to cross-examine witnesses; and there is no right of appeal to a court of law. While some measures are necessary to protect national security, the important question is whether purge procedures such as these are compatible with our fundamental democratic institutions.

A second issue for concern regarding the effect on civil liberties of a nuclear policy is the secret surveillance of members of the public who are not necessarily directly involved with any nuclear project but may be opposed to nuclear policy. The Royal Commission recognized that secret surveillance of members of the public was inevitable. It was stated that 'activities might include the use of informers, infiltrators, wire-tapping, checking on bank accounts, and the opening of mail'. Some of these 'activities' require closer examination.

The security services in the UK have long been largely beyond effective parliamentary control. They have powers of surveillance and capacity for storing information on individuals which go far beyond the immediate needs of security and pose a serious threat to individual liberties, including the right to protest against nuclear weapons. A particularly controversial issue is telephone-tapping.

Telephone-tapping in Britain by the security services and the police is not regulated by an Act of Parliament but, like press D Notices, by yet another *non-statutory* code of practice. This dates back to 1957 and is operated by the Home Secretary. Official figures indicate that during 1979 alone the Home Secretary authorized the issue of more than 400 warrants to intercept both postal and telephonic communications.[45] The legality of telephone-tapping was challenged in a recent case (*Malone* v *Metropolitan Police Commissioner* [1979] 2 All ER 620) and although the judge, Sir Robert Megarry, held that the procedure was not illegal in British law because there was no law expressly prohibiting it, he suggested that the system was so open to abuse that there was an urgent need for legislation. Indeed, he expressed the view that the code of practice which currently governs telephone-tapping was insufficient to comply with Britain's obligations under the European Convention on Human Rights. In fact, Malone has now taken his case before the European Commission, arguing that Britain is in breach of its obligations. The need for statutory regulation of the use of surveillance devices by the police was also recently emphasized by the Royal Commission on Criminal Procedure.[46] In spite of all these developments, the government has steadfastly refused to introduce legislation regulating telephone-tapping and an attempt to introduce legislative controls and safeguards in the British Telecommunication Bill 1981 was met with firm government opposition. In an endeavour to placate public disquiet about telephone-tapping, the government requested the Chairman of the Security Commission, Lord Diplock, to investigate the operation of existing procedures. But public dissatisfaction has not been soothed by his finding that existing controls on telephone-tapping are satisfactory. Lord Diplock's report was based on a number of random checks but no indication was given of either the number or the nature of those checks.

Moreover, the report does not deal with the question of unauthorized telephone-tapping conducted by official and unofficial agencies outside the operation of the Home Secretary's warrant procedure. Nor, indeed, does the report deal with the many other devices, apart from telephone-taps, which are used in electronic surveillance of members of the public. The use of such bugs is not controlled in the 1957 code of practice or by any other guidelines.

The possibility of abuse of telephone-tapping is self-evident. British Telecom has the capacity to make 1,000 interceptions at any one time.[47] In addition, telphone-tapping would appear to be the primary function of the American National Security Agency facility at Menwith Hill, near Harrogate. The station has the capacity to monitor 20,000 transatlantic circuits and also has a 32,000-line capacity in the GPO network which allows undersea cables as well as domestic circuits to be monitored. It has been estimated that the station has the overall capacity to monitor a quarter of a million British telephones.[48] The station has been occupied by US forces since 1955. No rental is paid and, presumably, its presence has been sanctioned by successive British governments.[49]

Basic civil liberties are clearly at risk when the police are able surreptitiously to store and use information relating to private individuals who have not committed any criminal offence. There is evidence to suggest that the police are collecting personal information on individuals who exercise the democratic right to protest against nuclear defence policy, and also that information held by the state for other purposes, for example in computers used by the Department of Health and Social Security and the Vehicle and Drivers' Licence computer of the Department of the Environment at Swansea, may 'wander'. It was alleged in a recent 'Panorama' programme, for instance, that the police took down details of registration numbers of vehicles parked near a CND rally. It has been common practice for many years for the police and security forces to photograph demonstrators at CND marches and rallies. In 1957, Hertfordshire police requested press photographers to release prints of pictures taken at meetings protesting against the Suez invasion and the development of nuclear weapons. It was reported that the police had not taken their own photographs because they were all preoccupied with noting the car numbers of those attending the meeting.[50] The police have advanced some remarkable excuses in justifying their practice of photographing demonstrators. Photographs of a CND poster parade in Middlesbrough were taken ostensibly as a 'record of traffic problems', while photographs of the Aldermaston marches were allegedly taken 'for social purposes'.

The Data Protection Committee (the Lindop Committee) reported in 1978 that the total list of information the government held on individuals was 'formidable'.[51] The DHSS alone holds some forty-eight million records, primarily for laudable purposes. But there is always a potential for abuse. A major issue is the use of computers by the police. The Police National Computer and the Thames Valley Police computer are officially said to contain information concerning 'crime, criminals, and their associates'. But the Chairman of the Thames Valley Police Authority recently divulged that the details of 142,000 people were stored in his local computer, including information on 22,000 people who had no criminal record.[52] In spite of recommendations by the Lindop Committee in 1978, the government has failed to introduce legislation controlling the storage of computerized information. The government has been content, yet again, merely to rely on non-statutory guidelines issued to chief police officers. Individuals are not entitled to know whether there is any personal information on them stored on police or security service computers, let alone challenge the accuracy of any information so held. It has also been recently demonstrated that information in a computer can easily be 'burgled'.[53]

(B) FREEDOM OF ASSEMBLY

It is generally held that it is an essential element of a free and democratic society that individuals should be able to assemble peacefully to express their views on political issues. In actual fact there is no legally enforceable right to demonstrate in Britain as there is in the United States. The law relating to freedom of assembly is dominated by the broad discretionary powers vested in the police and other public officials. The police have at their disposal a wide range of public order offences which can be used against demonstrators, including unlawful assembly, riot, rout, affray, obstructing a police officer in the execution of his duty, offensive conduct conducive to a breach of the peace, obstructing the highway, and so on. In many situations the police enjoy virtually unfettered discretion in deciding whether to arrest a particular dissident and on what charges. Chief police officers also possess an important statutory power under section 3 of the Public Order Act of 1936 to ban processions or marches. Wide discretionary power is present at upper levels of decision-making affecting the right to protest. Some local authorities have enacted by-laws prohibiting marches and processions without prior consent or requiring written notice of intended processions. The Attorney-General and the DPP have wide discretions in relation to prosecution policy. Finally, magistrates enjoy broad discretions in granting and withholding legal aid, in deciding whether to grant bail to an arrested person, and in deciding whether to require a defendant to enter into a binding-over order.

The liberty to protest is by no means a fixed commodity: it fluctuates according to the manner in which the police and other officials exercise their discretionary powers. The opportunities for abuse are considerable and abuse is more likely to occur when greater pressure is applied to official authorities in the form of public protest.[54] Many of these discretions have been used to stifle or punish opposition to nuclear defence policy. Some notable examples include the exercise of public order powers against the Committee of 100 during the 1960s. The government refused the Committee's request to use Trafalgar Square for an anti-nuclear rally in the summer of 1960. Five days before the rally was due, Bertrand Russell and thirty-two other prominent figures on the Committee were imprisoned for periods of up to two months for refusing to be bound over. Their outraged supporters scheduled a protest march for Sunday, 17 September, but these plans were foiled when the police promptly banned all marches in central London, and closed off several streets. There was a public outcry at what appeared to be a policy of active suppression.

Other examples of abuse of public-order powers in relation to opposition to nuclear defence policy are readily available. In Liverpool, Bootle docks is an area frequently used for public meetings. The police usually attend such gatherings to ensure the free passage of traffic. A prominent anti-nuclear protester was arrested and convicted of obstructing the highway after addressing an orderly lunchtime meeting at Bootle docks.[55] Her complaint that no other speakers had ever been prosecuted was to no avail. More recently, a Cambridge resident was arrested for threatening behaviour likely to lead to a breach of the peace when he put a poster in central Cambridge advertising a meeting on nuclear disarmament.[56]

It has also recently emerged that some public order powers which are exercised with other groups primarily in mind can have an indirect yet very significant impact on the individual freedom to protest against nuclear defence policy. This problem has arisen in consequence of a change in police policy in the face of planned marches by bodies such as the National Front. Rather than provide a police escort for such marches, the growing tendency has been for the police to ban all political marches under section 3(2) of the Public Order Act 1936. This change in policy is illustrated by the fact that the number of bans imposed in March 1981 alone almost equalled the total number of bans (nine) imposed in the twenty-nine years between 1951 and 1980. The issue for concern is that these bans are expressed in such broad language that they catch marches and demonstrations on nuclear defence policy. In April 1981, for instance, the National Front announced that they would march in Ealing. The Home Secretary approved a ban imposed by the Metropolitan Police Commissioner on public marches in the whole London Metropolitan Police District (an area of 786 square miles) for twenty-eight days. The CND, which had planned a march to Hyde Park during that period, challenged the ban, arguing that it was too wide. The Court of Appeal held that there was no evidence that the Metropolitan Police Commissioner had abused his statutory discretion and the ban was upheld.[57]

The case underlines the need to amend the Public Order Act to enable bans to be imposed in narrower terms.[58] It is unacceptable that individuals should be prevented from peacefully demonstrating against nuclear weapons merely because the Metropolitan Police Commissioner reasonably apprehends that some other march will incite a breach of the peace. The Public Order Act should reflect the fundamental constitutional principle that no person proposing to act lawfully should be prevented from doing so by the threats of others to act unlawfully.

A nuclear defence policy poses a clear and present threat to our democratic constitution and the rule of law. As the stakes are raised, as weapons become more powerful, more sophisticated, and consume more and more of the nation's resources, feelings for and against the process also run higher. Those who are attempting to promote the process must observe by all means available, survey, and, if necessary, stifle the opposition. Secrecy becomes not the occasional resort but the constant ally of government. In attempting to suppress opposition to its policy the government is driven to use powers which strike at the basic tenets of a democratic society. The cost in terms of the erosion of parliamentary democracy and the loss of fundamental civil liberties is too great a price to pay.

9 The Case against a Nuclear Defence Policy

II: Nuclear Projects and the Environment

Conventional arms, if not deliberately exploded, are relatively harmless. True, there are occasional explosions in munitions factories or arms dumps, but they are rare events, and in such an accident a death toll of one hundred would be considered extremely severe. In the ordinary course of events, the manufacture and stockpiling of the weapons of the pre-nuclear age caused little damage. With nuclear arms, the case is quite different. Not only might an accident (which need not involve nuclear detonation) kill *at any time*, but nuclear weapons are causing illness and death *now*: pollution inevitably arises at every stage of the nuclear cycle which creates weapons: from the mining of uranium to plutonium production, which involves not only initial processing of reactor fuel, but regular reprocessing of the material from warheads to remove unwanted fission products – and the long-term disposal of the various unwanted radioactive wastes during these processes. And this is not a temporary issue. The eventual disposal of the bombs made in the last thirty years poses problems which will remain to trouble generations well into the future, to which there is no foreseeable solution. Here is one of the most urgent reasons of all why the nuclear arms race must be halted and why alternative ways of ordering our affairs must be found.

The issues here concern the production of both nuclear power and nuclear bombs. The information necessary to specify the relative responsibility of each is not fully available (although some figures are given below), but the two processes are closely interwoven. We shall consider first some issues that apply to both, postponing discussion of the relations between them to the end of the chapter.

1 The Nuclear Process

The fuel in most nuclear reactors is uranium enriched in its rare isotope. In the production of nuclear electricity, fuel is converted into radioactive waste products. These include plutonium, an element which scarcely exists in nature, but one isotope of which – Pu 239 – forms the principal element in nuclear bombs. A useful account of the processes involved in various types of nuclear reactor is to be found in Walter Patterson's book, *Nuclear Power*.

Reactors form only one stage in a long sequence of processes starting with the mining of uranium ore and culminating in the (as yet unsolved) problem of the disposal of the radioactive waste. In the ores uranium occurs as two isotopes, one very rare (uranium 235), the other common (uranium 238). The ore must be mined and milled, and the oxide may be converted to a fluoride. For most types of reactor the proportion of uranium 235 must be enriched to a figure of around 2–4 per cent. (By contrast, military enrichment may be to a level of 99 per cent.) The enriched uranium is then fabricated into fuel rods for the reactors.

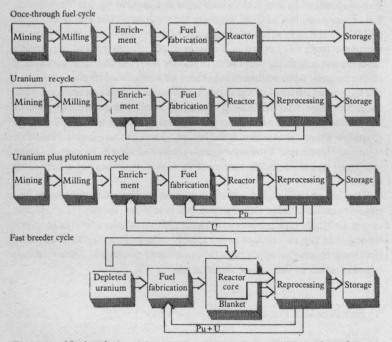

Figure 12. Nuclear fuel cycles: once-through, uranium recycle, uranium plus plutonium recycle and in a fast breeder reactor

In the reactor the uranium atoms, under neutron bombardment, are broken into two, much energy and further neutrons being released in the process. The neutrons produce further atomic fission and thus a continuing chain reaction. The energy is used to raise steam and thus to generate

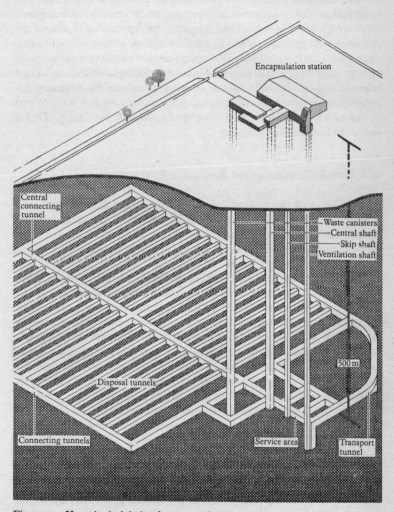

Figure 13. Hypothetical design for a spent fuel repository

electricity. As with any form of electricity generation, about two-thirds of the primary energy is degraded and lost as waste heat and the rest is transmitted as current.

As the nuclear fuel is burned, radioactive waste products accumulate in the fuel rods. Every year or two they must be removed and replaced. The spent fuel rods are highly radioactive and must be stored in cooling ponds for several months at least. They may then be reprocessed to extract the plutonium. At present, most civil reactors operate on the 'once-through' cycle. (See Figure 12.) If the fuel rods are not to be reprocessed they must be kept in cooling ponds for much longer – perhaps for decades. Their ultimate disposal is still a matter of uncertainty. An underground repository, constructed in stable geological formations, such as is illustrated in Figure 13, is considered by many to be the best possibility. This is discussed further in Section 4.[1]

2   A First Indication of the Radiation Problem

At each stage in the production of nuclear energy there are potential dangers to the workers and to people living near the factories, and further possibilities of radioactive contamination that would affect an even wider area – though as we shall see, the precise extent of the dangers currently involved is a matter of dispute.

The milling plants produce waste, or 'tailings', of which, by 1975, there were 100 million tons in the western USA. Radioactivity in the tailings can leach into the ground water. Direct gamma exposure arises if the tailings are used for land-fill upon which to construct houses. In one famous case in the USA at Grand Junction, Colorado, 5,000 houses were built on radioactive foundations, but mostly tailings are now piled in deserted areas. Hardest to control are atmospheric releases of radon gas, decay daughter of radium 226 (half-life 1,620 years), grand-daughter of thorium 230 (77,000 years) – all α-emitters. The carcinogenic potential of radon was regarded as very serious by the American National Academy of Sciences BEIR III Report. The Australian Fox Report stated that tailings pose a long-term threat to future generations. Stabilization of tips and a thick earth covering are first steps. Back-filling old ore-mines and chemical treatment are more permanent solutions; but the cost and size of the job will be vast, and buried tailings always risk leaching by ground water.[2]

Similar issues attend every stage of the nuclear fuel cycle. Before the dangers were fully realized, there were casualties amongst the miners, amongst workers in the enrichment and fabrication plants and in the reactors, and amongst the populations of surrounding areas. These have been carefully documented in a number of places.[3] Not infrequently publicity has been minimized by out-of-court settlements to the casualties of radiation exposure in the nuclear industry.

It is important to remember that even small releases of radioactive substances can be dangerous to man, as they may be taken up by animals or plants selectively, concentrated in the tissues, and eventually eaten by man. For example, strontium 90 is drawn up from the soil in grass and further concentrated in the cows that eat the grass; the radioactivity is then passed on in their milk. Ingested by the human body and with a half-life of twenty-eight years, strontium 90 mimics calcium and is incorporated in bone, where it irradiates the white-cell-producing bone marrow and may cause leukemia. Iodine 131, with a half-life of eight days, is collected in the thyroid, and may cause cancer there. In each case, the ingested radio-isotope lodges in a permanent site where it can deliver high doses to soft tissue for its life or that of the human host, whichever is shorter. Other radio-isotopes, even if not ingested, nevertheless augment the background level of radiation, thus causing increased genetic damage within cells. The debate concerning the significance of near background radiation levels in carcinogenesis is detailed in Section 4. Exposure to radiation which has been concentrated in the food chain has been one of the major issues in the Pacific atolls surrounding the site of the US nuclear bomb tests.[4]

Nuclear installations are allowed to emit small quantities of radioactive material 'routinely'. This can include the unexpected. By the 1970s standards at Windscale were low. Leaks occurred; also large amounts of caesium 137 from corroded spent Magnox fuel were discharged. An ion exchange plant to stop this will come into service in 1983. Windscale is also the source of americium 241, a long-lived α-emitter. Both radionuclides can accumulate in fish or shellfish, and thus in those who eat Irish Sea produce. Since 1965 reported cases of myeloid leukemia in Lancashire have doubled and, in some locations, trebled. In 1978–9 elevated levels of caesium 137 were found in people in the west of Scotland.[5]

3 Nuclear Accidents

Quite apart from the dangers of irradiation in the working of the mine, processing plant, or reactor, and of low-level radiation from routine emissions and mine tailings, there is a constant danger of accidents. 'Minor' accidents are very frequent. An analysis of American Nuclear Regulatory Commission 'Licence event Reports' for the period 1969–79 showed that 169 accidents were 'potential precursors' of core damage; that such accidents were fifty times more likely than the NRC WASH–1400 estimate (the Rasmussen Report) and that human error was important in 38 per cent of cases. Analysis of 1980 returns found 57 per cent of all LERs, minor and major, to be due to equipment failure, 20 per cent to human error. Major accidents, involving prompt loss of life, have so far been rare, but have occurred. For instance three people were killed in an explosion in a military reactor in Idaho in 1961.[6]

A major release of radioactivity certainly occurred in the Kyshtym area of the Urals, in 1957 or 1958, probably as a result of an explosion in a nuclear waste disposal site. Strict censorship about this event was maintained, but its magnitude is apparent from a number of studies, published in Soviet journals, of the resultant contamination, and its effects on various life forms.[7] An attempt has been made to explain the facts as a consequence of the leakage of reactor wastes stored in a lake in the early days of Soviet nuclear technology, and the subsequent spread of radioactive contamination in windblown spray.[8] A 1982 report from Los Alamos attributes the damage to appallingly lax procedures, but the scale of the damage renders such explanations extremely implausible.[9]

There have also been a considerable number of near misses, such as the fire in the core of a reactor at Windscale in 1957. Such events are played down by the proponents of nuclear power, often in a rather surprising way (see box). A more recent case was the severe 'LOCA' at Three Mile

---

'The level of contamination did not represent a hazard to life, but was such as to make the milk production in an area 10 miles by 30 miles unusable . . . due to the accumulation of radioactive iodine by grazing cattle.'[10]

(In fact 20,000 curies of radioactive iodine 131 were released in an accident largely due to a failure to apply already existing knowledge.)

Island, Harrisburg, in 1979. A 'LOCA' is a 'loss of coolant accident' which, in a pressurized water reactor, can swiftly expose the core, and so risk a 'melt-down': the core would then fuse into a mass of white-hot radioactive material which would *melt* its way *down* through the floor. In the accompanying gas or steam explosions the containment vessels would be ruptured, and radioactivity would be spread over a wide area.

Advocates of the PWR play down the Three Mile Island accident, believing that they could control a LOCA.[11] In this case a melt-down was avoided, but at one time (30 March–1 April) it was considered a strong possibility. There were releases of radiation into the atmosphere which led to the ordering of a partial evacuation of the area. At the time of writing it appears that the collapsed reactor core contains a heap of disintegrated nuclear fuel.[12] The Kemeny Commission placed central blame for the accident on the 'mindset' that nuclear power is safe: 'this attitude must be changed to one that says nuclear power is by its very nature potentially dangerous'. This 'mindset' afflicted all involved: operators, generating company and NRC staff, compounding minor equipment failures. It concluded that 'if the country wishes, for larger reasons, to confront the risks that are inherently associated with nuclear power, fundamental changes are necessary if those risks are to be kept within tolerable limits'.[13]

RISK

In an attempt during the mid-1970s to find a means to compare one hazardous activity with another, decision-makers, particularly those associated with the nuclear-power industry, began to employ the mathematical quantity of 'Risk'. The 'Risk' inherent in an activity was to be judged *in terms of the probability per year of an individual's premature death being occasioned while partaking in that activity*. At last decisions that had previously been weighed in a balance of argument could be assessed through a mathematical quantity. 'Risk' gained its greatest publicity in a televised Dimbleby Lecture given by Lord Rothschild in 1978. It was also used to defend nuclear power by Sir Francis Tombs, of the Electricity Council, and Mr Justice Parker.[14] Rothschild went to considerable lengths to 'prove' from his Risk figures that nuclear power had an extremely low Risk, not only in comparison with the probability of being killed in a traffic accident, but also, when account was taken of fatalities in mining, equipment manufacture, etc., far lower than for other means of electricity generation. He endorsed this sort of risk accountancy, accepting Dr Herbert Inhaber's quixotic conclusion that when all the prompt death risks associated with construction of windmills were summed, they appeared more dangerous than nuclear power. Rothschild's and Inhaber's mathematical quantities may appear authoritative – for statistics always look so – and thus appear to be blessed with an aura of truth. It is important to understand why they are highly misleading.

When calculating the Risk associated with nuclear-power

generation two considerable problems in formulating Risk estimates combine to erode their significance and accuracy. First, fatalities in traffic accidents – Rothschild's most important comparison – are occasioned by obvious physical injuries that occur at the moment of the accident. In contrast 'injuries' caused by radiation are generally not immediate, but result insidiously in an increased incidence of cancer many years later. Thus the risk associated with radiation in the nuclear industry is inherently less amenable to quantitative assessment than the risk involved in using the roads. The problem becomes compounded when all the processes associated with nuclear power, from uranium mining through to nuclear waste disposal, are taken into account. Uranium mining safety regulations vary from country to country and the boom in mining is too recent to uncover any long-term mortality statistics and therefore any fatality figures that could be used for Risk calculations. Similarly, nuclear reprocessing is an infant technology and the controlled release, as takes place at present at Windscale, of certain radiogenic isotopes into the environment leads to isotopes remaining for an unknown length of time in biological food chains that may, as with the Irish Sea fish and seaweed industries, lead back to man. Mr Justice Parker's reaction to a string of expert witnesses suggesting that knowledge of our ignorance should favour great caution was to cite other, less cautious scientists, and to assert that, since claims were not conclusively proven, they might be discounted in planning decisions; which he then did.

The second problem with the Rothschild 'traffic accident' approach to Risk is that for probability figures to be in any way meaningful they must be compiled from a statistically significant sample. If 10,000 nuclear power stations had been in operation for the past 100 years it might be possible to have a true idea of the frequency of major accidents. As the total operating period for all nuclear power stations adds up to only a few thousand years, and so far there have been no accidents causing immediate fatalities in the surrounding communities, one could argue, with irreproachable Rothschild logic, that the probability of an accident was zero – as in the early days of airship flights! This is exactly what Hoyle and Hoyle (in *Common Sense in Nuclear Energy*, 1980) also do. Of course, one melt-down will change all these risk predictions dramatically and end nuclear-power generation, just as the crashes of R–101 and the Hindenburg ended hydrogen-filled airship flight. There is a further problem. Rothschild's figures are calculated by taking probabilities of worst possible cases in equipment failures. If three pieces of equipment each with a breakdown probability of one in a thousand are needed to fail simultaneously for some imagined disaster, then the Rothschild risk is 1 in 10^9. But experience has taught us that human error often compounds equipment failure. That is what happened at Three Mile Island, and in a host of other nuclear 'near-misses'. So in strict logic such speculative figures should be compared only with an estimate of traffic-accident fatalities compiled from a knowledge of how cars work, how traffic flows, etc., but with no reference to actual statistics, which involve a human element. Even here, the comparison is misleading, for this sort of 'fault-tree' analysis implies that you know all the primary faults that can conceivably occur, and their probability, and that for each you can establish the secondary and tertiary effects. The Three Mile Island accident illustrates this ignorance also. One of the most dangerous aspects of the accident was the creation of a large amount of hydrogen. Yet, while the theoretical possibility was known, before this happened no one concerned with pressure water reactors seems to have considered the practical consequences of it.

To compare 'back of the envelope' projections with well-established statistics is mathematical sleight of hand, rather than the basis for more important policy decisions.

4 The Unsolved Problems of Low-level Radiation and the Disposal of Nuclear Wastes

There is no doubt that nuclear technology has learned from the mistakes of the past. Conditions in mining and extraction plants are much better than they were. As a result of the Three Mile Island accident, safety precautions are likely to be much improved. Nuclear technologists claim that the risks are very small. The misleading way in which proponents of nuclear power discuss 'risk' is examined in the accompanying box (pp. 239–41).

Even though efforts have been made and are being made to tighten up the safety regulations, no regulations can cover every possibility. This is especially the case when the regulations act against the profit interests of the company or of some of the individuals concerned. There is much evidence to show that in the past workers have been allowed to remain in partial or total ignorance of the dangers to which they were exposed. And, as just noted, the official report shows that the accident at Three Mile

Island was compounded by a series of human errors. In testimony in the autumn of 1981, supporting President Reagan's desire to expand the ailing American nuclear industry, the 'father of the H-Bomb', Edward Teller, now aged seventy-three, denounced the operators at Three Mile Island as 'fools' and underpaid; members of the Nuclear Regulatory Commission as 'fools' also for 'over-reacting'.[15] But it will never be possible to ensure that all nuclear operators are devoid of human failings.

While proponents of nuclear power are sometimes right in their claim that the media tend to latch on to first reports of radioactive releases or pollution and neglect their subsequent refutation,[16] it is also true that their dangers are often played down or even falsified by those involved in the nuclear industry. For instance the US Atomic Energy Commission at first claimed to have released only one milligram of plutonium from the Rocky Flats Plant, Denver, but were subsequently forced to admit to 100,000 milligrams.[17]

Many safety measures involve reducing the level of radiation to which the workers are exposed below a certain threshold level which is deemed to be 'safe'. Interestingly, this level has always been higher for workers in the industry than for the general public – in itself an admission that the former are not really 'safe', and that the dangers to the workers must be balanced against the supposed usefulness of the process to the community as a whole. (It goes without saying that it is never put to the workers in quite this way.)

The International Commission on Radiological Protection (ICRP), whose recommended limits for radiation exposure are accepted by the British authorities, continues to set the worker's rate at 5 rems/year, but given mounting epidemiological evidence of significant effects at low doses, now regards this as an absolute ceiling, rather than a working level as previously. In the US, radiological protection appears to be taken more seriously; for example, standards set by the Environmental Protection Agency for discharge of long-lived α-emitting radio-isotopes in the nuclear fuel cycle are many times stricter than could be met technically by the existing and proposed plants at Windscale.[18]

RESEARCH ON LOW-LEVEL RADIATION[19]
Between 1965 and 1977, Dr Thomas Mancuso of the University of Pittsburgh was asked by the US Atomic Energy Commission (AEC) to conduct an investigation of the long-term health of the atomic workers at the Hanford Works nuclear complex near Richland, Washington State. Collaborating with Mancuso by independently

analysing his data were two British scientists, Dr Alice Stewart and Dr George Kneale, who have for over thirty years been prominent in epidemiological radiation research. A population of 25,000 workers over a period of twenty-nine years was investigated.

The results caused concern, for Mancuso, Stewart and Kneale suggested from the Hanford data that the doubling dose for all cancers in males aged about 45 years was 33.7 rads. Since the doubling dose for that age group suggested by the BEIR (Biological Effects of Ionizing Radiation) Committee report then current as the official benchmark for health physics was around 500 rads, the alarm and interest created by Mancuso's study can be understood: it implied that a low total dose of radiation, delivered slowly – and therefore without difficulty – within 'permissible' occupational guidelines was carcinogenic. They also reported three other conclusions: that certain types of cancer had lower doubling doses; that the sexes exhibited different sensitivity to carcinogenesis; and that older subjects showed lower doubling doses than those aged 25–45 years when exposed.

The study was immediately and strongly attacked. Two assessments in 1978 (NRPB R–79 and Sanders) rejected all its major findings. Then in 1979 Professor J. Gofman of the University of California independently re-analysed Mancuso's raw data using a different methodology. Gofman rejected the sex difference finding because the female sample was too small; he argued that the exceptionally radio-sensitive cancers could be neither proven nor disproven, but in this study were a product of statistical aberration and that, consistent with BEIR, younger – not older – people showed lower doubling doses. But he broadly confirmed the major finding, calculating a doubling dose of 43.5 rads of external, low LET (γ- or X-ray, see p. 323) radiation, set within broad confidence limits. Gofman points out that given the limitations in the data, this figure cannot be regarded as conclusive. However, it would be prudent to regard it as the present best estimate, since the Hanford data are the best yet available. Only more case studies with data of the quality of Mancuso's could carry us further towards certainty.

However, the response to Mancuso and Gofman has not been marked by the spirit of a common quest for truth. When Mancuso's original findings began to indicate radiation risks below the 'permissible' threshold, his funding was cut off (July 1977) and he was then pressed to take early retirement (which he refused to do). Gofman's paper was subjected to detailed scientific criticism, all of which he meticulously refuted. Nevertheless, the Hanford study is under continuous attack from government and nuclear-industry scientists and is normally represented by them as worthless (see, for example, Saunders in *Atom*, 1981). This is to protest too much and thereby to raise legitimate suspicions about the motives for so doing.

Also received with hostility was another hypothesis about the effects of radiation, distinct from that of carcinogenesis: the hypothesis that it produces a generalized ageing effect. The largest study indicating this conclusion has been the Tri-State Study, which was carried out under US government funding at the Roswell Park Memorial Institute in Buffalo, New York. It was a three-year study of sixteen million people in New York State, Maryland, and Minnesota into the causes of leukemia. The proposal is not that one would die earlier as a *direct* consequence of radiation exposure, but that, because radiation breaks down the body's immunological defence mechanism (an integral component in the ageing process), the probability of contracting diseases of old age is increased at earlier ages. Funding for this study was also abruptly terminated.

Health physicists are now sharply divided on the low-level issue. In 1979 the BEIR III report, which warned of possible danger, was withdrawn after protest from less cautious scientists.[20] But it is difficult to know just how dangerous low levels of radiation are, for several reasons:

(a) Its effects are delayed: leukemia (cancer of the white blood cells) may not appear for several years after exposure, and cancers in the rest of the body for ten to forty years. With long-term follow-up studies there are always difficulties in the interpretation of the data because of vicissitudes occurring to subjects between exposure and assessment.

(b) Most of the evidence comes from people who have received relatively high doses of radiation. To predict the effects of low doses, it is necessary to extrapolate the curve relating dose level to incidence of illness backwards: since the precise shape of the curve is unknown, this involves a good deal of uncertainty.[21] In addition, previous risk estimates draw heavily on data from Hiroshima and Nagasaki. Until very recently it was supposed that the Hiroshima radiation was unique in containing a high proportion of neutrons (high *linear energy transfer* – LET – radiation) while the Nagasaki explosion released primarily gamma rays and X-rays (low LET radiation). On this logic, it was argued that it was illegitimate to relate Hiroshima evidence to nuclear projects involving exposure to low

LET radiation (see Appendix B), and the Nagasaki data were insufficient. Now evidence has thrown doubt on the assertion about the Hiroshima bomb. In fact computer simulations of the two Japanese explosions now suggest that they were rather similar in emitting principally gamma rays and X-rays. As a result, there are now no accurate data on the effects of exposure to neutrons, and previous estimates of the effects of other types of radiation have been called into question. The new data suggest that the dangers of low LET radiation may have been underestimated – perhaps very seriously so. But the experts cannot agree on the shape of the curve at low doses, or about whether or not there is a 'safe' threshold.[22] This was the cause of very heated exchanges at the 1981 meeting of the US Radiation Research Society.

It may even be that, far from low doses being relatively safe, they are proportionately more hazardous. There is some evidence of an initial 'hump' in the curve of biological effect against radiation dose at very low doses, which may arise from a small sub-population of extra-sensitive cells. Alternatively, the hump may represent a stimulation of the cell's capacity to repair radiation damage. This stimulated repair will increase the chance of a cell's surviving a low radiation dose, but if – as is likely – the repair is not entirely accurate, it will tend to lead to the perpetuation of mutations in the DNA, which may ultimately result in cancer.[23] The existence of a 'hump' and its cause have yet to be confirmed; we refer to it here simply to illustrate the caution which should be – and often is not – applied in assessing radiation risk at low doses.

(c) There is always a background of natural radiation, and many people are irradiated in the course of medical diagnosis or treatment. Because of variation in these background levels, it is often difficult to distinguish the effects of additional exposure. Of course, difficulty in establishing statistically that additional low doses have an effect is not evidence against the view that particular cases were specifically caused by additional exposure. The existing standard for exposure permissible for workers (5 rems per year) is thirty to fifty times more than the natural background radiation (100–160 millirems per year).

(d) People may differ in their susceptibility to radiation: a major effect on a few susceptible individuals would be hidden in a large-scale survey. Thus discussion of accidents or over-exposure in terms of average radiation dose per man[24] are doubly misleading: some individuals get much more than the average dose and some are more susceptible than others.

(e) Little is known about the effects of low-level external radiation, but even less is known about radioactive materials inhaled and ingested. A very small amount of radioactive material, once lodged inside the body, can give a large integrated radiation dose to soft tissues and be a potent cause of cancer. Indeed, most anxiety in relation to cancer has related to ingested radioactive elements as a result of man-made nuclear projects. Worryingly, internal 'hot spots' due to inhaled or ingested radio-isotopes are extremely difficult to monitor accurately. But in discussion both of nuclear-power-related radioactivity and of fourteen-day-post-attack 'civil defence' calculations, government and industry advice takes account of direct external radiation only. A favourite benchmark of comparison, used with rhetorical effect by Mr Justice Parker in his discussion of risks associated with radiation, is the greater level of background radiation to be found in granite houses in Aberdeen than in brick-built houses in southern England. But you don't *eat* granite.

While definitive conclusions are beyond our reach, the only reasonable one lies in the stand taken by Morgan, who was earlier instrumental in setting up the existing criteria, that 'there is no dose of radiation so low that the risk of malignancy is zero'.[25] The onus lies upon those who promote nuclear activities and who act as if there is a 'safe' threshold to prove it.

A further point to be made with respect to safety regulations is that they often involve improved ventilation or washing procedures in the mines or factories. These certainly reduce the level of radioactive material to which the workers are exposed, but in so doing they dissipate it into the environment.

Quite as important as the present-day hazards from radiation is the long-term problem of disposal of the radioactive wastes from the various processes involved in the mining and refining of uranium, and especially of the plutonium and other radioactive materials in the spent fuel rods from all nuclear reactors. Low-level wastes, like the clothing used by workers in nuclear installations, are often buried near the surface, a danger to ignorant or careless trespassers, as already witnessed at BNFL's Drigg site. As we have seen, at one time tailings were used to build dams and even for the construction of buildings. Later the dangers of the radiation in these materials were realized and in some, but not all, cases efforts have been made to remove them. But since their radioactivity will persist for tens of thousands of years, and includes radon, they must not be left lying around on the surface. They should be returned underground, thus adding yet further to the costs of the nuclear cycle.

Wastes with a medium level of radioactivity require a stricter degree of containment; and their bulk makes disposal a major undertaking. Much waste has been dumped in the oceans – from 1970 to 1981 the UK dumped 22,795 tonnes – but the containers have only a limited life-time, and since it is not fully known whether, and how, radionuclides might enter marine food-chains, heavy sea dumping is a gamble on dilution.[26]

Even more dangerous are the spent fuel rods from the nuclear reactors. As we have seen, they are highly radioactive, containing uranium and a variety of its radioactive breakdown products, including a high proportion of plutonium. It cannot be sufficiently emphasized that no satisfactory method for disposing of them is yet known. They are so highly active that before processing they must be stored for about a year in cooling ponds. The decay of the shorter-lived radioactive elements results in a reduction of total activity by a factor of several hundred during the first year after removal from the reactor. This and later decay of total activity, indicated by release of heat, is seen in Figure 14.

The British government has in 1981 endorsed the proposal of the Radioactive Waste Management Advisory Committee to store wastes above ground for fifty years. Sir Walter Marshall, formerly of the UKAEA, a vociferous proponent of nuclear power and the Conservative government's choice for Chairman of the Central Electricity Generating Board to replace Dr Glyn England, whom it found uncongenial, has suggested storage for a *century*. The difficulty of doing this with liquid

---

'Until we do find out what is to be done to dispose safely of these extremely dangerous substances we have to envisage that they be kept under a very sophisticated lock and key for centuries, and in the case of plutonium itself for perhaps a quarter of a million years – if intelligent beings should be with us that long...

'... methods may eventually be devised to dispose of these substances permanently should further generations find that desirable. It is simply that in spite of some good ideas, no single method has yet been established beyond reasonable doubt...

'The relevant research has only just begun, and even now the resources being devoted to such work are negligible compared with its importance.'

(Sir Brian Flowers, FRS, Chairman of the Royal Commission on Environmental Pollution)[27]

waste is shown by the concrete-covered steel tanks used at the Hanford Works in Washington State. These last twenty to thirty years and a number of serious leaks resulted in contamination of the Columbia River and surrounding areas.[28]

Plutonium 239 has a half-life of 24,400 years, but the material will continue to be dangerous even longer than that. Furthermore the magnitude of the problem requires emphasis. The amount of reactor-grade plutonium created was estimated in 1979 to be about 150 tonnes and the weapon-grade stockpile to be about 160 tonnes. Recall that only a few kilograms of plutonium 239 is sufficient to form a critical mass that might be triggered to cause an explosion; and only a *millionth* of a gram of the oxide powder free in air can be fatal if inhaled. As well as warning of the 'plutonium economy', the Flowers Commission recommended that a nuclear programme should not proceed until at least one acceptable method of waste disposal for the indefinite future had been demonstrated beyond reasonable doubt.[29] This recommendation has not been met.

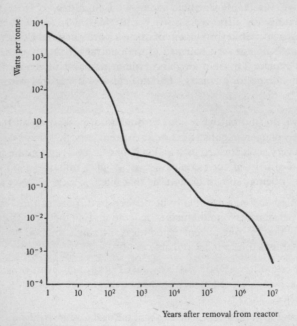

Years after removal from reactor

Figure 14. Heat generated by the radioactive decay of materials in spent fuel (log-log scale)[30]

Vitrification, or the creation of synthetic crystals (SYNROC) which contain radioactive waste in solid solution, and subsequent burial 1–3 km below the surface in impervious rocks is already thought by some to be well proven. One person who believes so is Mr Justice Parker. In his controversially robust judgement, comprehensively in favour of British Nuclear Fuels Ltd when it applied for planning permission to build a new reprocessing plant at Windscale, he on the one hand admitted that BNFL's borosilicate vitrification process (HARVEST) was not yet perfected, but on the other expressed no anxiety about problems with the process. 'The stage of development has, I consider, been reached, when success can be confidently predicted,' he wrote. This jaunty tone is official policy. But is such confidence justified? Sir Brian Flowers's Royal Commission expressed considerable caution; nor is there unanimity in the scientific community to back BNFL. Many with expert knowledge think that borosilicate vitrification is by no means fully proven: waste may devitrify when exposed to ground water at moderately high temperatures and pressures. A borosilicate glass spheroid containing fission products was exposed to water in a sealed gold capsule at 300 °C and 300 Bar. After one week numerous fissures were observed; after a fortnight the specimen had broken into fragments and seemed to be totally altered. These results contrast markedly with the low temperature and pressure tests about which AERE expresses satisfaction. They show that a waste/rock interaction can be rapid and extensive if the container is breached during the thermal period (i.e. the first 500–1,000 years). Furthermore, radiation effects on glass and host rock may change physical properties, leading to overheating and melting of the vitrified block.

Another sort of problem arises with SYNROC, namely, excess concentration of the waste materials in the surface crystals: this could perhaps be overcome by washing the block with nitric acid after it had stood for twenty years. The efficiency of this washing is, however, as yet unproven and the probable cost of the process would be at least 3 per cent of the cost of the energy produced by the fissile material from which the waste came.[31]

Also, finding a site for deep burial poses severe problems, for it should be safe from human or geological disturbance for many thousands of years. The Flowers Commission in 1976 demanded that urgent research begin but, impeded by public fear, progress has been slow so far to establish if it is safe to dispose of high-level wastes underground in the UK. But it will never be possible to guarantee that a given site will remain stable and dry for the required time. Parker accepted this and indeed saw it as an additional reason favouring the removal of plutonium from waste before disposal: the amount of plutonium available to be leached out would be thus reduced. The National Radiological Protection Board assumes the inevitability of leaching, so to reduce doses has suggested that coastal sites be selected for repositories in preference to inland ones: any leakage would then contaminate the seas rather than inland waters. The logic is that we should rely on dilution in the oceans for protection and discount the concentration of radionuclides in the oceanic food-chains.

In the UK, decisions about the disposal of high-level wastes have been deferred until adequate research has been conducted.[32] In the USA, the National Research Council's Committee on Radioactive Waste Management has recently stated that high-level wastes should be cooled for at least forty years, much longer than had previously been usual, and discussed the pros and cons of different types of longer-term storage. It is thus quite clear that the nuclear industry has been allowed to continue to expand while this problem, crucial for the well-being of future generations, remains unsolved. A new problem, which only in 1982 entered public debate, will arise when it becomes necessary to decommission power stations after their twenty-five-year life. This will mean doing something with a great deal of contaminated steel and concrete.[33]

This section may have left the impression that the waste problem is one addressed principally in relation to the nuclear power programme because much of the evidence that has been used comes from civilian sources; but this impression would be incorrect. Because of the tight secrecy which envelops all nuclear matters in Britain, it is not possible to state with much precision what proportion of the most dangerous wastes – high-level wastes – derive from military activities, what proportion solely from those of generating electricity. But in the USA, where there is much greater freedom of information, it is possible to give figures: of 10,322,700 cubic feet of high-level waste, 10,196,000 (98.8 per cent) is the by-product of the nuclear weapons programme, 126,700 cubic feet (1.2 per cent) has been produced by civilian reactors.[34] This places nuclear weapons squarely in the centre of what is often discussed as a non-military topic. In the next section we must examine more closely the relations between different nuclear projects.

5 Nuclear Power and Nuclear Weapons

Much of what has been said concerns the stockpiling of nuclear weapons as much as the 'peaceful' use of nuclear power. Both require similar processes and both are contributing to the radioactive pollution of the earth. But in the case of nuclear weapons, there is a further issue to consider. Up to 1962, the majority of nuclear weapon tests were carried out above ground. Between 1946 and 1962 the U S Defense Department alone carried out 183 atmospheric bomb tests including the only 'live' firing of a nuclear missile, a Polaris S L B M in Operation 'Frigate Bird' in 1962. Subsequent surveys have demonstrated marked increases in cancer (especially leukemia) amongst the military personnel involved in tests,[35] some of whom were deliberately exposed to simulated battlefield conditions, and among civilians in neighbouring areas: these include residents of Utah, Nevada, and Arizona, and Pacific islanders. In addition to the effects of exposure to the prompt radiation of weapons tests, some victims, for example the Marshall Islanders, the fishermen on the *Lucky Dragon*, and residents of Nevada were exposed to fall-out. The small town of St George, near Las Vegas and adjoining the Nevada Nuclear Testing Range, was blanketed with fall-out during the atmospheric tests in the 1950s; indeed, citizens were invited to watch the test explosions. They were assured that the tests posed no risk to them. However, over the ensuing years, the townspeople experienced a spate of deaths from leukemia and cancer and the birth of many mentally retarded children. The deaths continue to this day. At the time of writing, over a thousand citizens are suing the U S government. The government rejects liability.

But fall-out was not only local in effect. Cows near St George grazed contaminated pastures, and the isotopes which concentrated in their milk were passed on to the schoolchildren of Las Vegas. More generally, the bomb tests of the 1950s and early 1960s added appreciable quantities of radioactive matter to the upper atmosphere, where winds distributed it globally. Some scientists such as Dr Teller have maintained that this radioactivity is of trifling significance; others do not agree (see box on fall-out). Isotopes such as strontium 90 (which mimics calcium, is concentrated in milk, and incorporated into the skeleton) are now present in the bodies of untold numbers of people as a consequence of these tests.

FALL-OUT

A moratorium on atmospheric nuclear tests was agreed by the USA and the USSR. But in September 1961 the Soviet Union broke the moratorium and recommenced testing, with a quite massive series of explosions, including the largest-ever thermonuclear bomb, above 50 Mt. Shortly after the signature of the Partial Test Ban Treaty, the famous oceanographer Jacques Cousteau had a lunch engagement . . .

'. . . I wanted to meet with Dr Zennkevitch, a distinguished Soviet oceanographer who belonged to the numerous Russian delegation. Zennkevitch was a remarkable personality. Apart from being renowned among marine scientists the world over, he was a highly civilized individual, at ease with many scientific fields as well as with art, philosophy, and literature. He spoke several languages fluently . . . He had recently been elected president of the Academy of Sciences of the Soviet Union, one of the most influential bodies within the Soviet political machinery. ". . . Professor," I said, "I feel embarrassed to ask you a difficult question. In Monaco, we are daily measuring radioactivity in the air. During the Russian tests, the level became extremely high and probably dangerous all over the northern hemisphere. Why? Why all these bomb tests? Did the Soviet government know what they were doing?"

'. . . The old master drew himself up again on his chair. He looked me straight in the eye and said softly, but clearly, "Cousteau, the Academy of Sciences of the Soviet Union was consulted by our government prior to the tests." He paused a few seconds. "After careful evaluation, we warned our government that the proposed programme of atomic bomb tests would probably cause the death of approximately 50,000 children in the USSR."

'Fifty thousand children! My throat ached and my mouth went dry. Zennkevitch, the venerable president of the powerful Soviet Academy, also had tears in his eyes. He added slowly, "But, the answer was that if we did not test the bombs, it may soon have cost the Soviet Union many more lives . . ." '[36]

*

In the United States, the Chiefs of Staff and scientists like Dr Edward Teller had vigorously urged President Kennedy to resume testing. To ward off this pressure, Kennedy had appointed an expert panel under the physicist Wolfgang Panofsky, which had reported that there was no urgent technical need to resume tests. But once the Soviets recommenced the pressure became irresistible. Kennedy sanctioned underground and laboratory tests in September 1961, but in March 1962 was forced to permit atmospheric testing again.

'The informal test ban, Hubert Humphrey said to Kennedy . . . has been a "ray of hope to millions of worried people . . . The renewal of testing might very well turn the political tides in the world on behalf of the Soviets." Moreover, testing in the atmosphere would bring a new surge of fall-out, and this weighed heavily with Kennedy. Jerome

Wiesner, his scientific adviser, reminded him one drizzling day how rain washed radioactive debris from the clouds and brought it down to the earth. Kennedy, looking out of the window, said, "You mean that stuff is in the rain out there?" Wiesner said, "Yes." The President continued gazing out the window, deep sadness on his face, and did not say a word for several minutes. He hated the idea of re-opening the race: "We test and then they test and we have to test again. And you build up until somebody uses them."'

*

'When the AEC joined the Rand Corporation in a study of radioactive fall-out, they named the study Project Sunshine; for the measuring unit of strontium 90, they coined the term "sunshine unit". This emerged at a hearing of the Joint Committee on Atomic Energy, and the members of the committee proved resistant. Representative Chet Holifield said doubtfully, when the terms were used: "The word 'sunshine' has a cheery note to it, and I was just wondering if we were allowing, let us say, propaganda to creep into our scientific terminology. Why did you not put it 'happy' units, or something like that?"

'Senator Clint Anderson chimed in: "They've put out Project Sunshine as the most enlightened and happiest look on radiation damage." Dr Willard Libby, the chemist and AEC commissioner, protested that the choice of name was haphazard and had no propaganda purpose, and was not altogether inappropriate because the subject did relate to sunshine. Nevertheless, no more was heard of the sunshine unit after this.'[37]

In total, between 1945 and 1979 there have been at least 1,221 nuclear explosions,[38] an average of about one per week: 653 by the USA, 426 by the USSR, 86 by France, 30 by the UK, 25 by China and 1 by India.

With weapons there is the further problem of the disposal of the 45–50,000 nuclear weapons already deployed. At present it seems that every new nuclear warhead must pose to our descendants the problem of its eventual disposal for a period immensely longer than the history of modern European society.

But there are also other relations between nuclear power and nuclear weapons. This is an area in which conflicting views are to be found: some maintain that the peaceful uses of nuclear energy have nothing to do with the manufacture of nuclear weapons, others that the one could not happen without the other. Here we shall specify some of the relations between the two.

● (a) That the nuclear power industry grew out of the early research on atomic weapons is beyond dispute. It would not have existed in size or spread of development without it. Decisions to allocate resources to nuclear technology, rather than to the development of other sources of energy, were originally military/political decisions.[39] In many instances, that may still be the case.

● (b) Much of the technology necessary for nuclear power is necessary also for the manufacture of nuclear weapons. Personnel trained in nuclear reactor technology can readily acquire nuclear weapons technology.

● (c) Nuclear power stations provide a source of plutonium 239 for use in nuclear weapons. Different reactor types produce plutonium at differing rates. Indeed, in the British case, the original Calder Hall reactor design (called Pippa: three Ps – pile/power/plutonium) was explicitly intended to maximize plutonium production. The Magnox reactors of the 'civil' programme are of a closely similar design. They also incorporate a facility to allow refuelling 'on load', both to improve availability and to permit withdrawal of only partially burned rods, before much weapons-grade Pu 239 has turned into the less desirable Pu 240. (In fact the Magnox 'on load' system does not work well. But it is the thought that counts.) The core geometry of Hinkley Point A reactor is made to favour production of Pu 239. (What happens to such plutonium is explored in Appendix D.)

Plutonium extracted after reprocessing can be stored and handled relatively easily. The main process, called the Purex cycle, was originally developed during the Second World War and is the basis of the Windscale and Cap de la Hague reprocessing plants. From the most recent figures (Appendix D), Windscale has reprocessed over 21 tonnes of plutonium, of which $14\frac{1}{2}$ tonnes is said to be stockpiled. (This is about double the amount conceded in the Parker Report.)[40] Note that the two Western countries with big reprocessing plants (UK and France) are the only two to have independent nuclear forces. Both, especially the French, are also expending effort on development of 'fast breeder' reactors.

Of thermal reactors, the British Magnox design is superior to the pressure water reactor, and indeed to most other types, as a plutonium producer, but no thermal reactor can match the performance of the fast breeder reactor. In its core, it produces approximately 70 per cent Pu 239, but this weapons-grade material is contaminated with Pu 240, which is less predictable and can fission spontaneously. For large weapons, a degree of contamination in the radioactive material can be tolerated, but for lighter,

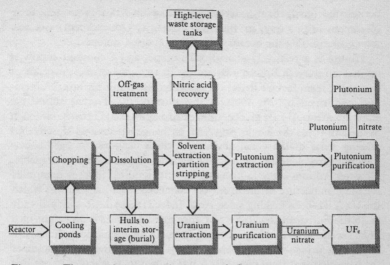

Figure 15. The stages in 'reprocessing' reactor fuel to extract plutonium by the Purex process[41]

more compact warheads, or for small 'battlefield' weapons, both particular Western priorities, the highest purity of Pu 239 is essential. The 'blanket' of natural uranium 238 which surrounds the core of a fast breeder reactor is 'bred' into plutonium – and this blanket plutonium consists of 95–98 per cent Pu 239. Thus, unlike other reactors, the fast breeder reactor produces high-grade weapons plutonium very efficiently as an unavoidable feature of normal use.[42]

The role of plutonium in illuminating the reasons why a civil/military distinction in nuclear projects is untenable deserves further attention. Let us take a particular example, the supply of British plutonium to the United States.

During 1958 and 1959 Britain and the USA signed agreements for cooperation on the uses of atomic energy for mutual defence purposes (see Appendix D). As was stated at the time, this agreement was a division of labour whereby Britain supplied the USA with plutonium in exchange for enriched uranium (mainly to fuel submarine reactors) and for tritium, a heavy isotope of hydrogen required for the manufacture of H-bombs. This was a barter trade, with an exchange rate of 1 g British plutonium for 1.76 g of enriched uranium, or a tiny fraction of a gram of tritium. In order to permit the (civil) British electricity generating boards to sell their plutonium in this way, in 1961 the Electricity (Amendment) Act was passed, permitting the boards to produce and sell isotopes.

Tritium is a relatively short-lived isotope, and a constant supply is needed to refurbish Britain's H-bombs. In 1976, the British government decided to manufacture tritium at Chapelcross, Dumfriesshire, an intention reaffirmed by Mr Nott at the time of the Trident submarine announcement. At first glance, this reaffirmation is odd because although in the late 1970s the Anglo-American exchange agreements lapsed, thus making sense of the construction of British facilities, in 1981 a new five-year agreement was signed; so American tritium should be available. However, tritium is the radioactive material required in large quantities for the manufacture of 'neutron' or 'enhanced radiation' bombs, which the USA has been making since 1978. Indeed, these devices may already be in the European stockpiles of Lance missile warheads and eight-inch howitzer shells. So this American requirement suggests a likely shortage of tritium for British needs, which may help to explain the reaffirmation of the Chapelcross tritium plant. (It is not known to us whether or not this plant is currently in operation.)[43]

An important reason for the new Anglo-American agreement is that the American appetite for plutonium will not diminish: indeed if President Reagan's rearmament programme is fully executed, that appetite will increase. But this trend is not exclusive to the Reagan administration. Under the Carter administration plans were initiated which are now being pushed ahead with vigour to expand and modernize the whole nuclear weapons production complex.[44] But in the meantime, there is a shortfall, and the British government has agreed to resume the supply of British plutonium. The Foreign Office has strenuously denied the implication intended here: that this material will help build nuclear weapons. It has stated that this plutonium is needed for the civilian fast breeder reactor programme. The plausibility of this is examined in Appendix D. But the nature of the FBR's plutonium production has just been described; so even if the Foreign Office is correct, even if the *atoms* in the warheads are different from those dispatched from Britain, they will depend on the latter for their existence; and even if the British plutonium fuels FBRs exclusively for civil use, it will permit diversion of other plutonium to military use.

In a most courageous letter to *The Times*, Dr R. V. Hesketh, a scientist employed by the CEGB at the Berkeley Nuclear Laboratories in Gloucestershire, wrote that he had, for years, assured his critics that civil and military nuclear energy were distinct, as Sir Alan Cottrell argued in his recent book *How Safe is Nuclear Energy?*, but he was now forced to conclude that, on the above logic, if plutonium were to be sold to the Reagan administration, 'I do not think it could be rationally maintained that we, the United Kingdom, have distinguished civil use from military use.'[45]

Advances in nuclear technology are likely in the near future to increase dramatically the availability of weapons-grade materials. The greatest immediate threat is from laser techniques already developed to enrich the U 235 content of uranium, which could be used to make weapons-grade material. These techniques are now being extended to separate the high-quality plutonium 239 from plutonium 240: by making much radioactive waste – the waste from any 'civilian' nuclear power station – 'reworkable', this would increase the availability of plutonium for weapons and make proliferation almost impossible to restrain.[46] Laser separation signals conclusively the end of the fiction of separable military and civilian nuclear projects.

While laser separation is the most worrying, in fact many aspects of commercial research could have a military spin-off. It was partly in recognition of such facts that President Carter decided to stop the reprocessing of spent fuel and to terminate work on fast breeder reactors, decisions which the Reagan administration has reversed. But although the dangers of the inadequate distinction between civil and military uses of nuclear energy are fully recognized,[47] political and commercial interests ensure they remain with us. President Reagan's recent decision to lift the legal ban on the production of plutonium by private companies, apparently a response to a shortage of plutonium caused by the increase in America's nuclear forces, can only exacerbate the issue.

• (d) Nuclear power is becoming widespread throughout the world, and even though it will only ever make a small contribution to the total supply of energy, it inevitably takes with it the potential for development of nuclear weapons by any state which possesses it.[48] This danger and the difficulty involved in the international control of nuclear weapons (i.e. in enforcing 'non-proliferation') were discussed in Chapter 8. If, however, nuclear power were not used, there would be virtually no occasion for uranium mining or for any of the processes or equipment necessary for the making of bombs. Any attempt to make nuclear bombs would be relatively easily detectable and would carry a high political cost as being clearly military in intent.[49]

A nuclear power programme is, even in the most cautious accounting terms, the *most expensive* way to generate electricity. In the UK, historically this has been so, is now the case and promises to be more so in the future. The leading expert critic has shown that, once the dubious statistical practices and wild assumptions of CEGB calculations are corrected, not only are the capital costs of nuclear stations much higher than coal-fired power stations, but that, in Britain, Magnox electricity has *never* been cheaper than electricity produced from coal, contrary to the view which the CEGB cultivates with the public.[50] Professor Jeffery's figures for generating costs show AGR nuclear to cost 137–144 per cent of new coal-fired plant;[51] nor is there any prospect of improvement, since present estimates do not embrace the huge and unsolved problems of the disposal of radioactive waste – a long-term financial liability of huge proportions[52] – and of decommissioning. A nuclear power station lasts only twenty-five to thirty years and must then be dismantled. No one has yet done this successfully and intentionally. The Lucens reactor in Switzerland suffered a catastrophic failure of the primary circuit on 21 January 1969. Fortunately, being under a mountain, the radioactivity could be contained and the mangled wreckage eventually dismantled. After the near-disaster of the fire in Number One plutonium production reactor at Windscale in October 1957, both it and its twin, Number Two, were filled with concrete.[53] The fate of the Harrisburg reactor is still unclear. Intentional decommissioning must involve containment of the radioactivity, and is likely to prove up to twice as expensive as the initial construction,[54] though the variation between estimates indicates that in the absence of real examples our knowledge can be but hazy.

Even ignoring such hidden costs and the various governmental subventions which went and still go into the several parts of the nuclear cycle (mining, ore-extraction, enrichment and fuel-rod manufacture, and also the development of reactors),[55] the most that is now officially claimed is that nuclear power could be marginally cheaper than power from conventional fuels; many authorities, including a US congressional committee in 1978, believe that it may prove more expensive. Once American utility companies began to see that they could be saddled with huge extra costs, and despite legal protection from full liability in the event of an accident under the Price-Anderson Act, the retreat from nuclear power has gathered speed. There have been only two uncancelled orders since 1974; no commercial nuclear power plant has been ordered in the United States since the accident at Three Mile Island. During 1981, five reactors under construction in Washington State were 'mothballed' indefinitely, while on the East Coast, from New England to North Carolina, reactors have been cancelled. The world's second largest nuclear-reactor constructor, General Electric, expects no more orders for the 1980s.[56]

The CEGB memorandum to the Select Committee on Energy estimated that the installed cost of the proposed pressure water reactor nuclear power programme was £1,000 per kilowatt capacity. We believe this is a conservative figure, and of course it does not reflect the weight of the full nuclear cycle. Nevertheless, if used, this gives a cost of £1.3 billion for a 1.3 Gw (gigawatt) station. Such a station, operating at 60 per cent load factor – an optimistic figure given that past operating experience of PWRs worldwide has been 46.7 per cent (Select Committee evidence again) – over a twenty-five-year lifetime would produce at 1980 prices £4.2 billion of electricity.

At the same time, the Conservative government has cut back on highly cost effective waste-saving and insulation schemes and, more particularly, has refused to back a gas-gathering pipeline for the North Sea oilfields to collect the gas at present being 'flared off' to a current value of £1 million a *day*. The capital cost of the pipeline would be £2.7 billion, i.e. approximately *one tenth* of the projected cost of the 15 Gw(e) nuclear programme. It would provide a total energy about the *same* as that from the lifetime of the nuclear stations. The estimated value of the gas that would be saved would be, at 1980 prices, £25 billion. So as a purely *financial* investment, the gas pipeline looks like a four – possibly six – times better return on invested capital.

But we must translate the comparison into *energy* terms. Apart from the 8 per cent of UK energy demand which has to be electrical (motors, lighting, welding, telecommunications, etc.), much of the rest is low-grade heat, and another, small, part is high-grade heat for industrial processes, either of which is much more efficiently produced from gas than from electricity, and low-grade heat even more so from low-grade sources, which gas is not. It is, in energy terms, quite idiotic to transmit electricity and then to turn it into heat because electricity is not a *source* of energy like coal or uranium; it is produced by consuming such sources and in the process, degrading most of their useful energy. Hence, electricity generation is, above all, an energy *user*. Four times as much coal is burned in order to heat a building by electricity than would be used to heat it directly.[57]

Therefore, seen as an energy investment, the gas-gathering pipeline is even more (perhaps *eight to twelve* times more) cost effective, assuming an optimistic outcome of the CEGB's own calculations. Furthermore, the pipeline would be relatively labour intensive, generating jobs and bringing useful orders to the domestic steel industry.

In sum, we have looked at the economics of nuclear power, starting from the present position in its own terms and moving out: at the comparative capital costs of plant; at real comparative generating costs; at the looming, vast and still barely quantified cost of the full nuclear cycle; at the strikingly bad return on investment in financial and energy terms, compared to available alternatives, offered by nuclear power. We are driven to conclude that if the nuclear programme is viewed as an energy programme, selected from among other available energy options, the government's policies in this field are incomprehensible. It is therefore interesting to note that when previewing the CEGB's case for the Sizewell B PWR, a board member did not mention the old claims (of cheapness and the need to meet rising demand) since neither is now publicly tenable. Instead he stressed 'security and diversity of supply' (i.e. dislike of the coal miners) and the need to retain a nuclear option.[58] Other motives that might have been mentioned are indicated in this chapter and in Appendix D.

In addition to the economic issue, nuclear power – as power – has many other disadvantages. Nuclear reactors are restricted by their design, because of fatigue problems, to supplying 'base load' electricity – i.e. the continuous basic minimum of electricity in an electric grid system. In the context of Britain, around three quarters of generating capacity has to be more flexible than nuclear stations permit. And a grid system supplying electricity, both in its scale and its product, is unsuited to many of the requirements of underdeveloped countries. Their need for electricity is predominantly in the form of small local stations and, far more than this, they need other non-electrical *types* of energy. The capital intensiveness of nuclear power exacerbates unemployment, as already noted. The enormous expenditure on research (though borne in part by military budgets) could have been better used if diverted into energy conservation or into developing new energy sources. After all the research and development that has been poured into nuclear power, it still contributes less than 1 per cent of the world's energy consumption, and it seems at the moment unlikely that it will ever supply more than about 10 per cent.[59] It would be nice to believe that the dangers of nuclear power and its unsuitability for many purposes have been recognized, but in fact it has been the simple issues of cost and reliability which explain the dramatic fall-off in nuclear power programmes.

It is perfectly clear that during the rest of this century no electrical solution to oil and gas depletion is possible in the time available, even assuming zero growth in demand: it would require about 250 Gw(e) at 70 per cent load factor of new capacity in the U K to substitute for oil and gas. Nuclear energy could never meet this – the 1979 plan is for 15 Gw(e) to AD 2000; no more could coal, since an equally impracticable four-fold increase in coal production would be required. This is quite apart from the impossible scale of power-station construction in either case. Only development of renewable energy sources, conservation, improvements in the efficiency of machines, reduction in the use of electricity for low-grade heating and a great expansion of district heating for that purpose – coupled with coal-fired generation of the modest irreducible requirement for electricity – offer any hope of making the substitutions in time. Alternative forms of power are now coming forward.[60] This would have happened much sooner if adequate American and British research money had been made available.[61] Instead, in Britain £2,500,000,000 has been spent over twenty-five years on nuclear R D and D (*excluding* fast breeder and fusion research) to provide in 1980 1.5 per cent of our national energy needs. In contrast R D and D on energy conservation in 1980–81 was £299,000, and the Conservative government has, in fact, *withdrawn* money from renewable energy research. Britain already lags behind more perceptive European countries in viable energy planning, and is set to trail even further. Compared to available low-energy strategies using reliable technologies, nuclear power makes no sense, but does make plutonium.[62]

The persistence of nuclear power may also reflect the simple fact that reactor technology is thought to be more exciting, intellectually stimulating, and prestigious in the world of energy technologists and scientists than improving boring old coal-fired power stations or, even worse, 'intermediate technology' – messing about with small-scale methane extractors for cow-dung. It is the Zuckerman argument about the lure of exotic weapons technology in the context of the Steel Triangle applied here. But burning cow-dung contributes more energy to the world today than nuclear power (although much less than burning wood) and the wasted methane which rises from the cows of the Ganges valley is sufficient to be detected by satellite! In fact if all the people employed by the U K Atomic Energy Authority had spent their time thatching houses, they would have made a greater contribution to the national energy regime. In addition to having a viable energy future, we would *not* have the radioactive wastes, the plutonium and the addition to that burden of contamination arising from all nuclear projects which irreversibly affects the form of life on this planet. The case against a nuclear defence policy concerns more than the folly of possessing bombs.

10 Alternatives

'A journey of a thousand miles must begin with a single step.'
– Chinese proverb

1 The Political Steps Ahead

In this final chapter we suggest ways in which we can begin to make a future different from the one which otherwise we seem to be doomed to embrace.

It is frequently argued by government spokesmen that any change of direction would involve risks. That is true. But every course of action involves risk, and we must decide which is the least hazardous. We have argued in this book that our present course involves a range of poisonous uncertainties and of rapidly increasing future perils, including the risk of nuclear war. We must, therefore, seek a new direction. But before we produce detailed alternatives, outlining the first steps away from existing policies, it is important that we have a clear view of the destination to which we want to go.

The first goal must be to remove the danger of nuclear weapons. President Kennedy spoke of 'the nuclear sword of Damocles, hanging by the slenderest of threads, liable to be cut at any moment by madness, accident, or miscalculation'. The threat from this hanging sword is in a category of its own: apocalyptic in the future, morally untenable and physically polluting in the present. Government action on nuclear weapons cannot be linked to their behaviour on any other matters. The diplomatic device of 'linkage' in this context ('we won't discuss nuclear weapons unless you amend your ways on human rights') is a luxury that the human race cannot afford. But beyond nuclear disarmament there is a wider objective which should also be embraced.

During the Second World War, President Roosevelt defined the war aims of the Allies. One of these was 'Freedom from fear, that is reduction of armaments down to the level at which no nation has enough armaments to make aggressive war against any neighbour anywhere.' To jaded ears in the 1980s it sounds like an impossible dream. Yet safety lies only in the achievement of General and Complete Disarmament, nuclear and conventional. This was the hope of the distant days when the memory of the world war was still fresh. This is today the goal to which 149 nations, including our own, pledged themselves in the Final Document of the First Special Session on Disarmament of the United Nations General Assembly in 1978 (see box).

> 'Removing the threat of a world war – a nuclear war – is the most acute and urgent task of the present day. Mankind is confronted with a choice: we must halt the arms race and proceed to disarmament or face annihilation.
>
> 'The ultimate objective of the efforts of States in the disarmament process is general and complete disarmament under effective international control.
>
> 'The principal goals of disarmament are to ensure the survival of mankind and to eliminate the danger of war, in particular nuclear war, to ensure that war is no longer an instrument for settling international disputes and that the use and the threat of force are eliminated from international life, as provided for in the Charter of the United Nations.'[1]

No single country can work effectively in isolation for general nuclear disarmament. The arms race is primarily in the hands of the two superpowers and the major decisions will eventually have to be taken by the United States and the Soviet Union. Nevertheless, by its independent actions, the British government can move towards making this country a safer place for its own citizens and, just as important, the independent actions of the British government can have beneficial effects on other countries. We suggest that specific steps can be taken by this country in the immediate future.

(A) NUCLEAR WEAPONS CONTROLLED BY BRITAIN

The Foreign Office Arms Control and Disarmament Unit repeatedly emphasizes in its *Bulletin* the impracticality of achieving disarmament at a stroke, through a single treaty for General and Complete Disarmament. With this we agree. However, we disagree with the alternative that the Foreign Office has proposed, namely, the pursuit of highly specific and limited arms control agreements.

Here is a six-point plan for this country that would carry us through the first step towards general disarmament. The proposals should be read in conjunction with the alternative defence strategy presented later in this chapter.

● (i) The Polaris submarines should be retired, the nuclear submarine facilities at Faslane dismantled, and the government should not proceed with the programme of nuclear-powered fleet submarines or 'their proposed facilities.

● (ii) Britain should cancel the programme to install Trident II missiles in new submarines.

● (iii) Nuclear bombs carried by V-bombers, Buccaneers and Jaguars should be decommissioned, the V-bombers retired as planned, but not replaced with a Tornado variant, and the other aircraft reassigned to solely conventional roles.

● (iv) Nuclear depth-charges carried routinely on anti-submarine patrols should be decommissioned. (Anti-submarine warfare tactics should be radically rethought, as suggested in our next section.)

● (v) Most urgent of all is the problem with the army. Its Lance missiles should be removed and access to nuclear shells from the American stockpile formally renounced. This action is inseparable from those under B (ii) and (iii), pp. 265–6.

● (vi) The carrying out of research for new weapons at the Atomic Weapons Research Establishment (AWRE) at Aldermaston should be halted. Personnel and facilities should be redirected solely to the problem of the dismantling and safest possible long-term disposal of fissile and contaminated materials (since there is no known method of absolutely safe disposal).

In the event of nuclear war, or even conventional war, nuclear power reactors and waste-storage sites such as Windscale are obvious and horribly dangerous targets. For this reason, but also because military and civilian nuclear projects are inseparable, poisonous, and uneconomic compared to alternative ways of making and using power, we take a stronger line than the Flowers Commission and favour a declaration of intent to aim for the progressive elimination of nuclear fission programmes from Britain's energy regime. It was a mistake to have started out on that road. Scientific staff of the U K A E A, C E G B, and A W R E should combine to attack the problem of radioactive waste already accumulated; the borosilicate AVM process will not do. Until resolved the Windscale site will have to continue to act as a temporary repository. A strictly supervised laboratory is needed for the manufacture of radio-isotopes for medical and other purposes. Simultaneously, investment should be made in a massive insulation and heat conservation programme, in fluidized bed combustion and desulphurizing flue scrubbers for coal-fired power stations, in combined heat and power generation plants, and in the vigorous development of renewable energy technologies, all of which would not only offset the small loss of current from the nuclear programme, but would also begin to move in the direction of replacing oil and gas supplies. There should be a coherent national energy plan, so far never provided by any British government.

Clearly, action in this wider, yet related, strategic area cannot be completed as swiftly as those actions listed in the six points.

(B) OTHER NUCLEAR WEAPONS IN BRITAIN

The second dimension of British political action relates to the way in which this country is used as a base for nuclear weapons systems and their essential ancillary detection and communication equipment over which the British government has no final control. In this we are not unique. West Germany in particular is a country in a similar situation, with an even higher density of nuclear weapons on its soil. Therefore, realistically, when we discuss this problem, we automatically move on to a European stage. Each European nation diminishes its own sovereignty when it relinquishes to America the power to decide its entire existence, and only by reasserting individual sovereignty can the member countries of NATO come to the discussion as free and equal partners, which is actually what the North Atlantic Treaty stipulated thirty years ago.

Here are three immediate goals:

● (i) No new nuclear weapons, land, sea, or air launched, should enter the NATO arsenal. In particular, the cruise and Pershing II missiles and the neutron warheads for Lance missiles and eight-inch shells should not be deployed.

● (ii) Britain should resume sovereignty over her own territory. The government should announce an intention to require the removal from British soil within a short period of that announcement of all American nuclear weapons. By a further date, it should require the dismantling of all American facilities connected with nuclear weapons. At the same time, it should be made clear that this return to the objectives of the North Atlantic Treaty, a stand already taken by a number of NATO countries, does not affect the obligation upon all Alliance members to assist each other with forces in mutual defence (in a real sense of the word) if necessary. We need to return to the spirit of the Treaty.

● (iii) This British action would not be sprung suddenly upon our European neighbours; it would be crucial that West Germany in particular understood and preferably participated in these moves. In the case of all Alliance states, the 'de-nuclearization' of their forces would be accompanied, at the first step, by transformations of their armed forces into forms appropriate to their particular circumstances, but upon the same principles as are set out for Britain in the next section. On the European stage:

● (a) A formal renunciation of the first use of nuclear weapons should be immediately signed with the Warsaw Pact nations.

● (b) Simultaneously, an agreement should be negotiated to prohibit short-range 'battlefield' nuclear weapons – arguably the most dangerous sort of all because a general escalation would result from their use – from a zone, of width to be determined, astride the inter-German frontier. Once established it should be extended to the northern and southern flanks of the Central Front.

● (c) This should be followed by establishment of a European nuclear-free zone from Poland to Portugal. This action is directed at medium-range systems.

(C) ACTION IN THE INTERNATIONAL ARENA

As well as the concrete national and continental actions proposed, there are actions which can only be taken internationally.

● (i) *A comprehensive test ban treaty.* This is vital. The superpowers cheated the world of it in 1963. An end to tests in any environment stops the development of new nuclear devices. The neutron bomb, for example, was developed with underground tests after the signing of the Partial Test Ban Treaty. Although difficult to enforce, the ban should, if possible, include controls on the computer simulation of nuclear explosions, a technology which the Americans and the British, and presumably other states also, have acquired, no doubt in part as a hedge against the day when resistance to a comprehensive test ban becomes politically too difficult. But that day is not yet here, for as the full scale of the 'electromagnetic pulse threat' (see pp. 140–42) to US communications and sensors dawns in the Pentagon, we must be prepared for fierce pressure from that quarter to conduct atmospheric tests again, invoking the 'supreme interests of the state' under the escape clause which was written into the Partial Test Ban Treaty. It must be resisted. Never again must the people settle for less than all.

- (ii) *An agreement to stop flight tests of new nuclear delivery vehicles.* No flight tests: no new missiles or bombers. Such an agreement could be monitored at once, by national technical means. This proposal is close to the demand for an immediate 'freeze' of all new systems which is a central plank of the American nuclear disarmament movement.

- (iii) *The opening of international debate over control and prohibition on production of fissionable materials for weapons purposes.* Laser separation technology makes all reactor fuel potential weapons material. The ineffectiveness of the Non-Proliferation Treaty was demonstrated conclusively in the Iraqi desert: the Israelis attacked the Iraqi reactor because they felt that treaty provisions were no protection against the production of bombs. Chapter 8 showed that if we are to avoid living in a nuclear armed crowd, action must be swift and radical. It will not be enough simply to 'internationalize' parts of the nuclear cycle. The way to strangle nuclear proliferation is to withdraw reactor fuel and technical expertise from existing reactors and place an embargo on the export of nuclear technology. But, in addition, there must be the creation of an international 'fission bank' to which all national stocks of plutonium and enriched uranium should be surrendered and of an effective international atomic agency to take over all uranium mining. This proposal revives in modern form the idea of the Acheson–Lilienthal Report of 1946.

2 The Military Consequences and Opportunities

The NATO doctrine of a flexible response with nuclear weapons has been accompanied by an extraordinary inflexibility of thought. By degrees it has become apparent that many reflective military men in NATO appreciate this fact. Usually they have aired their doubts publicly only upon retirement, but as critical views have become more widespread, some serving officers have also revealed their concern, as we have shown in Chapter 6.

In Britain, Field-Marshal Lord Carver has been a particularly articulate critic of current NATO doctrine. He has described the concept of flexible response as 'almost incomprehensible and certainly illogical'.

'At the heart of the problem is the dilemma that, if you wish to deter war by the fear that nuclear weapons will be used, you have to appear to be prepared to use them in certain circumstances. But if you do so, and the enemy answers back – as he has the capability to do and has clearly said he would – you are very much worse off than if you had not done so, if indeed you can be said to be there at all. To pose an unacceptable risk to the enemy automatically poses the same risk, or perhaps even a greater one, to yourself; but to attempt to reduce the risk, in order to make the threat of use more credible, by some form of limiting nuclear war – territorially or by types of targets or means of delivery – begins to make the risk more acceptable and therefore less of a deterrent. The more acceptable nuclear war may appear to be to the governments and military men of the nuclear powers, the more likely it is that it will actually come about, and, even if it is limited in some way, the effects on those who live in the countries in or over which the nuclear weapons of both sides are exploded will be catastrophic. To call the results defence or security makes a mockery of the terms.'

(Field-Marshal Lord Carver)[2]

While unorthodox in these views (see box), Lord Carver accepts the analysis of the Soviet threat as described by the Ministry of Defence and therefore believes strongly that conventional weaponry of the type currently deployed should be increased so that NATO can confidently abandon its 'low-yield' theatre nuclear weapons. However, he remains ambivalent about total nuclear disarmament. He has 'no doubt that possession of nuclear weapons by the USA and USSR deters them both from going to war with each other', but at the same time he perceives the danger of persisting with the policy of nuclear deterrence.

Lord Carver's description of the inescapable attributes of nuclear deterrence is forceful and correct. But in two respects our paths then part. Firstly, Lord Carver is not prepared to carry the thrust of his argument to its logical conclusion. 'Minimum deterrence', the position which he sees as a satisfactory end in itself, we see as only a step on the road. Secondly, a different view of the 'threat', such as we have advanced in this book, leads us to a different assessment of relative risk. 'Scenario No. 1' – the NATO conventional wisdom – is a vision of massed tanks of the Warsaw Pact rolling across the north German plains; 'Scenario No. 2' is of Soviet invasion and occupation of the British Isles. While we see the risks of either of these things happening as very low, and not because the Soviet desire to do them is 'deterred', but because there is no convincing evidence for the existence of that desire, we accept that, during the first step away from present postures, it would be prudent to provide a non-nuclear defence against those two eventualities. After all, there is considerable uncertainty about what will happen to the USSR in coming decades. Most immediate is the question of what will happen when the old men of Brezhnev's generation pass. For example, will this unleash the explosive forces of suppressed nationalisms within the USSR? The future is full of potential risks that must be avoided, but we differ from Lord Carver in our view of how that might best be done. These details appear later in this section. First, we must discuss some more general principles which should guide nuclear disarmament.

As early as 1962, Helmut Schmidt, later to be West German Chancellor, provided a way of thinking about this question. He said: 'The optimum goal of German defence policy and strategy would ... be the creation of an armaments structure clearly unsuited for the offensive role yet adequate beyond the shadow of a doubt to defend German territory.'[3] The object is to have a policy that is minimally provocative. The distinction is therefore between this kind of *defensive* deterrence, which can be a credible deterrent, and the NATO doctrine of *retaliatory* deterrence with nuclear weapons, which is plainly incredible as a deterrent, or, if credible, then lunatic. The distinction is one that Dan Smith develops in his thoughtful reappraisal of British defence strategy.[4]

The discussion about alternative forms of defence is necessary and long overdue. On past performance, it is neither right nor wise that attempts to find solutions should be left to Ministry of Defence officials working in secret. The officials seem incapable of escaping from the outmoded orthodoxy that has characterized so much of NATO strategic thought. The public debate has at least as good a chance to generate clear-headed and imaginative solutions.

The current discussion revolves round the priorities that should be given to three tactics for a modern non-retaliatory defence policy. Such a policy, of course, involves a political will to confine the use of all weaponry to defensive purposes.

● (a) Capitalizing on technological improvements in defensive weapons to make possible transformation of present armed forces.

● (b) Establishing a militia – a citizen's reserve army – that could be mobilized rapidly and used to defend the country in depth.

● (c) Arranging civilian affairs in such a way as to complicate the task that an occupying power would have in imposing its will on the civilian population.[5]

Our concern in this chapter is to specify only the very first step, and necessarily that involves a discussion confined principally to point (a). These proposals are not mutually exclusive, nor are the first two at any rate novel. After debating whether or not to adopt a nuclear defence, both Sweden and Switzerland have come to rely on militia and formidable modern defensive weaponry, carefully selected.

Sweden has total armed forces of about 65,000, of whom some two-thirds are conscripts. However, it can mobilize up to about 800,000 within seventy-two hours. It relies on a coastal defence navy with emphasis on fast missile or torpedo boats, submarines, mine-warfare vessels, and coastal artillery, and, operating from extensively protected bases (in one case inside a mountain), an air force which is primarily directed towards interception (twelve air defence squadrons as against six fighter/ground attack squadrons). The army, organized in local defence districts, is designed to fight defensive actions to exhaust an invader. Switzerland can mobilize up to 625,000 men of the militia army in only forty-eight hours. Swiss citizens engage in military exercises annually and keep their weapons and some equipment at home. Switzerland relies extensively on the careful preparation of 'slow-down' defensive battles involving modern precision-guided munitions (PGMs) to debilitate the attacker. Other countries like Yugoslavia are less extensively equipped, but can mobilize up to 500,000 people in territorial defence and have a formidable reputation for guerrilla fighting.[6]

Britain is not identical with Sweden, Switzerland, or Yugoslavia. Their models cannot be applied directly to our situation. There are differences in social structure: Britain is much more urbanized, not particularly mountainous, and only parts are suitable for guerrilla warfare. However, Britain is an offshore island. Over a period of 900 years this useful asset has proven its worth several times. Here we consider 'Scenario No. 2': invasion.

An invasion force would, as in 1940, require the transport of an army by air and landing craft (or hovercraft). For this to succeed, air superiority is essential. Hitler never obtained air superiority and he was never able to invade. In this respect Britain could benefit from the Swedish experience by moving towards a dedicated air defence and interceptor air force. The

RAF has seventeen strike/attack squadrons to nine interceptor squadrons (seven of which are British based). A change would require considerable investment in radar, communications, and effective IFF (electronic equipment to make possible identification of whether an aircraft is friend or foe), as well as in aircraft. Some moves in this area are already in hand, modernizing the system, and designing the P110/ACA air superiority fighter.[7] However, the need for tactical air power would not be entirely eliminated, because strike aircraft would form an important part of Channel and coastal defences, deploying air-to-surface guided weapons as a necessary adjunct to surface-to-surface weapons in deterring or stopping an invasion fleet. Furthermore, should a form of territorial defence be adopted by Great Britain at a later stage, close ground-support aircraft capable of taking off and landing on short runways, or vertically, like the Harrier 'jump-jet', would have a role to play alongside helicopter forces. Thus at Step One, reversal of the proportion of strike/attack squadrons to air defence squadrons in the RAF is required. This would have the effect of greatly reducing RAF (Germany); but, as we discuss below, this is not likely to weaken our ability to halt an assault, since Central Front tactics need revision also. A two-to-one bias to air defence would, in fact, exactly match the present structure of the Swedish Air Force.

The Swedish model of coastal defence with fast, small vessels, patrol submarines, mine-warfare ships and coastal artillery offers an example of how the Royal Navy could be reorganized to provide protection for coastal waters and offshore assets. The Soviet model is also of interest. Given the paramount fear of invasion felt by Soviet leaders, the USSR has accumulated more fast coastal protection vessels than the rest of the world combined. They support these ships with extensive shore-based naval aviation. Again, limited steps have been taken here, with a new class of mine-countermeasures vessels and an excellent new class of offshore protection vessel entering service, although in restricted numbers, and a new diesel patrol submarine (the Vickers Type 2400) in an advanced stage of design.[8]

The equipment to fulfil a naval coastal and offshore mission must be tailored to British conditions: the North Sea and the Western Approaches are not the Baltic. Thus, the Swedish 'Spica' class of high-speed patrol craft cannot serve as a general model, although there is a case for a narrow-seas fleet of such missile boats (in which Vosper's has a proven expertise) – rather as there was need for motor torpedo boats during the Second World War. What is required is, in addition, a larger class of vessel, with lower speed and, instead of gas turbines, diesel power (for reliability, fuel economy, and tolerance to a salty environment). There should be a design emphasis upon sea-keeping, especially bad-weather performance, and tolerance to damage. It should have primarily an off-shore patrol and surface attack capability; anti-submarine capability should be by self-contained helicopter detection/data processing/attack system, with only modest provision for ship-board sonar and computing. (With the advent of the helicopter, top speed has become a less important quality in a warship than it was during the period 1897–1945 – that is, during the ascendancy of the Parsons steam turbine.) Anti-aircraft defence would employ standard A-A guns and 'marinized' small PGMs. Such a ship is required in fair number and therefore the unit cost must be low. The temptation to elaborate the basic design – to change it from 'gothic' to 'baroque', as it were – must be resisted. Indeed, designing a cheap and effective ship is intellectually the most demanding challenge to the naval architect, and he must be in a position to exercise vigorous discipline throughout the programme. The new 'Castle' class of offshore protection vessel whose lead ship, HMS *Leeds Castle*, was launched in October 1980 at a cost of about £10 million, appears to fit this bill well. Its design represents a welcome return to realism and precise conception of role after the 'baroque era' in Royal Navy ship design.[9]

That era really arrived in the 1960s. The decision to abandon big deck carriers, made under Defence Secretary Denis Healey and expressed in the 1966 White Paper, created consternation in naval circles, from which emerged a two-pronged response: to find a way to circumvent the decision and to promote a radically new sort of surface fleet. Underpinning this strategy was the 1967 decision by the Royal Navy to adopt COGOG (combined gas or gas) all-gas turbine propulsion for its future major surface ships and, associated with that, to repair engines by modular replacement rather than work *in situ*. Around these two concepts were designed the increasingly and finally astonishingly expensive, extremely complex 'push-button' warships of the 1970s – the Type 42 Sheffield class destroyer, the Type 22 Broadsword class and Type 21 Amazon class frigates, and the 'through-deck cruiser'/pocket aircraft carriers of the Invincible class. This last has no clear role, but was the way that the Navy fought the carrier war in Whitehall.

In their enthusiasm for new propulsion and weapons technologies and for innovative construction (for example, a much greater use of aluminium than some more cautious naval architects thought wise), designers appear to have forgotten that Clausewitz's principle of 'friction' in warfare applies as much at sea as on land. Gas turbines are exacting machines requiring, for example, the greatest purity in their fuel; repair by replacement is a sound engineering argument, but raises considerable logistical demands; and it is unrealistic to hope that a warship will not be extensively damaged in combat. As Clausewitz explained, it is not prudent to require as a minimum an exacting level of performance by men or machines.

These classes were designed more around 'what can the technology do' (a force described in Chapter 5 above) than around any hard-headed thinking about roles in relation to defence needs in the real world. Some naval architects blame the vagueness in role definition, the construction and cost overruns, and the technical problems of these ships on the committee system of design, which was also an innovation of the 1960s; and they may have an important point. Cost escalation was huge. In 1981 the Ministry of Defence admitted that a Type 22 then cost £120 million. Critics of the 'baroque orthodoxy' – which now applies generally in Western arms industries – are fond of quoting Voltaire's dictum that 'the Best is the enemy of the Good'. Experience supports them.[10] The official role of the baroque fleet in the 1980s has finally become one of anti-submarine warfare by task force; but it was not in that role that it was mainly tested during the Falklands war of 1982.

This war graphically revealed that air superiority is the only effective defence against 'smart' air-launched anti-shipping missiles or sustained waves of air attack. The very costly and complex missile defence systems of the baroque fleet were insufficiently effective, and under attack, the Type 42 and Type 21 appear to have been woefully inflammable. Since a combination of submarines and long-range naval aviation is the best way to hunt submarines, the ASW carrier task force was thus seen to be not only obsolete, but also vulnerable. Three hard but simple lessons must be learned.

The first is that, as a result of the 'PGM revolution', surface ships – merchantman or baroque frigate – within range of hostile shore-based aircraft and without friendly air superiority are highly vulnerable. Such a situation is most likely to arise when conducting offensive operations. For 'power projecting' missions, such air cover can be relied upon only if carrier based. Without carriers, the Royal Navy is not equipped – nor should it be – for such expeditions at long range. (America is the only country that is.) The second lesson will be much less palatable to admirals who conceive of future naval warfare as a bigger version of the biggest carrier engagement of the Second World War, the Battle of Midway, or to politicians who, given the chance, prefer gunboat diplomacy. This lesson is that the 1966 decision to phase out big deck carriers was absolutely right, and must not be reversed, despite the fact that such a vessel, flying long endurance interceptors and airborne early-warning radar planes, would have been invaluable during the Falklands war. The third lesson, which is political and not technical, has been confirmed by British experience in the Falklands war; it is that realism must return to the design of Britain's conventional forces; that those forces should relate to the defence needs of Britain in the late twentieth – not the late nineteenth – century, and that the maintenance of a credible (conventional) naval deterrent should be financed by the cancellation of an incredible (nuclear) deterrent, which for any sane political or military purpose is self-evidently and demonstrably useless, and is also an outright danger, not least to its possessors.

While the Falklands war has heavily underscored what some naval architects already knew – that the day of the baroque designs must end – (i.e. no more should be built), there is the problem of what to do with those already acquired. We conclude that they had better be retained during shortened lifetimes for escort and ASW duties; that no new investment should be made in surface-ship ASW techniques (the polar opposite of present planned expenditure), but that effort be redirected to producing a different sort of protection against submarines. Eventually there may be a case for a 'gothic' escort frigate; but that time is not now.

At present Britain has large and irreducible requirements for imported food and raw materials (and, unless changes are made, when North Sea oil is spent, for energy too). There is heated debate about what threat there is thought to be to the sea-lanes which carry this trade, and if a threat, then to which sea-lanes. The presumed vehicle of this threat is the Soviet fleet of 266 attack submarines (172 of which are conventionally powered and so of restricted endurance).

This is, in fact, an assumption about the intended role of Soviet submarines in wartime which is contrary to extensive evidence from declared naval doctrine, from the design, armament, dates and rates of deployment of Soviet vessels. These suggest that the primary role of both attack and ballistic missile submarines has been, since the mid 1950s, not (as extrapolation from Western thinking might imply) respectively to disrupt sea-lanes or launch attacks against the continental USA but rather to try to destroy, first, American carrier forces and then, when the prime nuclear attack role shifted below the waves, the Polaris, Poseidon, and now Trident submarines. The Soviet submarine fleet is thus to be seen as a consistent part of the Red Fleet's role in the overall homeland defence strategy. Nevertheless, setting all this aside and accepting the Western view, if there is indeed a worldwide and consistent threat, it is at once obvious that Britain, like any middle-ranking European country in a similar plight, and even in an alliance, has not the remotest hope of defending all the major sea-lanes upon which she depends.

In fact, current Western ASW strategies increasingly resemble what we know of Soviet plans: both sides would try to destroy the other's submarines – each fearing those of the other for different reasons – by filling the seas with underwater nuclear explosions (sterilizing the oceans in military jargon, and literally). In the Western case, rocket torpedoes and depth bombs dropped from helicopters or from maritime aircraft would be used; in the Soviet case, ballistic and cruise missiles.[11] We do not believe that it is at all necessary for Britain to be forced into this ridiculous and abhorrent sort of strategy.

In the first place, as just indicated, it would be wise to try to examine the presumed submarine (and naval air) threat less excitedly and therefore to see it more accurately, and in perspective. In the second, the forms of European defence that will be shortly proposed in this section make military reinforcement from the United States, by sea, much less central to NATO defence strategy than it is at present. This will become increasingly so as the successful transformation of Europe's defences proceeds, and is thus a further incentive to get started without delay on that process. In the third place, in the 1960s and 1970s, important realignment away from the old British Empire trading partners and towards our European neighbours occurred. Consequently, although North American grain remains significant in the pattern of essential food imports, much less of that traffic is now from beyond the European and Atlantic zones. Finally, there are alternative, and better, means of defence to hand.

Therefore, if the threat of disruption is more limited, as we argue that it is, then something sensible can be done about it. Our view is that at Step One of disarmament, it would be prudent to retain an efficient anti-submarine and naval air interception barrier at the Greenland–Iceland–UK gap to protect the transatlantic and littoral sea routes. The anti-submarine barrier should be maintained using primarily an augmented Coastal Command of long-range submarine-hunting aircraft (and associated tanker aircraft, if required), a fleet of new long-range diesel-electric submarines and mine barriers (in war); secondarily, helicopters carried on offshore patrol vessels. In the event of hostilities, certain merchant ships could be fitted with modular helipads for ASW helicopters to provide their own limited organic defence. There is also another reason for this suggestion, as follows.

Since the mid-1950s the USSR has developed a long-range shore-based naval air force, primarily as a counter to what the Soviets perceived to be the increasing threat of American carrier-based air power which, before the advent of the ballistic missile submarine, carried the American sea-borne nuclear strike force and even after, with the creation of the long-endurance nuclear-powered carrier task force, was seen by them as a grave threat to their homeland. Some Soviet naval air force planes provide reconnaissance and other support (for example, mid-course guidance for ship- and submarine-launched missiles) for the Red Fleet; others are equipped for independent anti-shipping attacks. The aerial threat to convoys is presumed to come from them: first introduced in 1954, the Tu 16 Badger medium jet bomber continues to be the backbone of Soviet naval aviation. About 240 are in service, supplemented by forty Tu 22 Blinder supersonic bombers, introduced in the early 1960s, and with much shorter unrefuelled range, and about seventy Tu 22M Backfire B variable geometry supersonic bombers, each armed with one Kitchen long-range stand-off air-to-surface nuclear capable missile. It is thought that this aircraft will gradually replace the Badger. Proponents of a large blue-water surface fleet for the Royal Navy sometimes cite the need for anti-aircraft defence as a reason. It is important to keep a sense of proportion. To reach the North Atlantic sea-lanes, Russian aircraft would have to fly through the Greenland–Iceland–UK gap where they can be detected by early-warning radar. (The British Nimrod AEW system will be operational in the 1980s.) They then face air interception on the long passage from base; and if they reach the North Atlantic, at extended range, they will have limited flexibility of action. Geography dictates that the USSR cannot use in-flight refuelling as effectively as Western countries. Therefore it is obvious that early detection and interception are the most cost-effective investment. In fact, it is already being made, and our earlier proposals for an emphasis on interceptors in the RAF would enhance this capability. Area and point defences are by definition a less elegant solution, and of these, more baroque Type 22 frigates would be the least efficient investment, and should be avoided. Instead, helicopters embarked on merchantmen could provide platforms for airborne early-warning radar and, perhaps, for air-to-air missiles. Sea Harrier jump jets can also operate from a temporary, improvised carrier, but this may be too extreme a response. One more closely matched to the scale of the threat would be to provide modular anti-aircraft missile, gun, and radar systems to be fitted to merchantmen during hostilities to supplement a modest provision of anti-aircraft escorts (at present the existing Type 22s and in the future, if required, a 'gothic' escort frigate). In both anti-aircraft and anti-submarine protection, investment in very expensive capital ships like the Invincible class or nuclear-powered fleet submarines (at £175 million per copy, not considering the special facilities required for them), seems ill-directed.

The case against high-value surface ships is well-known, and was underscored by their vulnerability to missiles and bombs during the Falklands war. Britain cannot and should not design a navy to fight that sort of war. There is no case for new attack carriers or new assault ships and their escorts for long-range intervention. There is no case for anti-submarine warfare carrier task groups. This cannot be stressed too often or too bluntly. However, the case against nuclear-powered submarines is less well known. Part of it is general and was set out in Chapter 9. All fission reactors contribute to the world's burden of radioactive wastes, and reactors that are also at risk of being breached and their contents spilled into the oceans are especially to be avoided if one has a choice in the matter. The other part of the case may be expected to appeal more to Whitehall. For British requirements, in a military cost-benefit comparison, nuclear-powered submarines are a worse buy than modern diesel-electric vessels.

On 28 January 1982, Admiral Hyman Rickover, the prime promoter of nuclear propulsion in the US Navy and regarded as the 'father of the nuclear Navy', gave testimony before a congressional committee. He had this to say about his life's work . . .

'Now when we go back to using nuclear power we are creating something which Nature tried to destroy to make life possible . . . I do not believe that nuclear power is worth it if it creates radiation. Then you might ask me why do I have nuclear-powered ships? That's a necessary evil. I would sink them all. Have I given you an answer to your question? . . .'

Senator Proxmire: 'What do you think is the prospect, then, of nuclear war?'

Admiral Rickover: 'I think we will probably destroy ourselves, so what difference will it make? Some new species will come up that might be wiser . . . I think from a long-range standpoint – I'm talking about humanity – the most important thing we could do is start in having an international meeting where we first outlaw nuclear weapons . . . then we outlaw nuclear reactors too . . .'[12]

Nuclear propulsion gives three undeniable advantages: mission endurance, the ability to cruise continuously deep underwater and sustained high underwater speeds. Captivated by the dogma of nuclear propulsion ('the Best') as pressed in the past by Admiral Rickover, Western naval constructors have argued that these are indispensable advantages for which other qualities ('the Good') must be sacrificed. These other qualities are (1) much lower unit costs (hence more boats); (2) more easily and swiftly trained crews (lack of crews would be the second biggest obstacle in operations after shortage in numbers of ships); (3) silence (nuclear boats will always be noisier than diesel-electric boats using batteries); (4) better resistance to damage; (5) smaller size. This is important for three reasons: (a) a diesel-electric boat has a much better payload/ton ratio (for example, the German HDW Type 2000 can, with a much smaller crew, carry an equivalent array of sensors and torpedo payload to a nuclear-powered submarine three times its size); (b) smaller size enables it to operate over the continental shelf and in coastal waters (the Royal Navy's nuclear Swiftsure class is already at a tactical disadvantage within the 100 fathom line; and all shipping eventually has to approach a coast); (c) smaller size gives greater manoeuvrability in combat. Many of these qualities were shown to advantage in the Falklands war, when, it appears, an Argentine submarine successfully evaded the anti-submarine cordon protecting the British task force.

Britain needs the advantages of 'the Good'. For coastal protection or for choke-point operations at the Greenland–Iceland–UK gap, numbers of units and silence matter more than endurance or sustained high speed.[13]

However, in addition to spending more sensibly such money as will be spent on weapons by any Government, in the longer term it would be even more prudent to use defence money to reduce our requirements of imported goods so that the need for extensive ocean traffic and hence the need for naval protection would decrease. Thus, a programme of insulation for houses and moves towards a new energy regime, mentioned in the previous section, form part of a coherent defence policy for Britain. So too does the remodelling of British agriculture away from the capital and energy-intensive form which it has adopted over the last thirty years.

A well-formulated idea of what is wanted for Britain's defence should determine the size, nature, and deployment of forces. It also points to the sorts of mistakes that should be avoided. The baroque era in the Navy is one good example; another is provided by the expensive and convoluted history of the joint development with West Germany and Italy of the Tornado multi-role combat aircraft. Among its many other roles Tornado is supposed to be a long-range deep-penetrating bomber. The 1957 defence White Paper properly envisaged that bombers would be phased out of the RAF. But to many senior officers this seemed to be tantamount to downgrading the Air Force. Ever since, the RAF has fought this threat and, in the specification of Tornado, seemed to have got its way, although at risk of producing an extremely costly aeroplane that does many things, none very well, and which is too expensive to risk for some of them (like tactical battlefield combined operations). The reasons for wanting a modern long-range bomber were more tied up with prestige – the thought that any 'proper' air force must have such a machine – than with any careful strategic plans. Thus, as well as failing to perform satisfactorily in any of its various roles, and being needlessly complicated and costly, Tornado is also provocative. In fact like the F–111 before it – an American multi-role aircraft which failed to perform as hoped – Tornado looks likely to finish up primarily as a nuclear weapons platform. Indeed, should the British purchase of the Trident SLBM system be cancelled for any reason, the public should be aware of the possibility of a totally new all-European nuclear strike force being sprung upon them; the Tornado will be there anyway, and modification to the new British Sea Eagle air-to-surface tactical missile could without too much difficulty provide a British stand-off weapon – a sort of junior version of the B–52s which are now being fitted with air-launched cruise missiles. Such a scheme must be throttled at birth. It is another reason why Tornado is precisely the kind of weapon that Britain should not be producing or buying.[14]

However, invasion and occupation of Britain is usually regarded as a possibility only after the defence of the Central Front has collapsed. (At present, the question would never arise, since the war would have ended with nuclear oblivion before that stage was reached.) How, then, to allay the fears of those who believe that after the successful removal of nuclear weapons from the European theatre, the USSR would be foolhardy enough to attack Western Europe – 'Scenario No. 1'? Lord Carver's prescription is for a substantial increase in the inventory of major weapons like tanks. Is this the way to go?

The revolution in precision-guided weapons has very considerable implications for the British army if it continues to play a major role in the defence of allies in Europe. (We assume in this chapter that the question of withdrawing the BAOR arises only at a second or later stage of the disarmament process.) In a non-retaliatory army it is not necessary to match tank for tank. Many now believe that the experiences of the 1973 Middle East war showed that the age of the *Blitzkrieg* involving surprise attacks by fast armour, relying on shock, is over. Others dispute this.[15] The argument can be briefly stated as follows.

A precision-guided munition (PGM) is a projectile which has a better-than-even chance of striking a target at full range. The first generation of PGMs began to be developed in the 1950s. They are wire-guided, and controlled throughout the flight to the target by a skilled operator using a small joystick. This disadvantage is offset by greater resistance to 'spoofing' by countermeasures than more automatic later generations of PGM, and so many first-generation anti-tank guided missiles (ATGMs), such as the British Army's Swingfire system, are still in service. However, it was during the Vietnam war and, especially, the 1973 Arab–Israeli war that PGMs were first used extensively in combat, and only since that time have the operational and strategic consequences of these weapons begun to be widely appreciated. By the late 1960s a second generation was being developed, employing semi-automatic guidance: all the operator has to do is to keep his sight on the target and the missile is automatically steered to converge with the line of sight. Examples of second-generation weapons are the Franco-German HOT and Milan and American TOW systems. The latest development, as in the Swedish RBS 70 anti-aircraft missile, dispenses with wires and rides a laser beam to the target, which is illuminated by the operator. Missiles of the third generation, under development since the 1970s, require no precise guidance by the operator after firing because they home, for example, on to infra-red emissions of the target (e.g. tank engine exhausts), or on to reflections from a target illuminated with a laser designator by a third party. These are so-called 'fire and forget' weapons. Currently, the most sophisticated 'fire and forget' missiles are Western anti-shipping missiles like the French Exocet, which combine initial incrtial guidance, pre-set by the launching platform's computer, with active radar terminal guidance aboard the missile; but such technology is closer to that of missiles like the Pershing II than to the battlefield PGM.[16]

It is suggested that improvements in technology are having the following effects: (1) Improved armour-piercing warheads are becoming capable of destroying, or at least disabling, most armoured vehicles and their crews. (2) Weapons capable of attacking a tank from directions other than the front (where armoured vehicles are most protected), will compel further increases in armour, even though, at sixty tons, tanks are already prohibitively heavy. (3) The range of anti-tank weapons is increasing far beyond the range of the tank gun. Tanks, therefore, have to rely more on supporting forces, primarily long-range artillery, for successful operations. (4) Advances in terminal-guidance systems are making missiles more reliable, more portable, less susceptible to jamming, and more versatile under a variety of battlefield conditions. (5) The cost of an anti-tank missile is already much less than that of a tank, and the disparity will become greater in the coming years.

Critics of this view of precision-guided weapons have not been persuasive. For instance, Edward Luttwak writes: 'As for the advent of the new technology precision-guided munitions (PGMs), only those people who persist in confusing technical effectiveness with operational utility can believe in the great importance of those weapons.'[17] He goes on to argue that the use of such weapons could not decide a contest against an adversary whose operational method is to penetrate deeply by using armour-mechanized forces and then to encircle the opposition. Luttwak assumes that the new weapons operate over short distances and are immobile. Neither assumption is correct. The new third-generation laser-guided Copperhead projectile is fired from 155mm howitzers and has already shown itself to be deadly at ranges up to 10 miles.[18] Many of the precision-guided weapons, like the Milan and Swingfire anti-tank systems and the Blowpipe and Rapier anti-aircraft systems in the British armed forces, can be carried in fast vehicles. Intelligent use of them would rely on their great mobility, perhaps combined with the use of prepared defensive positions.[19] The Israeli Army, which is one of the most innovative and experienced in the world, has found that for border defence, a combination of mobility and prepared defences is both cheap and highly effective. Such a solution might be profitably considered for the Central Front. Luttwak also fails to consider the very sizeable complement of air-launched PGMs now in the NATO arsenal. The advanced TOW and laser-guided Hellfire helicopter-mounted anti-tank weapons will augment an already formidable armoury.[20] However, PGMs are not foolproof; like all weapons, they are open to counter-measures. Even so, we would argue that a squadron of armoured vehicles with PGMs is a better buy than one baroque tank.

In the past, fixed-wing aircraft have not been particularly effective in anti-tank warfare, but the third generation of PGM development has touched such operations, and they offer an example of how one must be careful not to be swept off one's feet by these new technologies: they have important limitations. There is considerable enthusiasm in the armed forces and among equipment manufacturers for close-air-support operations where the aircraft (Jaguar and Harrier) fly very low and fast to avoid attack and work with forward air controllers who 'mark' the target with a laser target marker and ranger. The laser energy is detected by a marked target seeker on the aircraft which guides the pilot and automatically releases the bomb, and/or by a passive seeker in the nose of the weapon, which then guides itself. A new generation of semi-active laser-guided weapons is promised.

We are sceptical about investment on a large scale in this type of anti-tank weapons system, firstly because there is too much that can go wrong with a forward air controller/aircraft combination, but mainly because the battlefield environment for manned aircraft has already become as disadvantageous as for the tank – another point made brutally by the Falklands war – and has every prospect of becoming more so. This type of close air support may continue to have a role, but it seems likely to be a decreasing one, which is why we do not believe that reversal in the proportion of air defence to strike/attack squadrons would weaken the Central Front's ability to deter or repel a tank attack.[21]

The revolutionary improvements in accuracy associated with anti-tank guided missiles have implications for other branches of our armed forces in Europe as they are at present constituted, as well as for the Air Force. We have suggested that ATGMs have already transformed direct fire artillery. Logically, this leaves a much reduced role for 'traditional' anti-tank guns. However, since in built-up areas, for example, guns can operate more effectively than missiles, the role of anti-tank guns may not be entirely eliminated.

Lightweight mortars used by infantry are mechanically the simplest form of artillery and can provide close indirect fire most efficiently (and cheaply). While mortars can be made more elaborate, the British Army, unlike others, has wisely chosen not to do this extensively. Equipment and tactics in this type of operation are well established. However, the defensive capabilities of indirect fire by longer-range artillery have been significantly improved. This is partly the result of the introduction of fast, reliable fire-control computers and associated muzzle velocity, meteorological, and target surveillance sensors; partly, and more recently, because of the development of guided projectiles. Since there are strong grounds for pessimism about the survival of fixed-wing aircraft over the battlefield, and since the exchange value of aircraft to anti-aircraft defensive weapons has become so disadvantageous, it follows that the artillery may have an increased role in a non-nuclear defensive army. This is because long-range artillery can perform counter battery and second echelon bombardment, and the new developments, including the prospect of terminal guidance of shells, give gunners greater flexibility and accuracy than ever before. These qualities join the inherent advantages of artillery: low vulnerability, which can be further reduced by increasing the proportion of self-propelled to towed pieces, all-weather performance, reliability, and cost-effectiveness in comparison with aircraft acting as 'flying artillery'.

Over the past thirty-seven years, the European land forces of the NATO Central Front have evolved from the columns of the D-Day invasion armies, halted facing their Soviet allies where they met. While the titles and positions of the units in that victorious force have remained unchanged, as if fixed in amber a generation ago, the armies of the 1980s have become vastly more complex – and in real terms more costly – than those of the 1940s; and there is valid doubt about how well they now serve their purposes.

Among senior NATO officers first of all, then increasingly among a concerned public, the realization has spread that one cannot have confidence that these NATO forces and the strategies of 'forward defence' and 'flexible response' which govern their composition and stationing are those most likely to provide the desired result: that is, credible deterrence of any Soviet intention to invade western Europe or, if invasion occurs, successful defence. (The credibility of the first depends upon the realism of the second.) These doubts are not for the reasons of 'inferiority' based upon misused force comparisons, which are canvassed by the British government and the NATO Secretariat and were exploded in Chapter 6 above, but for real and concrete reasons.

It is seen, not least from field exercises, that the Byzantine complexity of modern capital weapons like tanks and aircraft, and of their ramified and demanding chains of logistical support, means that good operational readiness is increasingly difficult to maintain, and that therefore expectations of performance cannot be great.

It is seen that all levels of the NATO armies and of NATO strategies are profoundly interlaced with nuclear weapons. In consequence these armies can be permitted only circumscribed autonomy of decision: that latticework of nuclear warheads determines that command must be formally vested in a sharply pyramidical hierarchy which therefore depends critically for its own success upon the maintenance of constant and extensive communication up and down its heights: but the necessary minimum of communication is precarious on the modern battlefield.

Thus it is concluded that if these NATO armies were to be put to the test, they would be savagely abraded by Clausewitzian 'friction'. The last time that logistics were planned too inflexibly, it led to the logistical chaos of the D-Day campaign, only overcome by heroic improvisation in the field.[22] Because the campaign was ultimately successful, that lesson seems to have been forgotten by the next generation of soldiers. But today the penalty for failing to pay timely attention to the likely effects of 'friction' upon men, machines, and strategies will not be the stalling of armoured columns without fuel or support trucks, but a frighteningly swift step across the nuclear firebreak to NATO's first use of nuclear weapons, the outcome of which will not be 'successful defence'. The realization has also spread that there are better alternatives.

Excision of short-range nuclear weapons and a conscious move to favour a trend already present in some NATO armies, namely, to capitalize upon the new technology defensive weaponry, will have two important and related consequences beyond creating a credible deterrent by offering the prospect of a credible, successful defence. Firstly, these changes will increase the relative size and importance of the infantry, which will also promote the local autonomy of small-group fighting units; top-heavy headquarters staff can be shed; communications requirements, being more manageable, can also be more secure and in consequence NATO forces will be more resistant to 'friction' and therefore better able to fulfil their defensive mission. Secondly, robust and 'friction'-resistant professional defensive armies created at this First Step of disarmament will be well constituted in command structures, strategies, and equipment for integration at a later stage into systems of territorial defence, some of which, such as the Franco-German concept of 'techno-commandos', have already received detailed investigation in continental Europe.[23]

In this section, we have specified in detail our view of what the first step, associated with the removal of nuclear weapons from Europe, might look like in terms of military consequences, and could look like in terms of modern technological opportunities. We do not wish to speculate about the second and subsequent steps on the path to general and complete disarmament, not because we believe, like Lord Carver, that the first step is the only necessary one, but for a different reason.

The future is murky. Whereas we can describe our ultimate goals, and are obliged to do so, the exact nature of opportunities for movement towards those goals, once we have made the first step, we cannot know. But when we achieve Step One, we will be able to describe the actions that will realize the second step. Once the coiled tension of the present begins to be unwound, the possibilities for future conventional disarmament will open out. But we reiterate the message of the 1978 UN Special Assembly: nuclear disarmament is an absolute priority.

We have stressed the prime urgency of a start on the immediate transformation of all NATO ground forces in Europe into a non-nuclear form, associated with an agreement to repudiate the first use of any nuclear device, an agreement which the East has repeatedly requested and which has been repeatedly refused. Once the levels of 'minimum deterrence' have been reached on both sides – and there is no need to insist that they arrive there simultaneously – then the final dismantling of nuclear systems (probably some submarines) will have to be open and simultaneous. But when that stage has been reached, a single, simple bilateral act will be politically feasible in the way that talk of simultaneous, complex multi-lateral agreement now clearly is not.

Finally, we must consider the question of whether a country or group of countries which renounced the use of nuclear weapons would be likely to face threats to adhere to a particular policy line or to face annihilation from either or both major powers. In the press this possibility is sometimes given the odd and inaccurate name of 'Finlandization'. As well as its being insulting to Finns, we see no value in this ugly term. There are four reasons why we do not believe that disarmament means a greater degree of political blackmail or leverage on the international scene.

The first is based on history. Since the devastating and horrible effects of nuclear weapons were revealed in 1945, any nation that uses them risks an international outcry. The political and economic effects of such an outcry could be as damaging to a totalitarian country as to a democratic one. Neild suggests that it is for these reasons that no nuclear power has seriously threatened a non-nuclear power since 1945.[24] He suggests that the threatened country would have made the threat well known to the rest of the world if anything like this had happened. Furthermore, for the restraint of a commonplace dictator committing a minor aggression, nuclear weapons are useless because their threat, being so grossly dispro-portionate to the insult, is hollow. The British Polaris submarines were no deterrent to the Argentine junta in 1982 when it attacked the Falkland Islands. It is not only in the East/West confrontation that nuclear threats are literally incredible.

It is also clear that fear of public opinion has had an inhibiting effect on some occasions when the use of nuclear weapons has been considered. A notable example was when Richard Nixon considered extensive bombing of the North Vietnamese irrigation system or the use of tactical nuclear weapons in order to bring the Vietnam war to an end. He concluded that both actions would be unwise and revealed why in his memoirs: 'The domestic and international uproar that would have accompanied the use of either of these knockout blows would have got my administration off to the worst possible start.'[25] In Nixon's case, as in the others cited by Neild, the political disadvantages were deemed to outweigh the expected military benefits.

The second reason derives from the importance of economic strength (or weakness) in the determination of political strength (or weakness) in international affairs. The fact that Britain was a nuclear power had absolutely no bearing on the outcome of the calamitous Suez operation of 1956. What mattered was the ability and willingness of the United States government to break the currency of this country if her Prime Minister continued to defy American demands for a cease-fire in Egypt. Similarly, the strength of Germany and Japan in international politics has grown out of their economic performance in a period of enforced limitation of their military development. Restraint in the growth of their military power was partly responsible for their current prominence in world affairs.

Thirdly, and on a related point, we should not forget that political blackmail is not a new phenomenon but rather a 'normal' procedure of international political life. The rhetoric of 'official spokesmen' rarely obscures the use of open and painful coercion in international disputes between countries regardless of their nuclear status. With or without the Bomb, international politics is, has been, and is very likely to remain, the art of orchestrated pressure. Nothing we advocate is likely to change this situation. What we urge is the limitation of its explosive potential.

Finally, standing on this harsh political field of conflict, it is prudent for citizens of this country, the economic difficulties of which are mounting steadily, to give up pretensions to act as the 'guarantor' of peace around the world, pretensions which are pointless, costly, and increasingly dangerous. The last thing that Britain needs for the future is political leadership that is unable to face present realities and so is incapable of allowing the lingering memory of imperial glory to fade peacefully away.

Surely the political (and military) future of this country is bound up first and foremost with that of our European neighbours on both sides of the Iron Curtain? We cannot go 'into' or 'out of' Europe; we were always and will always be there. We are no longer superior to our fellow Europeans in any sense of the term. In 1945, Britain was indeed one of the three great powers that liberated prostrate European nations from the evils of tyranny. Three decades later, it is imperative to revise our defence and diplomatic strategy to accept a new role in international affairs which, if less dominant, would be safer, and might be both more honourable and more effective. The real danger lies in retaining the illusion of power, which can never be a sound basis for the preservation of the security of the realm.

3 The Economic Consequences

(A) ABANDONING BRITISH-OWNED NUCLEAR WEAPONS

Official statistics on the costs of maintaining the Polaris submarine-launched nuclear strategic force make it look quite cheap: £270m or 2.2 per cent of the 1981–2 defence budget.[26] While it is true that the capital outlays for the programme (purchasing the Polaris missiles from the US, building the submarines, and developing and building the warheads) were incurred in the 1960s, there is reason to believe the true operating costs are higher than the direct costs given above. 'The Bomb' often figures in imagination as a large, inert object safely stored in some remote silo. In reality, it is a highly complex industrial system, processing and reprocessing dangerous materials. Constant servicing and modification, including long-distance transportation between manufacturing and reprocessing centres (Windscale, Chapelcross), maintenance areas (such as the Burghfield Royal Ordnance Factory), and storage areas (such as the naval dockyards at Rosyth, Chatham, and Devonport) are required to keep the weaponry ready to fire;[27] and in addition, there is a nuclear cycle for the submarine propulsion reactors. The first task of the Atomic Weapons Research Establishment at Aldermaston is not new research but – as the Commons Defence Committee was told last year – providing 'the scientific and engineering expertise needed to support the UK nuclear stockpile'. Some of these expenditures are almost certainly concealed under other headings in the defence budget (e.g. research and development, repair and storage facilities). It is also necessary to include the continuing costs of development of the 'Chevaline' programme, designed to give the front end of the Polaris advanced penetration aids and a manoeuvrable payload, in anticipation of improvements in Soviet ABM capacity – improvements which did not materialize. This programme has already cost £1 billion[28] and, for years, was disguised from the public and even from many members of the 1974–9 Labour Cabinet within the Defence Estimates from Parliament. In addition, at least £300 million is to be spent to provide the Polaris missiles with new rocket motors. These 'development costs' continue to be incurred. An alternative estimate to the government's, prepared at the Centre of Defence Studies at Aberdeen, of the cost of the British strategic nuclear force, is £855m or 7 per cent of the 1981–2 defence budget.[29]

Thus, the financial savings from scrapping the 'independent deterrent' are by no means negligible though relatively small in the context of the overall military budget. But, equally, the employment losses would be rather small also (16,000 civilian personnel and 2,700 service personnel),[30] and under a sensible strategy for UK economic recovery this highly skilled workforce could be deployed elsewhere.

(B) CANCELLATION OF TRIDENT II MISSILES IN NEW SUBMARINES

Following an earlier decision (announced in July 1980), to replace the Polaris strategic nuclear force with the Trident I (C3) submarine-launched ballistic missile system in March 1982, the government announced its decision to purchase the Trident II (D5) missile system from the United States; the submarine programme was accordingly modified to accommodate the Trident II missiles. Four 14,480 ton submarines are to be built in the UK, to be powered by British pressure water reactor atomic propulsion motors and fitted with improved sonar systems.

Table 12, based on information supplied by the British government, gives a breakdown of the Trident's capital costs.

Table 12. Trident Capital Outlays
(in £m, at mid-1980 prices and $−£ exchange rate)

Nature	Trident I[31]	Addition for Trident II[32]
Missiles	600	+ 390
Submarines	1,500	+ 500
Weapons systems	800	——
Shore construction (including 7-fold expansion of armaments depot at Coulport)	600	+ 110
Warheads	1,500	——
	5,000	+1,000

Note. In an attempt to reduce the apparent real cost of Trident II, the UK government has since announced that much maintenance work will be transferred to America, thus reducing shore construction work in Scotland.

Owing to inflation since 1980 and to a weakening in the sterling–dollar exchange rate, the capital costs of Trident have already escalated to £8,000m (by mid-1982). There is every reason to suppose that the price tag will eventually be considerably more: although the government has, through a fixed R & D levy, insured against escalating development costs on the missile system to be purchased from the US, cost escalation on the British-built part of the programme must be expected. For example, such large submarines (which have twice the displacement of Polaris submarines), have never before been built in the UK.

While the UK government has constantly sought to make light of the financial burden of this commitment, it is clear that it has already forced the government into major economies in the conventional defence programme and must surely continue to do so in the future. The financial savings accruing from cancellation would be considerable. The Navy budget stood to suffer most from the Trident decision, and therefore the Navy would stand to benefit most from its cancellation. Again, it must be emphasized that a new generation of attack carriers, amphibious assault ships, and surface ASW units would be the wrong way to redirect those resources.

(C) REMOVAL OF US NUCLEAR INSTALLATIONS

What would be the economic consequences of the withdrawal of US nuclear weapons delivery and communications systems from Britain? For the country as a whole, the *direct* economic consequences would be insignificant. US bases generate employment – especially in the construction industry – and expenditure by American military personnel creates income and employment near the bases; on the other hand, a large amount of what is consumed on US bases is actually imported from the US, and thus the local employment effects and benefits to the UK trade balance are fairly small. For 1980, UK statistics report a total of £263m of US military spending in Britain, of which £179m consisted of private spending by US forces in Britain.[33] The direct economic benefits from all US defence activities in Britain are thus not very great, though certain local economies are highly dependent on the business provided by US bases. Britain could therefore afford to request the withdrawal of US nuclear weapons bases, though the government would have to identify and provide selective financial assistance to local communities affected by this decision.

A more serious consequence could result if the US were to attempt to use economic and financial pressure to dissuade a British government from taking such a step. Some of these facilities are of central importance to US strategic planning and to the nuclear defence of the continental United States; and their withdrawal would bring to an end thirty years of close cooperation between British and US governments on nuclear questions. The request to withdraw would undoubtedly meet with strong opposition from elements within the US government, especially one like that of Mr Reagan, and it is conceivable that American leaders would bring pressure to bear on sterling, as was done in the Suez crisis in 1956. The US might even attempt to disrupt British trade. We think, however, that such a train of events would be unlikely.

In the first section we argued that the removal of U S bases is a European issue and, firstly, it would be obvious from the outset that economic destabilization would tend to unite the people of Europe; politically it would therefore be counter-productive. Secondly, given the growing interdependence at every level of the world economy, U S government action of that sort would be extremely damaging to the international economic system, which is already in an extremely fragile state;[34] there would, therefore, be influential voices in the U S urging caution. Thirdly, the U S has a great deal to lose from exerting economic pressure on Britain: currently the U S enjoys a healthy surplus on trade in goods and services with the U K (in 1979 this surplus, including profit remittances, was U S $6.1 billion). Fourthly, in 1956 Britain was heavily dependent on oil shipped through the Suez canal. Today, Britain is a net exporter of oil and is less open to 'energy blackmail' than any other European country. The windfall of North Sea oil, which at present we are squandering, could be used both to help create a national economy structured for the future and reclaim our national sovereignty; and if Britain chose to use her 'oil weapon' in support of other Europeans, she could help to protect them from energy blackmail also.

Furthermore, we recall that when a senior American officer addressed our Disarmament Seminar, he was asked what his reaction would be should the European allies inform the USA that they now felt able to undertake their own defence. His reply was that he personally, and in his opinion, the U S government also, would be delighted if the Europeans would take full responsibility for their own defence, but he believed that we lacked the political will to do so.

(D) THE ECONOMIC IMPLICATIONS
OF ALTERNATIVE BRITISH DEFENCE POLICIES

It would be misleading to suggest that we can provide a fully detailed costing of the alternative U K defence policies that we have outlined; even the U K government, with huge resources at its disposal, has repeatedly failed to forecast accurately the cost of given defence commitments. However, we have already estimated the financial savings from abandoning Britain's current nuclear posture (at least £800 million *per year*) and those from the cancellation of Trident (at least £8 billion up to 1995); against these savings must be set the cost of the safe dismantling of the warheads.

What would our proposals imply for the budgets of each of the three armed services? For the RAF, the re-orientation from offensive to defensive roles, with an expansion of air defence, can easily be accomplished within the present RAF budget – which provides for an expansion of *both* roles. Augmentation of Coastal Command would be an additional charge, but overall our plans may permit some savings. Similarly, for the Navy, the expansion of coastal protection and our proposals on anti-submarine warfare can be accomplished by savings from ceasing to build 'baroque' surface ships and nuclear-powered submarines. This is a path on which, before the Falklands war, the government was already engaged with regard to excessively costly vessels like the Invincible class, and it should be entirely feasible to contain these changes within the present Navy budget. Our proposal for the Army, if it continues to have a European role, is to concentrate on precision-guided anti-tank weapons rather than to engage in the purchase of, for example, the Challenger tank (at least £1.5 million per tank). This may be a source of economies. The present cost of British forces in Europe is 15.3 per cent of the defence budget, or about £1.9 billion in 1980–81.

Each year Sweden spends slightly less per head of population on defence than Britain (in 1981 $454 compared to $496), while Switzerland spends less than either ($291). One estimate of the cost of a strategy of *defensive deterrence* puts the cost (at 1981–2 prices) at £7.5 to £10 billion by 1989–90, compared with the projected cost of the government's current strategy of at least £14 billion.[35] But this is an overestimate of the savings from our proposals, since, while similar in many other respects, this costed proposal envisages a substantial withdrawal of British ground forces from Europe which, we have suggested, is a question that does not have to be resolved at Step One.

Despite the estimation problems, we conclude that this reorientation may provide the opportunity for some reduction in the overall level of military expenditure, although we would not wish to understate the far-from-negligible costs involved in disposing of existing nuclear weapons.

It seems likely that the pattern of alternatives to present defence policies proposed here will in the short and medium term require the services of a considerable number of those at present engaged in our defence establishments. Should it be decided at Step Two (which is beyond our present brief) that forms of home territorial defence should be adopted, a larger number of people would become directly involved in defence, although most of them only on a part-time basis. Equally, many of the measures of decentralization of administration, communications, and data protection which would be part of the preparation necessary to deny an invader the instruments of power – those which would ease the task of isolating resistance and identifying dissidents – would involve little special expense beyond that required for measures which, we have suggested in Chapter 8, are under present conditions in any case desirable for the protection of democracy in our country.

We have also pointed out that the reshaping of areas of our national economy into forms appropriate to the late twentieth century is integral to securing the proper defence of the realm. Thus, we must look for a moment at the longer term when, as the political objectives outlined in this chapter succeed, and as the tensions of international relations are relaxed, resources at present devoted to military ends can be redirected to address long-standing problems in British economy and society.

The human and physical resources currently devoted to military production have an important role to play in modernizing the British economy. The British education system produces fewer trained engineers and scientists than in our competitor countries, and the current imbalance in the allocation of research and development expenditure between civilian and military uses is rather alarming. Almost *half* of government-sponsored research and development is devoted to defence alone, while 60 per cent of qualified scientists and engineers in the mechanical engineering industry work on armaments, which represents less than 7 per cent of the output of this sector.[36]

In their attempt to produce an integrated conversion package for a particular industry, the workers at Lucas Aerospace have already shown that there are ways to use these skills differently. The Combine Committee that assembled the report, inspired by one shop-steward, Mike Cooley (subsequently sacked by the company), was naturally concerned to protect their members' right to work, but did so by proposing a range of alternative products on which they could become engaged in the event of cutbacks (for whatever reason) in the aerospace industry. They were also concerned to ensure that among the alternative products proposed were a number that would be socially useful.[37] Workers at the Vickers plant, which makes tanks, have also produced detailed suggestions of ways in which their skills can be more peacefully employed.

We believe that the fears of unemployment which are sometimes fanned by those who do not wish to see any change in our military dispositions are ill-founded. Ridding ourselves of nuclear weapons will not have significant consequences for direct employment since service personnel will be required for the real defence of the country, and expert staff at the AWRE at Aldermaston will simply stop sustaining the nuclear arsenal and start destroying it. The equipment and personnel needed for alternative forms of defence at Step One on the road to general and complete disarmament will probably require many of the resources currently devoted to the armed services. Thus, for example, shipyard workers will be building considerably more ships, especially submarines, in the immediate future under these proposals than they would under present nuclear-based government plans. For those people and factories that become surplus to the military requirement, both at once and increasingly in the future as circumstance permits, there are many concrete and hopeful signs of the way in which skills and plant can be redirected from warlike to peaceful purposes.

Conclusion

It is important to specify the actions required for the first step towards general and complete disarmament in a form that engages the existing present realities of our military dispositions and which is politically feasible (although not necessarily politically easy). But in doing this, the broader message of this book must not be forgotten: while we must start to act deliberately in the short run, in the long run we must escape from the grim polarities of the Cold War mentality. For this we can offer no political or military prescription; it is a question first for individual study and then for collective, informed questioning of the assumptions which guide our politicians today; but in the end, this escape matters most of all.

This was the message proclaimed by President Kennedy in the speech about peace which he made at the American University six months before his assassination, in which he warned the American and Soviet peoples alike '. . . not to see only a distorted and desperate view of the other side, not to see conflict as inevitable, accommodation as impossible and communication as nothing more than an exchange of threats. No government or social system is so evil that its people must be considered as lacking in virtue . . .' It was also the feeling of one of America's most distinguished military men, who was among the least flamboyant but most important architects of the Allied D-Day landings and subsequent campaign. General of the Army Omar Bradley, a soldier of the highest rank in the US Army and one of only five five-star generals in the post-war years, made a speech in Washington in 1957. We cannot improve on his message and we therefore give over our final pages to him:

The central problem of our time – as I view it – is how to employ human intelligence for the salvation of mankind. It is a problem we have put upon ourselves. For we have defiled our intellect by the creation of such scientific instruments of destruction that we are now in desperate danger of destroying ourselves. Our plight is critical and with each effort we have made to relieve it by further scientific advance, we have succeeded only in aggravating our peril.

As a result, we are now speeding inexorably toward a day when even the ingenuity of our scientists may be unable to save us from the consequences of a single rash act or a lone reckless hand upon the switch of an uninterceptible missile. For twelve years now we've sought to stave off this ultimate threat of disaster by devising arms which would be both ultimate and disastrous.

This irony can probably be compounded a few more years, or perhaps even a few decades. Missiles will bring anti-missiles, and anti-missiles will bring anti-anti-missiles. But inevitably, this whole electronic house of cards will reach a point where it can be constructed no higher.

At that point we shall have come to the peak of this whole incredible dilemma into which the world is shoving itself. And when that time comes there will be little we can do other than to settle down uneasily, smother our fears, and attempt to live in a thickening shadow of death.

Should this situation come to pass, we would have but one single and thin thread to cling to. We call it rationale or reason. We reason that no government, no single group of men – indeed, not even one wilful individual – would be so foolhardy, so reckless, as to precipitate a war which would most surely end in mutual destruction.

This reasoning may have the benefit of logic. But even logic sometimes goes awry. How can we assume that reason will prevail in a crisis when there is ordinarily so little reason among men? To those who would take comfort in the likelihood of an atomic peace to be secured solely by rationale and reason, I would recall the lapse of reason in a bunker under the Reich Chancellery in Berlin. It failed before, it can fail again.

Have we already gone too far in this search for peace through the accumulation of peril? Is there any way to halt this trend – or must we push on with new devices until we inevitably come to judgement before the atom? I believe there is a way out. And I believe it because I have acquired in my lifetime a decent respect for human intelligence.

It may be that the problems of accommodation in a world split by rival ideologies are more difficult than those with which we have struggled in the construction of ballistic missiles. But I believe, too, that if we apply to these human problems, the energy, creativity, and the perseverance we have devoted to science, even problems of accommodation will yield to reason. Admittedly, the problem of peaceful accommodation in the world is infinitely more difficult than the conquest of space, infinitely more complex than a trip to the moon. But if we will only come to the realization that it must be worked out – whatever it may mean even to such sacred traditions as absolute national sovereignty – I believe that we can somehow, some-where, and perhaps through some as yet undiscovered world thinker and leader find a workable solution.

I confess that this is as much an article of faith as it is an expression of reason. But this, my friends, is what we need, faith in our ability to do what must be done. Without that faith we shall never get started. And until we get started, we shall never know what can be done.

It is a terrible indictment that these words are still as relevant in their entirety today as they were twenty-five years ago. For how much longer are you prepared to let them remain so?

Appendix A1
The Assessment of 'Strength' of Strategic Nuclear Weapons

'What in the name of God is strategic superiority? What is the significance of it politically, militarily, operationally at these levels of numbers? What do you do with it?'

(Henry Kissinger)[1]

The numbers of strategic nuclear weapons belonging to the two superpowers are, with slight variation, quite reliably known, and are given in Tables 13 and 14. The simplest way of assessing 'strength' is to compare the **numbers of delivery systems**, which has been the approach in the SALT arms-limitation negotiations. One source suggests that although the United States has more strategic bombers than the Soviet Union (316 to 140) it is outnumbered in strategic missile submarines (85 to 41), in submarine-launched ballistic missiles (SLBM) (989 to 656) and in intercontinental ballistic missiles (ICBM) (1,398 to 1,054), leading to the conclusion that the Soviet strategic forces are 'stronger'. However, comparison of the numbers of strategic nuclear **warheads** (8,506 to 5,981)[2] suggests that the US is 'stronger'. The United States has always had more warheads, as is shown in Figure 16. In the 1960s this was due principally to its then enormous strategic bomber force, which was being cut back with the introduction of less vulnerable strategic missile submarines and ICBMs (hence the reduction in total number of US warheads in the 1960s), and more recently it is because the US developed multiple independently-targetable re-entry vehicles (MIRV) first. The numerical excess of US warheads is today due principally to the Poseidon submarine fleet whose submarines each carry sixteen missiles with up to ten warheads apiece.

However, since different types of strategic nuclear warhead have yields which may range from a few kilotons to 20 megatons, it might be argued that it is misleading to compare warheads by counting numbers as if each were equivalent. In particular, US warheads tend to be of lower yield, and hence less destructive than their Soviet counterparts. However, there is a contrary view that numbers matter more than yield because the explosion of any will initiate escalation. So therefore numbers increase that risk. But yield is used as an index, and so another guide to 'strength' is the **total yield** of warheads expressed in megatons, as shown in the Tables. The total yield of all Soviet strategic warheads is much greater than that of the U.S. However, because the blast from a nuclear explosion spreads out in three dimensions, whereas the area of ground destroyed by it has only two dimensions, the effect of that blast, or the overpressure (pressure above atmospheric pressure) of the shock wave destroys an area proportional to the two-thirds power of the yield of the explosion. For example, an overpressure of 5 pounds per square inch (psi) is sufficient to destroy most buildings,[3] and occurs at a distance of around 4 km from a 1 Mt explosion, so a 1 Mt explosion will destroy about 50 km² of city area. A 2 Mt explosion will, because of the two-thirds power relation, destroy an area of about 80 km², not 100 km² as might be expected. So although Soviet warheads have typically much higher yields than US ones, they are not that much more destructive. This limited usefulness of large warheads was, in fact, recognized by the Americans back in the 1960s, and as a result they began to direct their attention away from building larger and larger warheads, towards increased accuracy of their delivery systems. An 'equivalent megatons' (EMt) scale of destruction has been defined, where the EMt rating of any warhead is expressed as the number of 1 Mt warheads required to cause the same blast effect. This is a meaningful measure of the capacity of a weapon to destroy area targets, with a 1 EMt roughly equivalent to the ability to destroy 50 km² of a city. However, to use this scale to describe the whole of each superpower's arsenal is also inadequate, because the majority of both US and Soviet strategic nuclear weapons cannot be intended for destroying each other's cities: both superpowers have only about 200 cities each with a population of over 100,000, so only a small fraction of the warheads possessed by either side would be quite capable of destroying most of the industry and centres of population belonging to the other. One US Poseidon submarine *alone* deploys between 128 and 160 thermonuclear warheads, each having about four times the yield of the bomb which destroyed Hiroshima. So several such submarines provide more than enough warheads for that task. About fifteen of these vessels are on patrol at any one time.

An alternative approach to the measurement of strength involves comparison of the '**throw-weight**' of each missile. Throw-weight is the weight of the payload of a missile – the warheads, guidance systems, re-entry vehicles, and the post-boost vehicle which contains them all. It is thus analogous to the bomb load of a bomber, and is favoured by American strategists. Tables 13 and 14 show that the total Soviet throw-weight is nearly three times as great as that of the US, giving the impression that the Soviet Union is vastly 'stronger'. However this measurement is particularly misleading because, as already explained, the US has a policy of building small, light warheads which have low throw-weight. The weight of the warheads is in any case only a small fraction of the throw-weight of a missile; American missiles tend to be lighter because of the greater use of lightweight alloys in their construction and because of the microminiaturization of the electronics in their guidance systems. An example to illustrate the inappropriateness of throw-weight is the current programme to fit 300 of the US Minuteman III missiles with new Mark 12A re-entry vehicles which will add only about 35 lb to the throw-weight of the missile,[4] but will almost double the yield of the warheads. Throw-weight tells very little which is meaningful about missile systems. It does appear that the popularization of this concept by the US Secretary of Defense, James Schlesinger, in 1974 was a deliberate attempt to downgrade the strength of their own missiles compared with those of the Soviet Union, presumably in order to justify more arms expenditure to get out of a position of apparent weakness.

Instead of relating the strength of an arsenal directly to the physical characteristics of weapons – whether number of warheads, yield, or throw-weight – it is more meaningful to discuss strength in the context of possible strategies for the use of the weapons. The EMt scale provides a useful measure of the effect of weapons used against unprotected area targets; another measure is needed for assessing the effectiveness of attacks on well-protected point targets, such as enemy missile silos. This is 'lethality',[5] denoted by the symbol K, and defined for any weapons system by

$$K = Y^{\frac{2}{3}}/C^2$$

where Y is the yield of each warhead in megatons and C is the 'circular error probable' of the system, i.e. the radius from the target within which, it is expected, half the warheads aimed at the target would land, expressed in nautical miles. The 'hardness', H, of a target is defined as the maximum blast overpressure it can withstand before being destroyed; the probability P_k of a target of hardness H being destroyed by a targeted warhead of lethality K is given by

$$P_k = 1 - \exp\left[-.69K\,\{Hf(H)\}^{-\frac{2}{3}}\right]$$

where $f(H)$ is a correction factor for target hardness, typically of the order of 0.05.[6] If the lethality of the missiles of one superpower and the hardness of the silos of the other are known, then the effectiveness of a first strike of one upon the other's missile silos can be estimated.

The lethality of strategic bombers is not given in Tables 13 and 14 – it is difficult to envisage bombers being used in a first strike, because of their slowness and the ease with which they would be detected. However, some strategists believe that bombers could successfully attack missile fields by using a 'pin-down' tactic, whereby successively arriving ballistic missile warheads would prevent the launch of the missiles until the bombers arrived. But this seems impractical, since many would be shot down, because both superpowers have very sophisticated air defence systems, and the disastrous effects of dust from the Mt St Helens volcano on aero-engines exposed to it suggest that it may be impossible for air-breathing engines to fly through the dust from earlier nuclear explosions for any length of time. There are several other important points concerning the use of data on lethality.

Firstly, the probability P_k of a target being destroyed increases *theoretically* the more warheads there are targeted on to it. In practice, however, it may not be possible to have more than one warhead per target, because of the so-called 'interference' or, in Pentagonese, the 'fratricide' effect. The blast wave, the heat, and the pulse of electromagnetic radiation from the explosion of the first warhead to arrive near or on target may destroy or deflect other warheads arriving slightly afterwards, before they can explode. Consequently a strategy of counterforce has a chance of being effective only if there exist weapons of sufficiently high lethality for one on its own to have a very high probability (SSKP) (say greater than 97 per cent) of destroying its target. The most important counterforce weapons are ICBMs; ballistic missiles launched from submarines are less accurate, since there is uncertainty in the location of the submarine from which the missile is fired as well as in the guidance of the missile, giving SLBMs in general much lower lethality. The main exceptions to this are the American Poseidon and Trident systems, the newest of which, the D–5, will achieve high accuracy using the NAVSTAR satellite guidance system. The US cruise missile is also conceived of as an important counterforce weapon. This is discussed later.

Secondly, the definition of lethality shows that it is much more strongly dependent upon accuracy than on yield. A five-fold increase in yield will only raise K by a factor of about three, whereas a five-fold improvement in accuracy will increase K by a factor of 25 (Figure 17). With the exception of those Soviet ICBMs which have very high yield warheads, US missiles have higher K per warhead than Soviet ones, due to the better accuracy of US missiles. The accuracy of a missile is determined by the quality of its guidance system. The United States has a great technological lead in the design of inertial guidance systems – in the machining of very accurate gyroscopes and accelerometers to measure the motion of a missile and in the design of fast, light, on-board computers to calculate the missile's trajectory while in flight. Needless to say, the Russians are working as fast as they can to catch up.

Thirdly, there is the problem of the measurement of circular error probable (CEP) for different missile systems. This can only be done by flight-testing the missiles themselves. Because missiles are very expensive, relatively few have ever been fired, particularly by the Americans. US missiles are flight-tested along a westward flight path from the continental USA over the Pacific on to a test range in the Marshall Islands, and Soviet missiles generally on an eastward flight-path from west of the Urals to Kamchatka. For obvious reasons neither power has ever tested a missile on a flight path over the North Pole in the direction of the other. Targeting errors can be either *random*, due for example to slight mechanical imperfections in the guidance system, giving rise to error; or *systematic*, resulting from inaccuracies in determination of the earth's gravitational field along the flight path, and from magnetic drift, a phenomenon not discussed in the literature on rocket ballistics. One expert witness believes that forces arising due to the accumulation of an appreciable electrical charge as the re-entry vehicle moves across the earth's near-vertical magnetic field lines in the polar region, could cause bias errors on a scale that would quite vitiate 'counterforce' levels of accuracy[7] (see Figure 18). It is not at all clear, even to the US Air Force, whether bias error will be significant when a missile is fired over an untried flight path, although the likelihood is that it would be. Any missile for which the bias error is uncertain and possibly much greater than the circular error probable is useless as a counterforce weapon. The fact that the Russians carry out more tests of their missiles than the Americans is sometimes cited as evidence that they may have solved the problem of bias error and have very accurate missiles. This is rather like saying that someone who takes many driving tests before passing is clearly a better driver than someone who passes first time. It is much more plausible, particularly in view of the problems which are known to have arisen in Soviet aviation and space programmes, to regard this testing as evidence of the unreliability of Soviet missiles.

Indeed, speculations about the accuracy of Soviet missiles prompted fears of a new 'gap' – the next in the now familiar succession of bomber, missile, and ABM 'gaps'. Suddenly, in 1978, an 'accuracy gap' appeared. This 'gap' created a 'window of vulnerability' for the land-based US ICBM force. The 'accuracy gap' was publicized through articles in the technical press, reflecting a revision of the National Intelligence Estimate (NIE) which projected a *150 per cent* improvement in Soviet missile accuracies by 1985. This explains why, when Tsipis wrote in 1975, the 'worst case' (i.e. most accurate) estimates of Soviet CEPs were so much lower than those published by Collins in 1980 and included in this Appendix.[8]

In view of this difficulty in knowing the reliability of any quoted value of C, because of the strong dependence of lethality (K) on C, any calculated K value will be uncertain, and therefore we do not believe that K values should be regarded as absolute indices.

This is not a limitation of the concept of lethality, which remains important; it is a practical limitation due to poor data. The data are poor both because, as mentioned, tests are not, nor can be, realistic simulations, and furthermore, because information about the results of such tests as there have been are obvious prime candidates for manipulation.

Tables 13 and 14 illustrate the discrepancies in C values, and their effect upon K. The first of each of the pairs of 'lethality' columns gives values taken from the work of Col. J. M. Collins, for thirty years in US Army intelligence, then on the faculty of the National War College and now senior specialist in national defence at the Library of Congress. His reference book is regarded as authoritative by the Pentagon. The second of each pair is taken from the Stockholm International Peace Research Institute *Yearbook* 1980. SIPRI was established by the Swedish government to celebrate 150 years without war. It is government-funded, but wholly independent, with an entrenched constitution and an international staff of researchers. SIPRI material is used here because it is an authoritative source independent of either superpower.

Estimates of the total lethality of the US and Soviet strategic arsenals can be made by summing the lethalities of all the warheads of the different missile systems, but to do so without relating the potential to the targets (hardened silos) would be misleading. Yet such *relative* comparisons are exceedingly difficult to make with certainty. Consideration of total lethality in isolation can also lead to a further misleading impression. For example, the US programme to fit 300 Minuteman III ICBMs with Mark 12A re-entry vehicles, already mentioned, will when completed in 1983 have added around K 16,000 to the US total lethality. But because the US will still have the same number of missiles and warheads as before it can still only destroy the same number of targets (though their destruction is more certain, due to the higher lethality of each warhead). So it is more realistic to consider the effect of aiming one warhead (it has to be one only to avoid 'fratricide') on to each target, and to compare that.

For example, suppose a Russian commander wishes to destroy the 550 US Minuteman III silos, each hardened to 1,000 psi, using 550 SS–18 Mod 4 warheads, each with lethality K = 32. This K value comes from Collins, who lists the SS–18 Mod 4 as a deployed system; yet the 1982 *Department of Defense Annual Report* does not list the Mod 4 as being yet deployed. If it is, and for our example we shall assume that it is, then, in the opinion of the chief of the Ballistic Missile System Branch in the Defense Intelligence Agency, it has the best accuracy yet achieved in Soviet fourth-generation missiles, although the DIA regards this accuracy as being less than Collins suggests.[9] Nevertheless, using Collins's 'worst case' value and assuming 100 per cent reliability of missiles, the probability of destroying each silo is 0.7646, so 421 silos would be expected to be destroyed, and 129 to survive.

Suppose an American commander wishes to destroy the 211 SS–18 missiles housed in 450 psi hardened silos using 211 improved Minuteman III warheads each with lethality 48 (Collins's figure again). Assuming 100 per cent reliability of missiles, the probability of destruction of each silo is 0.9780, and it would be expected that 206 silos would be destroyed and only 5 would survive. To make the comparison fairer, suppose the SS–18s were sheltered in hypothetical 1,000 psi hardened silos. The probability of each being destroyed is now down to 0.8846, so it would be expected that 187 of the silos would be destroyed and 24 would survive. Thus, on Collins's figures, the Minuteman III is seen to be a much better first-strike counterforce weapon than the SS–18.

The MX missile system at present under development by the US represents the next generation of sophistication of ICBM. With fourteen MIRV warheads of 0.35–0.5 Mt and a CEP of only 0.05 nm (300 ft)[10] due to its AIRS (advanced inertial reference sphere) guidance system the lethality per warhead is around 200. This is sufficient to destroy any Soviet silo hardened to 1,000 psi with a probability of 99.99 per cent. The GLCM Tomahawk cruise missile due to be deployed in Europe from 1983 will, if it works as planned, also be a deadly counterforce weapon. Whether it uses the TERCOM (terrain contour mapping) guidance system to locate its target or the NAVSTAR satellite guidance system, which may now be being studied as an alternative, its radar homing terminal guidance system for the final approach to the target may give it a CEP of around 0.033 nm (200 ft).[11] With the 200 kt warhead this gives it a lethality of around 300, enabling it to destroy with virtual certainty any superhardened silo the Russians may care to build. Due to test failures, doubt also surrounds the performance of the Pershing II ballistic missile. If the defects are corrected it will be the most accurate rocket in any arsenal to date. Since most of the Soviet strategic rockets are land-based, such a threat is proportionally more serious for them than a threat to land-based missiles would be to the United States. (See Figure 20.)

The Soviet Union may thus be forced to introduce mobile ICBMs to remove the threat from very accurate missiles like MX, Pershing II, and cruise. Alternatively they may adopt a 'launch on warning' posture, to get their missiles away from the silos before the silos are destroyed; or again they may mount a first strike against areas such as south-east England and West Germany in which it is planned to disperse cruise and Pershing II missiles. Conversely, the Department of Defense having so stridently asserted that US missiles are vulnerable to a Soviet first strike, some American leaders may feel that the lead in total lethality which the USA will have after completion of the MX programme may justify a first strike, despite the inevitable retaliation from Soviet submarine-launched ballistic missiles.[12] The confirmation in 1982 by former Secretary of Defense McNamara that the US Air Force had promoted the formal adoption of the disarming first strike as official US policy twenty years before gives a chilling perspective and credence to what might otherwise seem to be a wild assertion. The escalation in lethality contributes to continuing colossal expenditure on new missile systems and to increased risk of war.

Lethality provides a means of assessing the effectiveness of a first strike; another index is needed to investigate the retaliatory second strike which would be expected to follow. A measure called '**retaliatory equivalent weapons**' has been devised,[13] equal to the average probability of a weapon destroying a target in a second strike, obtained by considering the types of targets available (e.g. hardened point targets, such as remaining enemy missile silos, unprotected area targets, such as enemy cities, and unprotected point targets, such as enemy radar installations), the numbers of each it is desired to attack, and the probability of each particular weapons system destroying each type of target. To assess the effect of a second strike it is also necessary to estimate the number of each type of weapons system left intact and their reliability in the chaos which will result from a first strike, especially since communications links between commanders and their forces will probably have been destroyed. Since all these are very difficult to estimate, it is not really meaningful to speculate about the result of a second strike, except to say that one would inevitably lead to massive destruction and many millions of casualties. Once a nuclear war has escalated to the point of contemplation of such a strike, it is sufficiently close to becoming a holocaust for it to be impossible to imagine anyone 'winning' in any meaningful sense.

The purpose of this appendix was to investigate which superpower has greater 'strength'. Unfortunately, no definite conclusion can be drawn, since, depending on which measure you use, either power can appear 'stronger'. The danger is that one superpower may use its apparent lead in some measure of 'strength' to delude itself into starting a war which it thinks it can win. However, what is abundantly clear is that there are so many more weapons than targets nowadays that the precise numbers either side possesses are relevant only as an indicator of the total danger to us all.

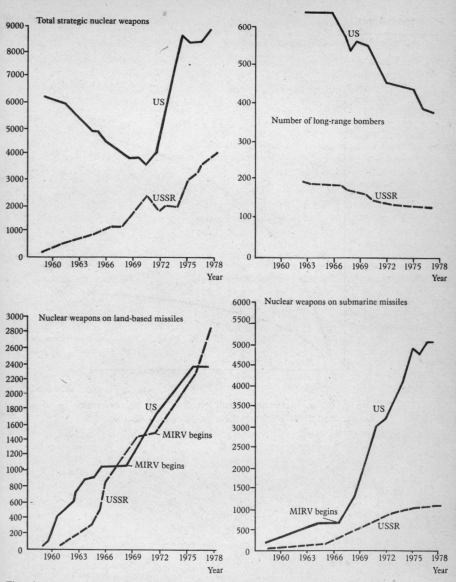

These charts cover *strategic* nuclear weapons. They do not include the even larger number of *tactical* nuclear weapons on both sides. The US has a total of approximately 26,000 nuclear weapons, the Soviets approximately 17,000.

Figure 16. Measures of the nuclear arms race[14]

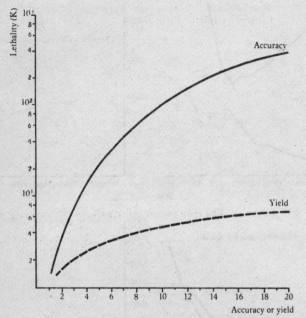

Figure 17. Increase in re-entry vehicle lethality[15] with improvements in accuracy and yield. (Note that the lethality axis is logarithmic in progression)

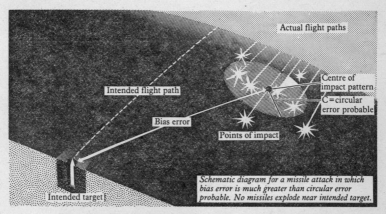

Figure 18. Bias error and random error in missile targeting

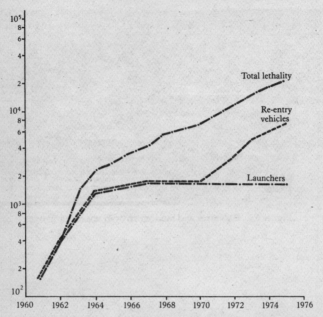

Figure 19. US strategic forces: numbers of launchers and re-entry vehicles, and total lethality.[16] (Note that the vertical axis is logarithmic; the increase in lethality is steeper than the line superficially suggests)

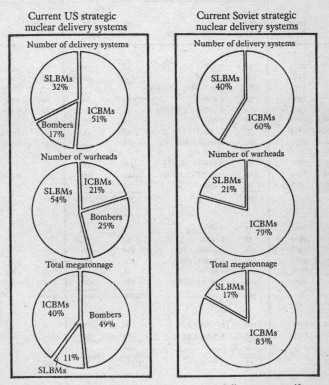

Figure 20. US and Soviet strategic nuclear delivery systems[17]

Table 13 Strategic Nuclear Weapons, USSR

System	First deployed	Collins 1979				SIPRI 1980	
		Delivery vehicles	Yield × warheads	Total warheads	Total yield (Mt)	Delivery vehicles	Yield × warheads
ICBM							
SS–9	1967	68	20 Mt	68	1,360	8	20 Mt
SS–11	1966	650	0.95 Mt	650	618+	580	1 or 0.2 Mt
Mod 3	1973		0.5 – 1 Mt × 3 MIRV				× 1 or 3 MIRV
SS–13	1969	60	0.6 Mt	60	36	60	1 Mt
SS–17 Mod 1	1975	120	0.75 Mt × 4 MIRV	480	360	150	0.5 Mt × 4 MIRV
Mod 2	1977	20	6 Mt	20	120		
SS–18 Mod 1	1974	26[b]	24 Mt	26[b]	624	60	15 Mt
Mod 2	1976	171[c]	0.90 Mt × 8 MIRV	1,368	1,231	240	0.5 Mt × 8 MIRV
Mod 3	1977	b	20 Mt	b			
Mod 4	1979	43	0.50 Mt × 10 MIRV	430	215	+	
SS–19 Mod 1	1974	210	0.55 Mt × 6 MIRV	1,260	693	300	0.5 Mt × 6 MIRV
Mod 2	1978	30	10 Mt	30	300		
		1,398		4,392	5,557	1,398	
SLBM							
SSN–4	1961	3	1 Mt	3	3	+	
SSN–5	1963	57	1–2 Mt	57	57+	+	
SSN–6	1968	468	0.50 Mt–1 Mt	468	234+	464	0.2–1 Mt × 1 or 2 MRV
SSN–8	1973	289	0.50 Mt–1 Mt	289	145+	326	1 Mt
SSN–17	1977	12	0.50 Mt	12	6	16	1 Mt
SSN–18	1977	160	1 Mt × 3 MIRV	480	480	144	0.2 Mt × 3 MIRV
		989		1,309	925	950	
Bomber							
TU–95 Bear	1955	100	1–5 Mt × 2	200	200+		
MYA–4 Bison	1956	40	1–5 Mt × 2	80	80+		
		140		280	280+		
Total		2,527		5,981	6,762	2,348	
Programmes in production[g]							
MX equivalent		presumed MIRVed				A new large solid-fuelled mobile ICBM, like the US	
SS–NX–20		MIRVed				(to be deployed in the Typhoon-class SSBN (20	

a IISS, *The Military Balance* (1980–81).
b 26 is the total of SS–18 Mod 1 and Mod 3.
c F. Kaplan, *Dubious Specter: a Skeptical Look at the Soviet NuclearThreat*, Washington, 1980.
d Bombers have not been included because Soviet bombers are so few and so old, and US air defences so adequate. The Backfire has intercontinental range only on a suicide mission, and is therefore excluded. It appears in Appendix A2. The USSR does not have a 'triad' in strategic thinking or in reality.

		Collins		Collins SIPRI		Collins SIPRI		Collins SIPRI	
Total warheads	Total yield Mt	Throw-wt (lb)	Total throw-wt /1,000 lb	CEP (nm)		Lethality per warhead		Approximate total lethality[f]	
8	160	11,000	748	0.4	0.7	46.05	15.03	3,100	100
1,160	464	2,200	1,430	0.76	1.0	1.7	0.41	1,100	1,100
		2,500		0.6		1.84			
60	60	1,500	90	1.0	no data	0.71			
600	300	6,025	723	0.24	0.3	14	6.99	6,900	4,200
		6,000	120	0.23	0.3	62		1,200	
60	900	16,500	429	0.23	1.3	170	3.59	4,100	200
1,920	960	16,700	2,856	0.23	0.3	18	6.99	24,100	13,400
		16,500		0.19	1.3				
		16,700	718	0.14		32		13,800	(e)
1,800	900	7,525	1,580	0.21	0.24	15	10.93	19,200	19,700
		7,000	210	0.14		240		7,100	
5,608									
		?[a]	?	1.5		0.44			(e)
		?[a]	?	1.5		0.44 +			(e)
696	325	1,500[a]	702	0.7	0.75	1.3 +	0.88 or 1.4	600	400
326	326	1,500[a]	434	0.8	0.80	1.0 +	1.56	300	500
16	16	3,000[a]	36	0.75	0.26	1.1	14.79		200
432	86	5,000[a]	800	0.75	0.52	1.8	1.26	900	500
1,238			10,900						
		bomb load							
		35,000		0.2[c]		(d)		(d)	
		20,000		0.2[c]		(d)		(d)	
								Approximate grand total	
6,878	4,494							82,400	40,300

MX, is reported to be under development. Also, the mobile SS–16 ICBM has been developed but not deployed.)
tubes each) after the mid-1980s)

e SIPRI believes that these weapons are no longer (SSN–4, SSN–5) or not yet (SS–18 Mod 4) deployed.
f Values have been produced from a formula worked to at least three significant figures. However, in recognition of the deficiencies in any data, results are rounded to the nearest 100. Values less than 50 have been omitted.
g *SIPRI Yearbook* (1981), p. 262; Department of Defense, *Soviet Military Power*, Washington, US Government Printing Office, 1981, p. 54.

Table 14. Strategic Nuclear Weapons, USA

System	First deployed	Collins 1979				SIPRI 1980	
		Delivery vehicles	Yield × warheads	Total warheads	Total yield (Mt)	Delivery vehicles	Yield × warheads
ICBM							
Titan II	1962	54[d]	9 Mt	54[d]	486	54	9 Mt
Min. II	1965	450	1–2 Mt	450	450+	450	1.2 Mt
Min. III	1970	550	0.17 Mt × 3 MIRV	1,650	280	550	0.17 Mt × 3 MIRV
Impr. Min. III	1979[a]		0.335 Mt × 3 MIRV				0.335 Mt × 3 MIRV
		1,054		2,154	1,216	1,054	
SLBM							
Polaris A–3	1964	160	0.2 Mt × 3 MIRV	160	96	160	0.22 Mt × 3 MRV
Poseidon C–3	1971	480	0.04 Mt × 10 MIRV	4,800	192	496	0.04 Mt × 10 MIRV
Trident C–4	1979	16	0.1 Mt × 8 MIRV[e]	128	13	16	0.1 Mt × 8 MIRV
		656		5,088	301	672	
Bomber							
B–52	1956	316	1.2 Mt × 4[f]	1,264	1,517	(SRAMS) 150	0.47 Mt × 12
						(bombs) 190	1 Mt × 4
		316		1,264	1,517	340	
Total		2,026		8,516	3,034	2,066	
Programmes in production							
MX		200[c]	0.335 – 0.5 Mt × 14[c]				
Cruise			0.2 Mt[b]				
Trident D–5		914[j]	to be selected Oct. 1982				

a Minuteman III fitted with NS–20 guidance system and Mark 12A re-entry vehicle. At the time that Collins and *SIPRI* 1980 went to press, a programme to replace 300 of the 550 Minuteman III re-entry vehicles with the improved version (whose characteristics are given here) had been announced but had not yet begun. It is intended to complete this modernization, which will not affect the total number of Minuteman delivery vehicles, by the mid-1980s.

b R. K. Betts, ed., *Cruise Missiles: Technology, Strategy, Politics*, Washington, 1981, pp. 152–4. Claims for a CEP in the range 0.015–0.1 nm are to be encountered. For choice of this figure see text. The cruise missile will be procured in three long-range nuclear versions: air-launched (4,348); ground-launched (560); and sea-launched (384). The first squadron of ALCMs mounted on B–52 bombers becomes active in December 1982. The cruise missile programme alone thus represents (assuming K = 300 per missile) almost a forty-fold increase over the lethality of the whole present US nuclear arsenal (taking the SIPRI-based calculation for 1980) on moderately bad, but not worst-case, assumptions.

Total warheads	Total yield (Mt)	Collins Throw-wt (lb)	Collins Total throw-wt /1,000 lb	Collins CEP (nm)	SIPRI CEP (nm)	Collins Lethality per warhead	SIPRI Lethality per warhead	Collins Approximate total lethality[g]	SIPRI Approximate total lethality[g]
54	486	8,275	430	0.8	0.70	6.8	8.83	400	500
450	540	1,625	731	0.34	0.21	8.7	25.80	3,900	10,200
1,650	280	1,975	1,067	0.12	0.16	21	11.98	35,200	19,800
		2,010	20	0.1	0.10	48	30.68		
2,184	1,306								
480	106	1,000[e]	160	0.5	0.48	1.4	1.58	200	800
4,960	198	2,000[e]	960	0.25	0.26	1.9	1.73	9,000	8,600
128	13	3,000[e]	48	0.15	0.26	9.6	3.18	1,200	400
5,568	1,623		3,416						
		bomb load							
1,800	840	60–70,000		0.1[f]	0.10			(h)	
760	760				0.10				
2,560	1,600							Approximate grand total	
10,282	3,223							49,900	40,300

		8,000[c]		0.05				200	
		3,200[b]		0.033[b]				300	
				est. 0.05					

c C. S. Gray, *Survival*, 20, 3, 105.

d *SIPRI Yearbook* (1981). Two Titan II missiles were lost in recent years in accidents.

e IISS, *The Strategic Balance 1980–81*, 1980.

f CEP for B–52s from SIPRI data. Confirmed by F. Kaplan, *Dubious Specter: a Sceptical Look at the Soviet Nuclear Threat*, Washington, 1980.

g See Table 13, note f.

h Bombers have not been included in the total because we do not believe the pin-down argument. If any B–52s get through Soviet air defences, it boosts the 'lethality' total.

j Hearing before the House Appropriations Committee, FY82, Part 9, p. 290. This number, to be placed in 20 SSBNs, represents the Navy's request.

Appendix A2
Nuclear Weapons in the European Theatre:
the Numbers Game

Debate about weapons in Europe has revolved around two apparently simple criteria: numbers of delivery systems and numbers of warheads. It has not been marked by that concern with the many qualitative criteria which bedevil the assessment of 'strength' in strategic systems and which were described in Appendix A1. One might therefore expect the judgement of relative 'strength' between East and West in these shorter-range systems to be more straightforward. But it turns out to be extremely difficult. This is partly because it is more difficult to obtain agreed figures for these nuclear weapons than figures for long-range strategic delivery systems. However, it is also because the official assumptions which underlie different bases of comparison are flexible.

Before proceeding, we must emphasize once more that we do not accept the assumption that 'strength through parity' in numbers of nuclear weapons brings security. The evidence brought forward in Chapters 3 to 6 shows that attempts to achieve 'strength through parity' involve unrestrained escalation and increasing dangers to both sides. What this appendix describes about relative 'strengths' is thus perpendicular to the main thrust of this book.

Yet both East and West assert that the maintenance of 'parity' – on one or other of the criteria for counting – is desirable. The Western officials equate this 'balance' with 'deterrence', which, as argued in Chapter 4, is to commit a simple but profound error, even if a 'deterrent' posture were desirable. Therefore, as we proceed further, as in Appendix A1, it must be continually remembered that all the most important questions for the real world are being begged by what is under discussion. It is assumed that the world of 'parity', if attained, would somehow yield stability and security. While this is not true, the pursuit of this chimera in itself increases risk. So, aware of the unrealism of the exercise, we proceed.

The reason why official figures are so difficult to reconcile, and why the chimera refuses to become tangible, is that the distinction between 'strategic', 'theatre', and 'tactical' nuclear weapons, which spokesmen assert to be of paramount importance, is slippery. The Department of Defense dictionary[1] bases the distinction between 'strategic' and 'tactical' upon the idea that 'strategic' operations are intended to have a long-range rather than an immediate effect on the enemy. But what does that mean in precise, practical terms? Should the criteria be related to the nature of the weapons (yield, range), or should they be based upon the nature of the targets (military of different types, civilian)? There is no uniform official definition, for a Lance missile may be 'tactical' or 'theatre' depending on whether its target is a troop concentration or an airport; a Pershing II or a SACEUR- controlled Poseidon may be 'theatre' if attacking Poland, but 'strategic' if attacking Moscow; and conversely, the same holds for Warsaw Pact systems, except that Soviet SS–20s cannot strike the USA. Yet these target-based definitions are at odds with the system-related criteria used in arms-control negotiations. This means that operational military distinctions are fluid, and so, when judging on the 'tactical/theatre/ strategic' distinction, ours must be also.

However, before we can examine the numerical evidence, a further and more important problem is encountered: there is a fundamental divergence over the assumptions upon which comparisons are constructed.

(a) The *official Western view*, mentioned in Chapter 6, is that comparisons must for the most part be between systems of similar capability. Western strategists are not quite consistent over this, since they sometimes justify NATO's tactical *nuclear* weapons by reference to supposed Soviet superiority in *conventional* weapons, and patently these systems are not alike. Within current comparisons of nuclear weapons a composite criterion is often used composed of the yield, range, and basing mode of the weapons of the two sides. These variables do a lot of varying. Now, inescapably, this view must assume that nuclear exchanges can be controlled, and that the 'war games' scenario of a reflective and gradual escalation, with pauses for thought, is, in fact, realistic.

(b) Carl von Clausewitz advanced an *alternative assumption*, namely that the effect of 'friction' in warfare is to render irrelevant complicated 'war gaming' plans, of which those to 'control' nuclear exchanges are a modern example. This view has been restated by General of the US Army Omar Bradley, more recently by British Admiral of the Fleet Earl Mountbatten, more recently still by the Soviet Lt General Mikhail Milshtein, by former Secretary of Defense, Robert McNamara, and his distinguished associates, and fairly consistently by most Soviet military strategists.[2]

If Clausewitz's assumption is held, then distinctions between yields, ranges, and basing modes are quite academic. For if there is only one 'firebreak' – between any other weapons and nuclear weapons – then the figures which matter most are the total of delivery systems, and totals of warheads *of all descriptions* and of both sides. More warheads, in this view, mean more targets at risk. More delivery systems mean more soldiers potentially able to release them and therefore, in direct proportion, more risk to all. This book has argued in detail that this is the assumption which it is prudent to hold.

In order to make clear the difference between the figures arising from the position advocated by this book and other positions, the table on pp. 318–21 is organized so as to list first different official estimates, from West and East, of the numbers of European theatre weapons. Comparison of these columns shows how totals can be dramatically altered by counting or not counting certain types of weapons. Then in the final column, we calculate the total risks, using the highest figures (i.e. the worst from our point of view), on Clausewitz's assumption.

Notes to table

(a) In an interview with *Der Spiegel* in November 1981, President Brezhnev observed that whilst the SS–20 had three warheads, their total yield was less than that of the SS–4 or SS–5 monoblock warheads which it replaced. IISS state a 19 per cent decrease in yield.

(b) Takes account of utilization, but not serviceability. The highest figures are used since these imply maximum risk. The IISS has, in its last two issues of *The Military Balance*, attempted to quantify the number of warheads likely to arrive on target by ascribing values to 'survivability', 'reliability' and 'penetration'. This is too speculative to be reliable and we suggest that the 'arriving warheads' index should not be given serious weight as an absolute measure. In this it is similar to the 'lethality' index used for strategic systems. In both cases the *concept* has obvious legitimacy, but the *data* are problematic. But the IISS 'arriving warheads' index is the less reliable since two of its three elements are entirely speculative. It is thus of very little use indeed.

(c) Assuming two-thirds are positioned in western USSR or in the 'swing zone' of central USSR.

(d) cf. estimates from W. M. Arkin, 'Nuclear weapons in Europe', in M. Kaldor and D. Smith, eds., *Disarming Europe*, 1982, and *SIPRI Yearbook* (1980), Table 4.1, p. 179.

(e) cf. estimate from W. M. Arkin, 'Nuclear weapons in Europe', op. cit., and SIPRI 1981 estimate, Appendix 8A, pp. 271–5.

(f) This is a SIPRI estimate of short-range Soviet nuclear systems confirmed by W. M. Arkin, 'Nuclear weapons in Europe', op. cit. Most of the warheads are kept within the USSR at special central depots guarded by KGB troops. An unknown but smaller, number is deployed within striking distance of western Europe. FROG and SCUD delivery systems without nuclear components are deployed on the central front.

(g) Mirage IVA cited as a one- or three-weapon system.

(h) Assumes that F111Bs would fly into Europe armed and then use the prepositioned stockpile of bombs.

(j) Assumes both French carriers in strike range.

(k) Sources: IISS, SIPRI: long and medium ranges; W. M. Arkin, 'Nuclear weapons in Europe'; material from Center for Defense Information.

(l) W. M. Arkin, 'Nuclear weapons in Europe'; and Center for Defense Information. Five hundred warheads stockpiled for both systems, including reloads; 380 Lance neutron warheads in production.

(m) Numbers of nuclear-capable 155 mm and 8 inch guns in Europe. (While some types of gun are not intended to fire projectiles as heavy as some of the early AFAPs, since, in theory, any gun of the right calibre can fire a shell of that calibre (after a fashion), this estimate does not distinguish between types of gun.) US: 35 artillery battalions (approx. 20 each) = 700 (both calibres); UK: 143 + 16; Belgium: 41 + 24; W Germany: 802 + 137; Greece: 366 + 92; Italy: 697 + 0; Netherlands: 358 + 41; Turkey: over 210 + unknown number of 8 inch. (Sources: IISS, 1981–2; Collins, *US–Soviet Military Balance*, New York, 1980.)

(n) Ninety armed helicopters and twenty-eight Nimrod (IISS).

(p) 'Clausewitz total' gives the total numbers of all systems and warheads, regardless of ownership, since this is the only realistic measure of the risks facing Europe, risks of two sorts, as explained in the text.

(q) Very few Soviet guns are nuclear-capable. Independent sources estimate about 150 dual-capable tubes. This sort of weapon is not part of Soviet strategy. The Joint Chiefs of Staff only claim 'introduction' of Soviet nuclear artillery in 1982, *Posture Paper*, p. 103. However, note that by spring 1982 NATO was crediting 300 tubes to the Russians.

Table 15. Nuclear Weapons in the European Theatre

Different official statements, 1981–2, in chronological sequence

Name and nature of delivery systems	'European theatre (land-based)' UK Defence Est. March 1981		'Long-range theatre nuclear force' Foreign Office (GB) July 1981		US–Soviet intermediate-range balance' State Department (US) November 1981		Soviet figures President Brezhnev November 1981	
	System	Warheads	System	Warheads	System	Warheads	System	Warheads
WARSAW PACT								
(a) Long- and medium-range	not mentioned				not mentioned		not mentioned[a]	
Land-based missiles	}		175		250			
SS–20	540 'missiles'		350 } (525)		350 }		496 }	
SS–5								
SS–4								
SS–12/	650 'medium-range missiles'						not included	
Scud B							not included	
Submarine-based missiles								
SS–N–5	not included		not included		30	18	18	
Nuclear-capable aircraft								
Tu 22/M–26 Backfire B	}		45		45			
Tu 16 Badger	350		350 }		350 }		461	
Tu 22 Blinder								
Su 24 (Su–19) Fencer	}		not included				not included	
MiG–27 Flogger D			not included		2,700		not included	
Su–17 Fitter C/D	2,000		not included		(Fencer, Flogger,		not included	
Su–7 Fitter A			not included		Fitter)		not included	
MiG 21 Fishbed			not included				not included	
Total	3,540		920		3,825		975	
(b) short-range								
FROG Mods (3), 5 and 7 missiles	}		not included		not included		not included	
SS–21 (not deployed outside USSR)	950		not included		not included		not included	
Nuclear artillery[q]			not included		not included		not included	
Warsaw Pact total	4,490		920		3,825		975	

					'Clausewitz balance'[k]		
IISS Military Balance 1981–2			'NATO and the Warsaw Pact – Force Comparisons', NATO				
Autumn 1981	Nuclear role		April 1982			Nuclear role	
System	v. Europe[b]	Warheads	System	Warheads	System	v. Europe[b]	Warheads
230	151[c]	455	300	900*	230	151	455
40	40	40	25		40	40	40
340	340	340	275		340	340	340
668	505	505	650		668 (72)	505	505[d]
					(650)	(72)	(72)
57	57	57	'a small number'		57 (33)(18)	57 (18)	57 (18)[e]
65	26	104	omitted, seen as 'strategic'		65	26	104
310	124	248	} 650		310	124	248
125	49	99			125	49	99
480	96	192			480	96	192
500	200	200	1,850		500	200	200
700	140	140	(includes Yak 20 Brewer)		700	140	140
165	33	33			165	33	33
750	150	150			750	150	150
4,430	1,911	2,563	over 3,750		(4,430)	(1,911)	(2,563)
	not included		} 650		all types	deployed	?
	not included				3,500[f]	?500	
	not included		300		inc. 150? 300?	?	?
4,430	1,911	2,563	over 4,700 *only warhead figure given		8,230	2,411	over 3,063

Different official statements, 1981–2, in chronological sequence

Name and nature of delivery systems	'European theatre (land-based)' U K Defence Est. March 1981		'Long-range theatre nuclear force' Foreign Office (GB) July 1981		'US–Soviet intermediate-range balance' State Department (US) November 1981		Soviet figures President Brezhnev November 1981	
	System	Warheads	System	Warheads	System	Warheads	System	Warheads
NATO								
(a) Long- and medium-range								
Land-based missiles								
S–2/3 (Fr.)	18		not included		not included		18	
Pershing 1A	180		not included		not included		not included	
Lance	below (SR)		not included		not included		not included	
Honest John	not included		not included		not included		not included	
Pluton (Fr.)	not included		not included		not included		not included	
Submarine-based missiles								
Poseidon C3	not included		not included		not included		not included	
Polaris A3 (GB)	not included		not included		not included		64	
M–20 (Fr.)	not included		not included		not included		80	
Nuclear-capable aircraft								
Vulcan (GB)			56		not included		55	
Buccaneer (GB)			not included		not included		not included	
Jaguar (GB)			not included		not included		80	
Mirage IVA (Fr.)			not included		not included		not included	
Mirage IIIE (Fr.)	260 'long-range' + 700 'medium-range'		not included		not included		46	
Jaguar (Fr.)			not included		not included		not included	
Super Etendard (Fr.)			not included		not included		not included	
F–4			not included		265		not included	
F–104			not included		not included		517	
F–111E/F	170		164		not included			
FB–111			not included		63		66	
A–6E	not included		not included		68		60	
A–7E	not included		not included		not included		not included	
Total	1,158		226		560		986	
(b) Short-range								
Nike Hercules surface-to-air missile	unknown what is included		not included		not included		not included	
Atomic demolition munitions (ADMs)			not included		not included		not included	
Artillery-fired atomic projectile (AFAP)								
155 mm			not included		not included		not included	
8 inch			not included		not included		not included	
Nuclear depth bombs (GB)			not included		not included		not included	
Total	1,200 (inc. Lance)		not included		not included		not included	
NATO total	2,358		226		560		986	
Warsaw Pact total								
Clausewitz total[P]	————————→		————————→		————→		————————→	

	IISS Military Balance 1981–2			'NATO and the Warsaw Pact - Force Comparisons' NATO		'Clausewitz balance'[k]		
	Autumn 1981	Nuclear role v. Europe[b]		April 1982			Nuclear role v. Europe[b]	
	System		Warheads	System	Warheads	System		Warheads
	18	18	18	not included		18		18
	180	180	180	180		180		360
		not included		100		117		500[l]
		not included				26		
		not included		not included		32		32
		not included		not included		40		400
	64	64	64	not included		64		64
	80	80	80	not included		80		80
	57	57	114	μ	$\mu = 200$	57	57	544 bombs
	60	30	60	+	$+ = 600$	60	30	in GB
	80	40	40	+		80	40	arsenal
	33	33	33	not included		33	33	33[g]
	30	15	15	not included		30	15	15
		not included		not included		45	23	45
	12	6	12	not included		36	12[j]	24
	364	109	109	+		364	109	900 bombs at 11 NATO
	318	95	95	+		318	95	and 7 US nuclear certified
	156	78	156	μ		156	78	air bases in Europe
		not included		seen as strategic		65	65	132[h]
	20	10	20	} 'not primary		20	10	20
	40	20	40	mission'		40	20	40
	1,512	835	1,036	1,080		(1,861)	(1,144)	(3,207)
		not included		not included		748		600
		not included		not included		300		300
		not included		} 1,000				2,500
		not included				approx[m] 3,700		1,000
		not included		not included		118[n]		422
		not included		1,100 (counts Lance and Honest John)		(4,866)	(4,748)	(4,822)
	1,512	835	1,036	2,180		6,727	(5,892)	(8,029)
						(8,230)	(2,411)	(over 3,063)

14,957	8,303	11,092

Appendix B
Radioactivity and Radiation

The basic substances of which matter is composed are the elements, which exist in the form of atoms. The smallest atom is that of the element hydrogen, and consists of a positively charged proton with a negatively charged electron, very light by comparison, in orbit around it. In the atom of any element, the number of protons is equal to the number of electrons, giving a zero net charge. It is the number and arrangement of the electrons that gives an element its chemical characteristics, determining, for example, the ways in which that element will combine with other elements to form the enormous variety of natural and man-made substances. In the atoms of all elements, apart from the simplest, hydrogen, the nucleus around which the electrons orbit contains both protons and neutrons (uncharged particles of roughly the same mass as protons); and in many cases an element exists in more than one form, with a constant number of protons and electrons, but different numbers of neutrons. These forms are known as *isotopes* of the element – for instance, uranium 235 (with 92 electrons, 92 protons and 143 neutrons) and uranium 238 (92 electrons and protons, but 146 neutrons).

The proportions of protons and neutrons in a nucleus determine how stable the nucleus is. Many isotopes are potentially unstable, or *radio-active*, and tend to decay, or undergo rearrangement of the nucleus to a more stable form. (Isotopes which are themselves not radioactive may be induced to decay by bombardment with neutrons or protons, which produces an imbalance of neutrons and protons in the nucleus.) Radio-active decay is measured by the *half-life* – i.e. the time taken for disintegration of the isotope atoms to reduce the amount of isotope to half. This is a constant for each isotope, and may be anything from a fraction of a second up to millions of years. For example, the half-life of plutonium 239 is 24,400 years, and so after, say, four half-lives (nearly 100,000 years), $\frac{1}{2} \times \frac{1}{2} \times \frac{1}{2} \times \frac{1}{2}$ or 1/16 of the original amount will still remain.

Radioactive decay is accompanied by the release of *ionizing radiation* of various kinds – positively charged α-particles (2 protons + 2 neutrons), negatively charged electrons or β-particles, and electromagnetic radiation (γ-rays, similar to X-rays). Different radioactive isotopes release different proportions of these radiations. Neutrons do not usually result directly from radioactive decay, but as the product of, for instance, collisions between protons and suitable target atoms. They occur in nuclear fission reactions. Ionization is not caused directly by neutrons, but as a consequence of collision of neutrons with atomic nuclei.

The various types of radiation penetrate living tissue to different extents: α-particles a fraction of a millimetre, β-particles up to about a centimetre, and γ- and X-rays far greater distances. However, the toxicity of radiation is not merely a question of its ability to penetrate, but depends on the capacity of the radiation to release its energy and so cause damaging ionization in the biochemical constituents of the body. This capacity is expressed in terms of linear energy transfer (LET) – the energy lost by radiation or charged particle per unit length of the medium it traverses. Roughly comparable with LET is the 'quality factor', which expresses the relative biological effectiveness (RBE) of radiation. The quality factor of X- and γ-rays (of low LET) is defined as 1. For slow neutrons it is 3, and for fast neutrons and α-particles (high LET) it is 10.

Although α-particles outside the body are not a serious hazard because of their low penetration, if released inside the body by an inhaled or ingested α-emitting isotope they are extremely toxic. The biological effects of radiation depend on dose. High doses cause gross disturbance of biochemical processes, resulting in cell death, radiation sickness, and death of the victim within a matter of weeks. The effects of lower doses are more subtle. They may be insufficient to kill cells, but the damage done to DNA (the molecule carrying coded genetic information within the chromosomes) may result in irreversible change in the genetic information or in the way it is expressed. An appropriate alteration of this kind in a single cell is sufficient to produce a clone of abnormally dividing cells which, after a latent period of perhaps many years, results in cancer. Genetic damage caused by irradiation of a foetus may in addition result in developmental abnormalities. Finally, genetic damage to the germ cells is likely to cause permanent, inherited defects in succeeding generations.

Some units defined

Curie: the unit of radioactivity – the amount of any isotope which will produce 3.7×10^{10} radioactive disintegrations per second.

Rad: the unit of absorbed radiation dose, used to measure the amount of energy from radiation absorbed in the body.

Rem: an important unit which defines the 'dose equivalent' of different kinds of radiation..The dose equivalent in rem is the product of absorbed dose (in rads) and the R B E or quality factor (see above). Thus, equal doses (in rems) of different kinds of radiation produce comparable biological effects.

Appendix C
The Position in 1982 on the Ultimate Disposal of High-level Radioactive Waste

Late in 1976 two major government commissions, set up to examine environmental aspects of nuclear power generation, published their reports.[1] The Australian government had established, under Mr Justice Fox, a distinguished Supreme Court judge, a commission to examine a proposal to mine uranium. The British government had received from the Royal Commission on Environmental Pollution, under the chairmanship of Sir Brian Flowers, its Sixth Report, which dealt with nuclear power and the environment.

In its origin the Fox Commission was more akin to Mr Justice Parker's 1977 Planning Inquiry at Windscale than to a Royal Commission. However, Justice Fox's treatment of his terms of reference was sharply in contrast with Parker's. Whereas Parker interpreted his brief as narrowly as possible, and thus felt no obligation to consider broader issues, Fox divided his report into two volumes, the second addressing the minutiae of the Ranger uranium deposits, but the first embracing the widest context of nuclear enterprise. In this, Fox's Commission came to many conclusions similar to those reached simultaneously by the Flowers Commission and, on certain questions, notably the threat of proliferation, voiced far stronger anxiety.

Regarding the disposal of radioactive waste, Fox stated:

> There is at present no generally accepted means by which high-level waste can be permanently isolated from the environment and remain safe for very long periods ... Permanent disposal of high-level solid wastes in stable geological formations is regarded as the most likely solution, but has yet to be demonstrated as feasible. It is not certain that such methods and disposal sites will entirely prevent radioactive releases following disturbances caused by natural processes or human activity.[2]

Flowers concurred, and the Royal Commission called this 'a profoundly serious issue, central to the environmental evaluation of a nuclear power programme'.[3] It stated:

> We believe that a quite inadequate effort has been devoted to the problems of long-term waste management.[4]

Elsewhere, the Commission added:

Neither the Atomic Energy Authority nor British Nuclear Fuels Ltd, in their submissions to us, gave any indication that they regarded the search for a means of final disposal of highly active waste as at all pressing, and it appears that they have only recently taken firm steps towards seeking solutions . . . We find this the more surprising in view of the large nuclear programmes that both bodies envisage for the coming decades.[5]

Consequently the Commission recommended that

. . . there should be no substantial expansion of nuclear power until the feasibility of a method of safe disposal of high-level wastes for the indefinite future has been established beyond reasonable doubt.[6]

Like Fox, Flowers observed that 'there are promising ideas for the disposal of these wastes, but it may take ten to twenty years to establish their feasibility'.[7]

A threat to its future, even from a body without legal force, such as a Royal Commission, concentrates minds in the nuclear industry wonderfully. Since 1976 considerable effort has been put into the planning of waste disposal in Britain. In Sweden an even harsher constraint was imposed. In 1977 the incoming coalition government passed a Stipulation Law, requiring owners of reactors to show how and where they could store radioactive waste with complete safety. In the emergency posed by an Act which threatened to kill off the entire Swedish nuclear programme the industry concentrated its research effort on trying to pass this test. It appears that an attempt to get spent reactor fuel reprocessed by the French firm COGEMA proved unsatisfactory. However, a report from the Swedish nuclear power industry in 1978 claimed that the disposal problem could be solved satisfactorily by the following elaborate method: spent fuel would be stored in water pools for forty years; then it would be loaded into copper canisters with walls 20 cm thick, each weighing 15 tons; each canister would be deposited in a separate tunnel 500 m below the earth's surface; each tunnel would be lined and stoppered with bentonite, which when constricted and exposed to water becomes almost totally impermeable. Thus treated, it was claimed, the spent fuel would be rendered harmless for thousands of years.[8] But seven of eight geologists consulted by the Swedish nuclear power inspectorate concluded that sites identified for such repositories did not satisfy the Stipulation Law.[9]

(After intense debate, a referendum was held in Sweden in 1980; 57 per cent of voters favoured a reduced nuclear power programme, by which twelve reactors would operate for twenty-five years, during which a combination of alternative energy sources must be developed to replace nuclear power plants.)[10]

It is generally agreed that radioactive waste is best stored by reducing in volume and embedding in a suitable matrix – cement, ceramic, crystalline, metal or glass. Since the matrix must accommodate without degeneration atoms of many kinds, all subject to radioactive transformation, glasses, with their freedom from systematic atomic patterns, seem to offer the best properties.[11] But crystalline media composed of many different constituents may offer some advantages.[12]

The earliest candidate as matrix was borosilicate glass, and the UK Atomic Energy Authority was able in the early 1960s to develop a pilot vitrification process. The Authority and British Nuclear Fuels Ltd planned to exploit this on an industrial scale in HARVEST (Highly Active Residue Vitrification and Engineered Storage).[13] Meanwhile French scientists had invented AVM (Atelier de Vitrification, Marcoule) and built a full-scale plant.[14] Perhaps stimulated into action by the Flowers Commission, the UKAEA rapidly showed to its own satisfaction that borosilicate glass possesses acceptable stability and freedom from degeneration at low temperatures and pressures.[15]

But the main forseeable danger in long-term storage underground lies in the great increase in degeneration of the glass at the high temperatures and pressures that result from radioactive heating. Research workers at Pennsylvania State University Materials Research Laboratory had shown that such effects occur at temperatures of about 300 °C and pressures about 300 bars.[16] Some scientists therefore looked for materials that would withstand such conditions better than borosilicates do. The group at the Vitreous State Laboratory, Washington, explored the properties of high-silicate glasses, and found such glasses to be markedly superior to borosilicates for use as stable matrices.[17] One difficulty in comparing possible matrices is that evidence gained over a few months (or years at most) may not be valid over periods of hundreds of years. But the rock rhyolite is a high-silicate glass, and field observations can discover how it has responded to many changes of environment during hundreds of millions of years. Nature has provided the laboratory that we cannot construct. The results confirmed the man-made laboratory results, but from this different direction, and suggested that high-silica glass is much more likely to be suitable for the long-term disposal of radioactive waste than borosilicate glass.[18]

Professor Ringwood of the Australian National University has followed a different course. He and his colleagues have fabricated artificial rocks designed to take up into stable form the various constituent elements of radioactive waste. Using titanates and zirconates in various combinations they have produced SYNROC.[19] It was claimed that at high temperatures and pressures SYNROC was far more stable than borosilicate glass. But other workers have questioned whether SYNROC would be much better than glasses at the temperatures and pressures likely to be met during the disposal of radioactive waste. They have also doubted whether any crystalline matrix can have the necessary flexibility to deal with the changing atomic structure of radiating elements.

There are many difficulties in forecasting the behaviour of a radioactive waste matrix during hundreds of years. At present it is not at all clear whether some variety of SYNROC, some high-silica glass, or some borosilicate would stand up best to the actual conditions of long underground storage. The weight of evidence at present seems to favour high-silicate glass, but recent writers urge caution and further experiment.[20]

Meanwhile the search for suitable storage locations should continue urgently, for a considerable amount of high-level waste has already accumulated in temporary stores. Such a location should be free from earthquakes, from underground water-flow, from physical or chemical change and from man-made disturbance. In the Flowers Report it was recommended that the Natural Environment Research Council and the Institute of Geological Sciences should undertake field studies. A good beginning was made, but it proved difficult to obtain planning permission for the drilling of necessary boreholes, owing to local opposition.[21]

The exploratory work of the IGS was cut short in December 1981, when the British government decided that work completed in other countries had shown that geological disposal was feasible in principle, and anyway that storage in solid form at the earth's surface for fifty years should also be considered.[22]

But British authorities had already preempted the necessary scientific research and had decided during 1980 to use a vitrification process with borosilicate glass. However, they opted for the French AVM rather than the British HARVEST process, for the sake of speed, to ensure earlier completion and operation of the plant, and because it was thought that there might be some financial saving.[23]

The packaging which will be produced by the Windscale vitrification plant[24] cannot be regarded as meeting the Flowers Commission's recommendation. On the one hand borosilicate glasses are still not certainly shown to survive high temperature and high radioactivity without degeneration and leakage of radioactive elements, and on the other hand no sites have been proven and specified for safe final storage. Engineered interim depositories, such as those used by the French, do not meet the criterion. We recall the words of the Royal Commission:

... there should be no substantial expansion of nuclear power until the feasibility of a method of safe disposal of high-level waste for the indefinite future has been established beyond reasonable doubt.

The storage of high-level wastes is too important a matter to be summarily dealt with, for whatever reason (railroaded through in the interests of, for example, protecting cherished programmes of reactor construction and development), or to be treated with less than the greatest possible scientific exactitude.

Appendix D
Nuclear Power and Nuclear Weapons:
Links in the Case
of British Plutonium Exports

A. An exchange of letters

While this book was in press, one of its contributing authors became engaged in a public correspondence of considerable significance, which occurred in the columns of the *Guardian* newspaper and is reproduced here with the permission of the authors.

The exchange of letters was stimulated by certain strong assertions made by the chief press officer of the United Kingdom Atomic Energy Authority. Two of his points were uncontroversial (that the Magnox reactor was designed to produce both power and plutonium and that plutonium for military purposes has been extracted by reprocessing facilities at the Windscale works); these were a repetition of what is already well known. However, another assertion was less easily accepted: a clear statement that at no time have Electricity Board reactors produced plutonium for nuclear weapons. It is notable that this statement is unqualified: it therefore means 'no nuclear weapons in Britain or anywhere else'. But in the final paragraph of his first letter, Mr Starr did, in fact, concede a different type of direct link from that which he was concerned to deny: he made the forthright observation that British 'civil' plutonium exported to the United States under the Mutual Defence Agreement (Amendment) of 7 May 1959 was in direct exchange for enriched uranium and tritium for the British military programme. Again, this is no revelation; it was in fact the clear and expressed intention of the Mutual Defence Agreement to facilitate this – of which more below. However, it is helpful to see the civil/military connection so frankly restated by the chief press officer of the UKAEA.

The publication of this letter caused Sir Martin Ryle and Dr R. V. Hesketh, a scientist working at the Central Electricity Generating Board's Berkeley Nuclear Laboratory in Gloucestershire, jointly to reply to it. They raised several specific questions about the composition of the British plutonium stockpile and about the 'civil' explanation given by Mr Starr for the application of British plutonium exported to the United States.

A further letter from Mr Starr addressed the questions raised in a curious way: on the one hand he failed to confront directly the analysis given by Dr Hesketh and Professor Ryle but instead offered oblique criticism by insinuation; on the other he made in the final paragraph an amplified, remarkably strong but unsubstantiated assertion.

Since Dr Hesketh and Professor Ryle believed that both the major and minor assertions were factually incorrect, they wrote again. They restated the main grounds for scepticism about the official version of the history of British plutonium exports, pressing the issue yet more closely, and, in response to the minor supporting claims made in Mr Starr's second letter, they were obliged to introduce specific evidence to dispose of these also.

LETTER OF 22 MAY 1982
FROM THE CHIEF PRESS OFFICER, UKAEA

Sir – Mr Howard Clark [in an earlier letter to the *Guardian*] invites me to comment on ('deny') certain propositions:

I confirm that all the plutonium required for British weapons since 1957 has been produced in reactors – other than those in the Electricity Boards' stations – which are also used to generate electricity. No plutonium for weapons use has at any time been produced in the Electricity Boards' reactors.

The Calder Hall/Chapelcross Magnox reactors were designed and built for the dual purpose of producing electricity and plutonium, including plutonium for weapons use as necessary. This dual role was clearly explained before Calder Hall was opened in 1956: for example in Mr Kenneth Jay's celebratory volume *Calder Hall* (Methuen, 1956), page 37: 'Accordingly, in February 1953 the government accepted a recommendation that a single PIPPA-type (Pressurized Pile for Producing Power and Plutonium) reactor should be built to produce military plutonium and electrical power.'

I also confirm that the facilities at Windscale are used for reprocessing irradiated reactor fuel from Calder Hall and Chapelcross for military purposes, as well as fuel from various sources for civil purposes. Information about the overall Windscale reprocessing programme, which would allow estimates to be made of the scale of work undertaken on behalf of the Ministry of Defence, cannot be published.

Mr Clark takes the government to task for not publishing the quantity of plutonium supplied to the United States before 1971 from the Electricity

Boards' Magnox stations. This plutonium, which the US authorities allocated to civil purposes, was supplied in exchange for highly enriched uranium for the UK defence programme: the scale of the plutonium shipments was thus related to the scale of the uranium supplies received in exchange, which the government indeed is 'unwilling to disclose'.

LETTER OF 16 JULY 1982 FROM DR R. V. HESKETH
AND SIR MARTIN RYLE

Sir – The letter by Mr G. R. Starr on behalf of the UKAEA (22 May) fits snugly into the pattern of 'bland, unsubstantiated official assurance' of which Lord Flowers complained in 1976. The letter admits that plutonium produced in the civil Magnox stations of the two electricity generating boards, CEGB and SSEB, has been exported to the US under the Mutual Defence Agreement of 1959. In exchange, Britain received highly-enriched uranium and tritium, and this has been used in the UK defence programme. The enriched uranium is used in submarines and the tritium in hydrogen bombs. The export of civil plutonium has thus quite directly assisted the UK military programme.

But what of the plutonium itself, exported for nominally civil purposes? On both sides of the Atlantic these civil purposes have remained unspecified for eighteen years, from 1964 to the present.

The export occurred in the decade 1963 to 1973, slightly later than the period in which the nine civil Magnox stations commenced operation – 1962 to 1971. After being optimized for electricity production, each Magnox reactor produces weapons-grade plutonium during roughly the first two years of its operation. (It takes some four years for a Magnox reactor to come into a steady state.) Thus weapons-grade plutonium was being produced by each of the civil reactors in succession during this same decade. The quantity of weapons-grade plutonium so produced should be between three and four tonnes.

Weapons-grade plutonium has a greater financial and military value than fuel-grade or reactor-grade plutonium, and it is not credible that the weapons material produced during the start-up phase of each reactor was simply mixed into a common stock of fuel-grade plutonium. Yet the previous chairman of the CEGB has publicly said that there is now no weapons-grade plutonium in the UK civil stockpile. Furthermore, official figures from *Hansard*, the UKAEA journal, *Atom*, and the Flowers Report indicate a discrepancy of three to four tonnes between the civil production of plutonium and the civil stock.

This coincidence of quantities and dates, and the absence of weapons-grade plutonium in the civil stock, together suggest that some three to four tonnes of weapons-grade plutonium from civil reactors was exported to the US between 1963 and 1973. The eighteen-year silence concerning the use to which this plutonium was put suggests that it was used for the purpose envisaged in the Defence Agreement, namely, 'research on, development of, or use in atomic weapons'*

So much for the water which has gone under the bridge. More recently, in December 1981, the British government said that 'the US Department of Energy may be facing a shortage of civil plutonium for fast reactor development'. For this reason the government has agreed, in principle, to the further export of UK civil plutonium.

Now the US programme of reactor development envisages *one* fast reactor, at Clinch River, and this is due to come into operation in 1990 if all goes well. According to usually reliable sources, the *present* US civil stock of fuel-grade plutonium is 17.8 tonnes, sufficient to fuel *three* reactors of the type proposed for Clinch River. Perhaps this is why the government statement says 'may be facing . . .' rather than 'faces . . .'

It is not immediately apparent that there is a shortage of plutonium for reactor development, but there is undoubtedly a shortage of plutonium for the weapons programme envisaged by the US administration in the next three years. Clinch River will only come on power five years after this immediate shortage.

A fast reactor burns fuel-grade plutonium but breeds a high-quality weapons-grade plutonium. It is one of several ways of obtaining weapons-grade plutonium from fuel-grade plutonium. Within a policy of world-wide deterrence the demand for military plutonium must be finite – there comes a point at which not even the superpowers need any more.

We have no evidence that the previous export of civil plutonium from the UK to the US was used for anything other than weapons, and we see no prospect that the proposed export (to which the government has agreed in principle) would be used for anything other than weapons. In our view, the distinction between plutonium for military use and plutonium for civil use needs to be far more clearly defined by the governments of the US and Britain, and the distinction needs to be open to the kind of public scrutiny envisaged in the Smyth Report of 1945.

* This quotation is misapplied. The quotation, from Article III, *bis*, paragraph B, sub-paragraph 4, refers to materials transferred from the USA to the UK, i.e. the enriched uranium and tritium whose military application is freely conceded by all parties. However, paragraph B of the same article states that transfers of materials from the UK to the USA shall be 'for military purposes'. Therefore, the point stands.

LETTER OF 6 AUGUST 1982
FROM THE CHIEF PRESS OFFICER, UKAEA

Sir – Mr Hesketh and Sir Martin Ryle devoted the first half of their letter of 16 July to elaborating a surmise that there has been an official silence of eighteen years designed to conceal some three or four tonnes of weapon-grade plutonium from the civil Magnox stations of the CEGB and SSEB exported to the US between 1963 and 1973 for use in atomic weapons or related R and D.

The House of Commons were, in fact, informed by the Prime Minister in 1964, before any deliveries began, that the US government had no intention of using, for weapons purposes, any plutonium from those stations (*Hansard*, Col. 621, 17–23 April 1964). This assurance was recently recalled by Mr J. Moore (Under Secretary of State for Energy) in a Parliamentary Answer (*Hansard*, Col. 168–9, 1 April 1982) which also gave a breakdown of the wholly civil disposition of the plutonium produced in them. Even more recently, Mr Moore has informed the House that the US Department of Energy have stated that the bulk of the plutonium is in US fast reactor facilities, a sizeable quantity has been used to make californium for medical purposes and the small remainder is in experimental civil uses at Argonne, Battelle, etc. (*Hansard*, Cols. 438–9, 27 July 1982).

For the avoidance of any further doubt about hypothetical discrepancies such as that advanced by your correspondents, may I say that none of the plutonium from the CEGB and SSEB Magnox reactors was exported, employed or applied for any atomic weapons or weapons-related R and D use in the UK, the US or any third country.

LETTER OF 19 AUGUST 1982 FROM DR R. V. HESKETH
AND SIR MARTIN RYLE

Sir – One does not have to 'surmise' that there has been an eighteen-year official silence concerning the use of civil plutonium exported from the UK to the US (Letters, 6 August); even the chief press officer of the UK Atomic Energy Authority does not cite any statement between 21 April 1964, and 27 July 1982.

On the former date Sir Alec Douglas-Home said: 'I am informed by the United States government that they have no intention of using the plutonium received from us for weapons purposes' (*Hansard*, Col. 1098). Had there been a binding agreement between the two governments, we may be confident that Sir Alec would have used a more direct form of speech, for example: '... the US Government has agreed...'

However, Sir Alec was only 'informed of an intention' and intentions may change, for the best of reasons. (What better reason than 'national security'?) One scarcely has to be an expert in sideways communications to grasp the meaning of Sir Alec's words.

The UKAEA letter of 6 August refers to 'a breakdown of the wholly civil disposition' of the plutonium produced in CEGB and SSEB reactors, but does not mention that the breakdown is incomplete. The final item of the breakdown is an undisclosed 'balance' of civil plutonium exported under the Mutual Defence Agreement.*

The UKAEA letter leaves unanswered two major points raised by our letter 16 July:

1. Is the previous chairman of the CEGB [Mr Glyn England] correct in saying that there is now no weapons-grade plutonium in the UK civil stockpile?

2. If the previous chairman's statement is correct, where is the weapons-grade plutonium that each Magnox reactor produces – by virtue of having been optimized for electricity production – during the initial years of its operation?

We would also ask:

3. Where is the weapons-grade plutonium from Wylfa, the last and largest

---

* Part of a written answer from the Under Secretary of State for Energy to a question from Robin Cook, MP

Plutonium inventory

		tonnes
In irradiated fuel:		
– in fuel loaded in CEGB and SSEB reactors	approx.	8.5
– in discharged fuel not yet reprocessed	approx.	3.5
Separated plutonium		
– in stock with British Nuclear Fuels Ltd as oxide		14.5
– in process with BNFL, e.g. as nitrate		0.5
– sold or leased to UKAEA for Fast Reactor Research and Development		5.5
– exported, other than to the USA		0.5
		33

Balance, consigned to the USA under the Mutual Defence Agreement before 1971 (note g)

Note g. 'Because of the barter arrangements under which this plutonium was consigned, it would not be in the national interest to publish this figure.'

of the Magnox stations? Wylfa came on stream in late 1971, and should have produced half a tonne or more of weapons-grade plutonium. The export of civil plutonium to the US is said to have been complete by the end of 1970. Accordingly, the Wylfa weapons-grade plutonium should at present be in the UK civil stockpile.

The UKAEA letter describes the several discrepancies as 'hypothetical'. We therefore note that the Under Secretary of State for Energy assured the Commons on 21 December 1981 that he would choose his words with great care (Col. 736). He then referred to '... 1,280 kg of United Kingdom *civil* plutonium ... exported *since* 1971 to other countries for civil purposes' (Col. 738, emphasis added). In a later statement (*Hansard*, 1 April 1982, Col. 169) 780 kg of this 1,280 kg is attributed to the military reactors at Calder Hall and Chapelcross, rather than to the civil stations. Should the statement of 21 December 1981, be preferred, or that of 1 April 1982?

If the statement by the previous chairman of the CEGB is correct (point one) does the 780 kg in fact contain the half tonne of Wylfa plutonium?

The UKAEA letter speaks of weapons-grade plutonium, but does not deny that weapons-grade rather than fuel-grade was exported.

We are asked to believe that 'the bulk' of the exported weapons-grade has been used in the fast-reactor programme, principally in the core of the reactor known as FFTF. The core of FFTF uses 0.6 tonnes of plutonium. The UK export is between three and four tonnes.

[Furthermore, speaking before the Procurement and Military Nuclear Systems Sub-committee of the House of Representatives Committee on Armed Services on 2 March 1981, Dr F. Charles Gilbert said, '*All* of our new fuel-grade plutonium comes from one reactor, the "N" reactor in Richland, Washington ... and that goes mostly into one reactor, FFTF' (HASC No. 97–2 p. 145, emphasis added)*. There are two discrepancies here. First, the source of the plutonium for FFTF and second, the grade of the plutonium used. Dr Gilbert's statement seems to us to be preferable to Mr Starr's; it would be foolish to use weapons-grade in a fast-reactor core when an ample supply of fuel-grade is available.

Dr Gilbert's remarks in regard to the plutonium received from the UK are equally interesting. Asked if the United States was receiving anything useful in exchange for its highly enriched uranium, he made a statement of which only the concluding sentence remained unexpunged: 'I cannot

---

* The 'N' reactor was switched to production of fuel-grade plutonium in December 1963. In a letter to Senators Hart, Simpson and Mitchell on 13 May 1982, the Natural Resource Defense Council stated that 'N' had produced 7.8 tonnes of fuel grade to the end of fiscal year 1980.

really speak very knowledgeably in the commercial or civilian area' (p. 146). Asked to address 'the defence area', Dr Gilbert then made *three* statements, all expunged from the record. It would almost seem that the plutonium supplied by the UK does have some connection with the United States defence programme. We recall that the Mutual Defence Agreement speaks of 'military purposes'.]*

The US Department of Energy, unlike its UK counterpart, is responsible for the design and fabrication of nuclear warheads, and for the associated production of weapons-grade plutonium. The statement of 27 July 1982 by the US DoE – to which the UKAEA letter of 6 August refers – is therefore a statement by a defendant, rather than an independent assessment.

The US DoE statement says that 'a sizeable quantity' of UK plutonium has been used to make californium for medical purposes. A large reactor could produce one kilogram of californium per year, say 10 kg in a decade. At one time, ten or so hospitals in the US and the UK used californium to treat malignant tumours; only one does so now. Probably less than 1,000 people have received californium therapy. The total amount of californium used in this therapy is less than one-tenth of a milligram.

The production of californium may well run into kilograms. It is a preferred radioactive source for use in reactors, and its non-medical uses vastly outweigh its medical uses.

The weight of the evidence is that civil weapons-grade plutonium has been exported from the UK to the US under the Mutual Defence agreement, and that it has been used in weapons.

Our letter of 16 July concluded with two proposals for the future: a far more clearly defined distinction between the civil and military use of plutonium; and a more open system of accounting and of public scrutiny. The UKAEA letter of 6 August, by its manner and by its content, only emphasizes the need for these reforms.

B. The Mutual Defence Agreement between Britain and the United States

At issue between the spokesman of the UKAEA and his critics are certain matters of fact: what actually has been *done* with particular quantities and types of plutonium by successive British and American governments, the

* These paragraphs were omitted from the letter as printed in the *Guardian*.

UK Atomic Energy Authority, the Electricity Boards, and the US Department of Energy? But also centrally in dispute is a question of interpretation: what were the intentions surrounding the Mutual Defence Agreements at the time of their making, intentions to be read both in the circumstances of their negotiation and in the texts themselves?

Mr Starr concedes that fissionable material sent to Britain from the USA was used for the nuclear defence programme, but he maintains that plutonium sent westwards across the Atlantic has never been used for military purposes. In his second letter he suggests that there was never any intention of doing this. Dr Hesketh and Professor Ryle agree with Mr Starr about Britain's imports from America but believe not only that British plutonium has been used in weapons, but that this was the intention of the Agreements. What do the Agreements actually say? Three separate but related acts of legislation must be described:

● 1. Amendment of the US Atomic Energy Act debated in June and signed by President Eisenhower on 2 July 1958.

● 2. The Anglo-American Mutual Defence Agreement of 3 July 1958, made possible by the American Act of the previous day.

● 3. The Amendment to the Mutual Defence Agreement of 7 May 1959.

In 1946, the year after the United States destroyed Hiroshima and Nagasaki with atomic bombs, and while that country still held a monopoly on the successful explosion of atomic devices, Congress passed an Atomic Energy Act (the so-called McMahon Act). During the period of the atomic monopoly, America's legislators tended to feel that the best way to protect the world from any danger arising from this new power was by maintaining that monopoly, and therefore the McMahon Act was designed to lock up atomic research within the deepest secrecy. Its passage also coincided with an incipient public hysteria about secrecy, intensified by news of the discovery of the Canadian spy-ring, including the treachery of one of the British atomic scientists, Dr Nunn May, who gave atomic secrets to the Soviet Union. Accordingly, the Act (notably clause 10(a)) inhibited any American cooperation with other parties in atomic matters.

As explained above in Chapter 3, America's monopoly did not last for long, but it was not until 1954 that official cognizance was taken of this in the form of amendment to the McMahon Act. The amendment was intended partly to open up nuclear-power generation in the USA for private enterprise, partly to facilitate the export of 'civil' nuclear expertise and technology under President Eisenhower's 'Atoms for Peace' programme and partly to enable the USA to cooperate in limited ways with allies in the military nuclear field.[1] An early outcome of this amendment was the announcement by President Eisenhower on 20 June 1955 of Military and Civil Atomic Cooperation Agreements signed with Great Britain on 15 June. The military agreement was restricted to the exchange of atomic information 'which the USA considers necessary for (1) the development of defence plans; (2) the training of personnel in the employment of, and defence against, atomic weapons; (3) the evaluation of the capabilities of potential enemies in the employment of atomic weapons'. The Civil Agreement also dealt principally with the exchange of information. This was to be by no means free: it would be confined to general properties of materials or the general character in the design of equipment. Information about the design or operation of specific plants was excluded. Some limited exchange of materials for research purposes and of specialized research facilities was envisaged. The following year, on 14 June 1956, the Agreements were broadened, and thereby began to become mingled. On the one hand, it was agreed that Britain might obtain, in exchange for 'depleted' uranium (i.e. containing less than 0.7 per cent uranium-235), equivalent quantities of enriched uranium (a sort of Aladdin's lamp trick: new uranium for old); on the other, there would be an exchange of information on military power propulsion reactors. Press commentators observed that in this way Britain could profit from American expertise in submarine propulsion package reactors (unquestionably military) while in return, the USA would benefit from the British lead in civil electric-power generation technology.[2]

In a rapidly deteriorating state of international relations during 1956 and 1957, described above in Chapters 3 and 4 (this was the period of Suez, of Hungary, of the bomber and then the missile 'gaps'), the British and American governments evidently felt that the bonds of atomic cooperation should again be strengthened, and in late October 1957, the British Prime Minister, Harold Macmillan, flew to Washington with a party of his senior Cabinet colleagues and with senior civil servants, including the Chairman of the UKAEA, Sir Edwin Plowden, to hold talks with President Eisenhower. After a meeting at the White House during the morning of 24 October, which was attended by the US Secretary of Defense, the Chairman of the Joint Chiefs of Staff and other senior American officials, among them Admiral Strauss, Chairman of the US Atomic Energy Commission, it was announced that a study group under the joint chairmanship of Plowden and Strauss had been established and assigned 'the duties of making recommendations in the field of nuclear relationship and cooperation'. The following day, the series of discussions ended with a 'Declaration of Interdependence', made jointly by Eisenhower and Macmillan.

The Declaration first expatiated upon the threat of international Communism and then stated that:

If the free nations are steadfast, and if they utilize their resources in harmonious cooperation, the totalitarian menace that now confronts them will in good time recede.

In order, however, that freedom may be secure and show its good fruits, it is necessary first that the collective military strength of the free nations should be adequate to meet the threat against them. At the same time, the aggregate of the free world's military expenditure must be kept within limits compatible with individual freedom. Otherwise we risk losing the very liberties which we seek to defend.

These ideas have been the central theme of our conversations . . .

The Declaration then enunciated several concrete steps to be taken. Observing that in scientific research 'the concept of national self-sufficiency is out of date', it urged greater cooperation in military research. The Atomic Energy Act (1954) would not permit this and therefore in the 'Declaration of Interdependence', President Eisenhower undertook to request Congress to amend it further. On his return to London, the Prime Minister described the Washington meetings as 'the most fruitful I can remember, and the most effective', forming a 'new start' in Anglo-American relations.[3]

In accordance with the Declaration, the President submitted to Congress proposals for amending the McMahon Act again. In hearings during the spring of 1958, the Atomic Energy Commission supported the proposals. Acting-Chairman Harold S. Vance testified that 'to assure proper training and planning for nuclear weapon use and for defence against nuclear war, added information must flow to many of our allies'. The House approved an amending Bill on 19 June by an overwhelming majority (345 to 12). After some disagreement with the Senate, a joint House/Senate compromise Bill was agreed on 26 June, of which the principle provision was to permit the administration to supply nuclear weapons' designs and fissionable materials for research, development and fabrication to countries that had already made 'substantial progress' in the development of such weapons. It was made clear in debate that only Britain fulfilled this condition. In addition, the Congress agreed the supply to allies of reactor designs and atomic fuels for submarine propulsion plants (for example, France benefited from this with an import of enriched uranium for its prototype submarine reactor in 1959).

The day after signing this second amendment to the McMahon Act, President Eisenhower sent to Congress a new atomic energy agreement with Britain concluded earlier that same day on the basis of the new

American legislation.[4] The agreement covered the transfer of nuclear materials and equipment from America to Britain, including a submarine propulsion plant and uranium-235 to run it, the enriched uranium to be paid for at the USAEC's applicable prices. The Agreement also provided for the exchange of necessary classified information in a wide range of nuclear matters. Of especial interest in gauging the drift of intention behind the Agreement was Article V, Paragraph C:

Except as may be otherwise agreed for civil uses, the information communicated or exchanged, or the materials or equipment transferred, by either party pursuant to this Agreement shall be used by the recipient party *exclusively for the preparation or implementation of defence plans* [emphasis added] in the mutual interests of the two countries.

In short, the military applications were envisaged as primary and any civil use as secondary. If this correctly shows the intention of the Agreement, it accords more closely with the views of Professor Ryle and Dr Hesketh than with that of the spokesman for the UKAEA in their 1982 correspondence. What this Agreement did not authorize was the export of fissile materials from Britain to the USA; but this was the major effect of the Amendment to the Mutual Defence Agreement signed in Washington on 7 May 1959.[5]

Coincidental with the passage through Congress of the original Agreement, on 17 June 1958 the British Ministry of Defence issued the following statement:

In order to provide insurance against future defence needs, certain of the civil nuclear power reactors now in the early construction or design stage are being modified so that the plutonium produced as a by-product is suitable for use, if the need arises, for military purposes. These modifications will not delay the construction of the reactors and will not affect their normal operation as civil power stations. This decision does not affect power stations at Bradwell, Berkeley, and Hunterston where construction and installation are already well advanced. Hunterston is so designed as to be suitable for this purpose anyway.[6]

These modifications, referred to in the text of Chapter 9 above, were principally to do with fuel-loading and storage provision, to accommodate the greater volume of 'through-put' required by the military cycle of operation. In the event, only Hinkley Point A received them. One reason for the reduction in the original plans for British plutonium production as conceived in the early 1950s was the successful explosion of a British hydrogen bomb. Having previously intended an arsenal of fission bombs (A bombs), the switch to fusion (the H bomb) meant that requirements for plutonium were much reduced; but commensurately, the need for tritium, obtained through the US/UK barter, was of greater significance. Thus, an adequate, but not excessive, provision for the production of weapon-grade plutonium, such as the revised plans offered, was indicated.

Under Article III *bis*, Paragraph A, of the May 1959 Amendment, four classes of material that might be transferred from the United States to Britain were mentioned:

1. non-nuclear parts of atomic weapons;
2. other non-nuclear parts of atomic weapons systems involving restricted data;
3. 'special nuclear material for research on, development of, production of, or use in utilization facilities for military applications'; and
4. 'source, by-product and special nuclear material for research on, development of, or use in atomic weapons . . .'

Under Article III *bis*, Paragraph B, the return traffic was authorized:

The Government of the United Kingdom shall transfer to the Government of the United States *for military purposes* [emphasis added] such source, by-product and special nuclear material ['special nuclear material' is a form of words which includes plutonium and enriched uranium] and equipment of such types, in such quantities, at such times prior to 31 December 1969 and on such terms and conditions as may be agreed.

(December 1969 was the term of the Agreement without renewal.) The effect of this paragraph is to underscore the message of Article V, Paragraph C of the 1958 Agreement.

When the White Paper containing the text of the Amendment was released, the political correspondent of the *Daily Telegraph* wrote that:

The immediate object is to enable both countries to produce nuclear weapons more cheaply than hitherto, by avoiding costly duplication of production capacity.[7]

Reporting without attribution what appears to be the same official spokesman (perhaps at a lobby briefing), *The Times* political correspondent explained that the supply of British plutonium to the USA would not affect the British atomic power programme or the price of electricity (this for the worried consumers . . .): it meant avoidance of costly duplication of production facilities, the USA producing uranium-235 and Britain making plutonium in association with the production of electric power. The plutonium would come either from Calder Hall or Chapelcross (the 'military' reactors) or from civil nuclear power stations which would go into operation in the future.

The British civil service's working distinction between the 'civil' and 'military' applications of fissile material was now fully evolved. It is extremely convoluted and a bureaucrat's delight. Below its spreading branches, it offers officials many shady places wherein to repose and thus to avoid public gaze and control of their activities. *Three* separate factors are to be considered singly or in combination:

1. The *isotope composition* of plutonium (whether fuel-grade at about 80 per cent Pu 239 or weapon-grade at 93 or 97 per cent).
2. The *legal ownership of the reactor* (whether operated by BNFL, in which case declared 'military' and outside the International Atomic Energy Authority's 'safeguards', or operated by the CEGB or SSEB, in which case declared 'civil').
3. The *bilateral Anglo-American agreements*: whether, regardless of origin or composition, material was transferred under the civil or the military agreement.

These factors are blurred together with ease, with the result that the distinction between civil and military use is, in fact, made more hazy rather than clearer by what appear to be strictly defined parameters.

The implication of this aspect of the 1959 Amendment was foreseen and concisely stated at the time by the science correspondent of *The Times*:

The most important technical fact behind the agreement is that plutonium of civil grade – such as will be produced in British civil nuclear power stations – can now be used in weapons...

When the first British civil stations come into operation Britain will have a relatively big output of plutonium. The United States, on the other hand, has a vastly greater output of the fissile isotope of uranium – uranium 235. The military effect of the agreement amounts therefore to a pooling of resources...

From an international point of view, it appears to follow that any country with civil nuclear power stations and a plutonium separation plant will be able to make some form of nuclear weapon without need to design or operate their designs for specifically military production ... The distinction between civil and military uses of atomic energy is thus rendered less clear-cut than it was.[8]

Further Reading

Books

M. Howard, *War and the Liberal Conscience*, Oxford, OUP, 1981.

M. Walzer, *Just and Unjust Wars, a Moral Argument with Historical Illustrations*, Penguin, 1980.
The principles which have been held to justify wars, with examples from the Greeks to the nuclear age.

J. Keegan, *The Face of Battle*, Penguin, 1978.
How are battles possible in terms of those who have to fight them? By analysing three battles (Agincourt, Waterloo, and the first day of the Somme) Keegan has written the most important work of military history of recent years.

*

A. J. P. Taylor, *From Sarajevo to Potsdam*, London, Thames & Hudson, 1966.
Controversial and indispensable.

P. Calvocoressi and G. Wint, *Total War: Causes and Courses of the Second World War*, Penguin, 1972.
The 'book to end war books' (A. J. P. Taylor).

Hugh Higgins, *The Cold War*, London, Heinemann, 1974.
A study of East–West relations from 1917 to 1960.

D. F. Fleming, *The Cold War and its Origins*, 2 vols., London, Allen & Unwin, 1961.
Well documented study of the evolution of US–Soviet relations since the First World War.

Seweryn Bialer, *Stalin's Successors*, Cambridge, CUP, 1980.
Highly penetrating and original examination of Soviet political system, including valuable section on Soviet perceptions of international affairs, and trends in Soviet foreign policy.

A. H. Brown and M. Kaser, eds., *The Soviet Union since the Fall of Khrushchev*, London, Macmillan, 1978.
An informed introduction to numerous aspects of modern Soviet society, with a particularly useful essay by David Holloway on foreign and defence policy.

J. P. Nettl, *The Soviet Achievement*, London, Thames & Hudson, 1967.
The best-single volume account of the evolution of Russian society since the turn of the century.

Volker Berghahn, *Militarism*, Leamington Spa, Berg Press, 1981.
A unique survey of the debate on the relationship between armed forces and society in Europe, the United States and the Third World.

*

M. Gowing, *Britain and Atomic Energy, 1939–45*, London, Macmillan, 1964; *Independence and Deterrence: Britain and Atomic Energy, 1945–52*, 2 vols., London, Macmillan, 1974 (with Lorna Arnold).
Professor Gowing's three books are the essential foundation for an understanding of Britain's nuclear affairs. The earliest volume is also an excellent account of the wider context of the wartime project.

Lawrence Freedman, *Britain and Nuclear Weapons*, London, Macmillan, 1980.
A readable narrative, continuing the story from where Gowing leaves it.

*

Lawrence Freedman, *US Intelligence and the Soviet Strategic Threat*, London, Macmillan, 1977.
A descriptive account of American intelligence operations, carefully documented from open sources. It is valuable for its factual context, although weak in its analysis.

F. Kaplan, *Dubious Specter: a Skeptical Look at the Soviet Nuclear Threat*, Washington, Institute for Policy Studies, 1980.
Brisk and thought-provoking.

R. C. Aldridge, *The Counterforce Syndrome: A Guide to US Nuclear Weapons and Strategic Doctrine*, 2nd ed., Washington, Institute for Policy Studies, 1979.
A brief and powerful interpretation of recent American weapons programmes by a former senior engineer at Lockheed Missiles.

M. Kaldor, *The Baroque Arsenal*, London, Deutsch, 1981.
An investigation of present-day weapons culture and its history.

*

SIPRI, *Nuclear Energy and Nuclear Weapon Proliferation*, London, Taylor & Francis, 1979.
Chapters in the form of essays cover all aspects of the proliferation question. Rather technical in places.

Albert Wohlstetter and others, *Swords from Plowshares: the Military Potential of Civilian Nuclear Energy*, Chicago and London, University of Chicago Press, 1979.
One of America's leading nuclear strategists of the 1960s examines the dangers of the 1980s.

*

H. Street, *Freedom, the Individual and the Law*, 4th ed., Penguin, 1977.
This is generally regarded as being the leading survey of the law relating to civil liberties in England. This comprehensive yet highly readable book examines the content of civil liberties in general, but the chapters on individual freedom of expression and assembly are particularly relevant to the nuclear arms issue.

B. Cox, *Civil Liberties in Britain*, Penguin, 1975.
This book, written by a journalist, is especially valuable for its collection of case histories illustrating the precarious and vulnerable nature of civil liberties in this country, not least in relation to the exercise of individual freedom to protest against nuclear defence policy.

M. Supperstone, *Brownlie's Law of Public Order and National Security*, 2nd ed., London, Butterworth, 1981.
This is a very detailed and rather technical publication, but the chapter on disclosure of information and official secrecy is of particular interest to those concerned about the nuclear arms race.

*

Ian Breach, *Windscale Fallout*, Penguin, 1978.
A detailed examination of the whole process of the Windscale public inquiry of 1977, including those parts left out by Mr Justice Parker in his Report. Covers far more ground than the title might imply.

J. Rotblat, *Nuclear Radiation in Warfare*, London, SIPRI, Taylor & Francis, 1981.
A meticulous account of the present state of knowledge about radiation by this country's leading authority. Easily comprehensible for the lay reader.

J. Rotblat, ed., *Nuclear Reactors: to Breed or not to Breed*, London, The Royal Society, 1977 (the Pugwash debate on FBRs).
Papers for and against the fast breeder reactor and what it implies, presented at a conference at the Royal Society.

J. Schell, *The Fate of the Earth*, Picador, 1982.
A remarkable essay which sets out the present state of knowledge and ignorance about the effects of nuclear war.

*

M. Kaldor, *The Disintegrating West*, Penguin, 1979.
Examines the changing power structure and the developing conflicts among the nations of the Atlantic Alliance.

Alva Myrdal, *The Game of Disarmament: How the United States and Russia Run the Arms Race*, Nottingham, Spokesman, 1980.
A history of the nuclear age by Sweden's former Minister of Disarmament, as seen from the vantage point of a participant in many of the negotiations that she describes.

Solly Zuckerman, *Nuclear Illusion and Reality*, London, Collins, 1982.
Lord Zuckerman's important argument about the role of scientists in the nuclear arms race is here set into a more extended presentation of his thoughts.

*

D. Smith, *The Defence of the Realm in the 1980s*, 2nd ed., London, Croom Helm, 1981.
A leading sceptic of Ministry of Defence plans and actions sets out his case.

A. Roberts, *Nations in Arms*, London, Chatto & Windus, 1976.
Examination of alternative forms of defence, particularly as they have been used in the past and might be used in the future.

M. Kaldor and D. Smith, eds., *Disarming Europe*, London, Merlin Press, 1982.
The first set of papers deals with the nature of the European arsenals, the second with forms of alternative defence.

A. Myrdal and others, ed. K. Coates, *The Dynamics of European Nuclear Disarmament*, Nottingham, Spokesman, 1981.
A collection of suggestions and statements from European groups and individuals campaigning actively for nuclear disarmament.

G. Scott, *How to Get Rid of the Bomb* (a Peace Action Handbook), Fontana, 1982.

Periodicals

ADIU Report. Bi-monthly newsletter of the Armament and Disarmament Information Unit, University of Sussex. Contains analyses, news, and a bibliographical section. Available from ADIU, University of Sussex, Falmer, Brighton, Sussex, BN1 9RF.

Arms Control. A new journal intended to 'probe and understand the nature of arms control', published three times a year. Available from Frank Cass & Co., Gainsborough House, Gainsborough Road, London E11.

Arms Control and Disarmament: Developments in the International Negotiations. Irregular publication from the Foreign and Commonwealth Office combining extracts from articles and speeches, documentation and news of the various negotiations. Available from Arms Control and Disarmament Research Unit, Foreign and Commonwealth Office, Downing Street (East), London SW1A2AH.

Arms Control Today. Monthly journal of the US Arms Control Association. Contains articles, analyses, and reviews. Available from Arms Control Association, 11 Dupont Circle, NW, Washington, USA.

Atom. Glossy and expensively produced monthly bulletin of the UKAEA distributed free of charge to all who wish to receive it. Available from Information Services Branch UKAEA, 11 Charles II St., London SW1Y 4QP.

Aviation Week and Space Technology. Weekly coverage of all aspects of hardware with robustly hawkish editorials. PO Box 503, Hightstown, NJ, 08520, USA.

Bulletin of the Atomic Scientists. Monthly, carries articles, discussions, and reviews on armaments and disarmament. 1020–24 E 58th St, Chicago, Ill., 60637, USA.

Defense Week. Weekly US publication. Contains articles and analyses. Available from 300 National Press Building, Washington, DC, 20045, USA.

Disarmament Times. Published eleven times a year by the Non-Governmental

Disarmament Committee at the United Nations. Concentrates on UN negotiations and UN-directed activities of non-governmental organizations. Room 7B, 777, UN Plaza, New York, USA.

European Nuclear Disarmament Bulletin. Quarterly publication for the European Nuclear Disarmament movement, carries articles, news, reviews. Available from Bertrand Russell Peace Foundation, Gamble Street, Nottingham NT7 4ET.

NATO Review. Bi-monthly official publication from the North Atlantic Treaty Organization. Contains articles, news, analyses. Available from NATO Information Service, 1110 Brussels, Belgium.

Protect and Survive Monthly. Contains articles, news, and reviews relating to civil defence. Available from Protect and Survive Monthly, 80 Fleet Street, London EC4Y 1EL.

RUSI Journal of the Royal United Services Institute for Defence Studies. Published quarterly, carries original articles, speeches, reviews. Available from the Royal United Services Institute, Whitehall, London, SW1A 2ET.

Sanity. Monthly magazine of the Campaign for Nuclear Disarmament, carrying reports, analyses, news of the movement. CND, 11 Goodwin Street, Finsbury Park, London N1.

State Research Bulletin. Bi-monthly. State Research is 'an independent group of investigators collecting and publishing information from public sources on developments in state policy', including internal security and the military. Available from 9 Poland Street, London WC1.

Survival. Bi-monthly journal of the International Institute for Strategic Studies. Contains articles, reviews, and a documentation section. Available from the International Institute for Strategic Studies, 23 Tavistock Street, London WC2E 7NQ.

Annual Publications

International Institute for Strategic Studies (IISS), 23 Tavistock Street, London WC3E 7NQ. IISS publishes *The Military Balance* and *Strategic Survey* each year, *Survival* (six times a year), and the 'Adelphi Papers' series.

Royal United Services Institute and Brassey's. RUSI and this old-established military publisher annually produce a *Defence Yearbook*, which, like the *SIPRI Yearbook* (below), contains essays as well as a review of weapons developments, a bibliography, and chronology. These yearbooks make interesting and contrasting reading.

Stockholm International Peace Research Institute (SIPRI), Sveavagen 166, S-113, 46 Stockholm, Sweden. In addition to a number of books on many aspects of armaments and disarmament, SIPRI publishes annually the *SIPRI Yearbook of World Armaments and Disarmament*. This series began with the 1968-9 edition and a cumulative index covering 1968-79 is also available: *World Armaments and Disarmament Yearbooks* 1969-79, SIPRI, Taylor & Francis,

London, 1980. As well as providing annually updated tables, the *Yearbooks* contain essays on all aspects of arms and disarmament. For this reason, the *Index* is important. Your public library should have the whole series.

United Nations (UN). Since 1976 the UN has published a *Disarmament Yearbook*. It also publishes *Disarmament*, a periodic review; both available from the Sales Section, United Nations, New York, 10017, USA.

World Military and Social Expenditures (WMSE). WMSE is an annual digest listing and comparing national military and social expenditures. It is available from WMSE Publications, c/o CAAT, 5 Caledonian Road, London N1 9DX.

World Military Expenditure and Arms Transfers. Published from the US Arms Control and Disarmament Agency. Available from the US Arms Control and Disarmament Agency, Washington, DC, 20451, USA.

Notes

All works published in London unless otherwise indicated.

Introduction

1. *Guardian*, 22 April 1981, p. 2.
2. *Newsweek*, 5 October 1981, p. 35; 'Public rejects idea of "winnable" nuclear war', *Gallup Poll*, 2 August 1981; *Observer*, 15 November 1981.
3. *The Times*, 22 May 1981.
4. *The Times*, 2 June 1981.
5. *The Times*, 9 June 1981.

1. Discrepancies

1. Speech to XXVI Party Congress, 23 February 1981 (L. I. Brezhnev's report of CPSU Central Committee), Information Dept, USSR Embassy, Washington, p. 28.
2. R. V. Harlow and N. M. Blake, *The United States: From Wilderness to World Power*, 4th ed., New York, 1964, p. 777.
3. *Sovetskii Entsiklopedicheskii Slovar*, Moscow, 1980, pp. 1246–7.
4. *Sovetskii Istoricheskii Slovar*, XIII, Moscow, 1971, p. 278.
5. Henry T. Nash, 'The bureaucratization of homicide', in E. P. Thompson and D. Smith, eds., *Protest and Survive*, 1980, p. 66.
6. Department of Defense, *Soviet Military Power*, US Govt Printing Office, Washington, DC, 1981; CBS TV 'Evening News', 29 September 1981, 7.00 pm; NBC 'Nightly News', 29 September 1981, 7.00 pm; *Whence the Threat to Peace*, Military Publishing House, USSR Ministry of Defence, Moscow, 1982.
7. J. Nott, British Secretary of State for Defence, *Hansard*, 1000, 59, 3 March 1981, col. 138.
8. L. Brezhnev, President of USSR, *Soviet News*, No. 6005, 12 January 1980.
9. S. Zuckerman, 'Defeat is indivisible', in *Apocalypse Now?*, Nottingham, 1980, p. 27.
10. W. Kennet and E. Young, 'Neither Red nor Dead: the case for disarmament' (Open Forum Pamphlet, Social Democratic Party), 1981, p. 10.
11. *Guardian*, 4 November 1981; *The Times*, 4 November 1981; interview in 'Sunday', Radio 4, 8 November 1981; 'The New Alternative' (prospectus of the Council for Arms Control); Professor N. Brown, 'The delusions of neutralism', *RUSI Journal*, September 1981, pp. 27–33.
12. *The Times*, 5 and 6 November 1981; *Wall Street Journal*, 9 December 1981.
13. BBC Radio 4, 'Six o'Clock News', 6 November 1981; *The Times*, 6 November 1981.

2. The Trail of Mistrust, 1914–73

1. J. M. Winter, 'The decline of mortality in Britain, 1870–1950', in M. Drake, ed., *Population and History*, 1982.

2. J. M. Winter, 'Unemployment, nutrition and infant mortality in Britain 1920–1950', in J. M. Winter, ed., *The Working Class in Modern British History*, Cambridge, forthcoming.

3. D. Fleming, *The Cold War and its Origins*, vol. 1, pp. 43–7 (quote p. 45).

4. Compare J. Weinstein, *The Decline of Socialism in America 1912–1925*, New York, 1967; A. M. Schlesinger, *The Crisis of the Old Order 1919–1933*, 1957; J. M. Blum and others, *The National Experience*, 1963.

5. A. Nove, *An Economic History of the USSR*, 1969, pp. 201–8.

6. R. Medvedev, *Let History Judge*, 1972.

7. I. Deutscher, *Stalin, a Political Biography*, Oxford, 1966, p. 328.

8. J. K. Galbraith, *The Great Crash 1929*, 1955; H. V. Hodson, *Slump and Recovery 1929–37*, 1938.

9. Compare W. Leuchtenberg, *Franklin D. Roosevelt and the New Deal*, New York, 1963; O. Handlin, *America. A History*, New York, 1968; T. H. Williams, *Huey P. Long*, Oxford, 1967.

10. W. Galenson, *The CIO Challenge to the AFL*, Cambridge, Mass., 1960.

11. Fleming, *Origins*, vol. 1.

12. D. Drummond, *The Passing of American Neutrality 1937–1941*, Ann Arbor, Michigan, 1955.

13. M. Dobb, *Soviet Economic Development since 1917*, 1966, p. 301.

14. R. Polenberg, *War and Society: the United States, 1941–5*, Philadelphia, 1972.

15. G. Alperovitz, *Atomic Diplomacy*, 1966.

16. B. Urlanis, *Wars and Population*, Moscow, 1971; M. Huber, *La Population de la France pendant la Guerre*, Paris, 1931; J. M. Winter, 'Some aspects of the demographic consequences of the First World War to Britain', *Population Studies*, 1976; A. Vagts, 'Battle and other combatant casualties in the Second World War', *Journal of Politics*, 1945; *Defense Almanac*, 1981, p. 42.

17. D. S. Clemens, *Yalta*, New York, 1970.

18. W. Churchill, *Triumph and Tragedy*, New York, 1953, p. 454.

19. L. Dawidowicz, *The War against the Jews 1933–45*, 1975.

20. S. Hoffman, 'Collaboration and collaborationism in France during the Second World War', *Journal of Modern History*, 1968.

21. M. M. Postan, *An Economic History of Western Europe 1945–64*, 1967, p. 100.

22. Compare: G. Kolko, *The Politics of War*, 1969; A. Ulam, *Expansionism and Coexistence. The History of Soviet Foreign Policy 1917–67*, 1968; H. Higgins, *The Cold War*, 1974; D. Yergin, *Shattered Peace*, Boston, Mass., 1977.

23. S. Melman, *Pentagon Capitalism*, New York, 1970; and his edited volume, *The Defense Economy*, New York, 1970.

24. J. M. Winter, 'The fear of population decline in Western Europe 1870–1950', in R. H. Hiorns, ed., *Demographic Patterns in Developed Societies*, 1980.

25. A. Gramsci, *Selections from the Prison Notebooks*, 1971; A. Kriegel, *French Communists*, Chicago, 1972; F. Claudin, *Eurocommunism and Socialism*, 1978; E. Mandel, *From Stalinism to Eurocommunism*, 1978; E. J. Hobsbawm, *The Italian Road to Socialism*, 1977.

26. B. Lomax, ed., *Eyewitness in Hungary*, 1980; R. F. Leslie, ed., *The History of Poland since 1863*, Cambridge, 1980; G. Golan, *The Czechoslovak Reform Movement*, Cambridge, 1971.

27. J. Hough and M. Fainsod, *How the Soviet Union is Governed*, 1979.

28. J. Gittings, *Survey of the Sino-Soviet Dispute*, 1968.

29. B. P. Nanda, ed., *Indian Foreign Policy: the Nehru Years*, Honolulu, 1976; P. J. Vatikiotis, *Nasser and his Generation*, 1978; V. Dedijer, *Tito Speaks*, 1957.

3. 'An Extremely Effective Explosive': the Early History, 1939-56

1. O. Frisch, *What Little I Remember*, Cambridge, 1979, p. 126.

2. Extract from Part I of the Frisch-Peierls Memorandum, reproduced as App. 1, M. Gowing, *Britain and Atomic Energy, 1939-45*, 1964, pp. 389-93; correspondence between Professor Peierls and Dr Prins, 18 December 1981. We are indebted to Professor Peierls for commenting upon the early pages of this chapter.

3. R. Jungk, *Brighter than a Thousand Suns*, 1958, suggested that this was a deliberate choice. See also B. Page, 'God is sophisticated – but not malicious', *New Statesman*, 19/26 December 1980, pp. 19-24.

4. L. R. Groves, *Now It Can be Told: the Story of the Manhattan Project*, 1963, p. 296.

5. Quoted Gowing, *Britain and Atomic Energy*, p. 382.

6. Quoted ibid., p. 385.

7. R. W. Clark, *Tizard*, 1965, pp. 215-17.

8. See box on the atomic bombings, pp. 65-70.

9. Letter to *The Times*, 6 November 1981. See further Chapter 6.

10. W. Churchill, *Triumph and Tragedy*, 1953, p. 553.

11. Quoted F. Knebel and C. W. Bailey II, *No High Ground*, 1960, p. 244.

12. Gowing, *Britain and Atomic Energy*, p. 86.

13. Oppenheimer quoted L. Giovannitti and F. Freed, *The Decision to Drop the Bomb*, 1967, p. 197.

14. The Committee for the Compilation of Materials on Damage Caused by the Atomic Bombs in Hiroshima and Nagasaki, *Hiroshima and Nagasaki: the Physical, Medical and Social Effects of the Atomic Bombings*, 1981; R. J. Lifton, *Death in Life: the Survivors of Hiroshima*, 1968; R. Neild, *How to Make up Your Mind about the Bomb*, 1981, chapter 4.

15. Information from Gowing, *Britain and Atomic Energy*, chapter 14; *New Cambridge Modern History*, vol. XII, pp. 815-18.

16. Quoted A. Myrdal, *The Game of Disarmament: How the United States and Russia Run the Arms Race*, New York, 1976, pp. 73-4.

17. D. Acheson, *Present at the Creation*, 1979, p. 154.

18. From Myrdal, *The Game of Disarmament*, pp. 74-6.

19. Quoted H. F. York, *The Advisors: Oppenheimer, Teller and the Superbomb*, San Francisco, 1976, Appendix.

20. For the accusation, directly citing the H-bomb issue, Gen. Nichols's letter, *Keesing's Contemporary Archives* (1952-4), pp. 13,617-18.

21. Based on York, *The Advisors*.

22. From ibid., pp. 79-87.

23. I. Bellany, 'The origins of the Soviet hydrogen bomb: the York hypothesis', *Journal of the Royal United Services Institute*, 122, 1, 1977, pp. 56-8.

24. N. Moss, *Men Who Play God*, 1968, p. 86.

25. From R. E. Lapp, *The Voyage of the Lucky Dragon*, 1968; *Keesing's Contemporary Archives* (1952-4), pp. 13, 485-6.

26. *The Autobiography of Bertrand Russell, 1944–67*, 1969, pp. 99–100.
27. E. Teller and A. L. Latter, *Our Nuclear Future*, 1958, p. 94.
28. Teller and Latter, *Our Nuclear Future*, p. 85.
29. *Keesing's Contemporary Archives* (1952–4), 17–24 July 1954, p. 13,681.
30. Full text of clauses in *Keesing's Contemporary Archives*, 1955–6, 'Essay on the Disarmament Negotiations', pp. 14,851–2; P. Noel-Baker, *The Arms Race*, 1958, chapter 2.
31. Text of the treaty and formation of the Unified Military Command, *Keesing's Contemporary Archives* (1955–6), 11–18 June 1955, pp. 14,249–51.
32. UN, *The United Nations and Disarmament, 1945–1970*, New York, 1970, p. 58.
33. Khrushchev's speech reproduced, *Keesing's Contemporary Archives* (1955–6), p. 14,746.
34. Correspondence reproduced, *Keesing's Contemporary Archives* (1955–6), pp. 14,855–6.
35. *Keesing's Contemporary Archives* (1955–6), p. 14,854, col. 2.
36. *Keesing's Contemporary Archives* (1955–6), pp. 15,173–87; pp. 15,192–4.
37. W. Churchill, speech on the defence estimates, 1 March 1955, *Hansard*, 537, col. 1898–9.

4. Changing Nuclear Policies: the Quest for Flexibility since the Late 1950s

1. H. F. York, *Race to Oblivion: a Participant's View of the Arms Race*, New York, 1970.
2. J. Voorhis, *The Strange Case of Richard Milhous Nixon*, New York, 1972, p. 179.
3. *The Department of State Bulletin*, 57, 9 October 1967, p. 446.
4. J. B. Wiesner and H. F. York, 'National security and the nuclear-test ban', *Scientific American*, 211, 4, October 1964, p. 35.
5. H. S. Commager, ed., *Documents of American History*, New York, 1946, p. 146.
6. For this, and an extensive study of American intelligence, see L. Freedman, *US Intelligence and the Soviet Strategic Threat*, 1977.
7. O. D. Lilienthal, *The Journals of David E. Lilienthal: Vol. II, The Atomic Energy Years, 1945–50*, New York, 1964, p. 376 (Entry for 30 June 1948).
8. I. F. Stone, *The Hidden History of the Korean War*, New York, 1970, pp. 274–80.
9. L. Freedman, *US Intelligence and the Soviet Strategic Threat*, 1977, pp. 65–7; R. Neild, *How to Make up Your Mind about the Bomb*, 1981, p. 24; J. M. Collins, *US–Soviet Military Balance*, New York, 1980, pp. 25, 146, 16.
10. K. F. Gantz, ed., *The United States Air Force Report on the Ballistic Missile*, New York, 1958, p. 223; *Keesing's Contemporary Archives* (1957–8), p. 15,933; R. Hirsch and J. J. Trento, *The National Aeronautics and Space Administration*, New York, 1973.
11. Freedman, *US Intelligence*, pp. 69–73.
12. Neild, *How to Make up Your Mind about the Bomb*, Table 1, p. 25. Its sources: missile gap projection of J. Alsop (the newspaper columnist and chief spokesman of the hawks) from Ralph E. Lapp, *The Weapons Culture*, p. 32; 'actual' figures: 1960 and 1961 from Freedman, *US Intelligence*, pp. 73, 100, and Lt Gen. Daniel O. Graham, Former Director, United States Defense Intelligence Agency, *Air Force*, May 1976, p. 35; later years from IISS, *The Military Balance*, Annex A, Table 5, p. 446.
13. Collins, *US–Soviet Military Balance*, Annex A, Table 5, p. 446.
14. R. McNamara, 18 September 1967, 'The dynamics of nuclear strategy', *Department of State Bulletin* 57, 9 October 1967, pp. 445–6; interview with McNamara by R. Sheer, *Los Angeles Times*, 12 April 1982.

15. R. A. Fuhrman, 'Fleet ballistic missile system: Polaris to Trident' (the 1978 von Karman lecture before the 14th annual meeting), AIAA, February 1978, pp. 2, 4, 15.

16. E. Fermi and I. I. Rabi, 'An opinion on the development of the "Super"', 30 October 1949, quoted H. F. York, *The Advisors*, San Francisco, 1976, pp. 158–9. Note, however, that when the GAC advice was rejected, Fermi went to work on the H-bomb.

17. Kennan, Einstein Peace Prize speech, Washington, 19 May 1981, reproduced in *Guardian*, 25 May 1981, p. 10.

18. A. Wohlstetter, 'The delicate balance of terror', originally published in *Foreign Affairs*, Jan. 1959, reprinted in *Survival*, 1, 1, 1959, pp. 8–17.

19. Quoted A. Myrdal, *The Game of Disarmament*, New York, 1976, p. 117.

20. J. Rotblat, *Nuclear Radiation in Warfare*, 1981, Table 27, p. 129; S. A. Fetter and K. Tsipis, 'Catastrophic releases of radioactivity', *Scientific American*, 244, 4, April 1981, pp. 33–6; *A review of Cmnd 884: the control of radioactive wastes* (a report by an expert group made to the Radioactive Waste Management Advisory Committee), Dept of the Environment, Scottish Office and Welsh Office, HMSO, September 1979; P. J. Lindop, 'Radiation aspects of a nuclear war in Europe' – paper given at the Conference on Nuclear War in Europe, Groningen, April 1981, pp. 7–8 and Fig. 8; graph from A. Tucker and J. Gleisner, *Crucible of Despair: the Effects of Nuclear War*, 1981, annex 2, p. 16; J. Rotblat, 'Physical and biological effects of a nuclear war on Europe' and Working Group 4 Final Report, 'Medical consequences of nuclear war with special reference to Europe: Unquantified effects on the biosphere', both at Second International Congress of Physicians for the Prevention of Nuclear War, Cambridge, April 1982; United States National Academy of Sciences, 'Long term worldwide effects of multiple nuclear-weapons detonations', 1975. An authoritative guide to the prompt and proximate effects of nuclear explosions is: Office of Technology Assessment (Congress of the United States), *The Effects of Nuclear War*, 1980. A layman's introduction to the unquantified effects on the biosphere is to be found in J. Schell, *The Fate of the Earth*, 1982, Part I. We are indebted to Professor Rotblat for criticizing an early draft of this map and text.

21. F. M. Kaplan, *Dubious Specter: a Skeptical Look at the Soviet Nuclear Threat*, Washington, 1980, Fig. 2, p. 6.

22. R. McNamara, 'Annual Statement to the Senate Armed Services Committee', 1 February 1968, reproduced in *Survival*, April 1968, pp. 106–14. Graph from D. T. Johnson and B. R. Schneider, *Current Issues in US Defense Policy*, New York, 1976, p. 142.

23. C. Paine, 'Pershing II: the Army's strategic weapon', *Bulletin of the Atomic Scientists*, 36, 8, October 1980, p. 25.

24. A. L. Friedberg, 'A history of US strategic "doctrine" – 1945 to 1980', *Journal of Strategic Studies*, 3, 3, December 1980, p. 42.

25. A. I. Waskow, 'American military doctrine', *Survival*, May/June 1962.

26. This chronology in strategies does not agree with that in *Deterrence* (Defence Fact Sheet 3), MoD, April 1981. However, it offers a way of understanding the claim that US strategy has *always* had a 'counterforce' element which is now prominent in the establishment case in the debate about nuclear strategy. See reference 30, below.

27. Speech in Strasbourg, 11 May 1979, reproduced in *Apocalypse Now?*, Nottingham, 1980, p. 10.

28. 'R and D' (Research and Development) Corporation. Funded by the Air Force and originally part of the Douglas Aircraft Company. Subsequently became a quasi-'independent' military think-tank.

29. Waskow, 'American military doctrine', pp. 112–14.

30. Friedberg, 'A history of US strategic "doctrine" – 1945 to 1980', is an excellent example

of the argument (a) that 'counterforce' targets have existed in operational plans since the early 1950s; (b) that massive retaliation (viewed as a 'doctrine') is a myth because (c) policy has always called for a 'mix'. This academic article offers a message congenial to the 1980s Pentagon, since on 15 October 1981 it was circulated to 'Key DoD personnel' as *Current News Special Edition*, No. 771.

31. Details of performance of presently deployed weapons in *SIPRI Yearbook* (1980), fig. 6, and IISS, *The Military Balance* (1980–81), pp. 88–9.

32. H. York, 'Military technology and national security', *Scientific American*, 221, 2, 1969, pp. 17–29.

33. Freedman, *US Intelligence*, pp. 86–96.

34. K. Tsipis, 'United States strategic weapons – offensive and defensive', *Disarmament and Arms Control* (Italian Pugwash Conference), 1970; K. Tsipis, *Offensive Missiles* (Stockholm Paper 5), SIPRI, Stockholm, 1974.

35. Gerard Smith, *Double Talk*, New York, 1980; see further in Section 3 of this chapter.

36. See Appendix A1.

37. Friedberg, 'A history of US strategic "doctrine" – 1945 to 1980', pp. 42–3, 47.

38. R. S. McNamara, 'Address at the Commencement exercises, University of Michigan, Ann Arbor, 16 June 1962', *Department of State Bulletin*, 9 July 1962.

39. C. von Clausewitz, *On War*, ed. and trans. M. Howard and P. Paret, Princeton, 1976, pp. 75–7; *SIPRI Yearbook* (1981), p. 40; 'The threat to Europe', Soviet Committee for European Security and Cooperation, November 1981: V. D. Sokolovskii, *Voennaya Strategiya*, Moscow, 1968, pp. 346–7, 349.

40. M. MccGwire, 'Soviet strategic weapons policy 1955–1970', in M. MccGwire, K. Booth, and J. McDonnell, eds., *Soviet Naval Policy: Objectives and Constraints*, New York, 1975, pp. 486–502; P. H. Vigor, 'The Soviet view of war' in M. MccGwire, ed., *Soviet Naval Developments: Capability and Context*, New York, 1973, pp. 22–3.

41. M. MccGwire, 'The evolution of Soviet naval policy, 1960–1974', in McGwire, *Soviet Naval Policy*, pp. 505–46; R. C. Aldridge, *The Counterforce Syndrome: a Guide to US Nuclear Weapons and Strategic Doctrine*, 2nd edn, Washington, 1979, pp. 21–4, 66–72. See Appendix A1; Paine, 'Pershing II', Table at p. 27.

42. Quoted *SIPRI Yearbook* (1981), p. 22.

43. *SIPRI Yearbook* (1981), Table 2.1, p. 21, data standardized with SIPRI 1980 data given in Appendix A, Tables 13 and 14.

44. *SIPRI Yearbook* (1981), pp. 18–19.

45. Hearing before the Sub-committee on Arms Control, International Law and Organization of the Committee on Foreign Relations, United States Senate, 93rd Congress, 2nd Session, 4 March 1974, p. 11.

46. Remarks by the Honorable Harold Brown, Secretary of Defense, at the convocation ceremonies for the 97th Naval War College Class, Newport, Rhode Island, 20 August 1980. Speech File Service, No. 11, August 1980. Office of the Chief of Public Affairs.

47. Hearing before the Committee on Foreign Relations, United States Senate, 96th Congress, 2nd Session, 16 September 1980.

48. Hearing before the Committee on Foreign Relations, United States Senate, 96th Congress, 2nd Session, 16 September 1980, p. 22.

49. *Strat-X Report*, R-122, Institute for Defense Analysis, vol. I, August 1967, *passim*; Fuhrman, 'Fleet ballistic missile system', p. 20.

50. Paine, 'Pershing II', p. 30; *SIPRI Yearbook* (1980), pp. 182–3. FY 1982 Arms Control Impact Statement, February 1981, 97th Congress, 1st Session.

51. What follows is mainly indebted to R. J. Art and S. E. Ockenden, 'The domestic politics

of cruise missile development, 1970–1980', and R. Huisken, 'The history of modern cruise missile programs', chapters 12 and 3 in R. K. Betts, ed., *Cruise Missile Development: Technology, Strategy and Politics*, Brookings Institution, Washington DC, 1981. On claims for cruise capabilities, see FY 1982 Arms Control Impact Statement and *The Modernization of Nato's Long Range Theater Nuclear Forces*, Committee on Foreign Affairs, US House of Representatives, 31 December 1980, US Govt Printing Office, 1981.

52. On the RAF Tornado, Dan Smith, *The Defence of the Realm in the 1980s*, 1980, chapter 5; M. Kaldor, *The Baroque Arsenal*, 1981, pp. 189–91. See also Chapter 10.

53. Senate Armed Services Committee, FY73 DoD Appropriations, Washington, 1973, pp. 2363–77, esp. p. 2371 (evidence of Col. Mullins).

54. FY73 DoD Appropriations, p. 2365; A. Cockburn, 'Cruise, the missile that does not work', *New Statesman*, 22 August 1980, pp. 10–11. Reports by the Comptroller General of the United States, C–MASAD–81–9, 28 February 1981, 'Some land attack cruise missile acquisition programs need to be slowed down'; MASAD–81–15, 2 March 1981, 'Most critical testing still lies ahead for missiles in Theater Nuclear Modernization Program'; C–MASAD–81–11, 'Issues affecting the Navy's antiship cruise missile programs', n.d.

55. Interviews by Dr Prins in Washington, October 1981.

56. E.g. by Harold Brown, Hearing of 16 September 1980 on PD59, p. 17; United States Military Posture for FY 1982 by Gen. David Jones USAF, Chairman of the Joint Chiefs of Staff, 'Theater nuclear forces'; UK Ministry of Defence publicity broadsheets, 'Cruise missiles: some important questions and answers', CS (REPS), PPI, October 1981, and 'Cruise missiles: the important questions'.

57. *SIPRI Yearbook* (1980), pp. 178–9.

58. Details of European warhead comparisons, *SIPRI Yearbook* (1980), p. 176; IISS, *The Military Balance* (1980–81), p. 19. See further Chapter 6 and Appendix A2; *Tactical Nuclear Weapons: European Perspectives*, SIPRI, 1978, pp. 115–16; FY 1982 Arms Control Impact Statement, III A.

59. GAO report, *Countervailing Strategy*, MASAD–81–35, 5 August 1981.

60. For a brief introduction to the Soviet military system, D. Holloway, 'War, militarism and the Soviet state', in E. P. Thompson and D. Smith, eds. *Protest and Survive*, 1980. For views of arms production in the USSR which argue for differences from the Western 'Steel Triangle' see Roy and Zhores Medvedev, 'The USSR and the arms race', *New Left Review*, 1981; M. Kaldor, *The Baroque Arsenal*, chapter 4; V. R. Berghahn, *Militarism: the History of an International Debate 1861–1979*, Leamington Spa, 1981, chapter 5, 'The military industrial complex', discusses the case for similarity or difference between the USA and USSR.

61. *SIPRI Yearbook* (1969/70), 'Past proposals for disarmament in Europe', pp. 402–14; *SIPRI Yearbook* (1968/69), 'Disarmament efforts', p. 176.

62. *Keesing's Contemporary Archives* (1961–2), p. 18,090; p. 17,932; p. 18,335; pp. 18,242–4 (Kennedy's speech of 25 July and details of the additional defence spending increases); pp. 18,271–8; pp. 18,307–10; p. 18,454 (details of Soviet tests, September–October 1961).

63. *Keesing's Contemporary Archives* (1961–2), p. 18,689.

64. J. Rotblat, *Nuclear Radiation in Warfare*, 1981, pp. 73–103; for the data on the pre-1963 tests, pp. 97–9.

65. Myrdal, *The Game of Disarmament*, pp. 88–92.

66. Based on M. Mandelbaum, *The Nuclear Question*, pp. 129–57.

67. Khrushchev's speech before the Supreme Soviet, 12 December 1962, *Keesing's Contemporary Archives* (1963–4), p. 19,288.

68. Mandelbaum, *The Nuclear Question*, p. 168.

69. 'Commencement address at American University in Washington', 10 June 1963, *Public Papers of the Presidents of the United States, J. F. Kennedy 1963*, Washington, 1964, pp. 459–64.

70. Myrdal, *The Game of Disarmament*, pp. 93–5.

71. 'An arms control agenda for the eighties', *The Committee for National Security*, 30 June 1981, p. 13.

72. A. M. Schlesinger, *A Thousand Days*, 1968, p. 779.

73. *SIPRI Yearbook* (1981), p. xxv.

74. *SIPRI Yearbook* (1972), pp. 533–41.

75. *SIPRI Yearbook* (1968/9), pp. 159–66. Test of the Non-Proliferation Treaty, pp. 349–54.

76. 'SALT II: one small step for mankind', *The Defense Monitor*, 8, 5, 1979, p. 1.

77. Formal accounts of SALT I: *SIPRI Yearbook* (1969/70), chapter 3, 'The main arms race, SALT I and European security', pp. 36–91; *SIPRI Yearbook* (1972), chapter 2, 'The Strategic Arms Limitation Talks', November 1969–December 1971; M. Willrich and J. B. Rhinelander, eds., *SALT: the Moscow Agreements and Beyond*, New York, 1974.

78. Article V (1): 'Each Party undertakes not to develop, test, or deploy ABM systems or components which are sea-based, air-based, space-based, or mobile land-based.' Agreed Initialled Statement D, annexed to the ABM Treaty, committed both parties to discuss limitation of any ABM system 'based on other physical principles' that might be invented — Willrich and Rhinelander, *SALT: the Moscow Agreements and Beyond*, pp. 282, 288.

79. C. Bertram, 'Arms control and technological change: elements of a new approach', in C. Bertram, ed., *Arms Control and Military Force* (Adelphi Library Vol. 3), IISS, 1980, esp. pp. 168–9.

80. *SIPRI Yearbook* (1981), 'Ballistic missile defence', pp. 264–71; Department of Defense *Annual Report, Fiscal Year 1982*, 'Advanced Technology Development Programs', pp. 245–50.

81. Gerard Smith, *Double Talk: The Story of the First Strategic Arms Limitation Talks*, New York, 1980, p. 154.

82. A revealing account of the White House view and role is to be found in J. Newhouse, *Cold Dawn – the Story of SALT*, New York, 1973.

83. Smith, *Double Talk*, pp. 162–3.

84. Separate conversations between Dr Prins and Paul Warnke, Herbert Scoville, Raymond Garthoff and Gerard Smith, Washington, October 1981.

85. *Keesing's Contemporary Archives* (1977), p. 28,428; Strobe Talbott, *Endgame: the Inside Story of SALT II*, New York, 1979, p. 56.

86. Talbott, *Endgame*, p. 57.

87. *SIPRI Yearbook* (1980), 'SALT II: an analysis of the agreements', p. 211.

88. The argument of these final paragraphs is indebted to that in the SIPRI review of the 1970s, *SIPRI Yearbook* (1981), pp. 60–61.

5. The Steel Triangle

1. Quoted S. Melman, *Pentagon Capitalism*, New York, 1970, pp. 232–4.

2. *Public Papers of the Presidents of the United States, Dwight D. Eisenhower 1960–61*,

Washington, DC, 1961. Farewell radio and television address to the American people, 17 January 1961, p. 421.

3. G. Adams, *The Iron Triangle: the Politics of Defense Contracting*, New York, 1981.

4. General A. Beaufre, 'A conception of strategy', *Revue de défense nationale*, December 1963; English translation, *Survival*, 6, 2 March–April 1964.

5. R. A. Fuhrman, 'Fleet ballistic missile system: Polaris to Trident', AIAA, February 1978; K. Tsipis, *United States strategic weapons: Disarmament and Arms Control*, 1970, Tables I and II, pp. 26–9; R. Aldridge, *The Counterforce Syndrome*, 3nd ed., Washington, 1979, pp. 21–44; *SIPRI Yearbook* (1979), pp. 7–14.

6. L. Freedman, *US Intelligence and the Soviet Strategic Threat*, 1977, pp. 127–51.

7. C. von Clausewitz, *On War*, ed. and trans. M. Howard and P. Paret, Princeton, 1976, Book 1, chapter 7, pp. 119–21.

8. Earl Mountbatten of Burma. Speech on the occasion of the award of the Louise Weiss Foundation Prize to the Stockholm International Peace Research Institute, Strasbourg, 11 May 1979, reproduced in *Apocalypse Now?*, Nottingham, 1980.

9. W. J. Broad, 'Nuclear pulse I: awakening to the chaos factor', 'Nuclear pulse II: Ensuring delivery of the doomsday signal', and 'Nuclear pulse III: Playing a wild card', *Science*, 212, May 1981, pp. 1009–12, 1116–20, 1248–51; S. Glasstone and P. J. Doran, eds., *The Effects of Nuclear Weapons*, 3rd edn., US Dept of Defense and US Dept of Energy, 1977.

10. *US Army Field Manual*, FM 100–5, chapter 10, p. 9.

11. S. Lens, *The Military–Industrial Complex*, 1971, chapter 2.

12. Lord Zuckerman, 'Science advisers and scientific advisers', *Proceedings of the American Philosophical Society*, 124, 4, 1980, p. 245. The case is put at greater length in Solly Zuckerman, *Nuclear Reality and Illusion*, 1982.

13. *SIPRI Yearbook* (1981), quoting Leitenberg, p. 351.

14. DoD, Directorate for Information Operations and Reports (DIOR), Report PO4, 'Educational and non profit institutions receiving prime contract awards over $10,000 for Research, Development, Test and Evaluation (RDT and E) work Fiscal 1980', May 1981.

15. Lens, *Military–Industrial Complex*, p. 126.

16. S. Burkholder, 'The Pentagon in the ivory tower', *The Progressive*, June 1981, pp. 25–31.

17. ibid.

18. Adams, *Iron Triangle*, pp. 314, 344.

19. Quoted K. Tsipis, 'The factors promoting armaments in the United States, and some proposals for disarmament', *Disarmament and Arms Control* (Italian Pugwash Conference), 1970, pp. 106, 108.

20. Senate Armed Services Committee, FY 73 DoD Appropriations, p. 2366; further references at chapter 4, note 54.

21. *Disarmament and Arms Control*, p. 109.

22. M. Kaldor, 'Technical change in the defence industry', in K. Pavitt, ed., *Technical Innovation and British Economic Performance*, 1980, p. 118.

23. 'The Defense Department's top 100', *Council on Economic Priorities Newsletter*, November 1980, p. 5; 'Defense Dept lists top 100 contractors for fiscal 1980', *Aviation Week and Space Technology*, 27 April 1981, pp. 200–201.

24. Aldridge, *Counterforce Syndrome*, pp. 28, 29.

25. Lens, *Military–Industrial Complex*, p. 5.

26. W. Proxmire (Senator for Wisconsin), quoted C. W. Pursell, *The Military–Industrial Complex*, New York, 1972, pp. 253–62.

27. R. L. Tammen, *MIRV and the Arms Race: An Interpretation of Defense Strategy*, New York, 1973, p. 76; Fuhrman, 'Fleet ballistic missile system', p. 19.
28. Adams, *Iron Triangle*, pp. 393–4, 398.
29. Adams, *Iron Triangle*, p. 97.
30. M. Kaldor, 'Technical change', pp. 112–3; Dan Smith, *The Defence of the Realm in the 1980s*, 1980, chapter 6.
31. Lens, *Military–Industrial Complex*, p. 18.
32. B. M. Russett, *What Price Vigilance? The Burdens of National Defence*, New Haven, 1970, p. 140.
33. A. R. Sunseri, 'The military–industrial complex in Iowa', in B. F. Cooling, ed., *War, Business and American Society*, New York, 1977, pp. 165–70.
34. Pursell, cit. *Cong. Record*; Adams, *Iron Triangle*, p. 84.
35. G. Kennedy, *The Economics of Defence*, 1975, p. 194; Special Almanac Issue, *Defense 81*, American Forces Information Service, September 1981, p. 19; W. Sweet, 'The pit and the pendulum: domestic politics of United States military policy', *Alternatives*, 6, 1980, pp. 51–2.
36. Sunseri, 'Military–industrial complex', p. 158.
37. Quoted in Adams, *Iron Triangle*, pp. 81–2. For the view of retired officers see J. K. Taussig, 'Post retirement employment', *Shipmate*, March 1981, pp. 21–3.
38. Pursell, *Military–Industrial Complex*, pp. 258–9.
39. H. F. York, *The Origins of MIRV* (SIPRI Research Report No. 9), 1973, p. 8; H. York, 'Military technology and national security', *Scientific American*, 221, 2, August 1969, pp. 17–29.
40. York, *Origins of MIRV*, pp. 16, 17.
41. Freedman, *US Intelligence*, pp. 86–96; H. York, *Race to Oblivion*, pp. 176–7.
42. Tammen, *MIRV*, pp. 71–3; York, *Origins of MIRV*, pp. 8–9.
43. Tammen, *MIRV*, p. 72.
44. York, *Origins of MIRV*, pp. 8–9; Fuhrman, 'Fleet ballistic missile system', p. 17.
45. Tammen, *MIRV*, p. 87.
46. Aldridge, *Counterforce Syndrome*, p. 27.
47. Tammen, *MIRV*, p. 93.
48. ibid., p. 76.
49. R. S. McNamara, 'Address at the commencement exercises, University of Michigan, Ann Arbor, Michigan, June 16th 1962', *Department of State Bulletin*, 9 July 1962.
50. Quoted York, *Origins of MIRV*, p. 21.
51. W. Proxmire, quoted in Lens, *The Military–Industrial Complex*, p. 10.
52. Freedman, *US Intelligence*, pp. 176–9.
53. Freedman, *US Intelligence*, pp. 176, 177; J. M. Collins, *US–Soviet Military Balance*, New York, 1980, p. 446. Appendix A1 discusses and illustrates the uncertainty about the accuracy of missiles. Collins, a hawkish analyst, tends to assume the maximum deployment and the minimum CEP for Soviet missile types.
54. *Strat-X Report*, R–122, Institute for Defense Analysis, vol. 1, August 1967; Aldridge, *Counterforce Syndrome*.
55. R. Halloran, 'Pentagon draws up first strategy for fighting a long nuclear war', *New York Times*, 29 May 1982.
56. R. P. Smith, 'Military expenditure and capitalism', *Cambridge Journal of Economics*, 1977.
57. Hearings before the Committee on Foreign Relations, United States Senate, 97th Congress, 1st Session on 'The foreign policy and arms control implications of President Reagan's strategic weapons proposals', 3, 4, and 9 November 1981, p. 4.

58. Professor Martin, *Listener*, 12 November 1981, p. 564 (The Reith Lectures, no. 1).
59. See Council on Economic Priorities, *Newsletter*, New York, May 1981, Table 1, p. 3, based on *Fiscal Year 1981 and 1982 Department of Defense Budget Revisions*.
60. L. Thurow, 'How to wreck the economy', *New York Review of Books*, 14 May 1981, p. 3.
61. 'Preparing for nuclear war: President Reagan's program', *Defense Monitor*, 10, 8, 1982.
62. See, e.g., Joyce Kolko, *America and the Crisis of World Capitalism*, New York, 1974, and Felix G. Rohatyn, *New York Review of Books*, April 1981, p. 14.
63. See R. Parboni, *The Dollar and Its Rivals: Recession, Inflation and International Finance*, 1981.

6. The Case for and against a Nuclear Defence Policy

1. M. Quinlan, 'Preventing War', *Tablet*, 18 July 1981, p. 689.
2. 'Defence in the 1980s', *Statement on the Defence Estimates 1980* (Cmnd. 7826–I), p. 8, para 120; see also *US Department of Defense Annual Report 1981*, pp. 65–6.
3. *Statement on the Defence Estimates 1980*, p. 8, para. 121.
4. *Statement on the Defence Estimates 1981* (Cmnd. 8212–I), p. 18, para. 307.
5. *Statement on the Defence Estimates 1980*, p. 15, para. 212.
6. *Statement on the Defence Estimates 1980*, vol. 2, p. 12, and *Statement on the Defence Estimates 1981*, p. 11. See also Defence Open Government Document 80/23.
7. *US Army Field Manual*, FM 100–5, 1 July 1976, HQ, Dept of the Army, Washington, DC, pp. 10-2, 10-6–10-8.
8. *Parliamentary Debates* (House of Lords), 20 July 1981, col. 62.
9. M. Bundy, G. Kennan, R. McNamara and G. Smith, 'Nuclear weapons and the Atlantic Alliance', *Foreign Affairs*, Spring 1982, reproduced in Congressional Record – Senate, 13 April 1982, pp. S3427–S3431; Secretary Haig, 'Peace and deterrence', speech at Georgetown University, Washington DC, 6 April 1982, Bureau of Current Affairs, Current Policy Document no. 383.
10. IISS, *The Military Balance* (1981–2), pp. 73, 124; *Statement on the Defence Estimates 1981*, Figure 3, p. 17; Dan Smith, *The Defence of the Realm in the 1980s*, 2nd ed., 1981, p. 170 and note 41.
11. M. Mandelbaum, *The Nuclear Question: The United States and Nuclear Weapons, 1946–1976*, Cambridge, 1979, p. 136.
12. Major-General Gert Bastian (West German Army, retired), 'Nuclear war in Europe: causes, combat, consequences and how to avoid it', *Defense Monitor*, 10, 7, 1981, p. 4.
13. For discussion of other interpretations of threats see D. Baldwin, 'Thinking about threats', *Journal of Conflict Resolution*, xv, March 1971.
14. C. von Clausewitz, *On War*, ed. and trans. M. Howard and P. Paret, Princeton, 1976, Book 2, chapter 3, p. 149.
15. *Statement on the Defence Estimates 1981*, p. 13.
16. Statements and Speeches, No. 78/7. Information Services Division, Department of External Affairs, Ottawa, Canada.
17. L. I. Brezhnev, speech on 6 October 1979, cited A. Myrdal, *The Game of Disarmament*, New York, 1976, p. 235. Repeated in an interview with *Der Spiegel*, November 1981; translation in *Guardian*, 23 November 1981.
18. *Hansard*, 484, 1950–51, col. 630.
19. Conversation between Mrs Sugden and Mr Den Besten, Secretary, Peace and Security Council, Royal Dutch Armed Forces, November 1981. Kapitein van de Koninklijke

Luchtmacht Meindert Stelling, lecture at State University, Utrecht, 21 October 1981, 'Kernwapens en het volkenrecht' (Nuclear weapons and international law).

20. Quinlan, 'Preventing War'.
21. L. Freedman, *Britain and Nuclear Weapons*, 1980.
22. M. Gowing and L. Arnold, *Independence and Deterrence: Vol. I, Policy Making*, 1974, pp. 179–85, tells of the British decision. A. Wohlstetter, *Swords from Plowshares*, Chicago and London, 1979, pp. 45–6, mentions the French one.
23. L. Brezhnev, address to the 26th Congress of the Communist Party, 23 February 1981.
24. See also Zuckerman, 'Science advisers and scientific advisers', *Proceedings of the American Philosophical Society*, 124, 4, 1980.
25. Statement of Pugwash Medical Working Group, reprinted in *Proceedings of the Medical Association for the Prevention of War*, 1981, pp. 157–8.
26. P. H. Vigor, 'The semantics of deterrence and defense', in M. MccGwire, K. Booth and J. McDonnell, eds., *Soviet Naval Policy: Objectives and constraints*, New York, 1975, pp. 471–8.

7. The Soviet Threat

1. M. Quinlan, 'Preventing War', *Tablet*, 18 July 1981.
2. 5th Report, Foreign Affairs Committee, House of Commons, 1979–80, HC745; F. Halliday, *Threat from the East? Soviet Policy from Afghanistan and Iran to the Horn of Africa*, 1982.
3. M. I. Goldman, *The Enigma of Soviet Petroleum – Half Empty or Half Full*, 1980; D. Park, *Oil and Gas in Comecon Countries*, 1979.
4. *Defense Monitor*, 9, 1980, pp. 4–5.
5. 'The Defense Budget Controversy', *Challenge*, May/June 1980, p. 43.
6. *Statement on Defence Estimates 1980*, p. 5, para. 108.
7. Interview with *Der Spiegel* magazine; press release, 'News and Views from the USSR', Soviet Embassy, Information Department, Washington, 2 November 1981, p. 7.

8. The Case against a Nuclear Defence Policy, I

1. 'Preparing for nuclear war: President Reagan's program', *Defense Monitor*, 10, 8, 1982, p. 2.
2. Ole Holsti, Professor of Political Science, University of British Columbia in Vancouver, cited in *UNESCO Courier*, August 1970, p. 22.
3. Hylke Tromp, Director, University of Groningen Polemological Institute, 'Nuclear War in Europe', *Defense Monitor*, 10, 7, 1981, p. 3.
4. 'NORAD's missile warning system: What went wrong?', Report by the Comptroller General of the United States, MASAD–81–30, 15 May 1981; 'Recent false alerts from the nation's missile attack warning system', Report to the Committee on Armed Services, United States Senate, 96th Congress, 2nd Session, by Senators Gary Hart and Barry Goldwater, 9 October 1980, Government Printing Office, Washington, DC.
5. W. M. Atkin, 'Nuclear weapons in Europe: what they are, what they are for', in M. Kaldor and D. Smith, eds., *Disarming Europe*, 1982; information from Center for Defense Information, December 1981.

6. 'Nuclear armament – an interview with Dr Daniel Ellsberg', Conservation Press, 1980, pp. 2–3.

7. *SIPRI Yearbook* (1977), chapter 3, 'Accidents of nuclear weapon systems', pp. 52–85.

8. 'US nuclear weapons accidents: danger in our midst', *Defense Monitor*, 10, 5, 1981, p. 4.

9. N. Solomon, 'Unstable explosive still on sub warheads called a very serious danger', *San Francisco Sunday Examiner & Chronicle*, 18 October 1981, p. A18; B. Wilson, 'LX–09, the hidden threat inside Poseidon missiles', *Glasgow Herald*, 20 November 1981; 'Poseidon radiation leak alleged', *Scotsman*, 20 November 1981; D. Campbell, 'Lucky ending in missile mishap', *San Francisco Examiner*, 29 November 1981; D. Campbell and N. Solomon, 'Accidents will happen', *New Scotsman*, 27 November 1981, pp. 10–11; letter from Meteorological Office, Edinburgh, to Mrs Sugden, 8 December 1981, and *Analysis of Anemograms at Glasgow Airport* (Abbotsinch), 1–8 November 1981.

10. L. Dumas, 'National security in the nuclear age', *Bulletin of the Atomic Scientists*, 32, 5, 1976, pp. 25–35; *Defense Monitor*, 10, 5, 1981, pp. 10–11.

11. ibid., pp. 7–8.

12. Sir Brian Flowers (Chairman), *Nuclear Power and the Environment* (Sixth Report, the Royal Commission on Environmental Pollution), 1976, paras. 506, 507.

13. See J. Coogin, quoted *Congressional Record*, 11 March 1975), pp. 53619–20; Flowers Commission, para. 320; R. W. Fox (chairman), *Ranger Uranium Environmental Inquiry*, First Report, October 1976, Australian Parliamentary Paper 309/1976, pp. 151–9.

14. A. Lovins, *Soft Energy Paths*, 1977, gives references. Fox Reports, pp. 131–5.

15. E. Davenport, P. Eddy, and P. Gillman, *The Plumbat Affair*, 1978.

16. See D. L. Crouson, 'Safeguards & nuclear materials management in the USA', Atomic Energy Commission Document, Washington, DC, 1970.

17. A. Giorgy and others, *No Nukes: Everyone's Guide to Nuclear Power*, Boston, 1979, pp. 123–9; C. Fager, 'Tracking the plutonium police', *San Francisco Bay Guardian*, 4 August 1977.

18. See, e.g., A. B. Lovins, L. H. Lovins and L. Ross, 'Nuclear power and nuclear bombs', *Foreign Affairs*, Summer 1980, pp. 1137–77; SIPRI, *Nuclear Energy and Nuclear Weapon Proliferation*, 1979; SIPRI, *Internationalization to Prevent the Spread of Nuclear Weapons*, 1980.

19. E.g. Acheson–Lilienthal report, 'A report on the international control of atomic energy', US State Dept, 2498, 16 March 1946.

20. F. Ikle, Foreword to A. Wohlstetter and others, *Swords from Plowshares*, Chicago and London, 1979, pp. ix–xii.

21. ibid.

22. op. cit., Table 1, p. 15.

23. ibid., p. xiii.

24. J. Petera, 'Was Iraq really developing a bomb?', *New Scientist*, 90, 1,257, 11 June 1981, pp. 688–90. R. Denselow and D. Coxon Taylor, 'Argentina is very close to producing its own nuclear bomb – with German help', *Listener*, 22 April 1982, pp. 2–4.

25. *Nuclear Energy and Nuclear Weapon Proliferation, Internationalization to Prevent the Spread of Nuclear Weapons*, SIPRI, 1980; Wohlstetter, *Swords from Plowshares*; Fox Report, p. 185.

26. See *Radcliffe Report on Ministerial Memoirs*, Cmnd. 6386, 1976.

27. See *Attorney-General* v. *Jonathan Cape Ltd* [1976] QB 752 (publication of Crossman Diaries).

28. *The Times*, 3 January 1978. For recent criticisms of public records legislation, see *Report of Committee on Modern Public Records*, 1981.

29. *The Times*, 22 December 1980; *The Times*, 30 December 1981.
30. *Guardian*, 2 January 1982.
31. M. Gowing, *Independence and Deterrence. Britain and Atomic Energy, 1945–52*, pp. 17–22, 179–80. See L. Freedman, *Britain and Nuclear Weapons*, 1980, pp. 52–5.
32. *New Statesman*, 31 October 1980; *Defense 81*, Almanac edition, p. 47. *Inventory of Air Force Military Real Property*, Headquarters, USAF, 30 September 1980, pp. 125–7; *Inventory of Military Real Property, Navy*, vol. 2, NAVFAC P-77, 30 September 1980, pp. 1–810013; *Inventory of Army Military Real Property*, US Army Corps of Engineers, 30 September 1980, pp. A419–20.
33. See Appendix A2.
34. W. Kennet and E. Young, *Neither Red nor Dead: the Case for Disarmament*, 1981, pp. 23, 39.
35. P. O'Higgins, *Censorship in Britain*, 1972, p. 36.
36. The best account is D. G. T. Williams, *Not in the Public Interest*, 1965.
37. Letter to *The Times*, 20 March 1970, by Sir Lionel Heald, QC.
38. *Franks Report* (Cmnd 5104), 1972, para. 14.
39. See C. Aubrey, *Who's Watching You?*, 1981.
40. H. Street, *Freedom, the Individual and the Law*, 1977, p. 226.
41. See *Brownlie's Law of Public Order and National Security*, 1981, pp. 259–62, and *The Times*, 7 December 1981.
42. *Guardian*, 17 February 1979.
43. Cmnd 6618, 1976, paras. 330–33.
44. Street, *Freedom, the Individual and the Law*, p. 244.
45. Cmnd 7873, 1980.
46. Cmnd 8092, 1981, para. 3.57. See also the Law Commission's Report on Breach of Confidence, October 1981.
47. *New Statesman*, 1 February 1980.
48. *New Statesman*, 18 July 1980.
49. *Inventory of Army Military Real Property*, Entry for Menwith Hill, p. C–2729. (The inventories include detailed descriptions of all US sites, listing buildings, their general purposes and costs.)
50. B. Cox, *Civil Liberties in Britain*, 1975, p. 299.
51. Cmnd 7341, para. 6.05.
52. *The Times*, 26 September 1981.
53. *New Statesman*, 30 October 1981.
54. See, generally, Cox, *Civil Liberties*.
55. *Arrowsmith* v. *Jenkins* [1963] 2 QB 561.
56. *Cambridge Evening News*, 7 March 1981.
57. *Kent* v. *Metropolitan Police Commissioner*, *The Times*, 15 May 1981.
58. See generally, *Discussion Paper on Review of the Public Order Act 1936* (Cmnd 7891), 1980; Fifth Report from the Home Affairs Committee, *The Law Relating to Public Order 1979–80*; HC 756–I and 756–II, August 1980.

9. The Case against a Nuclear Defence Policy, II

1. W. C. Patterson, *Nuclear Power*, 1976, pp. 91–5; Sir Brian Flowers (Chairman), *Nuclear Power and the Environment* (Sixth Report, Royal Commission on Environmental Pollution, Cmnd 6618), 1976, para. 397; Justice R. W. Fox, *Ranger Uranium Environmental Inquiry*

(First Report, October 1976, Australia Parliamentary Paper 309/1976), p. 110; papers in *Nuclear Energy* (special issue on waste management), 21, 3, 1982.

2. Honicker v. Hendrie: 'A law suit to end atomic power', Nashville, Tennessee, 1978; 'Atom waste site', *New York Times*, 6 December 1981; D. Comey, 'The legacy of uranium tailings', *Bulletin of the Atomic Scientists*, 31, 7, 1975, pp. 43–5; *Use of Uranium Mill Tailings for Construction Purposes* (United States Congress, 92nd Congress, 1st Session, Joint Committee on Atomic Energy, Subcommittee on Raw Materials, Hearings 28 and 29 October 1971), US Government Printing Office, Washington DC; National Academy of Sciences, *The Effects on Populations of Exposure to Low Levels of Ionizing Radiation* (BEIR III), Washington DC, 1980, Appendix; Fox Report, p. 109; G. A. Watford and J. A. Wethington, 'Radiological hazards of uranium mill tailings piles', *Nuclear Technology*, 53, 1981, pp. 295–302; for a dissenting view, which criticizes BEIR III, B. L. Cohen, 'Health effects of radon emissions from uranium mill tailings', *Health Physics*, 42, 5, 1982, pp. 695–702.

3. e.g. Australian Atomic Energy Commission Report AAEC/1P9 1975, cited M. Ryle, *Towards the Nuclear Holocaust*, 1980; testimony of Dr J. Gofman in the case of the *State of Oklahoma* v. *Theodore Agnew*, 19 September 1979, District Court, Rogers County, Oklahoma.

4. Report of the United Nations Scientific Committee on the Effects of Atomic Radiation (UNSCEAR), General Assembly, 13th Session, Supplement 17 (A/3838), New York, 1958, pp. 38–41, Annex D, pp. 102–110; National Academy of Sciences, Report of the Advisory Committee on the Biological Effects of Ionizing Radiation, *The Effects on Populations of Exposure to Low Levels of Ionizing Radiation* (BEIR I), Washington 1972, pp. 100–116; N. Kochupillai and others, 'Down's syndrome and related abnormalities in an area of high background radiation in coastal Kerala', *Nature*, 262, pp. 60–61; these findings are at variance with a study of Keralese rats by H. Grünberg and others, *A Search for Genetic Effects of High Natural Radioactivity in South India* (Medical Research Council Special Report No. 307), 1966, which found no effects – our interest, however, is in humans and the Kochupillai study is therefore preferred; G. Johnson, 'Paradise lost', *Bulletin of the Atomic Scientists*, 36, 10, 1980, pp. 24–9, cf. R. A. Conard, *A Twenty Year Review of Medical Findings in a Marshallese Population Accidentally Exposed to Radioactive Fallout*, Brookhaven National Laboratory, New York, 1975.

5. International Commission on Radiological Protection, *Recommendations of the ICRP* (Publication no. 26, R–63), Oxford, 1977; C. R. Olsen and others, 'Reactor released radionuclides in Susquehanna River sediments', *Nature*, 294, pp. 242–5; Radioactive Waste Management Advisory Committee (Sir Denys Wilkinson, Chairman), Second Report, May 1981, paras. 3.20–22; F. Charlesworth, W. S. Gronow, and A. W. Kenny, *Windscale: the Management of Safety*, Health and Safety Executive, 1981, p. 12, para. 5.1; p. 29, para. 12.2; p. 35, Appendix I, details some of the more significant on-site accidents at Windscale; C. G. Geary, R. T. Benn, and I. Leck, 'Incidence of myeloid leukaemia in Lancashire', *Lancet*, II, 1979, pp. 549–551; S. D. Reid and others, 'Cluster of myeloid leukaemia in Lytham St Annes' (letter), *Lancet*, II, 1979, p. 579; D. E. Williams and others, 'Whole body caesium 137 levels in man in Scotland 1978–9', *Health Physics*, 40, 1981, pp. 1–4. (The association suggested between these observations and the recorded increase in Windscale effluent was denied by scientists of the UKAEA, but their objections and alternative explanation were found not to affect the original paper (correspondence, *Health Physics*, 42, 5, 1982, pp. 735–8)). We are indebted to Dr J. Heath of the Strangeways Laboratory, Cambridge, for guidance in this area.

6. 'Oak Ridge analyzes accidents', *Nuclear Engineering International*, 27, 332, 1982, p. 11; F. von Hippel, 'Looking back on the Rasmussen Report', *Bulletin of the Atomic Scientists*, 33,

2, 1977, pp. 42–7; the 1980 Critical Mass (anti-nuclear group) study reported in 'Nuclear mishaps by the numbers', *Washington Post*, 2 August 1981; IDO report on the nuclear incident at the SL–I reactor, IDO–19302, USAEA, January 1962; Z. T. Mendoza, C. A. Stevens, and R. L. Ritzman, 'Radiation releases from the SL–I accident', *Nuclear Technology*, 53, 1981, pp. 155–62 (a brief description is given in W. C. Patterson, *Nuclear Power*, pp. 175–6).

7. Z. Medvedev, 'Facts behind the Soviet nuclear disaster', *New Scientist*, 74, 1058, 30 June 1977, pp. 761–4, and Z. Medvedev, *Nuclear Disaster in the Urals*, New York, 1979. See also review by Prof J. H. Fremlin, *Nature*, 282, p. 157.

8. F. Hoyle and G. Hoyle, *Common Sense in Nuclear Energy* 1980, pp. 62–5.

9. W. Stillman and D. M. Soran, Los Alamos National Laboratory report LA–9219–MS, cited *Nuclear Energy*, 21, 3, 1982, p. 151, and report in *Nature*, 296, pp. 696–7.

10. Description of the accident by S. E. Hunt in *Fission, Fusion and the Energy Crisis*, 1974, p. 58; see also K. F. Baverstock and J. Vennart, 'Emergency reference levels for reactor accidents: a reexamination of the Windscale Reactor accident', *Health Physics*, 30, 1976, pp. 339–44.

11. For a graphic fictional account of a melt-down, see J. Berger, *Nuclear Power: the Unviable Option* (Palo Alto, 1976), pp. 21–35; J. C. C. Stewart, 'A PWR for Britain', *Nuclear Energy*, 21, 2, 1982, p. 108. The PWR design has been dogged with problems over emergency core cooling, radiation embrittlement and cracking (perhaps for other reasons also) of pipes and pressure vessels, ballooning of fuel rod cladding, etc. etc. – and by continuous and quite ruthless attempts by nuclear agencies to suppress unfavourable reports and/or to silence any critic or engineer who has dared to 'leak' such knowledge to the public. One important PWR case was the defeat by Dan Ford and Myron Cherry of the US AEC's attempt to suppress the Brockett Report on safety problems with emergency core cooling. This exposé led to the removal of Milton Shaw, Head of Reactor Development at the AEC and to the reorganization of the AEC (House Report 95–1090, 26 April 1978; D. Boulton, D. Hart, and L. Woodhead, 'The US Nuclear Cover-Up', *Guardian* 21 October 1978, p. 7). Another case is of the hounding of Shoja Etemad, formerly a project leader in the French nuclear industry who led an investigation into primary circuit cracking in PWRs. Confronted by secrecy and a refusal to admit problems which might threaten the French PWR programme, Etemad took his knowledge to the public – and paid the price (S. Etemad, 'Deaf to the cracks of doom', *Guardian* 17 January 1980; on the question of embrittlement due to radiation, S. Etemad, *Guardian*, 18 March 1982).

12. *Staff Report . . . The Public's Right to Information Task Force*, US Government Printing Office, Washington, October 1979, pp. 125–66; J. G. Kemeny (Chairman), *Report of the President's Commission on the Accident at Three Mile Island*, US Government Printing Office, Washington, October 1979, pp. 81–148; reports on the clear-up in *Nuclear Engineering International*, 27, 323, 1982, pp. 21–5 and 27, 332, 1982, p. 3.

13. *Report of the President's Commission on the Accident at Three Mile Island*, US Government Printing Office, Washington, October 1979, pp. 7–8 and 9.

14. Lord Rothschild, 'Risk' (the Richard Dimbleby Lecture), *Listener*, 30 November 1978, pp. 715–18; Sir Francis Tombs, 'Nuclear power and the public good', *Nuclear Energy*, 17, 2, 1978, p. 89; Hon. Mr Justice Parker, *The Windscale Inquiry*, chapters 10 ('Routine discharges – risks') and 11 ('Risks – accidents'); Hoyle and Hoyle, *Common Sense in Nuclear Energy*, p. 29. Rothschild 'Risk' accounting is also defended in the Wilkinson Committee's Second Report (May 1981), p. 35, para. 8.9.

15. 'Ah yes, the godfather's magic will fix the nuclear industry', *Washington Post*, 27 October 1981, p. A3.

16. E.g. R. Lapp, 'Cancer and the fear of radiation', *New Scientist*, 91, 1260, 2 July 1981, pp. 14–15.

17. J. Gofman in testimony cited above at note 3.

18. J. Rotblat, 'The risks to radiation workers', *Bulletin of the Atomic Scientists*, 34, 7, 1978, p. 41; B. Wynne, 'The politics of nuclear safety', *New Scientist*, 77, 1087, 26 January 1978, pp. 208–11; 'Safety at Windscale. Yes, we were wrong', *Nature*, 290, p. 537.

19. T. Mancuso, A. Stewart, and G. Kneale, 'Radiation exposures of Hanford workers dying from cancer and other causes', *Health Physics*, 33, 1977, pp. 369–85; T. F. Mancuso, A. Stewart, and G. Kneale, 'Reanalysis of the data relating to the Hanford Study of the cancer risks of radiation workers (1944–1977 Deaths)', Vienna, 1978 (seminal earlier research by Stewart and Kneale included: A. Stewart, J. Webb, and D. Hewitt, 'A survey of childhood malignancies', *British Medical Journal*, 1958, pp. 1495–1508; A. Stewart and G. Kneale, 'Radiation dose effects in relation to obstetrical X-rays and childhood cancers', *Lancet*, 1970, pp. 1185–8; it was set in context, with confirmatory independent studies, in BEIR I, 1972, pp. 160–67); J. A. Reissland, 'An assessment of the Mancuso study', NRPB R-79, Harwell, September 1978; B. Sanders, 'Low-level radiation and cancer deaths', *Health Physics*, 34, 1978, pp. 521–38; J. W. Gofman, 'The question of radiation causation of cancer in Hanford workers', *Health Physics*, 37, 1979, pp. 617–39 (for an example of an attack on this paper and Gofman's reply: *Health Physics*, 40, 3, 1981); P. Saunders, 'The effects of radiation on man', *Atom*, 298, 1981, p. 200 (another example appears in *Atom*'s sister journal, *Nuclear Energy*, 17, 4, 1978, pp. 258–60); R. Bertell, 'X-ray exposure and premature ageing', *Journal of Surgical Oncology*, 9, 1977, pp. 379–91.

20. J. Rotblat, 'Hazards of low-level radiation – less agreement, more confusion', *Bulletin of the Atomic Scientists*, 37, 6, 1981, pp. 31–6; J. I. Fabrikant, 'The BEIR III controversy', *Radiation Research*, 84, 1980, pp. 361–8; E. P. Radford (chairman of the somatic effects subcommittee and overall chairman of the recalled BEIR III report), 'Human health effects of low doses of ionizing radiation', *Radiation Research*, 84, 1980, pp. 369–94; H. H. Rossi (member of the somatic effects subcommittee and leading signatory of the dissenting minority report), 'Comments on the somatic effects section of the BEIR III Report', *Radiation Research*, 84, 1980, pp. 395–406. (On the basis of the opinion of the *five* dissenting members, who favoured a quadratic curve to suggest carcinogenesis at low doses, rather than the gloomier linear model employed in BEIR I and endorsed by the other *seventeen* members of the subcommittee of BEIR III, the President of the National Academy of Sciences ordered that the report be withdrawn.)

21. Given this situation, the BEIR III committee considered three models for the curve: linear, linear-quadratic, and quadratic. Under Radford's chairmanship, the original report employed the simplest model compatible with the available epidemiological data (and Radford is an epidemiologist). This was the linear model. After Rossi's minority report, the rump committee chose as a compromise the more complex linear-quadratic curve. Both Radford and Rossi appended dissenting reports, Radford claiming that the carcinogenic effect of low LET radiation was now underestimated, Rossi that it was overestimated. Both scientists explained their views at the 1980 meeting of the Radiation Research Society and subsequently published them (in Radford's case with considerable supporting evidence) in the papers cited in note 20. The rump committee had been swayed in selecting the linear-quadratic compromise by reliance on Hiroshima and Nagasaki data, and the apparent difference in the observed rates of cancer mortality between them. This difference is now thrown into doubt (Rotblat, 'Hazards of low-level radiation').

22. W. E. Loewe and E. Mendelsohn, 'Revised estimates of dose at Hiroshima and Nagasaki, and possible consequences for radiation-induced leukemia', D-80-14, Lawrence Livermore

National Laboratory, 1980, cited Rotblat, 'Hazards of low-level radiation', p. 36; E. Marshal, 'New A-bomb studies alter radiation estimates', *Science*, 212, pp. 900–903 and correspondence on pp. 1364–5, and 213, pp. 6–8, 392–4, 602–4; J. Rotblat, *Nuclear Radiation in Warfare*, 1981. Two examples of a bland, nuclear establishment defence of *de facto* thresholds are B. L. Cohen, 'The cancer risk from low-level radiation', *Health Physics*, 39, 4, 1980, pp. 659–78, and B. Wade, 'Radiation and nuclear power', *Atom*, 301, 1981, pp. 289–99. (This article, written for the layman by a senior health physicist of AERE, Harwell, is especially interesting because, even following the BEIR III controversy [to which no reference is made], it gives the impression that a 'confident definition of safe conditions for working with radiation' can be given.)

23. K. H. Chadwick and H. P. Leenhouts, *The Molecular Theory of Radiation Biology*, Berlin, 1981, pp. 327–8.

24. D. Gloag, 'Risks of low-level radiation – the evidence of epidemiology', *British Medical Journal*, 1980, pp. 1479–82. An example of use of the average dose concept (in discussion of the Portsmouth Naval Shipyard case) is in R. Lapp, 'Cancer and the fear of radiation', p. 15.

25. BEIR I, 1972, p. 113; K. Z. Morgan (a founder of the science of health physics; Director of the Health Physics Division of the Oak Ridge National Laboratory 1943–72, past chairman of ICRP and the US National Council on Radiation Protection), 'Cancer and low level ionizing radiation', *Bulletin of the Atomic Scientists*, 34, 7, 1978, p. 30.

26. A. G. Duncan and S. R. A. Brown, 'Quantities of waste and a strategy for treatment and disposal', *Nuclear Energy*, 21, 3, 1982, p. 116. For a conclusion that failure of intermediate waste packaging on land might be expected to occur after ten years, see M. D. Hill, S. F. Mobbs, and I. F. White, *An Assessment of the Radiological Consequences of Disposal of Intermediate Level Wastes in Argillaceous Rock Formations* (National Radiological Protection Board, NRPB–R126), Harwell, September 1981, p. 5.

27. Sir Brian Flowers, 'A watchdog's view', *Bulletin of the Atomic Scientists*, 32, 10, 1976, pp. 24–7.

28. The Wilkinson Committee, Second Report, p. 22, para. 5.7; W. Marshall, 'The disposal of high level nuclear wastes', *Atom*, 300, 1981, p. 263; J. Berger, *Nuclear Power*, pp. 106–9; R. Gillette, 'Radiation spill at Hanford: the anatomy of an accident', *Science*, 181, pp. 728–30.

29. SIPRI, *Internationalization to Prevent the Spread of Nuclear Weapons*, 1980, p. 35 (gives calculations by Professor J. Rotblat); Flowers Commission, para. 533, Principal Conclusion No. 27.

30. SIPRI, *Nuclear Energy and Nuclear Weapons Proliferation*, 1979, p. 396, figure 8.

31. G. B. McCarthy and others, 'Interactions between nuclear waste and surrounding rock', *Nature*, 273, pp. 216–17; J. B. Morris and others (AERE), 'Durability of vitrified highly active waste from nuclear reprocessing', *Nature*, 273, pp. 215–16; W. G. Burns and others (AERE), 'Radiation effects and the leach rates of vitrified radioactive waste' *Nature*, 295, pp. 130–2; R. Walgate, 'Nuclear waste may be stored in synthetic rock', *Nature*, 274, p. 413. Further information on this crucial issue is given in Appendix C.

32. Flowers Commission, p. 155, paras. 407 and 408 (for the fate of the IGS project, see Appendix C and J. H. Black and N. A. Chapman, 'In search of nuclear burial grounds', *New Scientist*, 92, 1266, 13 August 1981, pp. 402–4); M. D. Hill and G. Lawson, *An Assessment of the Radiological Consequences of Disposal of High-level Waste in Coastal Geological Formations* (NRPB–R108), Harwell, 1980, pp. 18–21; letter from L. E. J. Roberts (Director of AERE), *The Times*, 18 September 1981.

33. 'Nuclear energy's dilemma – disposing of hazardous radioactive waste safely', Report to

Congress by the Comptroller General of the United States, General Accounting Office, Washington DC, 9 September 1977; Report to House of Commons Committee on Interior and Insular Affairs, 23 and 25 June 1981; Wilkinson Committee, Third Report, May 1982, chapter 4.

34. 'Military nuclear wastes: the hidden burden of the nuclear arms race', *Defense Monitor*, 10, 1, 1981.

35. G. G. Caldwell, D. B. Kelly, and C. W. Heath, 'Leukemia among participants in military manoeuvers at a nuclear bomb test', *Journal of the American Medical Association*, 244, 1980, 1575–8, report an increased incidence of leukemia (9 cases versus 3.5 expected) in a cohort of 3,224 men present at the Smoky atmospheric nuclear weapon test in 1957; R. E. Toohey and others, 'Radioactivity measurements of former military personnel exposed to weapon debris', *Science*, 213, 1981, pp. 767–8, counter the possibility raised by B. L. Cohen that this increase might be due to additional exposure from internal deposits of radioactivity.

36. Jacques Cousteau, 'Tears in the ice cream', in M. Reader, ed., *Atom's Eve*, New York, 1980, pp. 237–8.

37. A. M. Schlesinger, *A Thousand Days*, 1968, p. 403; N. Moss, *Men Who Play God*, 1968, p. 97.

38. *SIPRI Yearbook* (1980), pp. xxxii, 359.

39. M. Gowing and L. Arnold, *Independence and Deterrence*, 1974, *passim*.

40. A. B. Lovins, 'Nuclear weapons and power reactor plutonium', *Nature*, 283, pp. 817–23, and *Nature*, 284, p. 190 *erratum*; A. B. Lovins, L. H. Lovins, and L. Ross, 'Nuclear power and nuclear bombs', *Foreign Affairs*, Summer 1980, pp. 1137–77; *The Windscale Enquiry*, Parker Report (1978). See note to fourth letter in Appendix D.

41. SIPRI, *Nuclear Energy and Nuclear Weapon Proliferation*, Stockholm, 1979, p. 394.

42. SIPRI, *Nuclear Energy and Nuclear Weapon Proliferation*, p. 2, Table 1.3; W. Marshall, 'Nuclear power and the proliferation issue', *Atom*, 258, 1978, p. 101; 'Nuclear proliferation factbook', US Library of Congress, 23 September 1977, p. 382; *Nuclear Reactors: to Breed or not to Breed* (Pugwash debate on FBRs, The Royal Society, 28 September 1976), ed. Prof. J. Rotblat, 1977, p. 95; Flowers Commission, paras. 516–20 sounded very serious warnings about the fast breeder, and urged that this technology be delayed for as long as possible and, if possible, avoided.

43. Dr N. Dombey, 'Fuelling suspicion', *Guardian*, 3 December 1981; R. Edwards and S. Dury, *Fuelling the Nuclear Arms Race: The Links between Nuclear Power and Weapons*, 1982; J. Simpson, 'Power, plutonium and politics: nuclear arms production and the British civil nuclear industry', *ADIU Report*, May/June 1982, pp. 7–13 and J. Simpson, *The Independent Nuclear State: Britain, the United States and the Military Atom*, forthcoming.

44. 'Long range nuclear weapon planning analysis for the final report of the DOD/DOE long range resource planning group', 15 July 1980; Hearings on Department of Energy Authorization Legislation (National Security Programs) for Fiscal Year 1982 before the Procurement and military nuclear systems subcommittee, Committee on Armed Services, House of Representatives, 97th Congress, 1st Session, 2, 4, 5, 9 March 1981.

45. *The Times*, 30 October 1981.

46. SIPRI, *Nuclear Energy and Nuclear Weapon Proliferation*. On laser separation, see chapter 2, paper 4; C. Norman, 'Weapon builders eye civilian reactor fuel – a laser separation process could make plutonium from spent fuel suitable for bomb production', *Science*, 214, no. 4518, 16 October 1981, pp. 307–8; B. M. Casper, 'Laser enrichment: a new path to proliferation', *Bulletin of the Atomic Scientists*, 31, 1, 1977, pp. 28–41; Report on Molecular Laser Isotope Separator (MLIS) and Atomic Vapour Laser Isotope Separator (AVLIS), *Nuclear Energy*, 21, 3, 1982, pp. 148–50; D. Dickson, 'Lasers purify', *Nature*, 292, p. 401;

Report of decision to proceed with Laser Isotope Separation facility at Lawrence Livermore, *Nature*, 297, p. 255.

47. A. Wohlstetter and others, *Swords from Plowshares: The Military Potential of Civilian Nuclear Energy*, 1979, *passim.*

48. E.g. Acheson–Lilienthal report, 1946 (*A Report on the International Control of Atomic Energy*, U S State Dept, 2498, 16 March 1946); Fox Report, pp. 125–49, p. 189, finding 3.

49. M. Ryle, *Towards the Nuclear Holocaust*, pp. 18–23.

50. J. W. Jeffery, 'The real cost of nuclear electricity in the U K', *Energy Policy*, 10, 2, 1982, pp. 76–100. Professor Jeffery's conclusions have been continually denied in the scientific press by nuclear establishment officials and his researches have been impeded by CEGB reluctance to release specific information when requested. Three public attacks are noteworthy. The first occurred in *Nature* in response to a provisional communication of the findings of the *Energy Policy* paper (J. W. Jeffery, *Nature*, 287, p. 674). The Head of Economics and Energy Studies at the UKAEA raised technical criticisms (P. M. S. Jones, *Nature*, 288, p. 638), which Professor Jeffery successfully refuted (J. W. Jeffery, *Nature*, 292, p. 791). Dr Jones renewed his assault, but on his home ground (*Atom*, 306, 1982, pp. 89–91) in the form of a 'book-review' of *Nuclear Energy: the Real Costs* by Sir Kelvin Spencer and associates, to whom Professor Jeffery acted as advisor. Professor Jeffery comprehensively refuted this second attack (*Atom*, 309, 1982, pp. 154–5) and Dr Jones responded lamely, simply citing the CEGB Statement of Case for the Sizewell B Inquiry and observing that 'He and I have very different views on the attractiveness of electricity' (sic). A CEGB refutation of the *Energy Policy* paper was promised by Dr Jones. It appeared while this book was in press in the form of a brief letter about Magnox reactors (P. E. Watts, *Energy Policy*, 10, 3, 1982, pp. 254–6), which merited no further attention. We conclude that despite its best efforts, the nuclear establishment has not succeeded in undermining Professor Jeffery's case, which therefore stands as the present best estimate of the real cost of nuclear electricity.

51. Jeffery, 'The real cost of nuclear electricity in the U K', *Energy Policy*, 10, 2, 1982, Table 4, p. 81.

52. W. D. Rowe and W. F. Holcomb, 'The hidden commitment of nuclear wastes', *Nuclear Technology*, 24, 1974, pp. 286–93; Fox Report, pp. 109–10.

53. W. Patterson, *Nuclear Power*, 1976, pp. 162–6, 185–8; Atomic Energy Office, *Accident at Windscale No. 1 Pile on 10th October 1957* (Cmnd 302), November 1957.

54. 'Nuclear Power Costs', 23rd Report by the Committee on Government Operations, House Report 95–1050, 26 April 1978; Fox Report, pp. 98–9; B. D. Solomon, 'U S nuclear energy policy: provision of funds for decommissioning', *Energy Policy*, 10, 2, 1982, pp. 109–119; Wilkinson Committee, Third Report, May 1982, para 4.7; 'Decommissioning costs assessed . . .', *Nuclear Engineering International*, 27, 332, p. 10.

55. H. A. Feiveson, T. B. Taylor, F. von Hippel, and R. H. Williams, 'The plutonium economy', *Bulletin of the Atomic Scientists*, 32, 10, 1976, pp. 10–14; P. F. Chapman, 'Energy analysis of nuclear power stations', *Energy Policy*, 3, 4, 1975, pp. 285–98.

56. *Daily Telegraph*, 23 November 1981; 'More utilities defer', *Nuclear Engineering International*, 27, 329, 1982, p. 9; 'Three more reactors cancelled', ibid., 28, 323, 1982, p. 4; 'GE expects no equipment orders', ibid., 27, 332, 1982, p. 6; Power reactors 1982', Supplement, *Nuclear Engineering International*, 27, 330, 1982, Table 3, p. 3 (GE listed with eighty-one reactor orders and 16 per cent of the world market).

57. G. Leach, *A Low Energy Strategy for the United Kingdom*, 1979, *passim*; W. Patterson, *The Fissile Society*, 1977, chapter 2; M. Ryle, *Resurgence*, 80, May/June, 1980.

58. J. Baker at conference on the PWR and the UK, University of Birmingham, 24–5 March 1982, reported by C. Conroy, *Energy Policy*, 10, 3, 1982, pp. 257–8.

59. J. Rotblat, *Guardian*, 29 May 1980.

60. Sir Martin Ryle, *Is There a Case for Nuclear Power?*, 1982 (this article is also printed in *Electronics and Power*, July 1982, pp. 496–500); 'Solar pumps raise level of agriculture in Pakistan', *New Scientist*, 90, 1257, 11 June 1981, p. 693; 'Danes sail ahead with wind power', *New Scientist*, 91, 1260, 2 July 1981, p. 23; 'CEGB and wind power', *Nature*, 286, pp. 252–3; J. Becker, 'Enter the Nibe', *Nature*, 292, p. 577; Fox Report, p. 43.

61. *National Academy of Sciences News Report*, 1981, 31, pp. 6–9.

62. *UK Energy Statistics, 1975–1981*, 1982; A. B. Lovins, *Soft Energy Paths*, 1977; A. B. Lovins, L. H. Lovins, and L. H. Ross, 'Nuclear power and nuclear bombs'; Leach, *A Low Energy Strategy for the United Kingdom*; C. Lewis, 'A low energy option for the UK', *Energy Policy*, 7, 2, 1979, pp. 131–48; G. Doyle and D. Pearce, 'Low energy strategies for the UK – economics and incentives', *Energy Policy*, 7, 4, 1979, pp. 346–51.

10. Alternatives

1. Lord Mountbatten, Lord Noel-Baker, Lord Zuckerman, *Apocalypse Now?*, text of the final document, p. 44.

2. Field Marshal Lord Carver, *Guardian*, 14 December 1981.

3. H. Schmidt, *Defence or Retaliation*, Edinburgh, 1962, p. 169.

4. D. Smith, *The Defence of the Realm in the 1980s*, 1980.

5. e.g. A. Roberts, *Nations in Arms*, 1976; M. Kaldor and D. Smith, eds., *Disarming Europe*, 1982, essays in second part.

6. General F. Seethaler, 'Switzerland: the tactics of dissuasion', *New Statesman Papers on Defence and Disarmament*, No. 3, pp. 101–4; A. Roberts, *Nations in Arms*, chapters 3, 4, 7 and 8.

7. *Statement on the Defence Estimates 1981*, para. 625, p. 50, pp. 51–2; para. 619(c) p. 49.

8. *Navy International*, April 1976, special supplement 'Swedish maritime defence'; J. M. Collins, *US–Soviet Military Balance*, New York, 1980, p. 256; S. G. Gorshkov, *The Sea Power of the State*, Oxford, 1979 (translation of second revised Russian edition, 1976), pp. 197–8, 204–5.

9. 'HMS *Leeds Castle* launched at Hall Russell', *Naval Architect*, January 1981, pp. E22–E24; D. Brown and D. Andrews, 'Warship design to a price', *Naval Architect*, January 1981, pp. E17–E18; *Brassey's Defence Yearbook* (1981), pp. 173–4.

10. S. J. Palmer, 'The impact of the gas turbine on the design of major surface warships' (The 38th Parsons Memorial Lecture), *Transactions of the Royal Institution of Naval Architects [TRINA]*, 116, 1974, pp. 1–11; Vice-Admiral R. G. Raper, 'Designing warships for a cost-effective life' (Parsons Memorial Lecture), *Proceedings of the Institution of Mechanical Engineers*, 185, 1970–71, pp. 159–74; Sir Alfred Sims, 'The contribution of warship design to industrial technology' (5th Amos Ayre Lecture), *TRINA*, 3, 1969, pp. 149–61; C. E. M. Preston, 'COGOG on trial', *Navy International*, May 1975, pp. 24–7; Supplement on the Type 21, *Navy*, December 1972; M. K. Purvis, 'Postwar RN frigate and guided missile destroyer design, 1944–1969', *TRINA*, 116, 1974, pp. 189–222.

11. K. J. Moore, M. Flanigan, and R. D. Helsel, 'Developments in submarine systems, 1956–1976', in M. MccGwire and J. McDonnell, eds., *Soviet Naval Influence: Domestic and Foreign Dimensions*, New York, 1977, pp. 151–84; J. E. Moore, *The Soviet Navy Today*, 1975, pp. 23–4. We are grateful to Admiral E. Carroll for comments on these paragraphs.

12. J. E. Moore, ibid., pp. 227–38; IISS, *The Military Balance* (1981–2), p. 13; S. G. Gorshkov, *The Sea Power of the State*, Oxford, 1979, pp. 200–202; D. R. Jones, ed., *Soviet Armed Forces Review Annual*, No. 5, Florida, 1981, pp. 125–8; *Statement on the Defence Estimates 1981*, para. 626, p. 52.

13. J. Snouck-Hurgronje, 'On the diesel submarine', *RUSI Journal*, September 1977, pp. 49–51; A. Preston, 'Non-nuclear submarines, *Naval Architect*, July 1981, pp. E183–E185.

14. Smith, *The Defence of the Realm*, pp. 129–36.

15. J. J. Mearsheimer, 'Precision-guided munitions and conventional deterrence', *Survival*, 21, 1979, pp. 68–76; P. F. Walker, 'Precision-guided weapons', *Scientific American*, 245, 1981, pp. 21–9. Sceptical views are: D. Goure and G. McCormack, 'PGM: no panacea', *Survival*, 22, 1980, pp. 15–19; E. Luttwak, 'The nuclear alternatives', in K. Myers, ed., *NATO: The Next Thirty Years*, 1980, pp. 95–107. *Brassey's Defence Yearbook* (1981), p. 212.

16. Smith, *The Defence of the Realm*, pp. 165–75; *Brassey's Artillery of the World*, 1977, chapter 8; *Brassey's Infantry Weapons of the World*, 1979, p. 210.

17. Luttwak, ibid., p. 99.

18. Walker, *Scientific American*, 245, 1981. Harold Brown, Secretary of Defense, *Annual Report Fiscal Year 1982*, p. 247. *Brassey's Defence Yearbook* (1981), pp. 214–22 and Table 9, p. 301, 'Western anti-tank missiles'.

19. Mearsheimer, *Survival*, 21, 1979.

20. DoD, *Annual Report 1982*, pp. 139, 142.

21. D. A. Malcolm, 'Battlefield Laser Target Designation', *RUSI Journal*, June 1979, pp. 73–8; Major D. E. King, 'The survival of tanks in battle', *RUSI Journal*, March 1978, pp. 26–31; Captain L. O. Ratley III, 'Air power at Kursk, the confrontation of aircraft and tanks – a lesson for today?', *RUSI Journal*, June 1977, pp. 25–9.

22. M. van Creveld, *Supplying War; Logistics from Wallenstein to Patton*, Cambridge, 1977, chapter 7.

23. B. Dankbaar, 'Alternative defence policies and modern weapon technology', and A. Boserup, 'Nuclear disarmament: non-nuclear defence', introduce the European debate to English readers. Both in M. Kaldor and D. Smith, eds., *Disarming Europe*, 1982.

24. R. Neild, *How to Make up Your Mind about the Bomb*, pp. 116–20.

25. R. M. Nixon, *The Memoirs of Richard Nixon*, p. 347.

26. *Statement on the Defence Estimates 1981*, para. 802, p. 46, and Figure 19, p. 66.

27. D. Campbell, *New Statesman*, 1028.

28. *Statement on the Defence Estimates 1981*, para. 214, p. 15.

29. See D. Greenwood, *Reshaping Britain's Defences: an Evaluation of Mr Nott's Way Forward for the UK* (Aberdeen Studies in Defence Economics, no. 19), August 1981, Table 3, p. 8.

30. L. Freedman, *Britain and Nuclear Weapons*, 1980, p. 146.

31. *Fourth Report of the House of Commons Defence Committee: Strategic Nuclear Weapons Policy* (H.C. paper 36), 1981.

32. Statement by Mr Nott to the Commons, *The Times*, 12 March 1982.

33. CSO, *UK Balance of Payments, 1981 Edition*, Tables 3.2, 3.9.

34. Owing to these factors, measures to prevent Argentina's continued access to international financial markets during the Falklands conflict were extremely limited.

35. IISS, *The Military Balance* (1981–2), pp. 27, 44–5; D. Greenwood and P. Hennessy, 'Nuclear-free – but no pushover', *The Times*, 29 October 1981, p. 4.

36. Labour Party Defence Study Group, *Sense about Defence*, 1977, p. 45.

37. Lucas Aerospace Combine Shop Stewards' Committee (LACP), *The Corporate Plan*, 1976;

Mike Cooley, 'Design, technology and production for social needs – an initiative by the Lucas Aerospace workers', *The New Universities Quarterly*, **32**, Winter 1977, pp. 37–49; Dave Elliott, 'The Lucas Aerospace Alternative Corporate Plan', in *Alternative Work for Military Industries* (Richardson Institute for Conflict and Peace Research), 1977; M. Kaldor, *The Baroque Arsenal*, pp. 213–18.

Appendix A1

1. Henry Kissinger, cited Paul Nitze, *Foreign Policy*, Winter 1974, p. 136.
2. J. M. Collins, *US–Soviet Military Balance 1960–1980*, New York, 1980, p. 443 ff.
3. Tsipis, 'Offensive Missiles' (SIPRI, Stockholm Paper 5), 1974, p. 11.
4. F. M. Kaplan, *Dubious Specter: a Sceptical Look at the Soviet Nuclear Threat*, Washington, 1980, p. 29.
5. Tsipis, 'Offensive Missiles', p. 16.
6. Tsipis, 'Offensive Missiles', p. 15. Tsipis derived the formula

$$P_k = 1 - \exp\left[-\tfrac{1}{2}K\left\{Hf(H)\right\}^{-\frac{2}{3}}\right]$$

which is slightly incorrect, the error arising from the confusion of the *circular error probable* C with the *standard error* of the distribution of incoming warheads. Tsipis used a blast model which gave, correctly:

$$f(H) = 0.19/H - 0.23/H^{\frac{1}{2}} + 0.068 \text{ with } H \text{ in psi.}$$

7. Eliot Marshal, 'A question of accuracy', *Science*, **213**, September 1981, p. 1230. Dr J. Edward Anderson, Department of Mechanical Engineering, University of Minnesota, statement on technical reasons for doubting the feasibility of successful counterforce strikes by missiles, inserted for the record into *Hearings before the Committee on Foreign Relations, United States Senate, 97th Congress, 1st Session*, on 'The foreign policy and arms control implications of President Reagan's strategic weapons proposals', 3, 4 and 9 November 1981, p. 47.
8. C. Paine, 'Running in circles with the MX', *Bulletin of the Atomic Scientists*, **37**, 10, 1981, pp. 5–6; C. A. Robinson, Jnr, 'Soviets boost ICBM accuracy', *Aviation Week and Space Technology*, 3 April 1978, and 'Soviets testing new generation', *Aviation Week and Space Technology*, 3 November 1980.
9. Paine, *Bulletin of the Atomic Scientists*, pp. 6–7.
10. Marshal, *Science*, **213**, 1981, p. 1231.
11. R. K. Betts, ed., *Cruise Missiles: Technology, Strategy, Politics*, Washington, 1981.
12. Anderson, *Hearings before the Committee on Foreign Relations*, p. 48.
13. F. A. Payne, 'The Strategic Nuclear Balance, a New Measure', *Survival*, **19**, 3, pp. 107–10.
14. Center for Defense Information,
15. Tsipis, 'Offensive Missiles', p. 12.
16. Tsipis, 'Offensive Missiles', p. 19.
17. *SIPRI Yearbook* (1980), Figs. 4 and 5, p. xxvi.

Appendix A2

1. *Dictionary of Military and Associated Terms* (Joint Chiefs of Staff, JCS Publ., Department of Defense), Washington, 1 June 1979. Entry for 'strategic mission', pp. 328–9; D. Smith, *Defence of the Realm in the 1980s*, 1980, pp. 90–95.

2. Interview with Lt-General Mikhail Milshtein following the enunciation of Presidential Directive 59 by Secretary of Defense Brown, *International Herald Tribune*, 28 August 1980; on Soviet doctrine, see passages in Chapter 4 above and references there. Also see D. Holloway, 'Strategic concepts and Soviet policy', *Survival*, **13**, 11, November 1971, and 'Military power and political purpose in Soviet policy', *Daedalus*, **109**, 4, Fall 1980, pp. 13–30.

Appendix C

1. Sir Brian Flowers (Chairman), *Nuclear Power and the Environment*, Sixth Report, Royal Commission on Environmental Pollution, Cmnd 6618, September 1976. Justice R. W. Fox, *Ranger Uranium Environmental Inquiry*, First Report, Australian Parliamentary Paper 309/1976, October 1976. B. Flowers, 'Nuclear power and public policy', *Journal of the British Nuclear Energy Society*, **16**, 2, 1977, pp. 113–21.

2. Fox Report, p. 110.

3. Flowers Commission, para. 435.

4. ibid., para. 504.

5. ibid., para. 391.

6. ibid., para. 504.

7. ibid., para. 504.

8. W. Barnaby, 'Nuclear waste problem solved, claims Sweden's nuclear industry', *Nature*, **274**, 6 July 1978, p. 6.

9. T. B. Johansson and P. Steen, 'What to do with the radioactive waste', *Bulletin of the Atomic Scientists*, **35**, 1979, pp. 38–42.

10. 'Swedes vote for nuclear', *Nuclear Engineering International*, **25**, 298, April 1980, p. 3. 'Impossible to vote clear "yes" for nuclear in Sweden', *Nuclear Engineering International*, **25**, 296, March 1980, pp. 24–5.

11. L. E. J. Roberts, 'Radioactive waste – policy and perspective', *Atom*, **267**, January 1979, pp. 8–20. (Dr Roberts is Director of AERE, Harwell.)

12. R. Walgate, 'Nuclear waste may be stored in synthetic rock', *Nature*, **274**, 3 August 1978, p. 413.

13. Roberts, *Atom*, **267**, p. 18.

14. J. Daglish, 'High-level waste management research', *Atom*, **269**, March 1979, pp. 58–62.

15. J. B. Morris and others, 'Durability of vitrified highly active waste from nuclear reprocessing', *Nature*, **273**, 18 May 1978, pp. 215–16. Results cited by Roberts, *Atom*, **267**, p. 18.

16. G. J. McCarthy and others, 'Interactions between nuclear waste and surrounding rock', *Nature*, **273**, 18 May 1978, pp. 216–17.

17. J. H. Simmons and others, 'Fixation of radioactive waste in high silica glasses', *Nature*, **278**, 19 April 1979, pp. 729–31. P. B. Macedo, A. Barkatt, and J. H. Simmons, 'A flow model for the kinetics of dissolution of nuclear waste-forms; a comparison of borosilicate glass, synroc and high-silica glass', *Proceedings*, 5th International Symposium on the Scientific Basis for Radioactive Waste Management, June 1982, Berlin, W. Germany.

18. S. N. Karkhanis and others, 'Leaching behaviour of rhyolite glass', *Nature*, **284**, 3 April 1980, pp. 435–7. A. P. Dickin, 'Hydrothermal leaching of rhyolite glass in the environment has implications for nuclear waste disposal', *Nature*, **294**, 26 November 1981, pp. 342–7.

19. A. E. Ringwood and others, 'Immobilisation of high-level nuclear reactor wastes in SYNROC', *Nature*, **278**, 15 March 1979, pp. 219–23. C. R. Kennedy and others, 'Comparative leaching behaviour of SYNROC B and a borosilicate glass', *Nuclear Technology*, **56**, February 1982, p. 278.

20. G. de Marsily, 'High level nuclear waste isolation: borosilicate glass versus crystals', *Nature*, **278**, 15 March 1979, pp. 210–2. G. L. McVay and C. Q. Buckwalter, 'The nature of glass leaching', *Nuclear Technology*, **51**, December 1980, pp. 123–9. H. W. Nesbit and others, 'Thermodynamic stability and kinetics of perovskite dissolution', *Nature*, **289**, 29 January 1981, pp. 358–62. P. A. Tempest, 'A comparison of borosilicate glass and synthetic minerals as media for the immobilisation of high-level radioactive waste', *Nuclear Technology*, **52**, March 1981, pp. 415–25. J. H. Simmons and others, 'Mechanisms that control aqueous leaching of nuclear waste glass', *Nuclear Technology*, **56**, February 1982, pp. 265–70.

21. J. D. Mather and others, 'The geological disposal of high-level radioactive waste – a review of the I.G.S. research programme', *Nuclear Energy*, **21**, 3, June 1982, pp. 167–73.

22. ibid., p. 167.

23. Sir Denys Wilkinson (Chairman), Radioactive Waste Management Advisory Committee, Second Report, May 1981, p. 14. Roberts, *Atom*, **267**, p. 18. *Hansard*, **994**, 7, 27 November 1981, cols. 220–21 (Heseltine).

24. D. W. Clelland and A. D. W. Corbet, 'Vitrifying Britain's waste', *Nuclear Engineering International*, **27**, 331, August 1982, pp. 33–5.

Appendix D

1. M. Gowing and L. Arnold, *Independence and Deterrence*, Vol. I, 1974, pp. 104–12 (on McMahon Act); *Keesing's Contemporary Archives*, 28 August–4 September 1954, pp. 13,756–7.

2. Letter from President Eisenhower to Senator Clinton Anderson, Chairman, Joint Congressional Committee on Atomic Energy, 20 June 1955, quoted *Keesing's Contemporary Archives*, 6–13 August 1955, p. 14,361; *Agreement between the Government of the United Kingdom of Great Britain and Northern Ireland and the Government of the United States for Cooperation on the Civil Uses of Atomic Energy* (United States, No. 2, [1955], Cmnd 9507, 15 June 1955), Washington; *Agreement . . . for Cooperation regarding Atomic Information for Mutual Defence Purposes* (Cmd 9508, 15 June 1955), Washington; *Keesing's Contemporary Archives*, 6–13 October 1956, p. 15,133.

3. ibid., 26 October–2 November 1957, pp. 15,823–4.

4. *Agreement . . . for Cooperation on the Uses of Atomic Energy for Mutual Defence Purposes* (Treaty Series No. 41 [1958], Cmd 537, 3 July 1958), Washington.

5. *Amendment to the Agreement for Cooperation on the Uses of Atomic Energy for Mutual Defence Purposes of July 3 1958* (United States, No. 2 [1959], Cmd 733, 7 May 1959), Washington.

6. *Keesing's Contemporary Archives*, 15–22 November 1958, p. 16,501.

7. *Daily Telegraph*, 8 May 1959, p. 24.

8. *The Times*, 8 May 1959, p. 12.

Acronyms

ABM anti-ballistic missile
ACDA Arms Control and Disarmament Agency (US Department of State, Washington)
AEC Atomic Energy Commission
AERE Atomic Energy Research Establishment
AEW airborne early warning (radar)
AFAP artillery-fired atomic projectile
AGR advanced gas-cooled reactor
ALCM air-launched cruise missile
ATGM anti-tank guided missile
AVM Atelier de Vitrification, Marcoule (see Appendix D)
AWRE Atomic Weapons Research Establishment
BDM ballistic-missile defence
BEIR Biological effects of ionizing radiation
BNFL British Nuclear Fuels Ltd
CEGB Central Electricity Generating Board
CEP circular error probability (see Appendix A1)
EMP electromagnetic pulse
EMt equivalent megatons (see Appendix A1)
GCD general and complete disarmament
GLCM ground-launched cruise missile
IAEA International Atomic Energy Agency
ICBM intercontinental ballistic missile
ICRP International Commission on Radiological Protection
IISS International Institute for Strategic Studies
IRBM intermediate-range ballistic missile
LET linear energy transfer (see Appendix B)
LORAN long-range navigation
MAD mutually assured destruction
MARV advanced manoeuvrable re-entry vehicle
MIRV multiple independently targeted re-entry vehicle
MRV multiple re-entry vehicle
MX missile experimental
NAVSTAR satellite guidance system
NRPB National Radiological Protection Board
PGM precision-guided munitions
PWR pressurized water reactor

SACEUR Supreme Allied Commander, Europe
SALT Strategic Arms Limitation Talks/Treaty
SAM surface-to-air missile
SCAD subsonic cruise armed decoy
SCUD subsonic cruise unarmed decoy
SIOP single integrated operational plan
SIPRI Stockholm International Peace Research Institute
SLBM submarine-launched ballistic missile
SRAM short-range attack missile
SSKP single-shot kill probability
TERCOM terrain-following navigation system (cruise missiles)
UKAEA United Kingdom Atomic Energy Authority
ULMS under-sea long-range missile system

Index

More about Penguins
and Pelicans

For further Information about books available from
Penguins please write to Dept EP, Penguin Books
Ltd, Harmondsworth, Middlesex UB7 0DA.

In the U.S.A.: For a complete list of books available
from Penguins in the United States write to Dept
DG, Penguin Books, 299 Murray Hill Parkway, East
Rutherford, New Jersey 07073.

In Canada: For a complete list of books available
from Penguins in Canada write to Penguin Books
Canada Ltd, 2801 John Street, Markham, Ontario
L3R 1B4.

In Australia: For a complete list of books available
from Penguins in Australia write to the Marketing
Department, Penguin Books Australia Ltd, P.O. Box
257 Ringwood, Victoria 3134.

In New Zealand: For a complete list of books
available from Penguins in New Zealand write to the
Marketing Department, Penguin Books (N.Z.) Ltd,
P.O. Box 4019, Auckland 10.

Published by Penguins

SUPERPOWERS IN COLLISION
The New Cold War
Noam Chomsky, Jonathan Steele and John Gittings

As U S–Soviet relations continue to deteriorate and as the arms race escalates, our outlook on world politics becomes easily confused and vulnerable to the superpowers' propaganda. Here three leading commentators cut through the myths to tackle the most basic questions, analysing the roles of the United States, the Soviet Union and China in the deepening crisis.

'If we hope to recover into our own hands the future of our own lives,' the authors stress, 'then the Dangerous Decade must become the Decade of Debate.' Informed and accessible, *Superpowers in Collision* is a vital starting-point for that debate.

Published by Penguins

INTERNATIONAL PEACEKEEPING
United Nations forces in a troubled world
Anthony Verrier

Irish squaddies are shot in a squalid encounter in the Middle East and the newspapers are pious for a week until the next bit of international 'news' displaces them. Unlovely acronyms, ONUC, UNFICYP and UNIFIL are trotted out for a bemused and bored public, but they conceal a real and urgent, a terrifying and crucial, a randomly violent half-war.

These are the visible bits of an astonishing and largely hidden military crusade. It is the struggle for peace waged, sometimes uncertainly but unceasingly, by the United Nations Peacekeeping Forces. The funny armies made up of amazing mixtures of people speaking lots of different languages under, for most of them, an alien command, keep warring factions apart.

This book describes the ways these unsung heroes work, shot at by all but unable, for the most part, to shoot back. Verrier recounts their history, their defeats and their victories. He shows how the strategies work or are improvised and, above all, how vital is their role in international politics.

Published by Penguins

THE GLOBAL 2000 REPORT TO THE PRESIDENT

'If present trends continue, the world in 2000 will be more crowded, more polluted, less stable ecologically and more vulnerable to disruption.'

Commissioned by President Carter, this is one of the most explosive and important documents to have been produced in the twentieth century. In it the world experts on the Council on Environmental Quality and the Department of State reveal the stark options open to us. The struggle to sustain a decent life for human beings on our planet will be enormous – yet, as they conclude, 'there is reason for hope'.

'It may well be the most detailed and authoritative review of the planet problems ever prepared' – *Christian Science Monitor*

THE SHATTERED PEACE
Daniel Yergin

'The best account to date of American foreign policy in
the early Cold War ... Yergin focuses on the period
between Yalta and the Berlin Blockade ... his exhaustive
research, fresh interpretations and readable style set the
book apart ... it challenges both "traditionalist" and
"revisionist" interpretations and should be the point of
departure in subsequent debate' – *Military Affairs*

'Yergin ... tells his story with great flair. A master of the
anecdote, he peppers the text with details that bring these
men alive and puts their actions in a personal as well as a
circumstantial framework ... he has gone over the
immediate post war years with a diligent eye, making us
see that an opportunity might have been lost' – *The Times
Educational Supplement*

Published by Penguins

THE POLISH AUGUST
Neal Ascherson

What has happened in Poland?

Poland has erupted four times in the last twenty-five years, but only the events of 1980 have had comprehensive media coverage. As a result, many questions have been raised in the minds of Western observers. How were such changes possible? What forces lay behind them? In what way did the workers' strike relate to the demands for political democracy?

Although a colourful and vivid eye-witness account of the 1980 upheavals, it is to these questions that Neal Ascherson's brilliant and thoughtful analysis mainly addresses itself. Viewing the situation in perspective, he argues that the Polish working class has brought about a controlled revolution, but is not intent on taking power for itself; the real heirs to the gains of 1980 and 1981 are likely to be the intelligentsia, in or out of the Communist Party. It is this social and political ferment that poses fundamental questions about the future of the whole Soviet system in Eastern Europe.

THE BOOK OF LECH WAŁĘSA
With an introduction by Neal Ascherson

'Fighting without violence, but through love, solidarity and co-operation'

During August 1980 and the crucial strike in Gdańsk, Lech Wałęsa was born as a great Polish leader. He has since won the respect and allegiance of millions of people – as a defender of human and civil rights, as a propagator of national moral and political revival.

Written by his friends in Solidarity, followers and critics, this book affirms Wałęsa as more than the myth that the media have created. And out of these interviews, analyses and eye-witness accounts there emerges a dynamic portrait of the man who, in his 'inspired stubbornness' has become an international symbol of hope.

Published by Penguins

WILL THE SOVIET UNION SURVIVE UNTIL 1984?

Andrei Amalrik

First published in 1970, Amalrik's essay was hailed by the *Guardian* as 'a brave unique voice from the Soviet Union coolly and pessimistically explaining the reality of that society and (a little less coolly) outlining his vision of the apocalypse to come, with the rise of China and the revival of nationalism among the non-Russian Soviet peoples'; while the *Sunday Times* called it 'literally the first piece of serious political analysis, based on experience, observation and undogmatic deduction to have emerged from Russia for fifty years'.

In 1976 Amalrik left the Soviet Union. His original essay is reprinted here, as immediate and pertinent as ever, accompanied by a selection of Amalrik's major recent statements, written both in the Soviet Union and in exile.

PRISONER WITHOUT A NAME, CELL WITHOUT A NUMBER

Jacobo Timerman

Dragged from his home at dawn by an extremist faction of the Argentine army, Jacobo Timerman, the former editor of *La Opinión*, Argentina's leading liberal newspaper, was held for two and a half years – tortured, abused and humiliated – without charges ever being brought against him. Timerman's only category of guilt was being Jewish: a chilling echo of Nazi Germany and the Final Solution.

This harrowing record of Timerman's resistance, in solitary confinement, 'will come to rank with the testimony of Gulag and the Holocaust' – *The Times*

Published by Penguins

ISRAEL AND THE ARABS
SECOND EDITION
Maxime Rodinson

Twice in the last two decades the Middle East has
exploded into war. Perhaps it is not surprising, if you
consider the mutually repellent elements packed into the
area; Zionism; Islam; socialism; reaction; dictatorship;
democracy; not to mention the ambitions of Russia and
America. Essentially though, Professor Rodinson believes
that the conflict must be seen in somewhat simpler terms,
as rooted in 'the struggle of an indigenous population
against the occupation of part of its normal territory by
foreigners'.

This new edition of his invaluable and challenging study,
Israel and the Arabs traces the course of Zionism and
examines the changing ambitions and interrelations of the
Arab nations. It is the informed analysis, says the
Listener, 'of a distinguished French Orientalist and
Marxist (who left the Communist Party in 1958), with an
unrivalled knowledge and understanding of the two sides
in the present conflict'.

THE ARABS
Peter Mansfield

The Arabs, which draws upon Peter Mansfield's many
years' experience as historian and journalist in the Middle
East, is a concise and authoritative general introduction –
social, political and historical – to the modern Arab
world.

'Masterly in its order and clarity' – Jan Morris in the
Spectator

'Should be studied by anyone who wants to know about
the Arab world and how the Arabs have become what
they are today' – Steven Runciman in the *Sunday Times*

Published by Penguins

WHO'S WATCHING YOU?
Britain's Security Services and the Official Secrets Act
Crispin Aubrey

The security services, invisible, unaccountable, surrounded by a mystique of dark glasses and turned-up collars, have grown steadily in size; so too has their expenditure on the most sophisticated techniques of mass surveillance.

Their net falls on trade unionists, students, anti-nuclear protesters, Welsh Nationalists, investigative journalists and a host of possible 'subversives'. Crispin Aubrey stumbled into this web one dark and rainy night in 1977, was arrested by the Special Branch and charged under the Official Secrets Act. His subsequent trial, the 'ABC trial', attained a legal significance and had political repercussions far beyond the facts of the case.

THE HIDDEN PERSUADERS
Vance Packard

In a new epilogue to his classic study of the American advertising machine, Vance Packard reveals that, far from losing ground as the innocent Fifties grew into the sophisticated Seventies, its power has grown accordingly: an $8 billion business has turned into a $40 billion industry. Their technologists now include brain specialists, neurophysiologists, hypnotechnicians, voice-pitch analysts. Their victims are the new stereotypes; the liberated woman, the independent man, the militant mother, the chic suburbanite, for swinging New Waver.

Whether or not we fall into such categories, we are all to some extent persuadable – Vance Packard definitively and entertainingly explains why and how.

Published by Penguins

ARGUMENTS FOR DEMOCRACY
Tony Benn
Edited by Chris Mullin

'This book has been written for those of us who want to see the people of this country take control of our own destinies and use the power of democracy to resolve the many pressing problems we face in our daily lives, including unemployment, injustice and the threat of war.'

Based on speeches, lectures and articles written or delivered in the two years up to April 1981, *Arguments for Democracy* is a cogent, concise and readable critique of the current practices of parliamentary democracy and a persuasive analysis of the way in which our political institutions need to be reformed before Britain can be steered towards socialism.

'The issues tackled are always substantial and they usually end with practical (classical left-reformist) proposals for change' – *New Society*

'It is worth reading for its own sake, and not only for the light it throws on a potential leader of the country' – *Sunday Telegraph*

POLITICS IS FOR PEOPLE
Shirley Williams

Politicians everywhere must change their thinking if we are to move forward the achievements of the post-war years.

Shirley Williams represents a major influence on political thinking on the Left. In this book she throws the debate open, blueprinting for us what she sees as acceptable and workable solutions for the future of our country. Industrialism is at crisis point and we must be ready to face the challenge.

Stimulating, caring, honest and backed up by carefully marshalled facts, her book bears out her deeply held conviction – politics is, and *must be*, for people.